Romantic Suspense

Danger. Passion. Drama.

Stranded
Jennifer D. Bokal

Bodyguard Rancher
Kacy Cross

MILLS & BOON

STRANDED
© 2024 by Jennifer D. Bokal
Philippine Copyright 2024
Australian Copyright 2024
New Zealand Copyright 2024

First Published 2024
First Australian Paperback Edition 2024
ISBN 978 1 038 93554 0

BODYGUARD RANCHER
© 2024 by Kacy Cross
Philippine Copyright 2024
Australian Copyright 2024
New Zealand Copyright 2024

First Published 2024
First Australian Paperback Edition 2024
ISBN 978 1 038 93554 0

MIX
Paper | Supporting
responsible forestry
FSC® C001695
www.fsc.org

Published by
Harlequin Mills & Boon
An imprint of Harlequin Enterprises (Australia) Pty Limited (ABN 47 001 180 918), a subsidiary of HarperCollins Publishers Australia Pty Limited
(ABN 36 009 913 517)
Level 19, 201 Elizabeth Street
SYDNEY NSW 2000 AUSTRALIA

Cover art used by arrangement with Harlequin Books S.A.. All rights reserved.

Printed and bound in Australia by McPherson's Printing Group

Stranded

Jennifer D. Bokal

MILLS & BOON

Jennifer D. Bokal is the author of several books, including the Harlequin Romantic Suspense series Rocky Mountain Justice, Wyoming Nights, Texas Law and several books that are part of the Colton continuity.

Happily married to her own alpha male for more than twenty-five years, she enjoys writing stories that explore the wonders of love. Jen and her manly husband have three beautiful grown daughters, two very spoiled dogs and a cat who runs the house.

Books by Jennifer D. Bokal

Harlequin Romantic Suspense

Texas Law

Texas Law: Undercover Justice
Texas Law: Serial Manhunt
Texas Law: Lethal Encounter
Stranded

The Coltons of Owl Creek

Colton Undercover

The Coltons of New York

Colton's Deadly Affair

The Coltons of Colorado

Colton's Rogue Investigation

Visit the Author Profile page
at millsandboon.com.au for more titles.

Dear Reader,

Welcome back to Texas Law. I'm thrilled to continue this series with the same amount of excitement, danger and desire—but with a new cast of characters. In fact, the things I love most about *Stranded* are the hero and heroine.

Brett Wilson is a medevac pilot and forever the optimist. Eva Tamke, a nurse, has a lot going on in her life and isn't looking for a new relationship. But the duo is set up on a date. The chemistry is real, and a nice dinner turns into a night of passion. Because of a family emergency, Eva only has time for their single night. After he gets the news from Eva that their budding relationship is being pruned from the vine, even Brett's sunny disposition can't keep him from feeling disappointed.

When Eva shows up to fill in as the nurse on his flight crew, things are awkward. But after their helicopter crashes in the Texas desert, they have to rely on each other to survive the elements and escape from an at-large serial killer.

The attraction from before can't be ignored, and both Eva and Brett realize that they're better together than apart. Will it be enough to keep them alive while they're *stranded*?

Read and find out!

All the best,

Jennifer D. Bokal

To John
On this journey of life, I'm glad that you're by my side.

Chapter One

The scent of salsa, fried corn chips and cinnamon hung in the air. Eva Tamke wiped her mouth with a paper napkin and set it onto the empty plate. Warmth crept up her chest and settled onto her cheeks. The heat had nothing to do with the spicy food she'd eaten or the margarita she'd finished an hour earlier.

It was all because of the man who sat across the table.

Brett Wilson was a medevac pilot at San Antonio Medical Center—the same place she worked as an ER nurse. The medical center was so large that she'd never met him before tonight.

After months of being matched only with creeps on dating apps, Eva was beyond dubious when a mutual friend from work promised that Brett was perfect. But he was. Heck, they even shared a history of serving in the armed forces. He'd been full-time army, flying Black Hawks, and had served overseas more than once. She'd been in the Air Force Reserve, using the GI Bill to pay for college.

Thank goodness she'd worn her favorite dress—a coral sundress with spaghetti straps and tight bodice that fell to her knees. The color matched her lipstick perfectly and brought out the caramel highlights in her brown hair. Truly, in this dress, she felt confident. Even beautiful.

And for the first time in what seemed like forever, she wanted to be attractive for a man—this man. Brett was tall, over six feet if she had to guess. He had broad shoulders, blond hair, blue eyes and a square jaw. His jeans hugged his rear and the cuff of his blue T-shirt accentuated the muscles in his biceps.

"So, what do you think?" he asked, pointing to her plate. "Was I right? Or was I right? That was the best burrito in all of San Antonio."

"It was good," she said, being honest. The chicken had been fresh and tender. The cheese was mellow. The beans had a spicy kick. "Then again, you only have food from an army base for comparison," she said, bringing up the old joke that army fare was horrible, while the air force fed their people well. In all honesty, she didn't know if the joke was true or not. She'd never eaten at an army facility. They'd talked about their military service, swapping stories, and he'd felt like someone she'd known for years. Comfortable. Familiar. And excitingly brand-new at the same time. "There's a Tex-Mex restaurant near my apartment. The food there is excellent, too."

"Excellent is nice," he said, smiling. In the dark restaurant, his teeth were brilliantly white. "But this was perfection."

"Perfection is pretty hard to come by." With Brett, she liked being flirty and charming. She flipped her hair over her shoulder.

Brett reached across the table and traced the back of her hand. An electric current danced along her skin. "Trust me." Again, he gave her that smile. Her cheeks warmed even more. "I know perfection when I see it."

She let him slip his fingertips between her own. Her pulse spiked. For a moment, she almost forgot about the call she'd gotten earlier in the day.

Her sister. Katya told her that their grandmother had fallen. Baba was taken to the hospital near Eva's childhood hometown of Encantador, Texas. Thankfully, Baba had only sprained her ankle. But the doctor had been clear: their grandmother could no longer live alone.

It brought up an interesting predicament. Katya shared a three-bedroom house with her husband and three kids. The home, though filled with love, was already too crowded to add an elderly lady who needed care.

Eva lived in San Antonio and worked full-time.

Their father and his new wife had moved to California almost two decades earlier.

Aside from the three of them, there was no other family.

Her grandmother had always resisted moving into an assisted living community. Eva had to do something…

Her mind drifted back to the restaurant. Nearby, a server placed an upside-down chair on a table. Another server pushed a broom across the floor.

She inclined her head toward the workers. "Looks like they want us to get out of here."

She could easily spend another hour here, talking, sharing, getting to know him. They'd covered all the first-date topics— basics about their families and where they were from, favorite foods and movies. They had a lot in common. They'd both even served in the military years before. Between their easy back-and-forth and her attraction to him, she'd managed not to let her sister's call trouble her during the date.

"I guess so." Still holding her hand, Brett rose from the table. She stood as well. "I'll walk you to your car."

He led her through the empty restaurant and pushed the door open. It didn't matter that the sun had set hours earlier, it was still hot outside. Sweat collected at the nape of her neck and pooled at the small of her back.

"Where's your car?" he asked.

The restaurant sat in the middle of a shopping plaza adjacent to a sprawling neighborhood. At this time of night, the parking lot was all but empty. Her car, a dark blue sedan, was two rows back, bathed in the glow of a tall lamppost.

"It's over there," she said.

"I'll walk with you."

With her hand in his, they crossed the parking lot. Using a fob to start the engine, she unlocked the doors. The date, it seemed, was over. But she really didn't want the night to end.

"So," Brett said, stepping toward her.

"So," she echoed, closing the distance between them.

Brett leaned toward her, touching his lips to hers. A spark ran through her body, and despite the heat, she wanted him closer. Wrapping her arms around his neck, she ran her fingers over the nape of his neck and pulled him close.

He gave a low growl. She felt the sound in her middle. It traveled to her toes and left her knees weak. Sighing, she stepped back. "Thanks for taking me out. It's been a long time since I've had this much fun on a date."

"It doesn't have to end," said Brett. "We can go to my house for a drink." He pointed to the neighborhood next to the shopping center. "I live over there."

"I really shouldn't have any more alcohol. The margarita's out of my system, but…"

"Coffee, then," he said, before adding, "I even have decaf if you prefer. So it won't keep you up all might."

It was too hot for coffee. But she didn't care. Brett was more than handsome and funny. Talking to him was like getting together with an old friend, rather than meeting someone new. Then again, she didn't usually go home with men on the first date. At thirty-six years of age, she'd gained some wisdom. She knew that one-night stands were just that—a distraction for one night.

With Brett, she saw the potential for more.

But her life wasn't so simple. Her grandmother's accident had made things complicated, and she had some tough choices to make.

Brett's lips were oh, so kissable. His arms were strong, and his legs were long. Just standing next to him left her toes tingling. Maybe what she needed was a distraction for one night. And she found herself saying, "A decaf coffee would be nice." She scanned the parking lot. "Where's your car?"

"I walked," he said. "My house is less than five minutes from here."

"Well, then." She opened the driver door. "Get in. I'll give you a ride."

Even with the engine running the past few minutes, the air conditioner had done little to cool off the car's interior. As she settled into the driver seat, she dropped the car's fob into a cup holder. While fastening her seat belt, she tried not to look at Brett. She tried not to think about what was going to happen next. Because, honestly, she wanted more from him than just a cup of coffee.

After a six-month-long romantic drought, it was no wonder that she was going home with the handsome pilot. But it was more than that. It seemed like her world had actually spun off its axis.

Her grandmother was her emotional support. After her mother left, it was Baba who put the little family back together. When her father remarried and moved to California while she was in college, she kept going back to Baba's house for holidays and breaks. The fact that her grandmother was now the one in need of care left her facing an uncomfortable truth. Nothing in life was certain beyond change.

Maybe that was why she wanted to go home with Brett. She was tired of playing by the rules and ready to really live— even if it was just for the night.

With an exhale, she put the gearshift into Drive and eased forward out of the space. "Which way?" she asked.

He pointed to a stop sign. "Go out of the parking lot over there."

Within minutes, she was parking her car next to the curb in front of a small house with a manicured lawn.

"Welcome to Casa de Brett," he said.

Pushing a button on her dashboard, she turned off the ignition. "You have a nice place," she said. "I've been in an apartment since moving to San Antonio—and that was almost eight years ago now. I'm never sure how I feel about home ownership."

"I bought this place three years ago, and I'll be honest, you're right to feel both." He paused. "Do you still want to come in?"

Without the engine running, the air-conditioning had turned off. The car's interior started to get warm. Sweat dampened her skin until her dress clung to her back. If she wanted to leave, now was the time. Lifting the fob from the cup holder, she slipped it inside the crossbody bag draped across her chest. "I don't work until noon, so I don't have to get up early."

After all, she could leave anytime she wanted. She'd agreed to a cup of coffee and nothing more. Yet, the kiss had awakened something deep inside of Eva—something that had been asleep for far too long—and reminded her that she was a woman with needs.

He slipped from the passenger seat and closed the door. Waiting at the curb, he lingered as she came to stand next to him. Reaching for her hand, he led her up the sidewalk.

Somehow, a swarm of butterflies had been let loose inside her, their wings beating against her belly. She hadn't felt this much nervous excitement in years, and the sensation left her giddy.

At the door, he entered a code into an electronic keypad. The latch unlocked with a click. He pushed the door open, and several interior lights began to glow.

Brett kicked off his shoes next to a mat. Eva did the same. The tile floor was cool under the soles of her feet. The air-conditioning had been set to polar, and the sweat dried, leaving gooseflesh on her arms. The front door opened to a living room, and a coffee table sat in the middle of the wooden floor.

It was surrounded on three sides by a tan sofa and two matching chairs. A large TV hung on the wall.

"How do you take your coffee?" Brett turned left, passing through a dining room and into the kitchen.

Following behind him, she said, "Cream and sugar," before remembering her manners and adding, "please."

In the kitchen, he pulled a phone from his back pocket and set it on the counter. The device was inside a clear plastic case.

"I know this isn't any of my business," she said, picking up the cell, "but what gives?"

"Oh, that." He laughed. "A year or two ago, Wade had everyone over to his apartment complex for a cookout. There's a real nice pool, and we were all sort of goofing around. I ended up in the water and never thought to get rid of my phone before jumping in. Anyway, it ruined my phone and took forever to get all my information back." He picked up the phone and shook it. "Hence, the dry bag."

Wade was their mutual friend—the one who'd set them on the blind date. He was a new addition to San Antonio Medical Center's trivia team. After the first night joining the team at a local bar, she'd gotten to like Wade's sense of humor and eagerness for fun. She could well imagine a pool party gone awry. She also trusted him enough that when he told her that he knew the perfect guy, she let herself get fixed up with the pilot on his flight crew. Turns out, Wade had been right about Brett.

He was perfect for Eva.

She'd been quiet for a beat too long. Smiling up at him, she touched the waterproof pouch. "So, you have this just in case a crazy pool party breaks out."

"Yeah," he said. "Something like that."

A coffeepot sat on the counter next to the sink. A window looked out over the front yard, the sidewalk, the road and her car. He removed a container of decaf coffee from the fridge and scooped the grounds into a paper filter. "I don't have cream," he said, turning the maker on to brew. "I have skim

milk or some kind of flavored creamer my sister left when
she visited last month."

For Eva, flavored creamer was better. "That'll work."

As the earthy scent of fresh coffee filled the kitchen, Brett
opened the refrigerator door. He stared at the shelves for a moment before reaching inside. "There it is." He held up a plastic
container, handing it to her. "I think it's still good."

"This stuff keeps forever," she said, before reading the label.
Yep, it'd be good for another three months. "Hazelnut. My favorite."

The simple domesticity of the situation hit her in the chest.
She couldn't get wrapped up in thoughts of forever—or even
tomorrow. There was only tonight. In the morning, well, a different set of problems already waited for her. But she'd worry
about those then.

She moved closer to Brett, resting her hand next to his on
the counter.

Stroking her pinky with his own, he said, "Seems like
you're meant to be here."

"Seems like." A shiver of anticipation traveled up her arm.

He removed two mugs from the cabinet, setting them on the
counter. The coffee maker hissed, spitting out the last drops.
After picking up the full pot, he began to pour. "Tell me when."

"That's good," she said when the mug was nearly full. Flipping the lid, she opened the creamer and poured. Like liquid
silk, cream swirled through the coffee, creating moving art.
"Where do you keep your spoons?"

Brett opened a drawer and pulled out a spoon. He held it
up. "Do you want anything else?"

Was there a bit of an invitation in his question, or was Brett
just being a polite host? She took the spoon, letting her fingertips graze his palm. "Do you have sugar?"

From the same cabinet where he'd found the mugs, he pulled
out a ceramic dish with a lid. He set it on the counter next to

her. "I'm not judging," he said. "But even with decaf coffee, the sugar's going to keep you from getting any rest."

She stirred in a teaspoon of sugar and took a sip of coffee. Looking at him over the rim of her cup, she said, "Maybe I don't want to sleep."

"The night's long," he said, his voice smoky and filled with desire. "What do you plan to do with your time?"

She licked the spoon clean and set it on the counter, along with mug. "I was hoping that you had some ideas."

"I might be able to come up with something we can do."

"Oh yeah?" she asked, feeling flirty and powerful. "Like what? Maybe, this?"

She wrapped her arms around his waist and pulled him to her.

She claimed him with a hard kiss, which quickly turned more passionate than their first in the parking lot earlier. Eva opened her mouth, and Brett slipped his tongue between her lips. Like a storm cloud rolling across the plains, her thoughts darkened with worries. She shouldn't be here, not when her grandmother was in the hospital. No matter how much she wanted Brett—and she did want him—taking him as a lover was selfish.

Without any more thoughts, she stroked the front of his jeans. He was hard under her touch. She rubbed him through the fabric.

Kissing her deeper, he growled, "Damn it, Eva."

His words danced along her skin. She was going to do this and regret nothing. Shoving away the last of her worries, she unfastened the top button and pulled down on the zipper. She reached into his underwear and touched him, skin to skin.

Brett edged her back until her butt hit the kitchen counter. The scent of coffee hung in the air, mingling with the muskiness of their shared desire. He used a cord to lower the blinds over the front window. Then he stroked her breast, running his thumb over her nipple.

But she wanted to feel his touch on her flesh. She lowered a strap on her dress, along with the band of her bra, exposing herself to him. He traced her nipple with his thumb. Arching her back, she pressed herself into his hand. Lowering his head, he took her into his mouth. He sucked hard, before scraping his teeth over her breast.

Eva shuddered. Her skin was too tight, and she ached with the need to have him inside of her. "Do you have protection?" she asked.

He removed his wallet from the back pocket of his jeans, then took out a foil packet. "Right here," he said, holding up the condom.

Reaching under her dress, Eva pulled down her panties, shimmying them to the floor. She kicked her underwear away as Brett tore the packet open and rolled the condom over his length. He lifted her up, resting her on the kitchen counter. Eva wrapped her legs around his middle, pulling him closer, and he entered her in one stroke.

Holding on to the counter's edge, she moved with Brett. The friction between them built. With one hand behind her back, he pulled her closer. As he claimed her mouth with his own, she knew what it meant to be alive and not simply exist. It didn't matter that she never slept with a guy this quickly—this moment would stay with her for a long time to come.

She felt an orgasm building, a tightening of her muscles. She was so close to her release. Reaching between their bodies, she found the top of her sex. She rubbed, and a shockwave curled her toes. She cried out as she came.

Brett kissed her again, driving into her hard and fast. She gripped his shoulders as he pumped his hips. Finally, he threw his head back and came as well. For a moment, they held each other. Her heart raced, and her breath was ragged.

He kissed her gently. "I'll be right back," he said.

Eva dropped to the ground. Her legs were wobbly. She held on to the counter to stay upright. "Of course."

"Give me a second." He held the front of his jeans together and hustled out of the kitchen.

She slipped into her panties. As she was straightening her dress, Brett returned. He reached for her hand. Pulling her to him, he wrapped his arms around her waist before touching his lips onto her own. "I won't be able to look at a cup of coffee for the rest of my life without thinking of you."

"Well, aren't you a charmer?" she teased.

In truth, he really was. He was smart, funny, and they shared an undeniable sexual chemistry. But what was she supposed to do next? Honestly, she didn't know if she should stay or go home.

Her mug sat on the counter. She dumped the coffee down the drain and set her spoon inside the cup, leaving both in the sink. "Well, I better..."

"You don't have to leave," he said, interrupting. "I mean, I'd like you to stay. But I understand if you...can't."

That old saying came to mind. *Wham! Bam! Thank you, ma'am!*

Okay, she didn't want to be one of those people.

Before she could say anything else, Brett added, "I make the best pancakes in the world. I can make you breakfast in the morning."

She chuckled. "First, you know of a restaurant with the best burritos in San Antonio. Now, you personally make the best pancakes in the whole world?"

"It's a hidden talent," he said before giving his wide smile.

Honestly, she didn't want to go anywhere, not now, at least. After all, she'd given herself permission to enjoy Brett for the night. And for her, the night was far from over.

Chapter Two

Hovering in the space between sleep and awakening, Eva knew that she was neither in her own apartment or even her own bed. The scent of pine, a male and the muskiness from sex hung in the air. The sheets were softer than the ones she used, and the room was cooler than she kept her bedroom.

Opening her eyes, she gazed at the man whose head lay on the pillow next to her. Brett's mouth was open slightly. He snored softly. His blond hair was tousled from sleep and last night's lovemaking.

Propping her head on her arm, she studied him as he slept. His cheeks were covered with a sprinkling of golden hair. Brushing her fingertips on his stubble, she recalled his breath on her shoulder. His lips were the color of a rich, red wine. Then came another memory, of his mouth on her thigh. Heat surged through her veins.

And now what? She wasn't sure what to do.

Roll over and go back to sleep?

Wake him and ask for the promised breakfast?

Leave without saying a word?

Sure, the last option wasn't classy. But it seemed to be the easiest.

At least she'd put her panties back on after their last round of lovemaking. She was also wearing Brett's undershirt. Sitting up, she scanned the room. Clothes—his and hers—littered the floor. Slipping from beneath the blankets, she padded quietly across the carpeting. Scooping up the entire pile—she could figure out what was hers later—she entered the adjacent bathroom.

After closing the door, she dropped all the clothes to the floor. It took her only seconds to find last night's outfit and get dressed. To be nice, she refolded all of Brett's belongings and set them next to the sink.

Looking up, she caught her reflection in a mirror that hung on the wall. The signs were unmistakable. Her dark hair fell in a tangled mess over her shoulders. Her brown eyes were bright. Her lips were swollen from being kissed. Her cheeks were red from where stubble had rubbed against her skin. She also had a stupid smile on her face—the kind that only came after—well, she came.

After winding her hair into a knot at the back of her neck, she used an elastic band from her pocket to secure a messy bun. She looked presentable enough to drive home. Now, there really was nothing more for her to do—other than leave.

Opening the door slowly, she stepped into Brett's room and grabbed her purse. She found her phone and glanced at the screen.

It was 5:37 a.m.

She'd missed fifteen calls.

Fifteen calls?

Her stomach dropped, and immediately she thought of her grandmother.

Scrolling through the log, she saw that the first call had come in at 3:45 a.m. The last, only moments ago. They were all from Katya. As children, the sisters had been best friends. In fact, they were still close, texting each other while simultaneously streaming true-crime documentaries. It didn't matter that their lives were different. Katya was married with kids and lived in the same community where the sisters had grown up. Eva had moved to San Antonio for work. She'd never married, and she didn't have kids. Hell, she didn't even have a goldfish.

She glanced back at her phone, and a single tear leaked down her cheek. Katya wouldn't have called so many times unless it was with bad news. Eva's eyes burned with tears she wanted to cry.

But she refused to get emotional in Brett's bedroom and while he was asleep, no less.

Anything her sister had to say could wait another few minutes. She'd call Katya back as soon as she got into her car. Before she could leave, she first had to find her shoes. Carefully lifting the corner of the bedspread, she peered under the bed frame.

No shoes.

The phone in her hand began to vibrate with an incoming call from Katya. After sending it to voicemail, she sent a text. I'll call you in two minutes. Sorry.

Then, she typed out another message:

What's going on with Baba?

Katya immediately replied.

You can't talk now? At least you're alive.

Her shoulders sagged. Of course, Katya would be concerned when she hadn't heard from Eva last night. That was what happened when you watched too many murder shows. What made matters worse, everyone in Encantador had been upset by the serial killer Decker Newcombe, who'd terrorized the community. Twice, the murderer had brought carnage to the small town.

She tapped out a message.

I'll call you in a minute.

She hit Send.

"Morning." Brett's voice was deep and husky.

The word landed in her middle.

Rubbing his eyes, he sat up. The blanket pooled across his lap, exposing his broad shoulders and well-defined pecs. A love bite that she'd given him had turned into a bruise.

Her face flamed with the memory. She hitched her purse onto her shoulder. "I didn't mean to wake you."

"Looks like you're heading out. I guess you decided to take a rain check on those pancakes."

The thing was, their date had turned into a good night—no, make that an excellent night. But she didn't know him, not really. Everything was flipped upside down. She'd always been told that after she met someone, a friendship should develop. Once she felt secure with that relationship, and then, only if the chemistry was unmistakable, should she have sex. At least, that was how it always had worked for her in the past.

With Brett, though, it had begun the other way around, and that just felt wrong.

Holding up her phone, she said, "I've missed a bunch of calls. I need to find out what's going on." She looked around the room. Bed. Dresser. TV on a stand. Bookcase. "I just can't find my damned shoes."

He scooted across the mattress and stood. Brett wore only his boxers, and she drank in the sight of him. Those broad shoulders. That muscular chest with chiseled abs. The line of hair that led straight down the front of his shorts. They were all too tempting for her own good. She was vaguely aware that once again this man was able to distract her from her troubles.

"You took them off by the front door," he said.

His words snapped her out of her fantasy. "I what?"

"Your shoes. You left them by the door."

He was right. She had. "Thanks. Well, I better…"

"I can still make you some pancakes," he offered, walking toward her. He was so close that she could reach out and touch him.

She wrapped both hands around her phone, squeezing tight.

He continued, "I like to think of myself as a man who keeps his promises."

Her phone vibrated with another text.

Are you okay?

What's the name of your first pet?

Her heart thudded. That question was their go-to incase either one was ever in trouble. It didn't necessarily mean something bad had happened, just that Katya wasn't about to give up until they spoke. "I really have to see what's going on with all these calls."

He smiled. "All right, then," he said, then paused. "At least let me walk you to the door." He looked down at the floor. "Any idea where my T-shirt went?"

"Uh, yeah. I slept in it. I changed in the bathroom. It's on the counter with all your other clothes."

"All my other clothes?" he echoed.

How was she supposed to explain that one? "Umm…"

"You know what, never mind." After walking to his dresser, Brett opened a drawer. He took out a pair of sweatpants and pulled them on. Then, he slipped a fresh T-shirt over his head. She had to admit, he looked almost as good dressed as he did in his underwear. He gave her a tight-lipped smile. "C'mon. I'll see you out."

They walked from the bedroom, along the hallway, down a set of stairs and through the living room. She wasn't sure what to say but was equally unhappy with the silence. In the tiled foyer by the front door, her sandals sat near the wall. She slipped them onto her feet.

Brett rested his hand on the door handle. "I'm not sure what happens next. Do I kiss you goodbye? Should I shake your hand?"

She gave a quick laugh and closed the distance between them. "How about a hug?"

"Deal." He opened his arms and she stepped into his embrace. God, it felt good to have him hold her. "Are you sure you don't want to stay for breakfast? After everything, well, it seems like I should do more than just give you a hug and say goodbye."

She inhaled his scent. He smelled like pine and mountain air. The thing was, she really was tempted to stay a little longer. But would they be able to navigate a new relationship after having had sex? "Maybe I can…"

The phone in her hand vibrated with an incoming call. She glanced at the screen. It was Katya. She sent it to voicemail. The phone began to ring again a moment later. Now Eva was getting a little nervous. Katya was a worrier, but something bad *might* have happened.

Exhaling, she slipped out of the embrace. "I really do need to see what's up."

"I get it." This time, when he reached for the handle, he opened the door.

She stepped outside. The sun had yet to rise over the horizon, and the street was quiet.

"Well…" She was struck with the urge to pull him to her and place her lips on his. Maybe he'd give her some privacy to call her sister back. Then she could stay for those pancakes he kept talking about. The phone in her hand began to shimmy.

"Looks like you really do have to take that," Brett said.

She stepped off the stoop. "Thanks again for everything."

"I hope it all works out for you." He lifted his hand in a small wave.

Phone still vibrating, she hustled to her car, where she took the call on her in-car audio. "What has gotten you so worked up? You knew I was going to call you back."

"You said you'd call me back in a minute," Katya snapped. "I was worried."

According to her phone, it had been eight minutes since first texting her sister. "I was going to call you as soon as I could."

She glanced at Brett's house. The front door was closed. She pulled away from the curb, taking the same route she had the night before, only in reverse.

"Are you in the car?" Katya asked. Did her sister's voice hold an accusatory tone? "Why are you out so early in the morning?"

"I *am* a nurse," she said, not wanting to tell her sister about the tryst. "We do work overnight shifts sometimes…"

"Last thing you told me, you had a date. You never called me when you got home. I was thinking that maybe the guy was a serial killer or something." Katya paused a beat. "Sorry you had to work and didn't get to go out. With everything going on, I just got worried that something happened to you, too."

Eva rubbed her forehead as she drove. Katya was taking care of a lot. The least she could do was acknowledge that her sister cared. "Thanks for looking out for me. How's Baba?"

"We had a rough night."

Approaching a stop sign, Eva let her foot off the gas and dropped it to the brake. Her heartbeat thrummed, echoing in her ears. "What happened?"

"I got a call from the hospital. She tried to get out of bed by herself and fell again." Katya exhaled a sob. "She's refusing to stay in the hospital, and honestly, I don't know what to do."

A wave of shock rolled through Eva. She needed to say something, but her lips had gone numb. She still remembered her grandmother saying, *Home isn't a place, it's the people who love you most.*

Rolling through the intersection, Eva cleared her throat. "Is she okay now? Did she break any bones?"

"This time she's fine. But who knows what will happen when she tries to get out of bed again? And I know she'll keep trying."

They really were lucky that their grandmother wasn't seriously injured.

"How is she?"

Katya said, "Right now, she's sleeping. I've been here all night. When I realized that you hadn't checked in after your date, I got worried. I guess I should've known that you were working."

Eva's omission of the truth sat heavy in her gut. "You're a good sister. A great granddaughter and a fabulous mother," she said, "Go home. Get some rest. We can talk later."

"Before you hang up, the doctor wants to have a meeting with us. He scheduled it for this afternoon at two. You should be able to get down here in plenty of time..."

"My shift starts at noon."

"And you're just leaving the hospital now?"

"What? No..."

"You said that you were leaving work."

Damn. She hadn't exactly lied to her sister. But she had let her believe something that wasn't true. "Listen, I'm on the schedule for the next few days."

"Aren't there other nurses who can cover your shift?" Katya protested.

She didn't have any extra leave to use after taking time off a few weeks back. Her head started to ache. "The hospital's short-staffed at the moment."

Katya huffed. "I was really hoping for more support from you."

"What's that supposed to mean?"

"Well, like you said, you *are* a nurse. You'd understand everything the doctor will tell us."

Her sister had a point. Eva braked at a red traffic signal.

"I'll see about taking my break during the meeting," said Eva. "Then, I can call in to the meeting."

"That'd help a ton, thanks." She could hear the relief in Katya's voice.

Honestly, Eva was happy to be helpful. "Anything else?"

"Right now, Baba's in the hospital for observation. After a few days, she'll have to go somewhere. The doctor's hinting that the 'somewhere' is an elder care facility."

"I can't imagine she likes that idea at all," Eva said before asking, "What does she want to do?"

Katya gave a mirthless laugh. "She refuses to live anywhere but her own home. Jorje said she could live with us—even though it'd be tight. I mean, five of us already live in a three-bedroom house. But Baba doesn't want to live with me. And she doesn't want to go to the senior care facility, either."

"Sounds like our grandmother—stubborn and single-minded."

"Yes, it does," said Katya. "I'll talk to you at two." And then, she ended the call.

Still waiting for the traffic light to change, Eva glanced at the clock on her dashboard. It read 5:58 a.m. Not even 6:00 a.m., and already her day had been more eventful than the entire last week.

Her phone pinged with an incoming text. Would Katya just let up? Eva pulled over to the side of the road and glanced at the screen.

The message was from Brett. Her pulse raced.

Did you take care of your call?

She smiled. He really was a great guy. She typed out a reply.

Looks like it might be complicated.

He sent another text right away.

I'm good at complicated. Want to meet for lunch before you go to work? We can talk about it. I know a place that has excellent burgers.

He was charming and persistent. She started to reply:

What time?

Her thumb hovered above the Send icon. She liked Brett, truly. They were certainly compatible—both in bed and out. She could still feel his kisses on her lips. Her cheeks were rubbed raw by the stubble on his chin. But her life might be *too* complicated, even for a second date. There was her grandmother to think about.

A solution as to where the older woman could live had taken root in Eva's mind. It would be a big commitment on her part, so until she was ready, she wouldn't broach the idea to anyone—not even Katya.

If everything in her life was about to change, then she really couldn't start a new relationship.

She deleted her unsent message, typed out a new one and hit Send. Before she pulled away from the curb, she glanced at her reply still visible on her phone screen... and felt how final it was.

I had a great time last night, but I can't see you again. Sorry.

Chapter Three

Golden light streamed through a set of French doors that led to a backyard patio. A TV hung on the wall. Images flickered across the screen, though the sound was muted. In the kitchen, the coffee maker gurgled as it brewed. Sitting on the sofa in his living room, Brett read the text from Eva. His gut clenched with disappointment. How had he gotten her signals so wrong?

At least she was being honest at the outset. No need to waste time wondering if their first date would lead to a second one—or even a relationship.

Eva was a sexy woman who also happened to be a generous and passionate lover. But there was more to like about her than just the physical. She was smart, funny and interesting. In short, she was a rare combination of everything he wanted in a partner.

So yeah, it sucked that she didn't even want to give it a try.

Picking up the phone, he looked at the screen. The message was still there, mocking him.

I had a great time last night, but I can't see you again. Sorry.

There was nothing else for him to do besides forget that he'd ever met Eva Tamke.

The thing was, he didn't want to forget.

He checked the time. It was 6:14 a.m.

Damn. He hadn't been up this early since his days as a warrant officer in the army.

Rubbing his eyes, he wondered what he was supposed to do next. Sure, he could go back to bed for a few more hours of shut-eye. But after what happened, he doubted that he'd get much rest. Since he didn't have to be at work until 2:00 p.m., he had an entire day to fill.

Rising from the sofa, he padded into the kitchen. He filled a cup to the rim with coffee from the pot. He took a sip and let the caffeine buzz through his system.

Last night, he'd made a pot of decaf coffee that he and Eva had barely touched. She took her coffee with flavored creamer and sugar—more of a dessert than a drink. The sugar dish still sat on the counter. Her mug was in the sink. Lipstick ringed the spoon's neck where she'd licked it clean. Funny, she'd only been in his house a few hours. Now, it seemed like everything reminded him of her.

Coffee cup in hand, he returned to the sofa. Leaning back into the cushions, he looked at his phone. He'd missed a call from Gus, the newly hired flight nurse on the air ambulance's crew. Gus had left a message in the middle of the night. "Hate to bother you. But I have a work question. It's important. Call me back."

Brett didn't typically call people so early in the morning. But Gus had said it was important. Using the number from the message, he placed a call.

Gus answered after the second ring. "Hey, Brett." The dude's voice was raspy and weak. "Thanks for calling me back."

"No offense, my man. But you don't sound too good."

"No offense taken. My kid came home from school with the stomach bug. Everyone at home caught it. This is my first time taking a personal day. I'm not sure of the protocol."

"Usually, you call Darla at human resources. She's in charge of finding replacements for the flight crew." There was no need to make a sick man deal with requesting leave time. He continued, "I'll reach out and let her know. I hope everyone is healthy soon."

"You and me both," said Gus.

After hanging up, he placed another call.

It was answered after the second ring. "This is Darla."

"To be honest," said Brett, by way of greeting, "I'm impressed that you're at work already."

"Make that still," said Darla with a wry laugh. "And I'm impressed that you're awake at all."

"Well, I got an email. Gus is out with a stomach bug, and that means…"

Darla finished his thought. "You need someone to fill in until he comes back." She tapped on a keyboard. "A nurse with experience working on a medevac helicopter will be difficult to find on such short notice. But I'm on it," she added, ending the call.

Before he had the chance to set down his phone, it pinged with an incoming text. His pulse spiked. Was it Eva? He hoped like hell that she'd reconsidered his offer for a lunch date. Or any date, really. He glanced at the screen.

The message was from his sister, Shannon.

Text me when you get up. I need help brainstorming…

Brett groaned. He loved his sister, but he knew that an early-morning text was probably bad news. Right now, her life was difficult. She was in the middle of a messy divorce. Her soon-to-be-ex, Lucian, owned several car dealerships in the Dallas/ Ft. Worth area. As it turned out, not all of his deals were legit. What was worse, his shady activities spilled into his personal life. Shannon had given Lucian more chances than Brett could count because she always wanted to work things out for their kids—four-year-old twins, Paige and Palmer.

Instead of texting his sister, he placed a call. She answered after the first ring.

"Wow. It's not like you to be up this early."

"So I've heard." He wasn't going to tell his sister about Eva, especially since the relationship had crashed during takeoff. He paused before asking, "What's up?"

Shannon drew in a shaking breath. "It's Lucian. He hasn't paid for the preschool program. And if he doesn't pay..."

Her words unwound, like a spool of thread rolling across the floor. He knew his sister couldn't afford it on her own. If the kids weren't in preschool, they'd need childcare, which also cost money. She'd end up relying on Lucian, which was what the jerk wanted. To control the situation. Honestly, Brett wasn't surprised. Mad, yes. Shocked, no.

"Bad day for me not to have childcare," Shannon said. "I have an interview this morning for a bank job with more room for professional growth."

He knew his sister had had to ask their parents for financial help, and sitters were hard to come by at a moment's notice. If Dallas wasn't a full five hours from San Antonio, he'd offer to watch the kids.

"I'll pay the tuition," he said without hesitation. True, he'd paid the retainer for her divorce attorney. That check had wiped out his rainy-day fund. But he had cash enough to help his sister. After turning on the phone's speaker function, he opened a payment app. "If I can transfer the money directly to the school, I'll pay now. How much do you need?"

Shannon gave him the school's pay-share address, along with the amount.

He sucked in a breath. "That's more than my whole mortgage payment."

"I know. I know," said Shannon. "I'm going to have to switch them to something more affordable—unless Lucian starts to pay. But there's so much chaos right now. I just want their lives to be close to normal."

"I get it," he said. "I want what's best for my nieces, too." He typed the amount into the app, along with a note that it was for Paige and Palmer's account. Then, he transferred the money. "Done. And don't worry about paying me back."

"Thank you, Brett. You're really the best. Whoever ends up with you will be the luckiest lady alive."

Eva's face flashed through his mind. Rubbing the back of his neck, he tried to laugh. Even he could hear the tension in his voice. "Well, I probably won't meet her today."

"I better get going," said his sister.

"Good luck with everything. Let me know how it goes."

"Will do," she said. Then she ended the call.

Setting the phone down, he leaned back into the sofa. It wasn't even 6:30 a.m. Already, he'd had quite a day.

His phone pinged again with a new message.

He knew it wouldn't be Eva. Still, hope like an electric current ran through him.

It was a notification from the bank informing him of his new balance. Brett cursed. In helping his sister, he'd almost wiped out his account. True, being flat-ass broke was only temporary. Next week, he'd get a paycheck. But he hadn't meant to give away all his money.

Holding his thumb on the power button, he turned off his phone. The last thing he wanted was another early-morning text. Especially, since the universe seemed to be conspiring against him.

It wasn't like him to be pessimistic. But he knew why he was so sullen.

He hated to admit it, but Eva's rejection still stung. Her scent filled his home. The taste of her lingered on his lips. Yet, the relationship was over before it had begun. The real kicker was, he didn't know why.

Well, he wasn't going to sit here and think about it anymore. They'd had one hell of the night, and for whatever reason, she was done.

So he was he.

Decker Newcombe lay in a hospital bed and tried to focus. It was hard to think around the constant beeping of the machines and the dullness caused by the pain meds. The bed, which he rarely left, shifted every few hours to prevent bedsores. The disinfectant scent of manufactured pine, stale coffee and his own body odor surrounded him like a fog.

The last things he remembered clearly were smoke and fire. He'd been trapped in an inferno. The pain had been unrelenting and unbearable. In the moment, he was certain that his sins had finally caught up with him and he'd been dragged to hell.

As it turned out, he hadn't been that lucky.

He'd been brought to a hospital in San Antonio, which he figured was its own kind of hell. Hours, days and weeks melted together until he couldn't tell how long he'd been handcuffed to the bed. Time didn't flow like a river but rather rushed in and receded like an ocean's tide.

Still, he knew a bit about what was happening to him and why. The information came through snatches of conversation he overheard while nurses and doctors talked with the police officer posted outside his door.

As much as he hated to have a cop sitting outside his hospital room, in a way, he was flattered. It meant the police still viewed him as a threat—and he most certainly was. Even before Decker knew that he was a direct descendant of Jack the Ripper, a Victorian-era serial killer, he was a dangerous man.

Decker had plotted the ultimate murder, a crime that he was to commit live on the internet. It would make him the most famous killer of all time.

Things hadn't gone according to plan.

There'd been a fire in the warehouse where he was set up to stream the killing. A fight with his former friend and now ultimate enemy, Ryan Steele, left them both bloodied and bruised. In the end, he'd been shot by the undersheriff from Encantador, Kathryn Glass.

Certainly, they could've left him for dead, but the undersheriff and Ryan had pulled him out of the blaze. Then they'd called paramedics, who gave him medical care and transported him to a hospital. As a man comfortable with vengeance, he couldn't fathom their thinking when they decided to save his life.

A normal man would feel gratitude.

Decker felt nothing.

No, that wasn't true. In those first days after the fire, he felt gut-wrenching agony. Whenever the meds wore off, there was a pounding in his left side with every beat of his heart. His lungs had burned with each breath. His right hand and arm had felt as if they were still on fire.

But since he had nothing to do but lie in bed and think, more memories returned.

The hacker who'd helped him—a person he knew only as Seraphim—had sent him a message.

You have a son with Anastasia Pierce.

Along with the message was a picture of the birth certificate. On it, Decker was listed as the father.

Memories of Ana haunted him like a ghost. A dozen years ago, they had lived together for ten months. True, he'd been working as muscle for hire the whole time—strong-arming people who owed money to a loan shark. But with her, he'd almost felt normal. It was the one time in his life that he dared to have hope for some kind of future. For him, Ana was a single ray of sunshine breaking through the clouds of a raging storm that was his soul.

Then, one day, he came home, and she was gone. She'd

taken all her things, even the kitten he'd given her. She'd left him with the furniture, the dishes.

He still remembered the date it happened. Seven months before the birth certificate had been issued.

It didn't take a genius to figure out what had happened. Ana discovered she was pregnant and split. But the fact that she didn't want him involved with the kid hurt worse than all his other injuries combined.

Yet, she'd listed him as the father.

There'd always been an underlying goodness to Ana. She might have been finished with Decker, but she wouldn't lie about her child's paternity.

Since he had nothing to do with his time but think, he realized that the hacker might've been lying to him from the beginning. But what would Seraphim gain by lying? They wanted to spread chaos and had chosen Decker to help them. After finding Decker through an internet café, they offered to fund his next killing—so long as Decker was willing to murder his victim live and on the internet.

Since Decker was determined to be the most famous serial killer of all time, he was in on the plan.

Which brought him back to the original question. Why would Seraphim lie to Decker about something like a child?

Then again, Seraphim was a weird person. They hid their identity behind a long-beaked plague doctor mask. Their voice was always distorted by electronics.

Decker's computer had surely burned up in the warehouse fire. But he'd stashed a cell phone in Mexico with Seraphim's number. If he could get the phone, then he could ask the hacker to find out if the kid was really his.

How was he supposed to get out of the hospital and back to Mexico? He needed an escape plan. But his whole body throbbed like a bass drum. It must be time for more meds.

"You going in there?" a male voice came from the hallway.

It was the cop who guarded his door, Officer Kwan. Over time, Decker had come to recognize the different voices.

"It's happy hour," a female said. Nancy, the afternoon nurse, was always glib. The happy hour she referred to was Decker's cocktail of medications.

"I guess you heard the news?" asked Kwan.

"No, what news?"

"The doc says he's healthy enough to leave San Antonio Medical Center. He's getting transferred to a jail hospital."

Nancy said, "Honestly, I'm not surprised. His vitals are looking good. Do you know when he's leaving?"

"Soon," said Kwan. "This morning I was told that I don't have to come back tomorrow. But before they're sending him to jail, he's headed to Encantador for a hearing."

Decker heard the door open, and he looked over. Nancy was holding the door with her back, now saying something to the cop about the weather. He could see the toe of Officer Kwan's shoe. It was shiny, black and reflected the overhead lights.

So, he was going back to Encantador. That was an interesting twist. But how could he use it to his advantage?

With the soles of her sneakers squeaking on the tile floor, Nancy pivoted. Before she entered the room, Decker let his eyes drift closed.

"It's time for the fun meds," she said.

He didn't reply. He never did.

The smell of rubbing alcohol filled the room. "This might feel cold," she said, wiping his arm. "And here's a pinch."

He watched as she injected a solution into his IV tube. Cool liquid began to flow through his veins.

"I don't know why you talk to him," said Kwan. "He never replies."

"Well, I just want my patients to know that I'm here and I care." She patted the back of Decker's hand.

"Care?" the police officer snorted. "You know who this is, right? You've heard all about what he's done."

"It's not my job to pass judgment," she said. "Just to provide the treatment he needs." A moment passed, then she added, "There, all done." She left the room, the door closing behind her.

"Whatever," Decker heard Kwan say.

A phone pinged loudly with an incoming message. There was silence for a few seconds. "You won't have to worry about him too much longer," Kwan said at last. "That text was from my boss. Looks like the feds are sending an agent to take custody of your patient."

"And then what?" Nancy asked. "They're going to drive him in a convoy?"

"Even better. Looks like he's getting taken by helicopter."

Good to know, you gabby idiots. The meds were trying to have their way with him, but Decker Newcombe was too mighty an opponent for anything coursing through his system. *Focus*, he ordered himself. *Remember what they said and make a plan.*

His mind started to fill with an image of a small boat floating atop the warm waters of the Gulf. Fluffy white clouds. A clear blue sky.

C'mon, you're Decker Newcombe. You've got things to do. Including finding out if you're a father.

He fought the fuzziness of the pain meds with everything he had.

And he had *a lot*. If he wanted to survive, he had to think. But how could he, when his head was filled with thick, white clouds and a soft blue sky? The sun was a bright, white ball. Then he was absorbed by the light and the pain was washed away by the tide.

Chapter Four

The sun hung in a cloudless sky over downtown San Antonio. Heat shimmered off the pavement in waves. Brett sat in the driver's seat of his pickup truck and glanced at the instrument panel. It was 1:50 p.m. Ten minutes early for his shift at the hospital.

The main campus for San Antonio Medical Center filled up several blocks to his left. As he stopped at an intersection, waiting for a break in traffic, his blinker gave off a hypnotic *tick-tick-tick*.

Usually, he was happy for his shift to begin. But today he wasn't.

Honestly, he'd tried to forget about Eva. It hadn't worked. There was something about her that had gotten to him. They'd made a connection, and while she clearly wasn't interested in pursuing it—and he respected her choice—he wished he could figure out what had gone wrong.

Pulling onto a road that ran adjacent to the hospital, he followed the blue sign to the medical flight facility. The road ended at a small parking lot. Beyond that was a domed metal hangar. It housed offices, held equipment and, if necessary, because of severe weather, the helicopter itself.

Brett pulled into a parking spot near the door. A metal sign was affixed to a post: Reserved for Pilot in Command. He turned off the engine and stared out the windshield. The helicopter sat on the landing pad. It was painted white, with SAMC's blue logo on the door.

As he did each time that he looked at his helicopter, he knew he was a lucky guy.

He had a job he loved. His crew was more like family than coworkers or even friends. But Eva's abrupt entry and exit from his life stung. At least he'd get to fly today. Maybe that was part of his problem. He was only truly happy when he was in the air.

Without the truck's engine running, there was no air-conditioning. The cab grew brutally hot. A bead of sweat snaked down the side of his face, and he wiped it away with his thumb. He opened the door, but it was no better. An oven-like heat rolled over him in a wave.

As per regulations, he wore a flight suit. The fabric was flame retardant, but the material didn't breathe. Sweat ran down his back and pooled at the base of his spine.

A yellow sports car entered the back of the lot. The driver gave two quick blasts from the horn as it swerved into a spot. Brett lifted his hand in greeting.

The door opened, and Wade Shaw, one of the two EMTs on his crew, unfolded himself from the small car. Before working as a flight EMT, Wade had played college basketball. The paramedic claimed to be six-eleven, and Brett believed him.

Wagging his finger, Wade approached. He also wore a flight suit. "You look like crap, no offense. It makes me think you had a very late night with my new friend, Eva Tamke."

Heading toward the hangar, Brett knew he had to be diplomatic. "She's a nice lady. We had a nice time."

"Nice lady?" Wade repeated. "Nice time? She's absolutely perfect for you. Did she tell you that she used to be in the air force? She even worked on a flight crew as a nurse."

"She was in the Air National Guard," Brett said, correcting his friend.

Wade shrugged his shoulders. "Same difference. When are you seeing her again?"

"We aren't going out on another date."

Wade stopped midstride, leaving Brett walking alone.

Brett glanced over his shoulder as he spoke. "She has some things going on in her life. I do, too."

"What's going on that's more important than finding your soulmate?"

"Soulmate?" Brett opened the door. Thankfully, the inside of the hangar was dark and cool. "That's assuming a lot." He paused a beat. "My bastard of a brother-in-law won't pay for his kids' tuition."

"I thought your nieces were little. Why do they need tuition?"

"Apparently, fancy preschool costs a lot—like more than a house payment." Hopefully, it was enough information to move the subject away from last night's date.

"So, what does that have to do with Eva?"

He'd had lots of luck so far that day. Unfortunately, all of it had been bad.

He didn't want to get into what happened last night. Aside from the fact that the adage was true about discretion being the better part of valor and all. He didn't want to admit that the night had been great, but Eva didn't want anything more to do with him. He ignored Wade's question.

The rest of the crew was already at the flight facility. Stacy, the copilot, and Lin, the other EMT, sat on folding chairs at a table with thin metal legs. A line of cards ran down the middle of the table, a game of gin rummy already underway.

"It's too hot outside to do any preflight." Stacy said as Brett approached. "We got the game started."

The medevac crew worked nine-hour shifts, overlapping another two other crews to cover an entire day. On some shifts, the chopper was in the air more than it was on the ground. Those days were filled with flying some seriously injured or ill people to the hospital. But mostly, the worst part of the job was boredom. If there were no calls, the crew was left with little to do.

He said, "Gus is out sick. Darla's supposed to send his replacement. I've got some paperwork to fill out, then you can deal me into the game." Duffel bag in hand, he walked toward his small office at the rear of the hangar. "If the replacement nurse shows up, let me know."

His phone buzzed with an incoming text from Darla in HR. He read the message as he walked. Apparently, the crew was transporting a patient to a different facility. But first Brett had to talk to an FBI agent.

There were about a dozen things Brett had to worry about before getting his helicopter in the air. But only one thing mattered right now.

What in hell did the FBI want with him?

Eva stood next to a bed in the emergency department at San Antonio Medical Center. She read the LCD panel on the thermometer. The patient, a four-year-old girl, had a fever of one hundred and two. Lying on a bed, the child had a white blanket pulled up to her chin.

Eva picked up the tablet computer from the small workstation and entered the information into the intake form.

The girl's mother stood on the opposite side of the bed. "So?" she asked.

Smiling at the girl and her mom, she said, "Your daughter definitely has fever." Then, to the patient, she asked, "And your throat hurts, pumpkin?"

The girl nodded. "It hurts bad," she said, her voice raspy.

"A doctor is going to come in," she told the child. "He'll use a really big Q-tip to tickle the back of your throat." She suspected strep throat but wouldn't know until a test had been run. To the mom, she asked, "Has she been around anyone who's sick?"

"She just started preschool. It seems like everyone has a runny nose or a cough."

Eva gave the woman a sympathetic smile. "It's like that at the beginning of the school year."

"I tried to get her an appointment with her pediatrician, but they were booked for days. When, she stopped wanting to drink anything, I figured I couldn't wait."

"It's best to get checked out. We don't want a little something to become a big something," Eva said, assuring the mom that she'd made the right decision. "The doctor will be in shortly. If you need anything, let me know."

She left the exam room. A clock on the wall read 2:01 p.m. Her pulse jumped. How had the time gotten away from her? She was supposed to be on the call with Katya and Baba's doctor already. Each second slipped through her fingers.

The longer she thought about her plan, the more she liked it. She was going to move to Encantador and help take care of her grandmother.

True, there were things that she'd miss about living in San Antonio. She had a job and friends. But nothing tethered her to the community—not really. She wasn't like Brett; she hadn't bought a house. She didn't have kids in school or a partner who'd also have to relocate.

After talking to Katya and her grandmother, she would tell her coworkers. Then she'd put in her official notice.

The nurse's station was a long counter in the middle of a warren of beds and rooms. A lower counter served as a desk. It was always cluttered with papers, a desktop computer, tablets and several phones. The scent of disinfectant circulated on a constant stream of icy air.

Her coworker, Rex, stood behind the counter. He looked up as she approached. "What's the verdict?"

Setting the tablet on the counter, Eva said, "I'd bet it's strep, but the doc will have to give her a test."

Rex nodded. "I'll send him there next."

A Latino in his late fifties, Rex was like an uncle to many on the staff—Eva included. Earlier, she'd told him about her grandmother's fall and the call to discuss long-term care options. Rex understood that she wanted to be a part of the meeting, even if it was over the phone.

"Unless you need anything else, I'm going to step into the break room and call my sister," she said.

He gave her a warm smile. "I hope everything works out for your grandma."

"Me, too."

A phone on the desk began to ring. Rex sighed. "Hold up a minute, Eva. That's the internal hospital line. Let's see what's happening." Lifting the receiver to his ear, he said, "Emergency Department." He paused a beat and then said, "Yeah?" Brows drawn together, he cast a glance in her direction. "Sure, we can," he said before hanging up the phone. He turned to Eva. "That was Darla with HR. She called about you."

"Me?" Anxiety exploded in her middle, leaving her with too much energy. Was the call about Brett and their date? What if the hospital had a nonfraternization policy and someone had found out about their night together? "What did Darla want?"

"You're being reassigned for the rest of your shift."

"Reassigned?" She exhaled a long breath. So, the call had nothing to do with her one-night stand. "Sure, where do they need me?"

"At the heliport. Now."

"I'm not flight certified. Not anymore, at least."

Rex shook his head. "It doesn't matter. You worked on a helicopter when you were in the army."

"It was the Air National Guard," she corrected, "That was when I was in college, like, sixteen years ago."

"All's I know is that they're short-staffed and need a nurse. You got picked."

There were several medevac crews who worked for the hospital. What were the chances that Brett Wilson happened to be the pilot of this particular crew? "I'll head to the hangar after my call."

"No time for that," said Rex. "They need you now. They've been called out and can't take off without you."

She glanced at her phone. There were four messages, all from Katya. A sick feeling settled in her gut. Slipping the phone into her pocket, she said, "I'll go now."

"I knew we could count on you. They'll have a flight suit you can use." Rex gave her arm a squeeze. "I'll have Security give you a lift."

Hustling down a long hallway, Eva sent a text to her sister.

I've been reassigned for the day. I can't call in. I'm so sorry.

It didn't seem like she'd done enough. She sent another message.

I'll come down this weekend. See you Saturday.

Katya responded.

Baba has to stay at the hospital for a week, so we have some time. We'll talk when you get home.

A security guard, clad in a tan shirt and brown pants, waited next to the employee entrance. "You Eva?" she asked.

"I am."

"I'm Natalie and supposed to give you a lift. Follow me." The guard approached a set of glass doors that opened with a swish.

Eva stepped outside. The sun beat down onto the pavement. In seconds, sweat streamed down the back of her scrubs.

Since the hospital complex was larger than a professional sports stadium, security guards drove official golf carts and provided rides to patients and employees alike. One of those carts, painted white with the blue SAMC logo on the hood, waited at the curb.

Natalie got behind the steering wheel. Eva followed and slipped into the passenger seat. "Thanks for the ride."

"Hold on," the guard ordered. "I've been told to get you to the flight facility STAT."

As the cart lurched forward, Eva grabbed a metal bar that was attached to the dashboard. They jostled through the parking lot and down a side road. It took only minutes before the cart rolled to a stop near the door to the hangar.

A white helicopter was on the landing pad. A blond woman wearing a flight suit sat in the pilot's seat.

Honestly, Eva wasn't sure if she were relieved or disappointed that the pilot wasn't Brett. Nodding her thanks to the guard, she hopped down.

The woman in the helicopter looked up and smiled as Eva approached. "You must be our nurse."

Sun reflected off the white aircraft and the concrete tarmac. It made looking at the woman painful. Shading her eyes with her hand, she said, "Eva Tamke."

"My name's Stacy Janowitz. Nice to meet you. We got a call right after the shift change, so we're scrambling to get into the air. Go inside the hangar and ask one of the guys for a flight suit. You'll need to change quick so we can get off the ground."

Inside, a man with black hair stood next to a bank of metal lockers. Eva smiled and walked toward him. "I spoke to your pilot, Stacy. She said someone in here would have a flight suit for me." She paused. "Sorry, I should've introduced myself first. I'm Eva Tamke, the nurse."

The man said, "We really appreciate you filling in at the

last minute. I'm Lin, one of the EMTs." He opened the door to a locker where a flight suit hung on a peg. He handed her the uniform and pointed to the rear of the hangar. "There's a bathroom back there. You can use it to change."

"Thanks. I'll be ready in a minute, then Stacy can take off."

She started across the long, cavernous room. Like she told Rex, it had been more than a decade since she'd been part of a helicopter crew. She didn't miss flying, per se. But she was excited to get back in the air, and adrenaline coursed through her veins.

As she headed for the bathroom, she could see someone sitting behind a desk in an office with a long narrow window in the door.

Someone very familiar.

And because she was staring at Brett Wilson, he happened to look up. Her eyes locked with his, and the breath caught in her chest.

He stood, and she pushed open the door and stepped inside. "Is it too cheesy to ask what a nice guy like you is doing in a place like this?"

"I work here and happen to like the flight facility." He cleared his throat. "So, I guess the real question is—why are *you* here?"

She refused to let him unsettle her. Standing taller, she said, "Darla said the medevac needed a nurse with flight experience."

Resting his elbows on the desk, he laced his fingers together. Despite his less than enthusiastic greeting, she still found him handsome. He gazed at her with his deep blue eyes, and her pulse raced.

He cleared his throat. "I'm glad to see that we've got a nurse. From what you said last night, it sounds like you still remember the job."

He was right. But there were other things she remembered, as well. Like the feeling of his lips on hers. Or how she fit perfectly next to him in the bed. If all she could think about was the feeling of his hands on her skin, then maybe it was best if she didn't work with the helicopter crew after all.

"I'm not sure that this is the best idea—me and you working together, I mean." She winced as soon as the last word left her mouth. She hadn't meant to be so candid. But working with Brett was the last thing she should do.

She was needed, though, and there was no going back now.

Brett worked his jaw back and forth. "I don't think we have the luxury of you accepting this assignment or not. We have to transport a patient. I'm not completely sure what's going on." Before he could say any more, the phone on his desk began to ring. "Stay there for a minute. Let me get this, then we can talk."

"I'll give you some privacy." She stepped into the hangar, just outside of the office door.

Brett picked up the call. "This is Brett Wilson."

A voice came across on the phone's speaker, loud enough that she could clearly hear. "This is Jason Jones. I'm a supervisory special agent with the FBI office here in San Antonio, calling regarding the patient you're about to transport."

Why was the FBI calling about this patient? Maybe the less she knew about the call, the better. She took a few steps back, creating more distance between herself and the phone.

The FBI agent spoke again, and she froze. "You're going to be taking a patient from SAMC. I've got to warn you, this person is particularly dangerous. Because of the risks, we've chosen to transport them via air ambulance to cut down on travel time."

"Okay." Brett's tone was wary. "What else can you tell me?"

Eva took a step back. She shouldn't be listening to a call between Brett and an FBI agent. But then the agent spoke, and she stopped her retreat.

"The hospital you'll be going to is in a small town south of you. It's called Encantador."

Her pulse started to race. The helicopter was headed to the hospital where her grandmother was also a patient. It didn't matter what else the agent had to say. It didn't matter that she was a fool for tempting herself by being around Brett, a man she wanted but would never get to have again.

Pressing the flight suit to her chest, she hustled toward the bathroom. After opening the door, she closed and locked it. Leaning against the wall, she drew in a single deep breath.

Being part of the crew would get her exactly what she needed—the ability to see her grandmother.

Yet, she needed to stay away from Brett. Even moreso, since her rejection of him this morning. She really couldn't develop feelings for anyone with so much going on in her life right now. Working with him was going to make it that much harder to keep her feelings neutral.

She drew in a single, deep breath.

She could still refuse to take the assignment.

No. She wouldn't let the hospital down by bringing her personal life to work. Exhaling fully, she stripped out of her scrubs and worked her feet into the legs of the flight suit.

After all, she just had to work with Brett for a few hours. What could really happen in such a short time?

Chapter Five

Brett had just gotten off the call with the FBI agent, and he didn't like the situation one bit. Jones had explained who they were transporting. Brett always thought he'd seen and heard it all, that little could faze him.

He was wrong.

He knew that declining the assignment was an option. Not even the feds could force him to fly if he thought it was unsafe. But even though he was in charge of the aircraft, he liked his crew to be a democracy. Every person got a vote if the situation was difficult.

And damn, but this was one of the most difficult transports he'd ever make.

More than their notorious patient, it seemed that Eva had changed her mind about staying for the shift while he was on the call. Now, she was dressed in a flight suit. He couldn't help but wonder why she'd made a different decision, even though it shouldn't matter to him.

Still, he had a job to do. Up first was briefing his crew. They were all gathered near the folding table. He took a moment to look everyone in the eye. Wade. Stacy. Lin. He met Eva's gaze last. Despite it all, his gut tightened.

The baggy jumpsuits were made for function, not fashion. But even the bland fabric seemed to give her skin a glow, even though it hid curves he knew lay beneath.

His fingers itched with the memory of tracing the outline of body after they'd had sex the second time. Or maybe it had been after their third round. How was he supposed to work with her and pretend like he didn't know her intimately? Hell, her scent still clung to his skin.

Then again, he knew what had to be done.

He couldn't look at her as a woman he desired. He had to see her as a colleague and a member of his crew. As hard as it was, he refocused his gaze.

She still had her hospital ID hanging around her neck. She'd have to remove it before they were airborne. But other than that, she looked ready to work. He wasn't sure why she'd changed her mind about staying on the crew for the shift, but he certainly wasn't going to question her now. After the phone call with Special Agent Jones, Brett needed to focus on the mission.

"We're about to take a patient from the hospital. I want you to know what you're getting into before you step onto the aircraft." He paused. "I assume you've all heard the name Decker Newcombe."

It was an easy assumption to make. The serial killer had been in the news for years. The media became fascinated with him when he assassinated a district attorney in Wyoming and then escaped arrest by living off the grid. He'd reemerged and killed four people in southern Texas around Christmas, then continued his killing spree throughout the region. A few weeks ago, he'd been taken into custody following a botched murder that he'd planned to stream live on the internet. The murderer was injured during the ensuing chaos and then taken into custody.

"Well, Mr. Newcombe has been recovering from his injuries at SAMC. He's due to be officially charged with all his crimes later today. Then, he'll be taken to jail, where he'll finish recovering at the hospital there. The feds want him transported via medevac, and that's where we come in." Tension pinched his shoulders together, and he rubbed the back of his neck. "I don't like this at all, although I've been assured that the patient will be restrained. Plus, he'll be guarded by a US marshal the whole time. Questions?"

Lin lifted a hand. "Can we refuse?"

"I suppose we can," he said.

Lin continued, "I mean, we aren't police officers. We've transported some rowdy patients, but this is different."

The safety and well-being of his crew—both physical and emotional—was his top priority. It meant making sure they were all willing to fly, regardless of the circumstances. "That's why I wanted to talk with you all before we take off."

"I don't know about any of you," said Lin, "but I don't want to fly a serial killer around."

Wade countered with, "We've had dangerous people in the chopper before."

"Dangerous, sure. But deranged?" Lin shrugged.

"I hate to tell the hospital no," said Stacy, "especially since we're the only helicopter crew on right now. Can't the Texas Rangers take him?"

It was one of the things that Brett had brought up with SSA Jones. "They don't have anything with the medical equipment we have."

"We should vote," said Wade. "I'm a yes."

"No," said Lin.

"What about you, Stacy?" he asked.

She puffed out her cheeks before blowing out a long breath. "I'd like to have more time to think about this." She paused. "What would happen if we refused?"

"I guess transporting the prisoner becomes the feds' problem." He'd tried to keep from looking at Eva, if only because his pulse raced every time he saw her. But he turned to her now. "You've been quiet. What do you think?"

"I'm not really part of this crew," she said. "I'm just filling in for the day."

"But if we take off, you'll be on the helicopter. That means that you get a say-so."

She inhaled and exhaled. "You said that Decker Newcombe will be restrained. You said that a US marshal will be on board."

She hadn't really asked him any questions. Yet Brett said, "Correct to both."

"I'm still not sure if I should vote," she said. "But Decker Newcombe is one man who's going to be restrained. Plus, he's going to be guarded. I'm sure the marshal is trained to keep the situation under control."

"Handle him?" Lin echoed. "He's a killer."

"But he's also a patient," she said.

The list of things he liked about Eva was already long. Now, he had to add two more characteristics. She was brave and committed to her job.

"I guess I'm a yes, too," said Stacy.

"Majority rules," said Brett. "We need to be ready to take off in fifteen minutes. But, Lin, I won't make you go if you aren't comfortable."

Folding his arms across his chest, the EMT exhaled loudly. "I'm not happy, but I'm also not going to let y'all take off without me. I'm in."

"We need to be vigilant during this mission," Brett said. "But we always have to be aware. I know each and every one of you will be professional. Now, let's get ready." He glanced at his watch. "We've got fourteen minutes until the marshals will deliver the patient to the landing pad."

"C'mon," Lin said to Eva. "I'll show you where all of the medical equipment is stored."

"Hey, Eva," Brett called out.

She turned. "Yeah?"

He touched his chest. "Your lanyard," he said. "You can't wear it. It's a safety hazard. The cards can catch the light. And the cord can wrap around your neck."

"Oh." Eva pulled the ID over her head. Winding the cord around her hand, she shoved the whole thing into her breast pocket. "Thanks."

"No problem," he said.

He watched her walk away. Just like he'd noticed before, the flight suit hugged her curves and accentuated her round ass. Brett's mouth went dry.

"Weird that she's on our crew," said Wade, his voice not much more than a whisper.

"I was surprised to see her, that's for sure."

"And you aren't going to tell me what happened between you two?"

Clapping his hand on the taller man's shoulder, Brett said, "She's part of my flight crew. Anything I say about her now will get me an unpleasant meeting with Darla in HR. Nobody wants that."

"Looks like you lucked out, then," said Wade. "I won't bring it up again."

"I'm glad that at least one thing has gone my way today," he said. "Now, let's hope that nothing goes wrong with our infamous patient."

Eva pressed stethoscope to the patient's chest and listened to his respiration. For now, Decker was asleep, resting from the pain meds he'd been given prior to takeoff. Both of his wrists were handcuffed to the gurney he lay on.

She'd heard all the news reports about the serial killer who'd been on the run for more than a year. His story was personally important to her because the communities he'd terrorized—Encantador and the neighboring town of Mercy—were where she'd grown up. But it was more than that.

Decker had killed her grandmother's neighbor.

Then, he'd kidnapped another person from the same housing development.

Decker had killed several people, including a podcaster from San Antonio, before being caught by the undersheriff in Encantador. During his capture, the patient had been beaten, shot and burned. But the wounds had healed enough that he no longer needed acute care. Which, she supposed, was why he was going to be sent to regional jail to await trial.

She pulled the earpieces free before replacing her headset. As she tucked the stethoscope into a pouch that hung from a hook on the fuselage, she figured that her current patient was probably one of the reasons her grandmother had fallen.

Only a few weeks before, Decker had killed one of Baba's neighbors, a woman named Connie Wray. He'd recorded the killing and then sent the video to everyone in Connie's contact list. Getting that message had devastated her grandmother. In fact, after it happened, Eva had taken a week off to stay with Baba. It was one of the reasons she couldn't ask for more time off now. But she imagined that even with Decker in custody, her grandmother was still under some serious stress. Who wouldn't be? She'd lost a neighbor and a friend in such a violent way.

"What's the verdict?" The US marshal spoke into the mic that was attached to his headset. Augustin Herrera wore a black windbreaker with the marshal's seal embroidered on the chest. He was in his fifties, with dark eyes and a sprinkling of gray in his otherwise black crew cut. He had a close-cropped beard and wore a gold crucifix on a gold chain.

"His pulse and respiration are all normal," said Eva. Even with ear protection, the constant *whomp-whomp-whomp* of the rotors drowned out most other sounds.

"How long will this trip take us?" Augustin yelled into his mic.

It was Brett who answered. "Now that we're out of San

Antonio, it's about one hundred and twenty miles to Encantador. The flight should only last us half an hour. Forty minutes, tops."

Below the helicopter, San Antonio's downtown, a sea of glass and pavement, had been replaced by the suburbs. Neat houses had been built one next to each other until the properties looked like a quilt from ten thousand feet in the air.

While speaking to the marshal, Brett had turned to look over his seat in the cockpit. In his flight helmet, headset and sunglasses, he looked like the quintessential pilot. Competent. Fearless. Handsome.

Eva turned to Decker once more. True, she'd seen pictures of the killer—had even watched a documentary on his crimes while texting Katya. In those portraits, Decker looked terrifying. A slight man with blue eyes so icy she felt cold just watching the show. But cuffed to the bed and asleep, he didn't seem threatening at all. Still, she knew enough to be wary.

Stacy sat in the cockpit next to Brett. Situated directly behind the cockpit was the cargo hold, which made up much of the aircraft. It was not a big space, but had enough room for transporting a patient, equipment, and medical personnel. Lin and Wade were buckled into seats on the opposite side of the hold. A jump seat, bolted to the fuselage, sat next to the stretcher. Typically, Eva would have occupied that seat. But for now, Augustin sat next to his prisoner.

There was medical equipment for any kind of trauma or emergency. The jaws of life, its handle clamped shut, hung from the wall. There was also equipment to deliver a baby, Narcan for those who'd overdosed, medications, sutures, gauze, bandages and an AED for anyone in cardiac arrest. The medevac was better stocked than most ambulances, and she was glad to see that she had everything she might need. After all, once they dropped off the patient, she still had several more hours left in her shift and would likely be called out on other medical emergencies.

Stacy's voice came in over the mic. "Where'd that come from?"

Eva glanced out the starboard window at the darkening sky. She'd been so focused on the patient and equipment that she hadn't paid attention to anything beyond her patient.

Brett cursed. "I thought we had clear weather the whole way."

"We did," said Stacy, a note of panic in her voice. "The storm came out of nowhere."

"We'll be okay," said Brett. Then to the whole crew, he announced, "Everyone strap in and hang on. It's going to get bumpy."

Another jump seat was folded up behind the pilot's seat. Eva didn't want to leave her patient's side. But she wasn't ready to make the marshal move, either. She wrapped her hand into the webbing that held the AED onto the fuselage. She glanced out of the window again. In the distance, dark clouds filled the horizon. A fork of lightning lit up, yellow against the black.

"Brett," she said, feeling some of the same panic as she'd heard in Stacy's voice. How were they supposed to fly through that? "That storm is huge. Can't we go around it?"

"We're too close to alter our course now. Our only other option is to turn around, he said. "But it's moving fast."

"No way are we going back," said Augustin. "This prisoner is supposed to be at a hearing in less than an hour. If we turn around now, we'll never make it."

"But if it's not safe in the air, then none of us will make it to Encantador," said Eva.

Brett turned in his seat, facing the crew. "The front isn't too wide, only a few miles or so. I can make it through, I think."

"You think?" she echoed.

"Brett's a good pilot," said Lin. "He won't fly into anything he can't fly out of."

Before she could say anything, the patient grimaced in his sleep.

"Did you hear that?" Augustin tapped Eva's arm to get her attention. "He said something."

Eva removed her headset and leaned close to the patient. She couldn't hear anything beyond the noise of the rotors. "What'd he say?"

"Dunno." The marshal unbuckled his harness and moved behind her. "Is he okay?"

She slid in next to the patient.

Decker worked his fingers through the sides of the sheet. His eyebrows were drawn together, and he moved his lips.

She removed her headset and bent close, coming nose to nose with a killer. "Mr. Newcombe," she yelled to be heard over the noise. "My name is Eva Tamke. I'm a nurse with San Antonio Med, and right now, you're on a helicopter. We're taking you to a court hearing." She knew that even in his highly medicated state, he might be lucid enough to know that he was somewhere other than the hospital and therefore confused. "Can you hear me, Mr. Newcombe? Are you uncomfortable?"

His lips moved.

To the marshal, she said, "He's speaking but I can't tell what he's trying to say." She leaned closer. Decker's breath was sour and hot on her ear.

"Ana," Decker said. "Why did you go? Was it because of him?"

She stood up and looked at the marshal. "Do you know anyone named Ana?"

He shook his head. "Nobody comes to mind," he yelled. "But I'll tell my supervisors when we land."

That was when the bottom of the world dropped out from beneath Eva. One minute she was standing next to the stretcher. The next, she was lifted from her feet and slammed into the webbing on the ceiling of the chopper. The chopper bucked, buffeted by gusts of wind and troughs of air on all sides. She fell, landing, nose to nose, on top of Decker.

Before she could move, she heard a sharp crack, like a vase

being thrown to the floor. The stretcher beneath her began to roll. Her impact had broken the metal clasp that locked the wheels to the floor of the hold.

Decker's eyes opened. They were the same icy blue she'd seen in all his photographs. "What the hell?" he growled.

The stretcher was still rolling. She couldn't safely jump off. "My name's Eva Tamke. I'm a nurse—"

"I don't care who you are. Get off of me." He thrashed. The cuffs that tethered his wrists to the sides of the stretcher rattled.

The blood in her veins turned icy. It didn't matter that he was handcuffed to the bed. Decker Newcombe was a danger-ous and deadly man. She pushed herself back at the same mo-ment as the helicopter lifted. The loose stretcher rolled back, stealing her traction and keeping her on top of the killer.

Decker started to howl. His legs hadn't been shackled, and he kicked. Augustin dove toward the stretcher, hanging on to Decker's feet. It left her with nowhere to go.

Outside, rain washed over the starboard window in a sin-gle sheet. A bolt of lightning streaked by. The scent of ozone hung in the air, and still the killer struggled.

Holding on to the stretcher's railing, she launched herself over the side. The helicopter bucked, dropping hundreds of feet in a single second. She was never sure if it was the steep descent or the weight of her body. But as she dropped over the edge, the whole stretcher tipped to its side.

She screamed as Decker, hanging from his wrists, was pinned on top of her.

She could see two pair of feet as the marshal and one of the EMTs tried to heave the gurney up and over. She scooted back, slithering to get out from under the stretcher. A set of hands grabbed her ankles and pulled her free.

"Wade." Her eyes were wet with terror and relief. "Thank you."

He helped her to her feet. "I got you."

Like the crack of a whip, another bolt of lightning struck

outside the helicopter. "That's too close for comfort," said Brett. "I'm taking us lower to the ground."

Decker's gurney was still upside down. The patient was still chained to the railing by his arms. He snarled, the sound feral and full of fury.

They had to get him right-side up. "Everyone, grab a side," Eva said.

She gripped the foot of the stretcher. Lin unbuckled himself and took the head. Wade was at the right and Augustin at the left. Everyone grabbed on to the railing.

"One. Two. Lift." Eva crouched down, pushing with her legs and lifting with her back and arms. Her muscles strained with pain and effort. The gurney rose from the floor several inches. The railing bit into her palms, but they couldn't get any more height.

The stretcher—with Decker on it—was too heavy.

He was right. "Everyone, lower the stretcher carefully."

"Don't you put me back down," Decker screamed. "I'll kill all of you mother…" The rest of his curses were lost by a boom of thunder.

Despite his threats, they lowered the gurney to the floor.

The helicopter dropped into a trough of turbulence, and Eva's stomach landed in her shoes. They had to get the patient flipped over. But how? There was barely enough room in the hold for the four passengers.

"How's it going back there?" Brett asked.

"Not good, but we've got it under control," she said.

"I have an idea," Lin said. "What if we wedged something under the right side of the stretcher and then flipped Decker over?"

"Or we can go with the obvious," said Wade. "Unlock the guy from his handcuffs, and then we can maneuver the stretcher no problem."

"I'm not going to unlock those cuffs," Augustin said, pressing his hand to the front pocket of his pants.

The helicopter shuddered as another strike of lightning lit up the sky.

From the copilot's seat, Stacy cursed. "Holy crap. Holy crap. Holy crap!"

"What's going on?" Lin asked.

But Eva already knew. The control panel, which had been illuminated before, was now dark. The steady beating of the rotors had gone silent.

"That last lightning strike fried our electrical system." Brett gritted his teeth. "Everyone, brace yourselves. We're going to crash."

Chapter Six

Brett stared at the blank instrument panel, and his gut turned watery. They'd taken a direct hit from a bolt of lightning. His electrical system was fried.

He pressed his feet onto the torque peddles.

Nothing.

He jerked the stick from side to side. Front to back. He still had some control, but only a fraction of the maneuverability he once had. Thankfully, there had been enough thrust that they were still aloft and moving forward. But the aircraft was losing altitude fast. He didn't know how long inertia would be on their side.

Without his control panel, he had no way to gauge their altitude. Still, they wouldn't stay in the air much longer than a few minutes.

His training would get him through this. He was the pilot. He was in charge. The souls on the aircraft were his responsibility. Since staying in the air wasn't an option, he had to get the helicopter onto the ground as safely as possible.

It was going to be a bumpy landing at best.

And the chaos in the hold was far from optimal.

"Everyone." He had to yell to be heard over the wind and

the storm. "Strap in." Then to Stacy, he said, "Try to contact air traffic control. Let them know that we're going down."

She flipped several switches. "Mayday. Mayday. This is MEDEVAC November-Charlie-Charlie-One-Six-Niner-Two. MEDEVAC November-Charlie-Charlie-One-Six-Niner-Two. We've lost power and are going down." She also gave the last known coordinates. Looking at Brett, she shook her head. "I don't think anyone heard me."

Texas airspace was monitored by a web of radar towers. When the helicopter disappeared, someone would notice. What's more, they'd come looking for the crash site.

"See if you can find a place to land," Brett said.

Stacy turned in her seat, looking out the window. "Down there. At two o'clock," she said.

The storm had turned the sky black. Rain washed over the windshield. Beneath the aircraft were hills, rocks and desert. Then, ahead and to the right, he saw a flat piece of ground. No large boulders. At the edge of the clearing was a dry stream bed and beyond that, a steep hill. If they could make it to the opening, he could do a running landing and put the helicopter down.

It wouldn't be a perfect landing. Certainly, someone would get injured on the way down. Eva's face flashed into his mind. His chest filled with the need to protect her.

He had to focus, or nobody would survive the crash.

Pulling the control stick hard, he focused on the valley below. His arms burned with the effort. His heart slammed against his ribs until his chest ached. His pulse echoed in his skull.

The helicopter pointed its nose a little to the right.

Would it be enough for them to make the clearing?

The ground was coming up fast. A sure sign that they were losing altitude.

He wasn't worried about bringing back an intact helicopter, but he did care about bringing back a whole crew. Brett focused on the piece of ground where he wanted to put his skids in the dirt. It was as if the sheer force of his will could land the helicopter.

He gripped the control stick harder. "C'mon. C'mon," he urged. "Don't you give out on me now."

Beside him, Stacy tried to send out another SOS.

From the back of the helicopter came Wade's panicked voice. "It's all too heavy."

Brett knew that the patient had tipped over in the back of the hold and that the crew had been trying to get the gurney upright. Decker yelled like a wounded beast. Brett didn't have time to worry about the killer. But what would happen to everyone else if the stretcher wasn't secured?

Actually, he knew the answer. With a gurney tumbling around in the hold, it wouldn't matter if everyone was securely buckled into their seats. The outcome wouldn't be pretty.

Before he could say a word. Stacy had unbuckled her harness and backed out of the cockpit. "I'm gonna help them with that stretcher. Back in a sec!"

He was about to yell for her to return and buckle up when a gust of wind hit the chopper from portside. It nudged the aircraft to the right. His nose was facing the clearing, but the ground was coming up too quickly. He wasn't sure how to keep the helicopter aloft in any case. But maybe he'd finally gotten a bit of good luck. Their heading was correct, and their speed had dropped enough for a safe—or safe-ish—landing.

"Stacy," he yelled. "Get back in your seat. Everyone else, buckle up."

There was nothing else to do but pray that they all made it out alive.

"One. More. Second," Stacy groaned. "We've almost got it secured."

They didn't have another second. The skids hit the peak of the hill that ringed the valley. The aircraft staggered to the right, sliding down. A cloud of dirt and mud billowed around them as they hit the bottom of the hill and started to roll. The helicopter was like a pebble that had been thrown into a dryer.

From the back, there was crashing and cursing.

There was the sharp crack of metal snapping in two. The tail rotor cartwheeled away.

Interspersed were memories.

There was the moment he'd gotten the news that he was going from basic training to flight school.

The first time his instructor pilot let him take the controls, and he soared through the air.

Last night, when he'd shown up at the restaurant, a beautiful woman with dark hair and a coral dress smiled at him. She approached with her palm outstretched. "You must be Brett," she said. "I'm Eva."

As she slipped her palm into his, one word filled his mind. *Home*.

Brett didn't have time to examine any other memories from his life, both good and bad. He was in the pilot's seat. The helicopter bounced along the ground as if in a drunken frenzy.

Metal tore with a sickening screech. Brett turned in time to see the tail of his helicopter being ripped from the rest of the fuselage. At the back of his aircraft was a gaping mouth with jagged teeth.

Wind and rain blew in through the opening. The stretcher that had caused so much chaos was sucked out and into the storm. It skidded on its side before Brett could see it no more.

Then, the aircraft slowed, finally coming to rest on its side in the dried creek bed. The screaming had stopped, and the silence was more terrifying than the constant noise. At some point, the windshield had shattered and torn away. Rain fell into the cockpit.

Brett's breath came ragged and short. He quickly scanned his body. Every part of him was sore, but nothing pained him. Unfastening his harness, he dropped from the seat and looked into the hold. It was a tangle of wires, metal and metal equipment. There was no movement. No signs of life.

"Hello," he called out.

There was no answer.

The metallic taste of panic coated his tongue. He swallowed it away. He'd been trained to survive a crash. He knew what to do. Brett mentally listed all the tasks he had to complete. Turning back to the control panel, he made sure the engine was off and there was no power to the aircraft. Right now, a fire would be devastating to any survivors. Since the lightning had fried the electrical system, it was easy work.

Now, he had to find and give aid to the survivors. All the souls on this chopper were his responsibility. Moving from the chair, he stood in the small space between the pilot and copilot's seats. He called out again. "Hello?"

Nothing.

He took one step into the hold.

Stacy's body was sprawled out near the cockpit. There was a long gash across her neck. She stared at nothing. Without question, she was dead. He closed his eyes for a second at the horror. The side of her helmet was crushed. The visor was broken. Blood soaked her flight suit, turning the fabric black. He knew the awful truth but grabbed her wrist anyway. There was no pulse. Her skin had already started to cool. He reached under her chin, searching for a pulse on her throat.

Nothing more could be done. He gently ran a hand over her face, closing her eyes. Then he turned to look at the rest of the wreckage.

The hold of his aircraft was strewn with medical equipment. Cargo netting from the ceiling dangled down. Wires, ripped from the walls, hung freely. The stench of fuel filled the air, burning his throat and eyes. Thank goodness there was no power. A single spark would've ignited the fumes.

His jaw was tight. There had been seven souls on the helicopter, himself included. He had to account for them all. Yet he couldn't help but wonder about one person in particular.

Where was Eva?

Decker's left shoulder hurt like hell. His head pounded, like someone had turned his skull into a snare drum. His whole body ached, and he was somehow cold and wet. When was Nurse Nancy with the salty sense of humor going to show up with the, as she called them, fun meds?

Like the sun breaking over the horizon, the reality of the situation dawned on him. He'd been in the back of a helicopter. But why?

Oh, now he remembered. There'd been a brunette. She'd told him her name was Eva, and she was also a nurse. He was being taken to Encantador for a court hearing. And then? Well, Nurse Eva hadn't said. But Decker knew that during the hearing, he'd be charged with all his crimes and thrown into jail.

There had been a storm. Turbulence. Lightning. The chopper had gone down.

And now what?

He looked up. Rain fell, pelting him in the face. He was still cuffed to the stretcher by one arm. The other arm? Well, that was an entirely different matter. The railing had broken, and he now just had the bracelet attached to his wrist. He could live with that.

His legs were free.

Flipping around, he kicked the railing. Once. Twice. The effort left him winded. He hadn't been out of bed much in days and days. His muscles were weak. The headache had gone from feeling like he was a drum set in a garage band to becoming the target in bazooka practice.

It was all the damn meds he'd been given in the hospital. Nurse Nancy had turned him into a cracked-out junkie.

Lying on his back, he gulped in air and rainwater.

The water cooled and refreshed him, and then he turned

cold. Clad only in a hospital gown, Decker had on a single sock with treads on both the top and bottom. He didn't know where the other sock was now.

Turning so his feet touched the railing, he pressed with all his strength. There was a snap of metal, and then the weight of the railing pulled his arm to the ground.

His little-used muscles strained as he struggled to sit up. Leaning on the stretcher, he breathed. After a moment, he pulled his arm, still cuffed to a section of railing, to his lap. A spindly slat connected the upper piece with the bottom. Given time and something heavy, he could break the plastic and metal. But for now, he had neither.

He swayed as he stood. His vision grew foggy around the edges, but Decker refused to pass out. A moment later, his wooziness passed, and he surveyed his surroundings.

He was in the middle of a clearing, with hills on all sides. The rain had turned the hard-packed ground to silty mud. The helicopter's rotor and tail were both more than twenty yards to his left. To his right was the rest of the aircraft.

Honestly, Decker didn't like being stranded with no food, no water, no clothes and no idea where he really was. But he did have one thing that he hadn't had in a while. His freedom.

Still, the wrecked chopper was sure to bring a search party. If Decker wanted to stay free, then he had to be gone before anyone showed up.

Placing one foot before the other, he staggered toward the rear section of the broken fuselage. Once he reached the broken rotor, he could see the trench dug in the ground by the helicopter as it skidded over the ground. He started to walk the perimeter. There had to be something he could use to break the railing.

It was then that Decker saw him.

At first, Decker assumed that the lump was another rock. But it moved. Moaned. Once he started paying attention, he could hear the wheezing breath.

He walked to where the person lay on the ground.

It was a marshal. He'd have pegged the guy for law enforcement even if the dude wasn't wearing a windbreaker with the US Marshal seal embroidered on the chest.

The man's nose was bloody and misshapen. His leg bent at an unnatural angle, undoubtedly broken. With the rain, it was hard to tell what was blood and what was soil.

The man met Decker's gaze. His eyes were wide, filled with equal measures of terror and rage. "You," he panted.

Holding the piece of railing in one hand, Decker lifted his other hand. The broken chain hung from the cuff. "I assume you have keys for this. Why don't you hand them over, and I'll make it easy for you?"

"I'm not giving you shit," the marshal said. Blood mixed with his spittle.

"You can give the keys to me nice-like. Or I'm going to take them, and I won't be gentle." Maybe all the things that people wrote and said about Decker was right. He might be a twisted son of a bitch. Because, honestly, he loved messing with this guy. It wasn't just that the man, who was seriously injured, was trying to be feisty. It was that Decker had all the power. They both knew it.

"No." The man spit on the ground. Bloody foam clung to his lips.

"Give me the goddamn key."

"Okay. Okay." The marshal held up one hand in surrender. With his other hand he slowly pulled down the windbreaker's zipper. "They're inside my jacket."

"Go ahead." Decker was ready for anything.

When the man brandished a gun, he wasn't surprised. Without thought, he swung the railing. It caught the marshal's wrist. There was a crack, a scream, and the firearm flew from the man's hand. Decker couldn't see where it landed.

"Jesus, that hurts." The marshal cradled his wrist.

"You done being cute?"

"You broke my wrist."

"You pointed a gun at me. So I don't know why you're whining. You and I both know that you're about to die."

"Wait. Let me tell you something about me."

Decker had seen this all before, when the doomed tried to tell him about their lives and tap into his humanity. He'd lost every shred of compassion long ago.

"I have two children," the marshal said in a pleading voice. "Auggie Junior. We call him AJ. He's eleven years old. My daughter Gabriella is fifteen. They need me."

Eleven years old. Like Decker's own kid—if the hacker was right. Not for the first time, he wondered about his boy. Was he tall for his age? Or smart? Or kind? In short, was the kid all the things that Decker was not?

"Well, Marshal," Decker said, straddling the man's chest. "I'll tell you what *I* need—those keys."

Holding the railing in both hands, he shoved the end onto the man's neck.

The marshal didn't struggle long. There was no real satisfaction in killing a dying man. But as the marshal breathed his last, Decker felt the power of life over death. He knew he was invincible.

Once the man was gone, Decker patted him down. Funny thing, the marshal hadn't lied entirely. A set of handcuff keys were tucked into the pocket of his pants. Decker worked the key into the lock, springing the bracelets on both hands loose. He rolled his wrists and looked down at the dead man.

There was more that the marshal could provide Decker knelt, his knees popping. Lifting the man's foot, he checked the sole of his cowboy boot. Size eleven, only half a size bigger than Decker. Close enough.

He pulled one boot off and then the other. Decker grabbed the man's socks and worked his jeans off, leaving the belt in the loops. He eyed the dead guy for what else he could take. Decker wasn't above much, but he drew the line at used skivvies. He stripped out of his hospital garb. Shivering and naked, he rubbed rainwater over his skin. Then he pulled on the jeans. They were too big around the waist and too long. He folded the cuff and tightened his belt.

In the back pocket was a thick wallet. He kept the cash. He threw a stack of business cards, credit cards and a set of family photos onto the ground.

Next, he stripped off the jacket. It was warm and waterproof—two things Decker needed most.

In the pockets, he found three dollars in change and a cell phone. He threw the phone onto the ground next to the pictures. Getting rid of the device pained him, but he figured it was a work phone. Surely the marshals had installed some kind of tracking device.

Decker worked his feet into the socks and boots. It gave him a moment to think about the crash. The aircraft had somersaulted like a drunken monkey across the valley. He remembered the screeching of metal as the tail section was ripped free and the gust of wind that sucked him out of the jagged hole. There was no way anyone could've survived. It meant he was on his own.

Just like his grandsire, Jack the Ripper. All those years ago, when his ancestor had stalked the streets of Whitechapel, had he encountered setbacks?

After all, there was the story of the third victim. A woman's body had been found in the courtyard of a tavern. The man who found her had mistaken the corpse for the prone body of his inebriated wife. He'd gone inside the establishment for help, but not before his horse was spooked by something.

In the dark, it was impossible to tell if someone else had been in the courtyard that night. Hiding.

Had Jack the Ripper almost been caught?

Slipping into his jacket, Decker knew that the need to kill was part of his DNA. But there was also the need to survive and the ability to outwit law enforcement that had come down through the generations, as well. Until recently, Decker hadn't thought much about his own legacy, other than what the history books would recall of the terror he caused. But now, he knew that he had a son.

Had the kid inherited anything of Decker?

Did the need to kill run in his blood, as well?

After finding the marshal's gun, he began to walk.

There was only one place for him to go. He had to get to Mexico and get the phone that he'd stashed. It was the only way to reach Seraphim.

He had to know more about Ana. Because if she'd given birth to Decker's child and never told him about the kid, then he was going to make her pay.

Chapter Seven

Eva sucked in a breath. Her chest burned, and the stench of gasoline hung in the air. She lay on the floor of the helicopter's hold. They'd been trying to secure the stretcher when the aircraft went down. Nobody had been buckled into their seats, hoping they had a few precious seconds to complete their task. Honestly, she didn't know how she'd survived the impact.

Yet she remembered it all.

There was the weightless moment when the chopper dropped out of the sky. Then the thundering as they skidded across the ground. Her head throbbed, and her ears were filled with the sound of a million angry bees.

Around the buzzing, she heard Brett's voice. "Eva. Can you hear me? Are you okay?"

She pried her eyelids apart. Everything in her vision wavered, surrounded by a haze. Blinking hard, she opened her eyes again.

He knelt in front of her. Worry lines creased his brow.

"Brett," she croaked. Her throat was so dry. She coughed and swallowed. The taste of fuel clung to her lips. "How is everyone?"

He pressed his lips together so hard they turned white. Giving a single shake of his head, he said, "Not good. In fact, everyone's…" He worked his jaw back and forth. "The whole crew is dead."

"All of them?" She didn't know Lin or Stacy well at all, but Wade had been a friend. They were on the same team that played trivia at a local bar every Wednesday night. He was quick with an answer and quicker still with a joke or a laugh. She always enjoyed his company and couldn't believe that the lively EMT was gone. For a moment, she couldn't breathe. "Are you sure?"

"Positive," he said. "I checked everyone's pulse."

But there had been more than the crew on the helicopter. "What about the marshal? The patient?"

Brett looked toward the rear of the helicopter. She followed his gaze. The rear section of the aircraft had been pulled off. "I haven't found them yet," he said, his voice hollow.

Brett said he'd checked for a pulse. But what if it was there, and he'd missed the signs of life? After all, he was a pilot. She was the nurse. She had to check the rest of the crew herself. Besides, Augustin Herrera and Decker Newcombe were both out there somewhere. They might be alive and need medical care.

Pushing against the floor, she tried to sit up.

Brett placed a strong hand on her shoulder, holding her in place. "Just rest a minute. We need to make sure you aren't hurt."

If Eva were a patient at SAMC, then she would be given several scans—an X-ray, an MRI and a CAT scan at least. Right now, she didn't have the luxury of sophisticated medical equipment, and there were no acute pains. While that didn't necessarily mean she wasn't injured, it was a good sign.

She held out her hand to Brett. "Help me up. I want to recheck the rest of the crew, and if there's nothing to be done…"

"There isn't," he interrupted.

She ignored him and continued, "We'll gather some medical equipment and see if we can find the marshal and his prisoner."

Brett placed his palm in hers. His hand was strong, firm and, somehow, reassuring. A flash of memory came to her. They were standing in his kitchen, and he'd reached for her hand. In that moment, she'd felt such a strong rush of desire that his touch left her breathless. Even now, with her hand in his, her pulse raced. She wanted to ignore her reaction, but it was unmistakable.

He pulled, and she rose to her feet. After standing, she placed all her weight on her feet. A sharp pain shot through her leg. She gritted her teeth.

"What's the matter?" Brett held her hand tighter. "Does something hurt?"

Honestly, everything on her body ached. "It's my left leg."

He knelt in front of her. "Can I look at it?"

"Sure," she said.

Brett gently pulled up the leg of her flight suit.

Last night, he'd knelt in front of her for an entirely different reason. To her, it seemed like their tryst never actually happened. Maybe it was all an erotic fever dream. But still, his touch was familiar and all too real.

"Ouch," he said, prodding her shin. "You've got a heck of a bruise. I can't tell if you broke anything or not, though. Can you stand on it?"

The old test of broken bones not being able to bear any weight wasn't an exact science. Many people had multiple breaks and could move the appendage. Still, she shifted her weight to her left foot. Eva couldn't help herself. She cursed, and tears collected at the corner of her eyes.

"It's okay," said Brett, his voice as soothing as his hand had been reassuring. "I know we've got an air cast around here somewhere. It won't be perfect, especially if you've broken something. But it'll be better than agony." He held out a strip of cargo netting. "Hold on to this."

She wrapped her wrist through the webbing and let her arm

bear much of her weight. It was then that she looked around the helicopter.

Wade lay several yards away. His eyes were open, yet he stared at nothing. His gaze was already turning milky. Lin was next to him. His eyes were closed, but a pool of blood so dark red it looked like tar surrounded him. Even from where she stood, she could tell that he no longer drew breath.

Turned out that Brett was right. Everyone on the crew was dead.

As an ER nurse, she'd faced death more than once. But never had it been this personal—this close to her. How was it that the Grim Reaper had come for Lin and Wade and Stacy but ignored her? And what were the chances that the US marshal or the killer had survived being sucked out of the helicopter's rear?

She knew the answer to the last question.

The odds of either man being alive was low.

Grief and guilt hit her with a double punch, and she saw stars.

Brett dug through the debris of the crash. He held up a preformed plastic boot with straps. "Found it. I can get it on you if you want."

"Thanks." She held tighter to the strap and lifted her foot. It took Brett only a few minutes to remove her sneaker and put the boot on her foot. He tightened the strap, and the throbbing eased to a dull ache. Setting her foot down, she sighed. "That's better."

"Glad I could help."

Help. The word resonated through her chest. "How are we supposed to get out of here? Does anyone know where we are?" She paused and drew in a breath. "Do we even know where we are?"

"Best I can tell, we're north of Encantador by about sixty miles. The interstate is that way." He pointed toward the cockpit. Stacy was on the floor. Her flight suit was stained with blood. "It's about twenty miles from here."

Eva had driven that same stretch of highway more times than she could remember. It was the artery that connected her hometown with San Antonio. But really, it was a narrow lane that ran through the middle of a vast desert. Even if they headed in the right direction, what were the chances of them finding the road? Not good. "What about making a call? Or is there a beacon onboard?"

"I checked my phone. No bars," he said. "What about you?"

Eva's phone was tucked into one of the many pockets on her flight suit. She removed the device. The ceramic shield was shattered. The screen had turned an eerie shade of green, and it flickered. She held up the device for Brett to see. "My phone's pretty much trashed."

"Even if we can't make a call, the FAA will notice that we went down. They'll have a reasonable idea of where we are and come looking. On top of that, there's an emergency beacon that will send out a ping with our location. So long as we stay close to the aircraft, they'll find us in a day or two."

"A day or two?" she echoed. But really, it wasn't that bad. She knew that it was protocol to stock the air ambulance with water, emergency rations, medical equipment, blankets. If it turned out that they were stranded for a few days, they'd survive.

She looked around at the carnage. "Let's gather up all the food and water. We need the med kit." A large plastic case, like a jumbo tackle box, was hanging on the wall. It was white with a red cross painted on the top and sides and had a red plastic handle. She pulled it free. "Where are the blankets stored?"

"We'll get those in a minute," said Brett. He held a box of food, wrapped in plastic, atop a case of water. "Let's pile everything outside. I'm not spooked or anything, but I'd like to set up camp away from the bodies."

The corpses were another problem. Too soon the scent of

blood would attract wild animals. "We'll have to do something with them, you know," she said. "We can't just leave them in the helicopter to rot."

"I know," he said. "I just haven't figured out what's best." Even though there was a gaping hole at the back of the helicopter, Brett jiggled the lever handle for the service door. It didn't budge. He slammed his palm against the hull. "Dammit."

The aircraft rocked, and Eva froze. Sure, Brett had hit the wall. But it had been a slap of frustration. He definitely hadn't used enough force to move an entire helicopter. In the distance, she could hear the chug of an approaching locomotive. "Is that a train?"

"It can't be," said Brett. "There's no track around for miles."

She had grown up in the area and knew he was right. And yet. "What's that sound?"

He stood still. "I don't hear anything."

"You don't?" Maybe she had a concussion and was having auditory hallucinations. She went still and listened again. The sound was still there. "That. Do you hear that? It sounds like an engine."

"Maybe," said Brett. "Yeah, I hear it now."

The helicopter shimmied, and she looked out the window. Her blood turned icy in her veins. A wall of mud, water and debris filled the creek bed and was headed straight for them.

"Run!" she shouted, pushing Brett away from the door.

They moved through the back of the helicopter, both of them slowed by what they carried—Brett the food and water, and Eva the med kit. Her injury and boot didn't help, either.

The hull vibrated with the oncoming flash flood. She could smell the debris, earthy and rotten, as it rolled forward.

In the boot, she was too slow.

"Get out of here." She refused to let Brett die on her account. And for a single moment, she was glad that her last night was spent in his arms. "Go without me." The words tasted sour.

"That's not going to happen." His eyes blazed. He dropped

the cases of food and water and lifted her from the ground. "Wrap your arms around my neck and don't let go. We are both getting out of here alive."

She held on to his neck, trying not to let the med kit bang against his back. As Brett picked his way out of the helicopter. She glanced once at the approaching water as he sprinted up the bank. The stream filled as she crawled the final feet. Lying on the muddy ground, she stared as roiling black water rushed past.

She rolled onto her back and clutched the med kit to her chest. The storm wasn't done with them yet. Rain still fell, dampening her hair and pooling on her flight suit.

There was a screech of metal being torn from metal. She sat up and watched the water push the chopper downstream, taking with it the bodies of the dead crew. And the homing beacon, as well. When the authorities zeroed in on a location, it would be miles from the actual crash site.

Eva surveyed her surroundings. They truly were in the middle of nowhere. She looked at Brett. He was lying on the ground, chest heaving with each breath. She had the strongest urge to rest her head on his shoulder and let him rub her back. He'd done as much the night before, right after they'd made love for the second—or was it the third?—time.

"Thanks for saving me," she said.

"I wasn't going to leave you."

"What now?" she asked.

"I say we climb to the top of that ridge." He pointed to a set of hills. "See if we can pick up a cell signal."

In the distance, she could see the helicopter's tail. But there was more. She wiped the rain from her face and looked again. She could see a wheel and a metal bar.

"Is that the stretcher?"

"I think so," said Brett.

She held up the plastic box with a bright red cross. "Thank goodness I didn't lose this."

"Agreed." Holding out his hand, he offered, "I can carry it."

For a moment, she thought about declining. After all, she was a grown woman and didn't need a man's help to survive. But this was different. If she truly wanted to make it out of this situation alive, she was going to need Brett. Finally, she handed him the pack. His fingers grazed the back of her hand.

After everything, she didn't expect a current of electricity to buzz up her arm. But it did. "Thanks," she said.

She couldn't be distracted by her libido.

Too much was at stake.

"Let's see if there's something in here for you to take," he said.

Honestly, Eve wasn't worried about herself. If that was the stretcher in the distance, a few seconds could be the difference between life and death for the patient. "We should go," she said. "I need to check and see if anyone else survived."

Brett had already taken a knee and opened the med kit. He rooted around, shifting the contents. It gave her a moment to study him, even though she wanted to sprint to the stretcher. Yet, he was right. She wasn't getting far with her foot the way it was.

His shoulders were broad. His chin was well defined. He still had a small bruise where she'd bitten the side of his neck the night before. Her body heated at the memory.

But there was more to Brett than just his good looks or that fact that he was excellent in bed. Last night, she'd found him to be charming and funny. But today, she'd seen him in a crisis and knew he was so much more. He was a good leader. Competent. Caring. He'd risked his own life to save hers.

Eva had learned early on that relying too much on others was a sure way to be disappointed. But she had no choice other than to work with Brett.

That meant she had to keep her emotions in check.

Brett stood, holding up a packet filled with OTC pain meds. "This should help."

She took the packet, careful not to touch his hand. Eva
didn't want to get distracted by that connection between them
again. "Thanks."

As they walked, she ripped open a corner and popped the
pills into her mouth. She swallowed them without water as
best she could.

They continued to walk. The boot was heavy, but it stabilized her foot and the pain was gone. From several yards
away, she could see the back of the stretcher. It lay on its side.
The corner of a sheet flapped in the wind. The gurney was
surprisingly intact, at least from the back. The only real damage she could see was a broken railing. She couldn't see the
patient from where she stood. She wasn't sure if Decker was
unconscious or if he'd died in the crash.

The rain had lessened to a drizzle. She wiped her wet hair
from her face and approached the stretcher. "Mr. Newcombe."
Her voice filled the vast emptiness. "It's Eva, the flight nurse.
I'm here to help you." She rounded to the front side of the
stretcher.

It was empty.

Had Decker been thrown from the stretcher on impact? It
seemed so. But where was his body now?

She scanned the clearing. A dark mass lay on the ground.
Even from where she stood, she could tell it was a person. She
grabbed Brett's wrist. "See that?"

He followed her gaze. "It's the marshal."

He sprinted to the body. Eva hobbled after him. From a
few paces away, she slowed. The missing railing lay next to
his body.

Brett knelt next to Augustin and set the med kit on the
ground beside him. He placed two fingers under the man's
chin, then looked up at Eva, and she knew. Still, Brett shook
his head and said, "He's dead."

They were the only survivors of the crash. Completely alone
in the wilderness. Aside from the dangers of exposure, there

were wild animals to contend with. Her gut clenched around a hard knot of grief and fear.

But there was more.

Augustin Herrera was clad only in his boxers and shirt.

"I don't think Decker got thrown off at all." With the toe of his boot, Brett nudged the railing lying next to the marshal. "That didn't just come loose. The handcuff has been unlocked."

Eva knelt next to Brett and stared at the body. There was bruising on the neck. "His windpipe has been crushed," she said. She'd seen similar injuries while working in the ER. "He was killed."

Her mouth was dry, and her palms turned clammy. She and Brett weren't just stranded and alone in the Texas desert. There was serial killer on the loose. She turned in a slow circle. Hills surrounded the clearing in which they stood. There was nothing else to see, other than thick clouds and dirt, turned to black silt by the recent rain. Yet, she knew that Decker had to be nearby. Was he watching them, even now?

She glanced at the marshal. Was her fate going to be the same?

No. She refused to become Decker's next victim. Between her and Brett, they had years of military service, training and skill sets that could get them out of here alive.

It was ironic. This morning, she'd tried to sneak out of his house. This afternoon, she'd thought about turning down an assignment because it meant working with her one-night stand. Now that they were stranded together, she was grateful he was the man she was trapped with.

Chapter Eight

SSA Jason Jones sat in his office in the FBI's building in downtown San Antonio. More than three hundred agents and support staff worked in a high rise located two blocks from the federal courthouse. Jason had a corner office on the seventeenth floor. The wall of windows gave him a view of the San Antonio River along with the restaurants and shops that made up the River Walk.

A computer sat on his desk, its screen filled with a report filed by one of his agents. The 302 outlined how a drug cartel was buying stolen weapons from a street gang. He'd have to meet with his counterparts at the ATF and DEA, but for now, he couldn't concentrate. He jiggled the mouse. The time appeared in the lower corner of his screen: 3:34 p.m.

"Dammit," he cursed quietly. He should have heard something by now.

He picked up the phone on the edge of his desk. The line went directly to his assistant. "Luke, I need you to check on something for me. Find out the status of the medevac flight with Decker Newcombe."

"I'm on it," Luke replied.

Jason turned his seat so he could gaze out the windows.

For a moment, he watched people on the street below, but he didn't really see anything. Honestly, until Decker had been arraigned, charged with his crimes and finally sent to jail to wait for his trial, he wouldn't be happy.

Hell, he wouldn't be truly happy until the killer had been found guilty in court.

He was the one who had signed off on the plan for the killer to be flown by air ambulance to Encantador, but he also knew that no plan was foolproof—especially where Decker Newcombe was involved.

Jason stared out the window and watched as tourists wandered on the streets below.

At a sharp knock on his office door, he swiveled to face his desk. "Yeah?"

His assistant stepped inside. Luke was a bright kid with loads of ambition and one day wanted to be an FBI agent. In short, Luke reminded Jason of a younger version of himself. A recent graduate of Texas Midland State University, Luke had been a summer intern while in college. So, when the assistant position became available, Jason offered him the job. After amassing three years of work experience, Luke could apply to become an agent. At that time, he'd put in a good word for the young man. Until then, there was work to be done.

"What have you got for me?"

"It's not good, sir." There was an uncharacteristic break in his voice. He held his phone to his chest, like it was a special toy and would give him courage. For the first time, he looked younger than his twenty-two years. Which was fine, because Jason felt older than dirt. "I spoke to the people at San Antonio Med. They lost contact with the helicopter. It hasn't landed at the hospital in Encantador, either. I put a call into the Texas Aviation Division. They don't have much of anything for me."

Jason's head throbbed. "Except what?"

"Except, there was a pop-up storm that showed up on the

route in their flight plan. They're trying to find out if the helicopter is still in the air."

Jason struggled to process all the information. He supposed that was why his first question wasn't the best. "Pop-up storm. That sounds made up. What is that?"

"Well." Luke swallowed. "Usually, storms are caused by a cold or warm front moving into an area. That's what's called a trigger. With a pop-up storm, there is no easily identifiable trigger. But they're not uncommon on hot and humid days. Or at least that's what the lady with the aviation division said."

With a wave of his hand, Jason cleared away all the information. "You know what, forget I asked." He needed to organize his thoughts. One worry was at the top of his mind. What if Decker had gotten away?

Luke's phone began to ring. He glanced at the screen. "It's the aviation division."

"Put it on speaker."

"This is Luke," he said after swiping the call open. "And I've got you on speaker. My boss, Supervisory Special Agent Jason Jones can also hear you." He set the phone on the desk.

"My name is Lola Sanchez. I'm one of the aviation officers for the state. I checked on the air ambulance from SAMC. We've lost contact. I have the coordinates where the helicopter was last located by our radar."

Jason typed them into his computer as she spoke. A map of southern Texas appeared, along with a red dot sixty miles north of Encantador.

"I've contacted the FAA," Lola continued, "and they're trying to find the tracking device on the aircraft's black box. Right now, I'm sending out a search party. I'll contact you when I hear something."

He was glad that everyone was taking the missing helicopter seriously. But he wasn't about to be left out of the investigation. Besides, he had to be transparent about the situation. "Ms. Sanchez," he began.

"Call me Lola."

"Lola," he said. "There are some things you need to know about that flight. There was one patient onboard being taken to Encantador for arraignment."

"I know," she said. "I saw the flight plan."

"The patient was Decker Newcombe. Which is why we have to be vigilant."

"Understood. What should I tell my search-and-rescue team?" she asked. "They aren't law enforcement."

She was right. Jason didn't know what they would find once they got into the desert. But in his gut, he knew it wasn't going to be good.

A plan came to him, fully formed. He rose from his seat. "I'm on my way to Encantador now. But it will take me a few hours to get onto the scene. The first thing I'm going to do is get in touch with the US Marshals. One of their people was on that aircraft." He pointed at Luke. The younger man nodded. "Then, I'm going to call in an agency who works in that area."

He opened his desk drawer and removed a shoulder holster and his service firearm, a standard issue SIG Saur. He slipped his arm into the holster and tightened the strap. The gun was heavy, cold and felt like death. He pulled his suit jacket off the back of his chair and slipped it on over his sidearm.

"What agency is that?" Lola asked.

"Tell me," Jason began, "are you familiar with a private security agency called Texas Law?"

Ryan Steele, an operative with Texas Law, sat in his office, a renovated motel outside of Mercy, Texas. There wasn't much to Mercy. Aside from the long strip of reconfigured offices, the Center for Rural Law Enforcement shared a parking lot. Across the road was a gas station with a small restaurant, and next door to that was the post office.

Leaning back in his chair, he knew that he'd been fortunate to get a second chance at life. At one time, he'd been wanted by the police. If he were being honest, he should really be in jail. But he'd made a deal, gone straight, and now he was working a legit job. He was also in love with the local under-sheriff, Kathryn Glass.

Who'd have ever thought that of all people, he'd end up in a relationship with a cop?

The man who'd offered Ryan the deal and was now his boss sat on the other side of the desk. Isaac Patton had founded Texas Law a few years before. The agency's first task had been to find the elusive killer Decker Newcombe.

Back in the day, he had acted as Decker's business manager when the man was just a paid assassin. Funny to think about how murder for hire seemed like an easy way to make cash.

But they'd been contacted by a motorcycle club, The Transgressors. They'd wanted Decker to kill a district attorney in the small Wyoming town of Pleasant Pines. There had been other deaths—a security guard and Decker's accomplice—and the murder had been captured on CCTV.

Decker and Ryan had both been wanted men. While Decker disappeared into Mexico, Ryan had been arrested. It was then that Isaac offered him a chance at redemption. In exchange for allowing himself to be the bait that would draw Decker out of hiding, Ryan was promised that his record would be cleared.

It had been several long years with Decker on the run. But finally, the killer had been captured. The wheels of justice were already turning. Soon enough, Decker would be rotting in a small concrete jail cell.

In fact, the hearing to formally charge Decker with multiple murders was the whole reason that Isaac sat on the opposite side of the desk. He wanted to be in the courtroom when the killer was taken away.

The desk phone rang.

"Hopefully," said Isaac, "that's the call we've been waiting for."

Ryan rather expected the caller to be the love of his life, Kathryn, with word that the helicopter had landed at the hospital. But he was at work, and his boss was within easy earshot. He had to be professional. "Hello," he said, answering the phone. "You've reached Texas Law, this is Ryan."

"It's Jason."

"Jason," Ryan repeated. "I've got Isaac with me. We're just waiting for word from the heliport in Encantador."

Kathryn and the sheriff, Maurice "Mooky" Parsons, were waiting at the hospital. As soon as Decker was off the aircraft, they were going to personally escort the killer to the courthouse. Once he'd been charged, Decker would be turned over to the Texas Department of Corrections, where he'd be housed in jail while waiting for his trial.

"I'm glad that Isaac's with you," said the fed. "Can you put the call on speaker? There have been some developments."

A hard knot lodged in the middle of Ryan's throat. Between Jason's tone and his cryptic words, he knew something was up. He swallowed before saying, "Sure thing."

He activated the speaker function and set the handset back onto the cradle. "Jason, you've got both of us now. What's going on?"

"The helicopter's incommunicado. The hospital can't raise it via radio. The FAA can't find it on radar. They flew into a pop-up storm, which apparently is a real thing, and lost contact somewhere about sixty miles north of you. We've reached out to the Marshals Service to get the contact information for their person onboard. But we're still waiting."

"What can we do?" Isaac asked.

"I've got the last known position of the helicopter." Jason read off the coordinates. "It's in the middle of nowhere, but I'd like you to take a team and investigate." He paused and drew in a breath. "Hopefully, it's just a fluke because of the storm. But until we hear from the helicopter, we're all in the dark."

Ryan knew that Jason was wasting energy with hope. If Decker Newcombe was involved, they were only going to find chaos and destruction.

Brett's chest ached. It was like the loss of each of his crew members—each of his friends—was a blade to the heart. But he couldn't give in to grief. He had to formulate a plan. Eva was relying on him. And though no one might know it yet, so was all of Texas law enforcement and the people in this community. A serial killer—with a gun and who knows what else the marshal had had on him—was on the loose.

Eva gestured toward the creek. "Without the helicopter, there's no homing beacon. How's anyone supposed to find us now?" Her voice held an edge of panic.

He hated to leave the crash site, although Eva was right. Without the beacon, the authorities might not even know where to look for survivors. Since he'd dropped the food and water to carry her out of the wreckage, they weren't prepared to wait for a rescue. But to save her life, he'd do it all again.

"Our best plan is to get to the top of that." He pointed toward one of the hills that ringed the small valley. "It's the best chance we have to pick up a cell phone signal."

"What about him?" She pointed to the body of the US marshal. "We can't just leave him here."

Brett hated the idea of *burning daylight*, as his old flight instructor used to say. Especially since in this case they were actually using time that could be spent finding a cell signal. But it was also true that they couldn't leave Augustin Herrera to rot, be torn to pieces by wild animals or both.

It took an hour to gather enough rocks to bury the body. They placed the family photos they'd found nearby in Augustin's hand. Brett kept the marshal's cell phone. Too bad he didn't have the chance to bury the bodies of his crew. They'd been washed away with the helicopter.

That knot of grief came back, filling his throat until it was difficult to breathe.

"Should we say something?" Eva asked.

"Sure," Brett agreed before taking in a deep breath. "I didn't know Augustin Herrera well—or even at all. I don't know if I should be praying to God or just talking to the universe. But he had a family. He did his job well, and he didn't deserve to die this way. Have mercy on his soul. Have mercy on us all."

"Thank you." She placed her hand on his shoulder. Her touch was soothing and at the same time, left him wanting more. "I'm sure he'd appreciate that you took a few minutes to look after him this way."

He accepted her compliment with a nod. "We really should get going."

The storm clouds had cleared, leaving the sky a deep blue. The downpour had washed away much of the heat, but it wouldn't last for long. Then again, the sun was hanging low on the western horizon. Too soon, they'd be dealing with the dark.

"Which way?" Eva asked.

It was a reasonable question. He just didn't have an answer.

From where they stood, all the hills were more than two miles away. The closest one—and tallest—was to the north. But it was in the opposite direction of the highway and the next town, Encantador. Still, going south meant that they'd have to deal with the creek. Hopefully, once they were out of the valley, his phone would find a signal. "Let's go this way."

They started walking. For the first several minutes neither spoke. Brett assumed that Eva was lost in her own thoughts, much like himself. Now that they were out of the helicopter, it was ludicrous to think that they'd crashed. Wade, Stacy and Lin had been so full of life just hours before. And now they were gone—he didn't even have bodies to mourn over. Even though he knew it wasn't true, it was easier to believe that this was all a bad dream. Any minute, he'd wake up. He'd be back in his house with Eva sleeping next to him.

Maybe this time around, she'd stay for pancakes.

"You know, you can change your outgoing message on your phone. Tell everyone that the helicopter went down and let them know where we've gone."

Brett was startled out of his own head. "What was that?" he asked before processing her words. And then, "You know, that's a great idea."

"Thanks." She smiled. Brett couldn't help himself, and he smiled, too. "The hospital offered a self-defense class last year. The instructor suggested changing our voicemail if we ever had a stranded car. Because even if we don't have any bars, the voicemail is still on."

He stopped walking and pulled his phone from a pocket on his flight suit. It was still in the dry bag. He erased the old message, then spoke into the phone. "This is Brett Wilson, pilot for San Antonio Medical Center." He gave the key information, including the flight number and approximate last known location, then saved the message.

It was followed by a long tone and an automatic voice reply: *Your message was not recorded. Please try again.*

He continued to walk. Eva was at his side. He started over, "This is Brett Wilson..." The second message he recorded was much like the first. He hit the save icon. There was the same tone, the same warning that his message hadn't been saved.

"Dammit," he muttered. The heat of anger began to rise in his chest. "What the hell is wrong with this?"

Eva placed her hand on his arm. Her touch was a balm to soul and soothed away much of his frustration. "It's okay if it doesn't work now. We can try again later."

He looked at the place where her fingertips rested on his flesh. It was like she belonged at his side. Then again, she was a nurse. He imagined she had good bedside manner with all her patients and could calm even the most agitated person.

"Yeah," he said, letting his arm slip away from her touch. "We can try later."

He powered down his phone. There was no need to use up the battery now. Then, he shoved the marshal's phone into the dry bag with his own. It was a tight fit, but he got the closure secure.

He started walking. Eva stayed at his side.

After a moment, he asked, "How's your leg?"

"It's okay. A little painful but not excruciating. Right now, it's not my biggest concern. If we make it back, I'll get someone to look at it."

If we make it back. He reached for her arm, pulling her to a stop. "We'll survive this. There is no 'if we make it back.' It's 'when we get home.'" He squeezed her arm a little tighter. "It'll be okay. I swear."

It was a promise he would keep—no matter what.

Chapter Nine

For Eva, climbing to the top of the hill in the desert heat had been difficult. Her legs ached—especially the injury to her calf. Eva worked out a few times a week to keep up her endurance for her shifts, but the wild terrain was nothing like an air-conditioned gym. There was a pull at her side from all the exertion, and she struggled to fill her lungs with air. But if they were able to get a cell signal at the top of the ridge, all the discomfort would be worth it in the end.

She watched as Brett pulled his phone out. He exhaled. "God, I hope this works."

She moved closer. From where she stood, she could see the screen, although it was upside down. He hit the power button, and the device winked to life. He cursed a moment before she saw it.

"No bars," she said, her cheeks and eyes burning.

"No bars," he repeated, then looked at her, his expression softening. "Hey." He rubbed her shoulder. "It's okay. It'll be okay."

He must have been able to read her emotions and knew that she was upset. Then again, Eva had never been blessed with a poker face.

"Okay?" she croaked. Yes, her military training had prepared her for some trying situations. And she'd seen it all as an ER nurse. But they had no idea if Decker was long gone or if he was hiding—and waiting to kill the last two people who could offer an assessment of what had happened after the crash. "How is any of this okay?" She looked over her shoulder, almost expecting to see Decker sneaking up on them from behind. She looked back at Brett. "We have no food. No water. We're twenty miles from the nearest paved road and sixty miles from the next town. And Decker is... somewhere."

Then there was her family who needed her, and she couldn't be there for them.

Brett said nothing, just reached for her hand and pulled Eva into his chest. She leaned into him, not sure if she ever wanted him to let go. After a moment, he said, "Between the two of us, we'll be okay, Eva."

She believed him, and yet she had to ask. "How are you so sure?"

"If we walk toward Encantador, we'll pick up a cell tower eventually. One call will bring the cavalry."

Eva swallowed. "You're right." Although it meant going back the way they'd come. "What about the stream?" She looked at the sky. The sun was close to dipping below the horizon. Even after sunset, it wouldn't be fully dark for hours. But eventually night would arrive. It would get colder—and they didn't have the right gear for hours in the chill. "What about the dark?"

"For now, the sun going down is best. It'll be too hot to walk during midday. And as for the stream..." He exhaled. "We can follow the water until we find a safe place to cross. Besides, if there's no more rain, then the creek will dry up."

She'd lived in this area most of her life and knew his thinking was correct. "I guess we better get going."

"If you need to rest," he said, "we can wait a minute."

"No," she said, shaking her head. "If I sit down now, I might not get back up." Sure, she was joking. But like all humor, there was some truth to what she said. "Let's just keep moving."

They worked their way to the bottom of the hill. Going downhill was easier on her cardiovascular system but harder on her knees and legs. By the time they reached the small valley, her quadriceps and injured shin ached with the same level of pain.

In the distance, she could see the helicopter's tail rotor and part of the hull. From where she stood, it looked like modern art—a statement about man trying to conquer the unceasing desert. She could also see the grave of Augustin Herrera. The sun's last rays cast shadows over the resting place.

"Have I thanked you for saving me?"

"You have," he said. "But there's no need."

"I guess I owe you, don't I?"

"No, you don't." He glanced at her from his periphery. There was something in his look, but she couldn't read his expression. Still, her cheeks warmed under his gaze.

"What is it?" she asked.

He shook his head. "It's nothing."

"Well, obviously, it's something. Go ahead," she urged. "Spit it out."

"Look, you don't owe me any explanations. But we had such a great connection last night. This morning was another story. I'm just curious what happened."

She glanced away for a moment. If she'd asked him out on a second date after their amazing night together, and he'd sent her that crappy text in response, she'd wonder, too.

She wasn't sure why she'd been so reluctant to tell him how complicated her life was. Her grandmother. Her sister. Moving to Encantador. Maybe because, very early this morning, she hadn't yet been through hell with him and discovered she could count on him.

But that was complicated, too.

Brett hadn't planned on bringing it up at all. But, yeah, he wanted to know. That kind of instant chemistry, with real conversation and mind-blowing sex, was rare. But she clearly had her reasons, and he needed to let it go. "Forget I said anything."

She shook her head. "I should've been honest with you from the beginning. There are things going on in my life—family things." They kept walking. "My grandmother fell yesterday." She exhaled. "It seems like it happened weeks ago, not just a day. Anyway, the fall was bad enough that the doctor said she can't live alone anymore. According to my sister, she refuses to go to an elder care facility. And honestly, if we did try to send her there, she'd be miserable." Eva took in a deep breath and sighed.

He waited a moment to see if she had anything else to say. She didn't. "That's awful," he said. "I'm sorry." He knew all about families trying to work together to help each other out. "Do you have a plan?"

"The thing is," Eva said, "there's only me and my sister, Katya. She's married with three kids. Right now, her house is bursting at the seams. Adding my grandmother would be too much. I really think there's only one thing I can do."

He already knew what she was going to say. And still, he prodded, "And that is?"

"I'm going to have to relocate to Encantador. There's a hospital in town—the one where we were supposed to land—and they're always short-staffed. I could get a job there."

Her plan was much like the one he expected to hear. It made sense why she didn't want to pursue a relationship. Yet knowing that she wouldn't be in San Antonio anymore hit him like a punch. He shook it off. "I understand completely, Eva. And I admire how devoted you are to your family." That was absolutely true. He was the same way.

That she appreciated what he'd said was clear in her expression. "My grandmother took care of me and Katya after our mother left. She was available when I needed somebody the most. I'm not going to ignore her now." She sighed again. "Anyway, that's why I left this morning, why I texted that there wouldn't be a second date."

"I'm sorry you're stuck here right now. Instead of with your grandmother. I'll do everything in my power to get you to your family."

She reached for his hand and squeezed it. "I believe that. And for the record, I really don't make it a habit to sleep with guys on the first date. It's just not me—usually—but with you…" She scratched the back of her neck as they walked. "Well, you're different. If I was planning on staying in San Antonio, I would've stayed for pancakes."

He smiled. "Your grandmother sounds like an amazing person." He looked at her, as if gauging how personal he could get with a question.

"Ask anything," she said.

"I'm wondering where your mom went."

Eva rarely spoke about her mother. Even though she loved her, their relationship had ended decades before. "I told you that we immigrated to the US from Ukraine. Before that, my father worked at a university in Odessa. He was a professor of world history. My mother had a job in a factory. I'm not even sure what she did, because I was so little, but my memories of my mother are that she was happy. The principal of Encantador High School knew my father. He sponsored my family to come to the US and gave my father a job. My dad spoke English. My sister, Katya, and I grew up in a bilingual home. But my mother never learned the language."

"That must've been lonely for her."

Eva nodded. "As a kid, I didn't see it. She was our mom and was there when my sister and I came home from school. Being enrolled in the public elementary, our English became very good very quickly. 'You're becoming too American,' she would say. Even as a child, I knew it wasn't a compliment.

My parents started to argue a lot. They never even bickered in Odessa." She paused, remembering those late nights as her parents screamed at each other from the bedroom. Her father spoke English and her mother Ukrainian.

"What about your dad? What did he think of living in the States?"

"My dad? He loves America—and Texas most of all. It didn't matter that there wasn't a Ukrainian church for miles around. On Sundays, he found a new religion. Football."

Brett barked out a laugh. "Your dad sounds like a good guy."

She paused her story, wondering what her family knew about the crash. Certainly, they'd all heard by now, and what was more, they'd be worried. How had her grandmother taken the news? Eva didn't want the crash to be what caused her baba's health to fail.

"My dad is great," she continued after a pause that was too long. She quickly added, "My mom is great, too. It's just that America wasn't the place for her. After five years of being miserable, my dad sent her back to Odessa for a visit. Katya and I both wanted to go with her. After all, there was family we wanted to see, too. She refused to take us. Refused to even consider it. Before she left, I think I knew that she wasn't coming back." That familiar knot of grief filled her throat. Her eyes stung, and she blinked hard. It had been years since she'd cried over her mother, but here she was with her eyes watering.

"Anyway," she croaked. "She moved back to Odessa and filed for a divorce. After a few years, she remarried. My mom and her second husband have three other children."

"That must have been really hard on you," Brett said, sympathy in his voice.

It was. Her mother going back to Ukraine was the reason she never felt as if she had a home.

"It's not easy for me to talk about all this, but I'm glad I did. I'm pretty talked out, though," she added. She liked the idea of walking in silence for a bit, having his quiet, strong presence beside her.

He squeezed her hand in acknowledgment and didn't say another word. Another of those gestures that made her feel... special to him.

Walking silently turned out to be a good thing. Brett had to focus on what was important, and that was getting them home. They'd returned to where they started at the creek, next to the crash site. Water, dark and muddy, still swirled in the riverbed. A slice of the dry bank fell into the water and was washed away.

He scanned the horizon, looking for a safe place to cross. There was none. "Let's stick to the bank. We're heading in the general direction we want to go. Eventually, we can get to the other side."

Eva faced west and held her hand up. Her palm was flat and facing her. "We have three hours until sunset," she said. He knew the old trick of measuring the time by the distance of the sun to the horizon. "That means it's five o'clock, give or take a few minutes. They have to know we're missing. The helicopter was due to land at three thirty."

She was right. By now, a search party had been dispatched to find them. But they'd go to the helicopter's homing beacon. That meant they'd be looking in the wrong place. He didn't need to add that extra bit—especially since they both knew it was true. "I'm sure people are trying to find us right now."

"Maybe if we stick to the riverbed, we'll find the helicopter," she said. "Then, they'll find us, too."

Walking slowly, he watched the water eddy hypnotically. Eva was a pace in front of him. Her limp, which hadn't been bad before, was more pronounced. "Your leg looks like it hurts. Do you need to rest?"

"Like I said before, if I sit down now, I won't get back up."

"It's also true that if you reinjure yourself or make your injury worse, then we might not be going anywhere."

"Hey." She placed her hands on her hips in mock indignation. "I'm the nurse. I'm the one who gets to give the serious talks about health."

He allowed himself a chuckle.

She continued, "But you're right. I could use a break."

He pointed to a stone that sat on the ground ten yards ahead. "You can rest over there."

She hobbled to the sandstone boulder. Easing down on the flat top, she moaned. God help him, it was the same noise she made while they were having sex.

"That's the best," she said.

Setting the med kit next to her feet, Brett shook the feeling back into his hand. "You rest for a few more minutes, I'm going to scout the bank and see if there's any place for us to cross."

He walked along the bank, watching the dark and swirling water as it rushed past. The movement of the water was almost peaceful and gave him a moment of clarity. He appreciated the fact that she'd been honest about her situation. And her commitment to her family really did move him.

He'd promised her he'd get her to them. And he would.

Chapter Ten

Brett scanned the river, up and downstream, looking for a way to cross. So far, the only thing he'd seen was water, silty and full of debris. The branches of a low-hanging bush hung in the torrent. He glanced at the twigs and leaves caught in the muddy foam. Then, he looked back. His eyes had seen something that his mind had missed.

There, in the middle of the debris, was the carton of ready-made meals from the helicopter. The cardboard box was double wrapped in plastic and bobbed as the current pushed it into the branches.

"Come here," he shouted, waving to Eva. "I've found something."

Panting, she walked toward him. She held the med kit by the handle, and it slapped her thigh with each lurching step.

"How's your leg?" he asked.

"Doesn't hurt. The boot's awkward, but I'm glad I have it."

He was relieved she wasn't in pain.

She was looking out at the water. "What is that?"

"The rations," he said. Sure, it wasn't much. Just four sets of breakfast, lunch and dinner. But if everything in the box had stayed dry, it'd be safe to eat. At the thought of food, his stomach contracted painfully. "I need a stick or something to pull the box close enough to reach."

"If a stick helps us get something to eat, I'll find a whole damn tree," she said. "You know, I was supposed to have pancakes for breakfast."

He looked at her.

She gave him a wink to show that she was teasing.

He shook his head.

"Too soon?" she asked, setting the medical kit on the ground.

He liked the easy rapport that they'd developed. It was one of the reasons he'd wanted to make love to her after the first date. It was also why it still stung that the relationship was over before it began. "Yeah." He chuckled to show he was teasing, as well. "Too soon."

Eva walked along the bank, heading back the way they'd just come. Brett took a few steps in the opposite direction. He hadn't even started to look when she called out, "I think this will work."

She held up a twisted branch, almost a yard long. Even better, one end split into a fork. He met her as she walked back toward him. "That's perfect," he said, reaching for the stick.

His fingers grazed the back of her hand. He needed to ignore the electricity that shot from his fingertips and up his arm, but it was damn difficult.

Standing on the edge of the riverbank, he reached out with the stick. He touched the top of the box, pulling it free of the branches. "When it gets close, you'll have to get it out of the water."

She knelt next to where he stood. "I'm ready."

He pulled on the stick, moving the box closer and closer. The current pulled against the carton, trying to drag it downstream. Brett kept the pressure on the top of the box, careful to pull it to him without breaking the seal and ruining everything inside. "Just a few inches more," he said, speaking more to himself than Eva. "Get ready."

And then, the box dipped, sinking under the surface. It bobbed back up, inexplicably several feet away. Sweat dampened his brow and pooled at the nape of his neck. He couldn't lose the rations. Having food was the difference between life and death. He reached out farther. Then a little more.

He felt the bank crumble a moment before the earth splashed into the water. Brett went with it.

In an instant, he was in water up to his chest. The current buffeted him from all sides. The water swirled around his legs, trying to upend him and pull him into the murky depths.

On the bank, Eva stretched out her hand. "Grab a hold of me. I'll pull you to the shore."

Getting out of the water was the prudent thing to do, he knew that. But he wasn't about to let the rations get away. He reached out with the stick, catching the box on the top. He pulled it to him, then grabbed it in his hands. He shoved the box toward Eva. "Take this."

"Give me your hand," she insisted.

He ignored her demand and pushed the box closer. "Take it. I can't climb out and carry the box at the same time."

Eva muttered a curse, but she dragged the box through the water and lifted it onto the shore. "Now you," she said, leaning back over the creek. "Give me your hand."

Brett took a step forward. And another. Eva was so close that he could almost reach her hand—almost, but not quite. He moved his foot forward once more and plummeted into the murky depths.

The water was freezing cold and black as midnight. The current swept him off his feet, pushing him downstream and keeping him submerged. He tried to gauge where he was, but he couldn't even tell what was riverbed and what was sky.

His mouth filled with water, cutting off breath, and Eva's face flashed through his mind.

If he drowned in this stupid river, Eva would be alone. The only way they could survive in the desert was if they stayed together.

He had to focus. He had to live.

Long ago, he'd been trained on what to do in this exact situation. The steps he needed to take came back to him at last. Brett stopped moving and let his feet follow the current. Then he held on to his knees. Slowly, he started to rise. He could see light breaking through the darkness. He kicked his legs and reached out with his arms. After breaking through the surface, he sucked in a lungful of air.

The first thing he saw was Eva. She was kneeling on the bank and scanning the water. Her face was pinched with concern. "Omigod," she said. "I thought you were gone for good."

Of all the things that surprised Brett, the one that struck him most was how little he'd traveled underwater. He was only a few yards from where he'd gone under. "I'm harder to get rid of than all that," he said with more bravado than he felt.

Eva leaned forward, holding the end of the stick. "Can you reach this?"

Brett stretched out, careful to maintain his footing. His fingertips brushed the end of the branch. He pulled himself forward. Then he grabbed hold with his whole hand.

From the bank, Eva dragged him toward her and dry land.

In seconds, he was close enough to touch her. Reaching out, he placed his palm into hers, her grip strong but soft. She pulled, and finally Brett made it to the edge of the river. He lifted himself out of the water.

Kneeling on the bank, he was suddenly exhausted. He rolled to his back and listened to his heartbeat.

"Jeez, I thought I'd lost you." She brushed the hair from his forehead. He relaxed under her touch. "It was terrifying to think that you were gone—that I'd never see you again." She exhaled, an unmistakable tremble in her breath. "I should give you an antibiotic, just as a precaution. Who knows what's in that water."

He lay on his back and stared at the sky as Eva retrieved the medical kit and returned to him. She held a pill in her hand. "Take this."

He lifted onto his elbow and, placing the medication on his tongue, forced the pill down his throat.

"How are you?" she asked.

"That depends," he said. "If the food is intact, then it was all worth it."

"Let's see." Using a utility knife that hung from her flight suit, Eva sliced through the plastic wrapping, wadded it up and shoved it into her pocket. "The box looks dry."

"Let's see what's inside," he said.

She sliced through the seam of tape, opening the box. "Looks like granola bars. Cereal. Apple sauce in a cup. There's other stuff, too." She held up a granola bar. "You want one?"

He took it and tore through the wrapper, his stomach gurgling.

That was when he heard it—a rumble rolling across the plain and echoing off the surrounding hills.

Eva turned her face skyward. "Great," she mumbled. "If there's thunder, more rain is coming."

But Brett had served full-time in the army. He'd been deployed to combat zones more than once. The noise wasn't thunder. His blood was like ice in his veins. "That's not another storm," he said. "That's gunfire."

Eva stared at him, her eyes wide with fear or disbelief, he couldn't tell which.

Before either could say a word, there was another report. The ground exploded in a cloud of dirt and stone as the bullet struck near their feet.

Decker looked down the sites of his gun as sweat dripped from his hairline and burned his eyes. His vision was blurry.

His whole body ached, as if thousands of angry wasps had been let loose under his skin. It was no wonder that he couldn't shoot for crap. He wanted—make that *needed*—his meds.

He'd watched the nurse—he remembered her name was Eva—and the guy who was probably the pilot for over an hour now. When he'd seen their figures moving across the plain, he'd planned to avoid them altogether. But then he noticed the red cross emblazoned on the box that the guy carried. He knew it was a medical kit of some kind and that meant pain-killers were inside.

He had to get that med kit. But how? With his damned headache—like his skull was being squeezed in a vise—he couldn't think.

Already two bullets had been wasted. He couldn't afford to fire and miss again.

The prudent thing to do was let them run. Chasing after the duo wasted time he didn't have. But that med kit was better than a treasure chest. Besides, he wouldn't make it all the way to Mexico if he couldn't concentrate because of his pain—not to mention the withdrawal symptoms from not getting his regular dose of meds. All he needed was a little something to take the edge off.

In missing his shots, he'd lost the element of surprise. Those two knew he was armed and looking for them. He drew in a deep breath and tried to think like people on the run. Their only chance of survival would be to get to the highway, which was roughly twenty miles to the south.

That meant he knew where they were going. He need not waste any more bullets trying to kill them from afar. All he needed to do was watch and wait. His headache eased a bit.

Decker was once again the predator, and he was ready to stalk his prey.

Using their contacts with the Texas Rangers, the team from Texas Law found a helicopter that was willing to pick them up in Encantador and take them to the last known location of the missing medevac helicopter. The chopper had room for four people. The pilot and one passenger in the front, along with two seats in the back.

Ryan sat next to the pilot, a woman named Farrah Kaufman. She spoke into a mic attached to her helmet and broadcast through the headsets that he and Isaac wore. "We've got a location for the downed chopper's black box. Just a few minutes more. There's a field nearby, and we can land."

Just like the pilot predicted, the remainder of the flight only took minutes. They circled above a small clearing, and even from the air, Ryan could see the remains of the helicopter. It lay on its side in the bottom of a ravine, covered in dirt, turning the once white aircraft to gray. A trickle of water flowed around either side of the hull as if the chopper was a great metal island.

"Christ Almighty," Isaac whispered into his mic. "What the hell happened?"

That was what Ryan wanted to know. The back rotor was missing along with the rear section of the hull.

"Don't know," said Farrah. "Maybe the helicopter got pushed here by the river. There was a big storm that blew through here not too long ago. When that happens, every crevasse can become a raging river."

Ryan nodded. "How'd it even get in the water? And where is everyone?"

"That's what we're going to find out," said Isaac.

The pilot brought the aircraft to the ground. The minute that the skids touched the dirt, Ryan and Isaac unfastened their harnesses and opened the cargo door. The downdraft from the rotor washed over them, the roar of the engine deafening.

Ducking low, Ryan jumped to the ground and ran to the wrecked aircraft, his stomach twisting into a knot. Isaac was at his heels.

Approaching the helicopter, his sprint slowed, then he

stopped altogether. From the looks of it, Farrah had been right, and the helicopter had been submerged. Mud was caked in the hold. The windscreen was broken. He peered into the torn rear fuselage. There was a body, male and tall, tangled in cargo netting. Ryan's heart slammed into his ribs, and he jumped back.

"What is it?"

He swallowed, trying to slow his racing pulse. "Looks like there are fatalities."

Isaac approached, then exhaled and shook his head.

"Can you tell," Ryan began, "if they died during the crash or was it a deliberate act?"

He knew that Isaac wasn't a medical examiner, but the investigator had seen his share of gruesome deaths.

"We'll have to leave that to the coroner," Isaac said. "I'm going to ask Farrah to radio in that we need an ME," said Isaac. "Hold up, and I'll be right back."

"Sure thing," Ryan said, even though he had no intention of waiting. He had to know about Decker. Was he the cause of the crash or another victim?

As soon as Isaac sprinted away, Ryan moved forward. He entered the helicopter through the jagged hole at the back. The floor of the hold was filled with water, a sheen of fuel shimmering on the surface. He saw a second body, face down in a puddle. Even without seeing a face, Ryan could tell from the flight suit and build that it wasn't Decker.

He moved away from the body, toward the cockpit. There was a female, also dead. Bile rose in the back of his throat. He coughed and looked away.

"What the hell are you doing in there?" Isaac yelled from the rear of the helicopter. "You can't contaminate the scene."

Ryan carefully walked to the back of the hold. "I had to know, man," he said, stepping into the sun. "I needed to find out if Decker was in the helicopter or not."

"And?" Isaac asked.

A sick feeling settled in Ryan's stomach as he shook his

head. "There are three dead bodies in there." He'd seen the flight manifest. On board were two pilots, male and female, a female nurse, two male EMTs, the patient they were transporting—Decker Newcombe—and the US marshal sent to guard the patient. Even though it was obvious, he said, "That means four people are missing."

Isaac cursed before flicking his fingers toward the wreckage. "What are the chances that anyone made it out of that crash alive?"

"If we're talking about Decker," Ryan said, "then the odds are pretty damn good."

"The guy's like a cat with nine lives. How many has he used up already? Seven? Or is it eight?"

Ryan used to be friends with Decker—or as close as anyone could come to being friends with a sociopath. He couldn't count how many times the other man should've perished, but he never did. Then again, Ryan was the most recent person to spare the killer's miserable life. Decker had tried to commit a murder online, a crime that Ryan had interrupted. In the ensuing chaos, Decker had been shot and was stuck in a burning warehouse.

Ryan could've left him behind.

But he hadn't.

He pulled the murderer from the flames and got him medical care. Now, his former friend was on the loose and as dangerous and deadly as ever.

If he was going to stop him, he had to focus.

Which brought up another point. Issac was right. The crash had totaled the helicopter, and the wreckage had been caught in a flash flood—that was the only thing that could've pushed the aircraft downstream. Even an evil bastard like Decker didn't stand much of a chance.

"C'mon," Isaac said. "Let's follow the streambed. That way we can see if there are any other bodies lost in the water."

Ryan nodded as if in agreement.

Isaac was a good person. A much better person than Ryan would ever be, even on his best day. Because of that, Ryan didn't bother to inform his boss that his top priority wasn't to find any other victims of the crash.

He only wanted to locate Decker's cold corpse. And this time, he'd make sure that he stayed dead.

Chapter Eleven

Eva ran, cursing with each step. It was the damned medical boot. Sure, the air cast stabilized her injured leg, but it made her slower than usual and clumsy. The hard plastic rubbed against her flesh and with each step, she could feel blisters forming. The med kit slapped against her thigh and hip, but at least she had it. The worst was the injury itself. Pain stabbed into her ankle and radiated upward until her teeth hurt.

But she ignored all the discomfort and ran. It didn't matter how much her foot bothered her; it was nothing compared to what would happen if she was struck by a bullet.

Holding the box of food in one arm and her free hand in the other, Brett pulled her along. The stream was on her left and the open plain on her right. Ahead was a thick willow tree. It didn't provide much protection, but at least it gave them some cover.

Decker was out there, somewhere.

"Get down," said Brett as they skidded behind the branches.

Eva gulped air, the same way she used to drink from a garden hose when she was a kid.

"How are you?" asked Brett. His hair was damp from the creek. Otherwise, he wasn't even breathing hard.

"I'm fine," she panted.

"Are you sure? You didn't get shot, obviously. How's your leg?"

"Fine," she said again, the single word a wheeze. "You know…" she sucked in a breath "…if I survive this, I'm going to get in shape."

"What do you mean? You look pretty good to me."

Despite the circumstances, his compliment started a new round of fluttering in her stomach. But she pushed aside all thoughts of past and future. What she needed was a plan for right now. "What're we going to do?"

Brett sat back on his haunches and exhaled. She'd noticed that about him. Whenever he was thinking, he let out a long breath. Almost like he was letting go of any bad ideas. "We can't sit here all night and wait for Decker to come find us."

"Agreed."

"We also have to go south, toward Encantador, or at least find the highway."

She nodded her head, saving her breath.

He paused for a moment. "We can cross here," he said. "The creek's already drying up. I hate to come out where Decker can see us. But walking on this side of the streambed makes us an easier target." He inclined his head to the opposite bank. "At least over there, we have cover, and we're getting closer to town."

A big part of Eva wanted to stay behind the willow tree. But Brett was right. Staying where they were made them an easy target. If she was going to have to face the likes of Decker Newcombe, it wouldn't be because she was cowering behind a bush. "Okay," she said, sitting up taller. "When do we go?"

"We'll wait a bit. We can both use the rest." Brett held out his granola bar. The wrapper was crumpled from where he'd clutched it in his palm. "Take some. We both need energy, and who knows when we'll be able to eat again."

She held out her hand, and he poured the broken pieces into

her palm. For a moment, they both ate in silence. Too soon, she chewed the last piece of granola; her mouth was dry. Not for the first time, she wished that they had found the case of water, as well.

The longer they sat behind the tree, the less she wanted to cross the creek and climb another hill. It was the only way to get home, but they'd be exposed. Before losing her nerve, she said, "We should go now."

Brett peered through the low-hanging branches, scanning the hillside. He stood, holding the box of food in one arm. He gripped the med kit's handle with the other hand. Finally, he said, "Let's go."

Her heartbeat raced, thrumming at the base of her skull. She followed Brett, stepping from behind the relative safety of the tree. He was tall, his shoulders broad. If Decker shot at them again, it would be Brett who would take the bullet.

The thought that he might die left her eyes burning. It was more than being alone and lost—although that would be bad enough. It was that the world would be a worse place without him in it.

"I'll go first," he said, standing on the bank. "If anything happens…"

"Don't," she interrupted. She couldn't have him speak disaster into being. As if to counter his thought, she said, "Nothing bad will happen."

He turned to look at her. "Then be careful."

"Brett." She reached for his arm and placed her lips on his cheek. The kiss was over as soon as it began, and yet her pulse raced. "For luck," she said.

He held her gaze for a moment, but she couldn't read his expression. "Thanks." He turned.

"Brett," she called out again. There was so much she wanted to say to him—that she was happy they'd met. She had enjoyed their one night together. And sincerely, she was sorry that it wouldn't work out between them. When he turned to face her again, she couldn't find the right words. Instead, she held out her palm. "I'll carry the med kit."

"You sure?"

"Just hand it over."

He gave it to her, then gently squeezed her wrist. "It'll all work out."

She tried to smile and gripped the handle tighter. "I hope you're right."

Turning, he stepped into the water and started to wade into the current. The stream came up to his ankles. His calves. His thighs. When he was submerged to his waist, he lifted the box of food overhead. Eva followed, clutching the med kit to her chest. The water swirled around her legs, pushing her downstream with each step. It was colder than she expected, and within seconds, her feet were numb.

Brett reached the opposite bank and climbed out of the water. If he could do it, she could, as well. Back in college, when she'd been with the Air Guard, she'd been trained what to do in case of a water landing. But that was years ago, and the lessons were fuzzy. Still, she tried to remember what she'd been taught. Filling her lungs with a deep breath, she focused on each step. The water crept up her legs. It leaked into the boot she wore on her injured foot. She tried not think about what might be floating in the water, or who might be watching them.

Then the current was up to her waist. It filled her flight suit. For an instant, she felt pain as an imaginary bullet tore a hole through her shoulder. She knew that trying to make their way to civilization was the only way to survive. But being this vulnerable left her hands trembling.

When the water reached her chest, she balanced the med kit on her head. The current was strong. One wrong step, and she'd get dragged underwater. Still, she wasn't going to turn back. Which meant there was no way to go other than forward. She took another step.

Just as the creek bed dipped down in the middle, it rose on the opposite side. The water receded. Chest, stomach, thighs and calves.

She splashed out of the water, clawing clods of dirt as she scrambled up the embankment. Dropping the med kit, she bent over and held on to her knees. Only then did she remember to draw a breath.

"Hey." Brett placed his strong hand on her shoulder. "What's the matter?"

"Decker is getting to me. It's been a while since I was a part of a military unit. Sometimes I can still call up my training, and my fear abates. But a serial killer shooting at me while I'm exposed crossing a stream?" She stood up straight. The water that had filled her flight suit poured onto the ground until she was standing in a puddle. The fabric clung to her like a second skin. "I just got scared there for a minute."

"Understandable," he said, glancing at her with concern. "If you're okay, we should get going. It's twenty miles to the highway, and that's a lot of walking. I want to get up and over this ridgeline before it gets dark."

She nodded and looked around. No serial killers in sight, but for all they knew, Decker was watching and waiting for the right moment to strike again.

With Eva at his side, Brett had been walking for hours. Luckily, his smartwatch still worked, and he could tell that they'd hiked over four miles.

The sun had dipped below the horizon, leaving the sky a riot of colors. Pink. Orange. And at the edges, purple. The ground, however, had been leached of color and definition. Missteps could happen easily. Eva had already injured her ankle; they couldn't afford another wound.

"Can I ask you a question?" she said as they descended a hill.

He wasn't in the mood to converse, but the sound of her

voice soothed him in a way nothing else had before. "You can ask me anything."

"Have you ever been part of a search-and-rescue team?"

He nodded. "I have."

"Can you tell me what's probably going on with the team out looking for us?"

"Well," he began, "I imagine that they've located the chopper's black box by now. If they've found the bodies of the crew, they might think we're dead, as well. They'll figure that we were pushed out of the aircraft by the floodwaters."

"So, nobody's looking for us now?"

"They'll conduct an aerial search, certainly. At least for a few days."

"And then what?" she asked, her voice small.

"Before then, we'll get found. Or we'll pick up cell service and make a call."

"I feel like you're lying to me," she said.

He was. Brett had no clue if or when they'd find cell coverage in the middle of nowhere. A plane would definitely be searching for them, but spotting him and Eva while they were trying to hide from a serial killer would be difficult. The two of them couldn't exactly walk out in the open, waving up at the skies at the first sight of an aircraft. Not unless they wanted Decker to know where they were hidden—which they did not.

He didn't respond. In the world of uncertainties, there was one thing he knew. He'd do anything to protect Eva, even if it was from the awful truth.

"You know that I can handle this situation, right? You know that if you aren't upfront with me, I can't be any help. In fact, I'll only be a burden." She paused. "I grew up around here. I know that cell coverage is spotty at best. I know that there's a lot of ground to cover to look for someone who's gone missing. Plus, you didn't mention the serial killer with a gun."

He exhaled, putting one foot in front of the other as they climbed another steep incline. "I think our only chance of survival is finding the interstate—and then, a friendly motorist who'll give us a ride."

She frowned. "So, you're saying that our chances are basically crap."

He wasn't about to give up or give in. "So long as we're alive, there's always a chance."

"I admire your optimism, Brett," she said, her voice reedy. "But I don't know that I buy it. Me, I'm more of a realist, with a toe across the line into pessimism. It happens when you work in the emergency department."

"In a situation like this, we always need to hold on to hope."

"Sounds like something from the inside of a greeting card," she said. "Maybe you should look into a second career."

"See, you're being optimistic, too. If you didn't think we're going to make it, then there wouldn't be any reason for a second career."

She barked out a laugh and then grimaced. Holding her side, she said, "Don't make jokes. It's hard enough to climb all these damn hills without laughing."

They crested the top of the rise. Night was closing in from all sides. The last remnant of the sun was only a sliver of orange on the western horizon. Brett stopped and inhaled. The air was loamy and heavy with humidity. Wiping the sweat from his brow, he scanned the sky. There were no early stars, only clouds. "I think we're going to get another storm before morning."

Eva cursed. "The only good thing with that is we can try to collect some rainwater."

"Now you're definitely being an optimist. I knew I'd rub off on you."

She chuckled. "Let's see what's in the case of food. Maybe there's something we can eat now and use the container to catch water."

"There is," he said, confident that he remembered what was inside the box. He set the case on the ground and squatted next to it. His quadriceps burned but the stretch would be good for his thighs. After all, they had miles yet to travel. He removed a plastic cup filled with applesauce. He held it up to Eva. "Here you go."

She peeled back the foil lid and tipped her head, dumping the contents into her mouth. He found a second applesauce pouch and quickly depleted it.

She held out the empty cup to Brett. "We better keep moving. Once it starts to rain, we won't be able to go anywhere."

He knew she was right. He placed both cups back in the box and lifted it. She picked up the med kit next to her feet. "Let's go," he said.

As they began to walk, he knew that their chances of being found were slim. But it wasn't because people weren't looking. Part of him wanted to leave a trail for the search team to follow, even just the two empty applesauce pouches. But Decker might spot the litter first.

And kill them long before they'd ever be found.

The storm came sooner and with more violence than Eva imagined. She and Brett had just descended a hill and were walking through a narrow pass when the first fat drop hit her cheek. As she wiped the drip away, the water still clinging to her hand, the deluge began.

She held the med kit over her head. "Where the hell did that come from?" she asked. Then, "Forget I asked. I've learned all I want to know about sudden storms."

Brett nodded his grim agreement. They were both silent for a moment, and she had no doubt he was also thinking of the crew he'd lost and the marshal. Finally, he said, "We gotta get to higher ground."

He was right. If this storm dropped as much water as the one that downed the helicopter, then they risked getting caught by another flash flood.

Tucking the box of food under one arm, he held out his hand to her. "Come with me."

She swiped the rainwater from her face, then reached for him.

He held her palm tightly against his own and, leading her over ground now slick with mud, began to climb the next hill. It was steep, the ground uneven. Climbing up this hill would be difficult in the best of circumstances—and in the dark and in the middle of a storm, these conditions were far from the best.

Her toe caught on the edge of a stone. She pitched forward, landing hard on her hands and knees. The med kit hit the ground and tumbled backwards, end over end before coming to rest on its side.

"Dammit," she cursed, rising to her feet.

"You okay?"

Her knees ached. By morning, she'd be stiff and covered with bruises. Her injured leg burned, the ibuprofen she'd taken earlier had worn off. Her hands were raw and bloody. "I'm fine," she lied. It would do no good to complain about minor injuries. "Let me get the kit."

She turned, careful about her footing, and climbed down the hill to where the med kit lay. With a groan, she picked it up. When she stood, she stared into the darkness. Had there been something there in the shadows? A man? Gooseflesh rose on her arms as she strained to see into the storm. There was nothing. Now.

But had Decker been there and darted into the shadows? She quickly turned around, needing to see where Brett was.

Brett was closing the distance between them. "I think there's a cave right behind you."

She looked into the gloom again. There, ten yards away, was what she had seen. She wiped at her eyes again. Now that she knew what she was looking for, it was easy to pick out. The rock formation was about six feet tall, but—she laughed quietly—how had she mistaken that for a person?

Brett stood above her on the hill and pointed to the cave. "C'mon. We can at least get out of this weather."

Eva scrambled up behind him. For moment, she thought about all the critters—none of them friendly—who might also take shelter in the cave. She pushed the thought away.

Brett must've been thinking the same thing. When she reached the mouth of the cavern, he'd already pulled out his phone and was using the flashlight to scan the space. It wasn't much, just a few feet of sandy ground. But it was thankfully empty and dry. He glanced at the screen. "Still no bars," he said before powering down the device. "Let's get inside."

She ducked down to keep from hitting her head on an over-hanging rock. Once inside the cave, she could stand up, but there wasn't much more room than that. If she pressed one shoulder against a wall, she'd be able to touch the other side with an outstretched arm.

She set down the med kit and shook feeling back into her hand. Brett set down the box of food. The cardboard was start-ing to pucker from the rain.

"There were a few little plastic cups in there," he said, rum-maging in the box. "We can use them to collect rainwater."

She knelt on the ground to help. The cups were stacked in a corner. She pulled out two and handed them to Brett. "Here you go."

Standing in the cave, he held both cups out into the down-pour. It took only moments for them to fill with rainwater. He handed her a full cup, and she threw it back like a shot of alcohol.

It hit her stomach like a bomb, and for a minute, her mid-dle contracted painfully. "I should've known better," she said, gripping her side, "and drank slowly."

"Here." He held out his own cup. "Sip this."

"I can't take your water."

He held his hand out to the sky. "I think there's plenty more where that came from."

She laughed. "You're right." She passed him the empty cup while taking the one that was full.

Brett kept his body in the cave, arm once again outstretched into the rain. While the other cup filled, she sipped the water. It was cool and refreshing. Soon, Brett lifted a full cup in salute. "Cheers."

She waited as he sipped the water. Once he was finished, she said, "Give me the cup. I'll refill them both."

"I got this," he said.

She held out her hand. "My arms can be in the rain. It's only fair. And it's not like my boot can get any wetter."

He opened his mouth, ready to argue. Obviously, he was raised to be a courteous man. But she was a force on her own. She'd taken care of herself her whole life. Sure, it was tempting to rest while he got wet. But she wasn't about to give into any weaknesses now.

He handed her his cup. "If you insist."

"I do."

Unfortunately, her arms weren't long enough for her to stand under the rock ledge and still have her hands in the rain. It meant that more of her had to get wet. The water had long ago washed away the sweat, the grime and the heat of the day. Now, it was just cold and unpleasant.

With both cups filled, she handed one to Brett. "Drink up."

"I think you said something like that last night when they brought a margarita to the table."

"Did I?" she asked, sipping the water. As long as the rain held, they'd be able to stay hydrated. Tomorrow would be another day, but for now, they were okay. "God, last night feels like it happened to a different person."

Settling on the ground, she unstrapped the Velcro that kept her air cast in place. She took it off, hoping the boot might dry quickly. With a sigh, she wiggled her toes.

"How's the leg?"

"I don't think anything's broken." Without the boot, her

shin throbbed with each beat of her heart. Her skin tightened as the injury began to swell. "Still hurts like hell."

"How about some more ibuprofen?"

"Definitely." She unlocked the med kit's latch, finding the OTC pain meds in a foil packet. She washed them down with the last swallow of rainwater. There were also bandages for the blisters and antiseptic wipes to prevent infection.

"I'll fill that up again." Brett took the cup from her hand. His fingers grazed hers.

Despite the pain, the fear and the exhaustion, her heart skipped a beat.

"Thanks," she said, not daring to meet his eye. Because if she did, would he see how much she still wanted him?

Chapter Twelve

For the next thirty minutes, the rain continued to fall. Brett switched back and forth with Eva, sharing the job of collecting rainwater one cup at a time. Even as the downpour continued, he went from parched to sated to overfull.

"When I went to basic training," he said as the downpour eased into a drizzle, "we were told that hydration was the most important part of staying alive."

Shaking her head, she gave a quiet laugh. "I remember basic training. It was brutal."

"You didn't like it?" Brett asked. "I kinda thought it was fun. Like scouting on steroids."

She smiled. "Times ten for me. But I actually loved getting pushed to my limits, learning what I was capable of—more than I ever would have thought at eighteen. I might have pursued an air force career, but I was always so worried about my family. Baba needed me, Katya had a lot on her shoulders... It was hard to leave after my service, but I did get to serve, and I know I made the right choice for my family."

Funny, Brett hadn't thought about college for years. After graduating high school in Dallas, he'd gone to school at Texas Midland State College. His first year, he'd had too much fun, and his grades suffered. His father, an attorney and a stern man at best, refused to pay for school if his son was going to, quote, "screw around." He'd given Brett a choice, go into the military or get a job.

Brett enlisted the summer of his twentieth birthday. In the army, he found more than just the discipline his father wanted; he found his life's passion—flight.

Of course, he also learned some important lessons during basic training. One was to eat whenever he had a chance.

"Are you hungry?" he asked. "How about a little box of dry Cheerios?"

Eva pressed a hand to her stomach. "Actually, I'm not sure how hungry I am. Though under the circumstances I guess I should eat something. Especially since I took some meds."

He rummaged through their food supply, pulled out the small box of Cheerios, then looked at her. "Tell you what— how about we share it, since you're not hungry? Then if you decide you want something else, we'll dive into another bag."

She shrugged. "Sure."

He opened the box and shook some into her hand. They ate, split one more pouch of applesauce, and he felt more or less satisfied for now.

Eva looked better, too, with more of a sparkle back in her eyes now that she was full, hydrated and not getting rained on.

"Well," he said. "We're here for the night. We'll keep walking in the morning."

"Sounds good." Eva sat with her back to one wall of the cave. She'd bandaged her own blisters and was keeping her injured ankle out of the air cast for now. "I didn't realize how tired I was until I sat down."

"You get some sleep," he said. "I'll take first watch."

She opened her mouth, ready to argue. Before she said a word, he held up his palms. "I'll wake you in a few hours," he promised. "Then I'll catch some sleep."

She gave him a weary smile. "Thanks."

Standing at the mouth of the cave, he took a minute to assess their surroundings. Calling it a cave was a bit of an overstatement. It was more of a narrow gap in the middle of a rock formation. But it provided them with some cover from the elements.

He stepped outside. The air was cool and clear. Folding his arms across his chest, Brett inhaled deeply and looked—as he always did—toward the sky.

The clouds had moved away, leaving an ebony carpet filled with diamonds. He found the Big Dipper. The Little Dipper and the North Star. Staring into the darkness, he fixed north in his mind. To get to the interstate, they had to go south by southeast. He took another step into the night and turned in that direction.

He stared into the darkness—watching and listening. There were no sounds. No sights.

Wait. That wasn't right. On the horizon, in the direction of the highway, he saw a golden glow. The light was faint, but there, nonetheless.

He stared at it for a moment and then, a moment more. It was moving through his field of vision from left to right. His heart began to slam into his chest.

Were those headlights on a moving vehicle?

They had to be. If he were forced to guess, it was most likely something large like a long-haul trucker. But it meant that they were headed in the right direction.

Brett did a little quick math. On flat ground, the horizon was approximately three miles away. It was night, pitch dark, and he had the benefit of elevation, which meant the road was farther.

He estimated that it was at least a dozen miles to the interstate. None of it was flat ground and there were more hills to climb. But the thing was, it could be done.

He wanted to let out a victorious whoop.

But it made no sense to call out, letting Decker know where they were. He turned around, retracing his steps to the cave.

Eva looked up as he entered. "What is it?" she asked, her voice a whisper.

He knelt next to her. "I saw it," he said, whispering the words into her ear. "I found the highway from the ridgeline. It's not going to be easy, but it's doable. How's your ankle?"

"It hurt," she said, "but I can walk."

The idea of leaving now was tempting. But with Decker out there, somewhere, he knew it was best to stay hidden. It gave them time for the killer to lose their trail completely. "We'll leave with first light."

Sitting up, she drew her thighs into her chest, resting her chin on her knees. He sat next to her, his shoulder pressed against hers.

His pulse continued to race, but this time, it had nothing to do with being close to a murderer. Now, it was all about Eva.

After a while, he traced the back of her hand and leaned in close. "You can go back to sleep," he said, his voice low.

"Sleep?" she echoed in a whisper. "I won't be able to get any more rest. Not right now, at least."

"I'm sorry I woke you." He whispered the word into her hair. "I was just excited about the road, you know?"

She nodded her head. He could feel the movement on his chest. Feel her breath on his skin. He wrapped an arm around her shoulder, and she leaned into his chest. Without any thought, Brett placed his lips on the top of her head.

She tilted up her face just slightly, her gaze meeting his. God, she was beautiful. Bending to her, he placed his lips on hers. She sighed and he deepened the kiss.

Brett's kiss sent a bolt of lightning straight to Eva's middle. Tonight, here in this cave, they were safe. There'd been no sign of the killer. No sound. She had barely relaxed, but as time passed, she wasn't as tense.

All she wanted was to let loose again, be distracted from everything. And she well knew that Brett Wilson could make that happen.

They'd talked about where they stood. If Brett had kissed her, it meant they were on the same page. That he needed this, too.

Without another thought, she broke away from the kiss. Rising to her knees, she placed her hand over her zipper to muffle any noise out of an abundance of caution. Then, she opened the front of her flight suit. She shrugged out of the sleeves and pulled the fabric down to her waist.

Using her thumb, she traced his mouth. She wanted to tell him that having him in her life, even if it was just for a few days, had been a high point. Sure, there was a lot of bad happening now. But he had been nothing but good.

Brett pulled her to him, placing a kiss on her stomach. He drew his tongue up her abdomen. He pulled the cup of her bra back, exposing her breast. Brett ran his teeth over her nipple, and she bit her lip to stifle a cry of pleasure and pain.

He worked her zipper down lower before running his finger inside of her panties. Eva spread her knees farther, giving him full access to her body. He slid a finger inside of her. With his thumb, he rubbed the top of her sex. His touch ignited a flame in her belly, until she burned with a need to have him inside of her.

The orgasm claimed her. Her fingers tingled, and her skin felt too tight. She sucked in a breath, just a hiss of sound. Even that was too much. She buried her face in his hair. She held him and shuddered as the last spasms left her body.

Cradling the back of her head, he placed his mouth next to her ear and whispered, "Take off your clothes."

His hot breath washed over her, and yet gooseflesh rose on her arms.

She wanted to feel him again, skin to skin.

Eva kicked off her shoe, careful not to make a sound. She

pulled the zipper down the rest of the way before shimmying out of her flight suit. The cool evening air caressed her skin.

Brett knelt next to her. He slowly traced her body with his fingertips. Shoulder, belly, hip and thigh.

She shivered in anticipation and lay back on the sandy ground.

"So beautiful," he whispered, he slipped his finger inside of her.

She wanted to moan. To scream with pleasure. Biting the inside of her lip, she ran her fingers through his hair.

Brett slipped another finger inside of her, filling her completely. He kissed the top of her sex, sucking and licking.

A bolt of pleasure electrified her body. She bucked, lifting her hips, and brought his mouth closer still. Although his kisses and touches could never be deep enough.

She felt her next orgasm building, a swelling that started in her middle and grew as it traveled through her body. But she wanted more. She wanted him inside of her when she came. Eva tugged on his shoulders.

Brett looked up from between her thighs. The sight left her lightheaded.

"Come here." She mouthed the words. "I want you."

Brett slid up the length of her body, kissing her as he went. Her pelvis. Her stomach. Her chest. Her breasts. He rested on top of her, his face only inches from her own. God, he was gorgeous. The muscles of his chest and shoulders were defined. The hard planes of his face were all the sharper in the shadows.

She kissed him again, deeper than before. The taste of her own pleasure lingered on his tongue. "Take me," she said, her words nothing more than a whisper on the wind.

Brett unzipped his own flight suit, stripping it down past his ass. She wrapped her legs around his waist. She was so wet that he entered her in one stroke.

They moved together. In the moment, there was nothing beyond her and Brett. He pumped his hips, driving into her harder and faster. She could feel an orgasm rising inside of her, the swell of a wave coming in fast and strong. Then, the surf crashed over her.

She wanted to cry out as the orgasm pulled her under and left her breathless. Pressing her mouth to his shoulder, she stifled her cries.

Brett drove into her harder. Faster. His breathing was harsh and ragged. He came, collapsing on top of her. He kissed her gently. The silence and the kiss communicated more than words ever would.

She stripped all the way out of her flight suit. After all, it was still wet and needed time to dry. It didn't bother Eva that they couldn't speak. She wasn't sure what she would say now anyway.

She sat on the ground; Brett took up a spot next to her. Their shoulders touched. The lovemaking left her spent. It felt as if she were no longer made of bones and muscles, but was something soft and malleable. Her brain had turned to mush as well, and her eyelids were heavy. Sleep was creeping toward her again from all sides.

She realized she had the luxury of feeling this way because she could trust Brett.

"You look tired," he said, his voice soft.

"I feel tired."

"Rest," he encouraged. "I'll keep watch. But I think we're safe tonight."

She nodded and placed a kiss on his cheek. In the moment, she felt safe and protected. Resting her head on his shoulder, Eva finally closed her eyes and slept.

Ryan and Isaac were once again in the helicopter piloted by Farrah. They'd been forced to stay grounded because of an unexpected storm, but now, they were on the move again. A team from the state police and the coroner's office had taken charge of the wreckage; there was nothing more they could do at the site.

"I've done a bit of math," said Farrah into her mic. "We're flying to the last place that the air ambulance showed up on radar. From there, I'll head south. Hopefully, we'll find a clue as to where the chopper went down—and if there are any other survivors."

"All eyes peeled on the ground and in the river," Isaac said, his tone terse.

The helicopter was equipped with a spotlight that swept back and forth over the ground.

Ryan sat on the left side, peering out the window. He wasn't sure what they hoped to find. After all, it was dark. Still, he could see enough to know that for miles, there was nothing other than rocks and dirt and the occasional scraggily tree or scrubby bush.

Then he saw a flash of light reflected off metal.

"Farrah, ahead and to the left," Ryan said. "I saw something."

"Roger that," she said. She eased the helicopter to the left and lowered their altitude.

He held his breath and stared out the window. A black shape lay in the middle of a small valley. "That's it," he said, tapping his finger on the window. "Do you see it?"

"I see it," said Farrah.

"Me, too," said Isaac, leaning over from his seat. "Now to find out what it is."

"On it," she said.

As soon as the skids touched the ground, Ryan unbuckled his harness and removed his headset. Isaac already had the cargo door open. Ryan jumped out of the aircraft first, ducking low to avoid the downdraft. As he ran, he pulled a flashlight from a backpack he had slung over one shoulder. He shone the beam into the darkness.

Isaac was right behind him with his own flashlight.

From five yards out, Ryan could tell that it was the tail rotor and rear section of a helicopter. He stopped and swept the flashlight beam over the ground, searching for other clues.

A stretcher lay on its side, the legs and undercarriage visible. He couldn't tell if anyone was on the stretcher.

Nearby, rocks were arranged in a pile.

"Interesting," Isaac said, staring at the rocks. "Almost like a memorial."

Ryan sucked in a breath. "But for who—or how many? And who survived the crash to make the memorial?"

"Right now," Isaac said, "all we know for sure is that the stretcher has to be Decker's."

Ryan nodded, then looked around slowly. "And he's nowhere to be seen."

Isaac removed his firearm from the holster on his hip. Holding the gun with one hand and the flashlight in the other, he kept the barrel and the beam pointed toward the ground. "Let's check it, but be careful."

Ryan let Isaac take point—after all, he was the one with the gun. But the stretcher was eerily still. If Decker was still handcuffed to the railing, he hadn't survived the crash. For a moment, he recalled their childhood. Both had been hungry for glory and riches. In a way, they were kindred spirits. But in those days, Decker still had a soul.

How would Ryan feel to see the corpse of a man he once loved like a brother but now loathed? He rounded the stretcher and stopped short.

Standing at his side, Isaac cursed and slipped his gun back into the holster.

The sheets were empty. One of the railings was missing. A set of handcuffs lay on the ground.

In that moment, Ryan knew exactly what had happened. But still, he needed proof. He shone the flashlight beam at the pile of rocks. A shiver ran through him. "Not just a memorial. A *grave*."

"I'm thinking you're right," Isaac said.

They spent a few minutes removing the rocks. Like Ryan had predicted, it was a grave. But he didn't recognize the man who'd been buried.

"Do you know this guy?" Ryan asked.

"Yeah," said Isaac. "It's Augustin Herrera, US marshal."

"Another thing we know for sure," Ryan said, "is that Decker sure didn't bury the marshal."

Isaac nodded. "Right. Let's replace the stones."

They got it done, covering the dead man once more. Farrah would radio in that another body had been found, and the US marshal would be taken away in a body bag. Until then, there was no reason to disturb his resting place.

Dusting his hands on the seat of his jeans, Ryan said, "There were seven people on that helicopter, right? So far, we've found four bodies. It means that Decker's either dead, or he survived and took off. It also means that either the pilot, the nurse or both survived. One of those two buried the marshal." He paused a moment before adding, "We have to get to the other survivors before they become Decker's next victims."

Chapter Thirteen

Every step sent a shock wave of pain and nausea roiling through Decker's body. A cold sweat coated his flesh like a second slimy skin. He climbed to the top of a hill and scanned the dark terrain.

It was filled with hills and rocky outcroppings that all looked like each other. But his eyes had gotten used to the dark, and his ears had become accustomed to the silence. He waited, watching and listening. There was no movement. No far-off sounds of voices.

He needed the meds in the kit. He'd been following the nurse and the pilot for miles. But then the effing storm had come out of nowhere, and he lost their trail.

He tried to recall the last several hours. Each time an idea came to him, his head felt like it was being split in two by a cleaver. His mouth hurt. His feet were sore. He wished like hell that he'd stolen the marshal's shirt. The baggy windbreaker had rubbed his shoulders and pits raw.

If he were a sensible man, he'd ignore the pain and the withdrawal symptoms and just get his butt to Mexico. All he needed was the phone to call Seraphim.

What the hell was wrong with him? Relying on pills was weakness in his mind. Yet, here he was—weak, sick and lost.

Indecision rooted him to the spot. What was his next best plan? He could keep walking and make it—somehow—to Mexico. Or he could turn around and try to find the med kit. He'd have to take it from the pilot and the nurse, but hey, he was the one with the gun. That pleasant thought almost lessened the pain shooting up and down his arms and legs.

He looked over his shoulder. The terrain was much as what lay before him. He couldn't think about going back when he'd already made it this far.

Wind blew along the spine of the hill, cutting through the thin jacket. Decker started to shake with the cold. Wrapping his arms around his chest, he tried to conserve his heat and contain the shivers. He did neither. His stomach revolted.

Dropping to his hands and knees, he vomited acidic bile onto the dirt. He was too exhausted to stand, too exhausted to move. He rolled onto his back, the gun digging into his flesh. He didn't mind—at least the pain was real.

Lying there on the top of a hill, he stared at the night sky and the endless stars.

Decker wasn't a complex man. He understood two things—dominance and death. But as he lay on his back, he wondered if there was more to life than taking what he wanted. For the first time in years, he wondered if things would have been different—if he would have been different—if Anastasia hadn't left him when she did.

His stomach roiled again. Decker rolled to his side as vomit trickled from his mouth. He wanted to scoot away from the puddle of barf, but he was too tired. His feet and legs were numb. Oblivion was coming to claim him, and he welcomed the void.

He wouldn't get much farther without something to stop the pain.

He had to find the med kit in the morning. If it meant killing the pilot and the nurse, so be it. As consciousness finally faded, he brought Ana's face to mind and whispered, "Someday soon, I'll find you."

Ryan glanced at his smartwatch: 3:47 a.m. He hadn't slept since the night before. But it didn't matter. He wouldn't be able to rest until Decker Newcombe had been found and captured.

A mobile command center had been set up near the crash site. Aside from Ryan and Isaac, Jason Jones was there with a cadre of FBI agents. A coroner had been flown in to collect the body of US Marshal Augustin Herrera. There was also a representative from the Marshals Service, Maria Reyes, the supervisor from the San Antonio office. The group also had two Texas Rangers and an agent from the ATF. Mooky Parsons, the local sheriff, rounded out the team.

Lights on tall poles had been set up around the perimeter.

The alphabet soup of law enforcement left Ryan jittery. Not long ago, all these people had been out looking for him, as well. Sure, he'd changed teams and was even working for Texas Law now. But his distrust and dislike of the police was like a splinter that had been driven in deep. It bothered him when touched and was damn near impossible to get rid of or ignore.

It was a supreme irony that he was dating the local under-sheriff. But Kathryn Glass was the exception to nearly every rule he'd created for his life.

The coroner, Sheila Garcia, was clad in full PPE with a mask, surgical cap and latex gloves. Approaching Maria, she held a small clear, plastic bag. "Here are the personal effects we found on the body."

Ryan stood more than five yards away, but he could see that there wasn't much beyond a wallet and a few photos.

"This is it?" asked Maria. "What about his clothes? His gun? His phone?"

"For now," said the coroner, "I'm leaving the deceased in his T-shirt and underwear for dignity's sake. But everything else is gone."

"Gone," the marshal echoed, as if the word was foreign to her. She shook her head slowly and looked at Jason. "Poor Auggie." And then, "We have to assume that Decker Newcombe stole all his belongings."

Before he could think better of it, Ryan said, "That's not true."

All eyes turned to Ryan. He hated having so many cops stare at him. In the past, it had never ended well.

"Excuse me?" Maria said. "What did you say?"

Well, he'd opened his big mouth already. There was no turning back. "Decker wouldn't take the phone."

She snorted a laugh. "How would you know?"

"Because I know him."

Isaac said, "Ryan's with Texas Law now. But he used to be Decker's business manager and friend. He knows him better than anyone."

"Oh." Maria looked at Ryan, sizing him up from the top of his head to the toe of his boots. Her face was pinched like she'd tasted something sour. "I heard about you. You're the one who got a sweetheart of a deal."

Jason said, "He's also the reason Decker was in custody in the first place. You want to find the guy who killed your agent, we do, too. And like it or not, Ryan's the person we need to find the killer."

In a day that had been full of surprises, Special Agent Jones standing up for him was one hell of a shock. Ryan wasn't used to praise. He couldn't help it and stood a little taller.

The marshal sniffed. "If you're such a specialist, what do you know about Decker?"

"He didn't take Herrera's phone for starters," Ryan insisted. "He'd know it could be used to track him."

"What else?"

"He definitely didn't bury your guy, either. It's not his style."

"What does all of that mean?" Maria asked.

"It means that there are other survivors of the crash. They

took time to bury the body, and they're the ones who have the phone."

"That would make sense," said Jason. "The pilot and nurse haven't been found."

The marshal nodded slowly. "The good news is, assuming there's power, we can track the phone."

"It might not bring us to Decker, but it'll do some good," Ryan said, surprised that he was genuinely glad to help someone in need.

"Let me make a call." A large metal satellite phone was hooked on Maria's belt next to her firearm. She pulled it free and walked outside the ring of lights. The night was still and silent, and it was impossible to miss the tones as she pressed the sat phone's keypad.

After a moment, she said, "Sorry to call so late—or maybe it's early—but I need a location on Herrera's phone." She paused. "There's no cellular coverage here, you'll have to call me back at this number with coordinates." Another pause. "Thanks. I appreciate it."

She walked back to the group. "I assume you all heard that?" Without waiting for an answer, she continued, "It'll take some time, but we can find the phone—and whoever's got it." Maria turned to Ryan. "Now, I have to ask you an important question. Where is the subject now?"

After Jason had built him up as an expert on everything Decker Newcombe, it pained Ryan to admit the truth. "Honestly?" he said. "I have no idea."

Even before he pried his lids open, Decker's eyes hurt. His teeth ached from clenching his jaw all night. His mouth was dry, his tongue thick. He shivered and wrapped the jacket tighter around his torso. He didn't know how he'd survived the night without his meds, but somehow he had.

It reminded him of the old joke. He was only alive because heaven didn't want him, and hell was afraid he'd take over.

After wiping grit from his eyes, Decker looked at the sky. It was still black, but only a few stars were still visible. He'd slept for hours and somehow felt worse for the rest.

As he sat up, a wave of nausea crashed over him. He started to heave and rolled onto all fours. Nothing came up. He was so thirsty—for water and meds both—that it felt like a knife in his gut. There was no way he'd make it to Mexico without something for the cravings.

The gun he'd shoved into his waistband pulled his pants lower. Tightening his belt, Decker reviewed what he knew.

Yesterday evening, he had been following the pilot and the nurse until he lost them in the storm. If he wanted to find them again, he had to double back. Yet, he knew that getting the med kit wasn't just something he wanted. It was something he needed.

He pushed to standing. His vision blurred, and the ground beneath his feet rocked like a boat on the ocean. It was the damned addiction to the meds, he knew. Still, he thought he might retch again. Or he would if he had anything left in his stomach.

Inhaling deeply, he placed one foot in front of the other.

Focus, dammit. Stay sharp.

But he couldn't concentrate. Every joint felt as if it were being crushed. His eyes ached too much to scan the horizon or study the ground for clues.

Then he heard it. A sound—something had clattered.

He stopped walking and listened.

Silence.

Was it them? The pilot and the nurse? He knew the general direction the sound had come from. Maybe he'd get lucky. He pulled the gun from the small of his back and gripped the handle with both hands. Carefully, he crept along the ridgeline. His steps were slow. His footfalls crunched on the gravel and hard-packed earth.

Now he heard a skittering sound. It stopped suddenly—purposefully.

He retreated several steps, trying to find the spot where he heard the noise.

The sounds had come from his left, farther up the hill. From where he stood, he could see a narrow gap in the rocks. There was a flash of blue against a white background and a red cross. It was one of the flight suits. Someone was barely visible at the edge of the opening. Keeping guard.

He removed the magazine from his gun and counted the bullets. Five rounds left. He reinserted the clip and lined the sight up with the red cross. His hands shook. His eyes stung as his vision wavered and turned the target fuzzy.

Decker didn't like his chances of hitting anything. He didn't like the idea of wasting any more bullets, either. If he was going to get the med kit, he had to get close.

Quietly, he climbed the hill. From there, he could look down and see everything. The pilot lay on his side, sleeping. He snored. Beside him, the nurse kept watch.

There was no way he could sneak past the nurse. Nor could he shoot them both, not with his withdrawal shakes.

In short, he didn't have a plan.

Yet, Decker did have certain things on his side—like time and patience. He settled behind a boulder. From there, he could watch and wait, finding the perfect time to strike.

Eva sat at the edge of the cave and watched as the sun crested over the horizon. A minute ago, a raccoon had rushed past her and knocked over the med kit, making it spin a bit. She'd hurried to silence the noise. Not just because Brett was sleeping and had barely gotten a couple of hours in. But because Decker Newcombe could be out there.

She hoped he'd moved on, giving up on trying to kill

them to get as far away as possible. Otherwise, he risked getting recaptured.

But Decker was an irrational serial killer. She couldn't count on him being reasonable, even about his own life.

She let herself watch the sunrise. For a moment, it was just a line of gold, and then it erupted into light. The day was going to be brutally hot. Even at this early hour, the temperatures had started to rise. She knew they shouldn't walk in the hottest part of the day, which meant that they had to take advantage of the light now.

After she and Brett had made love, she'd slept for several hours. Brett, gallant guy that he was, would've let her continue to sleep. But in the middle of the night, she'd awakened. She'd insisted that it was her turn to keep watch. Brett must've been exhausted because he agreed to let her stay up.

Now, she hated to wake him.

Brett lay on his back. His cheeks and chin were covered in stubble. She ran a finger over his chin.

He opened his eyes slowly.

"Hey," she said as his gaze rested on her face.

"Hey," he echoed. He glanced at the watch on his wrist. He pressed the crown on the side once and then, once more. "Damned battery" he said, his voice hoarse. "Any idea what time it is?"

"It's daybreak. So maybe five in the morning," she guessed. "How're you feeling?"

Sitting up, he scrubbed his face with both hands. "Better," he said. "Thanks for letting me sleep. We should probably get going."

"Agreed," said Eva. "But we should eat something first." They still had two days' worth of rations left.

"Let's eat while we walk." He stood. "But first, you'll have to excuse me. Nature calls."

Brett's absence gave her time to get ready for a day filled with walking. After straightening one sock, she slipped on a sneaker. As she reached for the air cast, a shadow—head, shoulders, arms—stretched out on the floor of the cave.

"That was fast," she said, turning.

A man stood at the cave's entrance. The sun shone on him from behind and obscured his features. But even without seeing his face, she knew the man wasn't Brett.

Decker Newcombe stepped forward into the cave. His icy blue eyes were dull. His hair hung around his shoulders. The stink of infection and vomit surrounded him like a fog. Holding a gun, Decker aimed the barrel at her chest.

She tried to scream, but all she could manage was a croak. "What do you want?"

"The medical kit. Give it to me."

Eva reached for the kit and held it up. "Take it."

"Push it here."

She set it back on the ground and shoved it toward the killer.

He knelt and lifted it by the handle. With his eyes on her, and the barrel aimed at Eva's head, he tucked the box into his chest. With his thumb, he unlocked the latch and flipped the lid open. Casting his gaze to the box, he shoved the contents around. He looked back at her; his gaze was filled with fury and pain. She'd seen that look more than once in the ER.

He asked, "Where's the good stuff?"

"Good stuff?" she repeated, though she could guess what he was looking for. "You want pain meds?"

"Yeah, and none of that over-the-counter crap."

"San Antonio Medical Center has a policy not to carry narcotics in ambulances," she said. Years ago, several EMTs had been robbed for the drugs they carried. "We don't take anything strong out of the hospital. Everything you were prescribed was separate from this. I don't know where those meds went but I guess they were lost in the crash." She paused, not sure why she was trying to reason with a killer. Still, she was nurse and she had to try. "But you were hurt in the crash… I can help you."

She didn't want to tend to a killer, but she took her oath to help seriously.

"I didn't get some other damn injury," he said. "What I need are drugs. And it's all your fault. If the hospital hadn't pumped me full of crap, I wouldn't need it now."

Had Decker become addicted to pain meds? It happened so often that she wasn't surprised. "There are things you can take to help with the cravings." With her hands lifted, she rose to her feet. "Let me show you."

"You're the nurse," he said. "Eva, right?"

"That's right." Even she heard the tremor in her voice.

She'd been in tough situations before over the years. The only way to survive was to keep her cool. But this man was much worse than a belligerent patient who'd come to the emergency department. She didn't have the support of other nurses or doctors or hospital security. Decker Newcombe was a serial killer, and she was alone. Even if she treated him to overcome his craving, she couldn't expect him to be thankful. Hell, she shouldn't expect to survive.

Still, the med kit contained an opioid receptor antagonist, naloxone, a drug that would minimize Decker's withdrawals. Swallowing her fear, she said, "I can help you, if you let me."

"Well, that's so kind of you to offer. Now get up, Nurse Eva." He pressed the gun into the top of her head. The iron was cold, and the barrel dug a groove into her skin over her skull. "You're coming with me."

Chapter Fourteen

Brett stood on a ridge and looked in every direction. The sky was a soft shade of blue and the sun had yet to crest over the horizon. In this light, the red rocks were a deep shade of ocher. The few plants hardy enough to grow in this area of the desert were brown at the edges. But the interstate was out there, somewhere. He knew where it was.

There were several hills between where he stood and where they needed to be. To find the road, they'd have to traverse miles of grueling terrain. They had food but hadn't saved any of the rainwater. The sun and the heat would be their worst enemies—that was if they could avoid Decker Newcombe altogether.

Now that he had his bearings, Brett walked back to the cave. He stopped at the entrance and froze. Eva was gone. The med kit was gone.

Two sets of footprints were impressed in the sand.

One set had to belong to Decker. Had the killer been watching and waiting? And more important, where were they now? Brett hadn't been gone long—a few minutes, no more. They couldn't have gone far.

He followed the set of prints to a bare rock ledge. Without

the sandy dirt, there were no more footprints. Like a magician's trick, there the trail was gone. He walked to the edge, shading his eyes to scan the horizon. There were rocks and hills and brush. But no sign of Eva or Decker.

He had to get her back. But how?

A scream ripped through the silent morning. It echoed off the hills, seeming to come from everywhere. He ran, not even sure if he was going the correct direction.

A root snaked along the ground. He didn't see it until it was too late. His toe caught, and he fell, skidding along the rocks. Ignoring the pain in his knees and the pinpricks of blood that filled his palms, he pushed to his feet and started to run.

"Eva!" he yelled. "Can you hear me? Where are you?

"Brett!" she screamed.

The one word was all he needed to find the right direction. Swerving to the left, he ran up a steep hill. Stones came loose under his feet, rolling down behind him. Clawing his way to the top, he reached the summit.

At the edge of a cliff stood Eva. Her eyes were wide with fear. Decker clutched her from behind. One of the killer's arms was wrapped around her neck. In the other hand, he held a gun. The barrel was pointed at Brett's chest.

"Stay where you are, flyboy."

"Are you okay, Eva?" Of course, she wasn't. "Did he hurt you?"

"I'm fine," she said. "You have to get out of here."

"I'm not going anywhere without you." And then, to Decker, Brett said, "Let her go and take me." He took a step forward.

"I told you to stay where you are. You move again, and I'll shoot you both."

Brett lifted his hands in surrender. But so long as he drew breath, he wasn't about to let Decker hurt Eva. He just didn't know how he was supposed to fight back when the killer had a gun—and Eva was his hostage.

"You don't have to do this," Brett said, trying to be reasonable. "You can let her go. We won't follow you. We can't tell the authorities where you've gone."

"I don't care about you," said Decker. "All I want is the meds and the nurse to make sure I get well."

"You aren't taking her." Brett's voice was clear and confident. It was in total contrast to the fear that gnawed at his belly.

"I don't know that you're in any position to make demands." Decker turned the barrel, pressing the gun into the side of Eva's head. "You take another step, and I'll shoot."

"You aren't going to kill her." Brett was certain that Decker needed—or maybe wanted—Eva alive. Then to her, he said, "It'll be okay. I'm here. I'll keep you safe."

She nodded as if she believed him.

He had to keep his promise, but how?

Decker snorted. "You think I got a problem murdering someone? Flyboy, you don't know who you're dealing with."

"You aren't going to kill her," he said, "because you need her."

"Actually," said Decker, "you're right."

Pointing the gun at Brett, he pulled the trigger.

A flash of fire erupted from the muzzle. A boom like a thunderclap rolled across the desert, and white-hot pain knocked Brett down. The rocky ground bit into his flesh. Blood trickled down the side of his sleeve. Carefully, he touched the top of his arm. The raw flesh stung. Damn. He had no idea how bad the injury was, but blood wasn't gushing. That was a good sign.

"Oh my God, you shot him!" Eva screamed. "You really shot him!"

Without thinking, Brett launched himself at Decker. The killer still had the gun in his hand, but Brett had a split second to get Eva away from him.

Just like he'd been taught in high school football practice, he wrapped his arms around Eva's torso and pulled her away. "Run, Eva, and don't look back!" He hoped like hell that she would be fast enough to escape. If she was going to get away, he had to keep Decker from going after her.

It had been years since he'd been given any instruction on hand-to-hand combat. Even then, his lessons had been perfunctory. But he remembered enough.

Brett kicked the man's knee—hard. Decker folded like a house of cards on a windy day and crumpled, the gun dropping to the ground.

"You son of a bitch." Spittle flew from Decker's mouth. He scrambled to his feet and lunged forward, slamming his head into Brett's middle. All the air left his body in a single gust, leaving him dazed and flat on his back. The killer was on top of him, wrapping his hands around Brett's throat and pinning him to the ground. "I'll kill you for that."

Decker's fingers dug into Brett's flesh. Brett slammed his fists into the other man's arm, trying to break his hold. It did no good. Blackness crept in from the sides, and every part of his body burned, screaming for air.

"Let him go, Decker." Eva stood at his side with the gun in her hand.

Decker loosened his grip.

Gulping down breaths and coughing, Brett rolled to his knees.

"What do you think you're going to do with that gun, Eva?" Decker asked.

"I should shoot you," she said, "for everything you've done."

"But you won't," said Decker. "Remember, you were going to help me. That's the kind of person you are. Helpful. Compassionate."

"Maybe I was," she said, "but that was before you took me as a hostage and tried to kill Brett."

Rising to his feet, Brett rubbed his throat, not sure if he could speak. "Give me the gun, Eva." His voice was hoarse as each word scraped over his bruised larynx. "You don't want to kill Decker."

"And you do?"

She touched on a difficult question. Just like the proverbial dog that finally caught the car, Brett didn't know what to do now that the killer was held at gunpoint. Of course, he hated the idea of shooting an unarmed man. But even though Decker didn't have a weapon, he was still dangerous and deadly. They couldn't let him go. Nor could they keep him as a prisoner.

Like she'd been reading his mind, Eva asked another question. "What are we going to do now?"

Brett turned to meet her eyes. Their gazes locked and held.

An instant was all the time that Decker needed. He lunged at Eva, grabbing her around the middle. Unprepared, she fired the gun, sending a bullet into the sky.

Holding on to her, Decker kept going. He grabbed the gun and shoved her off the cliff.

Brett rushed forward, but he wasn't fast enough. By the time he got to where she'd stood, Eva was gone. Ten feet below, she lay on a rock ledge. She didn't move. He couldn't even tell if she breathed.

He turned to Decker. "You did this." His voice was stronger than he could believe.

Decker pointed the gun at him. "You should've let me take her. At least she'd be alive."

Enraged, Brett was about to lunge for Decker when a twig snapped nearby.

Decker shot wildly in that direction, but it was just a critter of some kind. The distraction gave Brett the chance to run behind an outcropping of rocks. He glanced out from behind it. Decker had decided his odds weren't good, even with the gun, and was running away with the med kit.

For an instant, Brett was rooted to the ground. Did he chase after the killer or climb down to Eva?

Well, when he thought about it that way, there really wasn't a choice at all.

Drawing in a deep breath, he turned to lower himself over

the edge of the cliff. His legs dangled uselessly into the void for a moment, then his feet connected with the side of the mountain. Placing one foot, then the other on a small, narrow ledge, Brett eased down the side of the cliff. He could just make out a series of cracks in the rock wall that might let him reach the shelf where Eva lay.

He scooted his feet along the ledge until it ended, then stretched one leg out to reach his next toehold. But when his toe hit, the rock crumbled away.

Suddenly weightless, he could feel himself falling.

Throwing himself forward, Brett clung to the wall of stone. His heart hammered in his chest. Sweat streamed from his hairline, burning his eyes. He blinked hard.

Drawing in a deep breath, he looked down at Eva.

She hadn't moved.

Was she even alive?

He had to ignore all the doubt. He wouldn't survive if he didn't focus. Shifting his foot out to a farther hold, he took a breath and started to climb down. When he only had a few feet left between him and Eva, he jumped.

The landing sent a shock wave through his feet, knees and hips.

Kneeling next to Eva, he watched her chest rise and fall. Thank God. She was still breathing. He touched her shoulder. "Eva? Can you hear me?"

She didn't stir.

By 6:00 a.m., there had been no new intel. It left the law enforcement officers with nothing to do but hurry up and wait.

Ryan hated the inactivity.

He heard a sharp trill at the same instant Maria reached for the satellite phone hooked to her belt. "What have you got for me?" she asked into the phone. A moment later, she yelled, "We've got coordinates for Augustin's phone! Someone get me a map."

"I have one." Jason spread a topographical map on a folding table set up under one of the lights.

"I need a pen," Maria said.

Ryan removed a pen that had been tucked into a side pocket on his cargo pants. "Here you go."

Maria took it, nodding her thanks.

"Go ahead," she said to the person on the other end of the call. The marshal repeated a series of numbers, scribbling them onto the margins of the map. Finally, she said, "Thanks. You've been a lifesaver." She ended the call. Maria circled a point on the map. "This is where the phone is located."

"That's less than five miles from here," Jason said at a glance. "Farrah, can you fly to that point?"

"Fly? Yes. Land? No." She pressed her finger onto the map. The contour lines were close together, denoting a steep slope. "There's no flat surface. But if I get into the sky, I can conduct a grid search."

"A team should head in that direction on foot," Ryan spoke up. "If Farrah finds anything, she can let the ground team know."

Farrah said, "I'd want someone in the chopper with me. There's no way I can fly and manage a thorough search at the same time."

"I'll go up in the helicopter," Jason said. "I can take some of my agents with me."

Maria said, "I've got the sat phone and the only way to make contact from the ground. I'll lead the team that goes in on foot."

"Ryan and I will come with you," said Isaac.

"I'd appreciate that," she said.

With a plan in place, everyone started to move. Before Ryan took a step, Maria placed her hand on his arm. "You got a minute?"

"I guess."

"I know I busted your balls earlier, but you've had some

good ideas. I'm not usually wrong, but it seems like I misjudged you. In my book, you're all right."

It wasn't exactly an apology. It wasn't exactly a compliment, either. But it didn't matter, Ryan would take it. "Thanks," he said. "That's nice of you."

"Don't get all mushy." Maria folded up the map and slid it into a pants pocket. "And if you fall behind, I'm not waiting around."

Isaac approached with two backpacks. He handed one to Ryan. "Are we ready?"

Maria picked up a backpack that was sitting on the ground. "I'm ready—and I'm not waiting for you, either."

Isaac placed his hand on Ryan's shoulder, holding him back. "What was all that about?"

"It seems like Maria Reyes doesn't hate me as much as she did before," Ryan said, partly joking.

Resting the backpack on the table, he examined its contents: a water bottle, a first aid kit, a space blanket, a compass. At the bottom of the bag was a 9mm Beretta 92 tucked inside a holster. He loosened the belt on his jeans, wove it through the holster and fastened his belt again.

"You ready?" Isaac asked. "Because I don't think that the marshal is kidding about leaving us behind."

But what concerned Ryan the most was that Decker Newcombe was still out there. If the two men ever met again, one of them wouldn't come back alive.

Decker sat in the shade of a large boulder and waited. It was the perfect place to ambush the pilot—apparently the guy's name was Brett—if he came after him. But honestly, Decker didn't think he would.

After five minutes, he stopped looking. Resting against the rock, he unlocked the med kit. His hands shook. He wanted pain meds, but now he knew that he needed something else.

He rifled through the contents, looking for the naloxone that Eva had mentioned. He found it, read the dosing instructions and inserted the tip of the nasal spray into a nostril.

Inhaling sharply, he squeezed the dispenser.

The spray filled his sinuses with cold droplets. He inhaled again until his lungs filled.

He exhaled. There was no relief. His head still throbbed. His joints still ached. His hands still shook.

But maybe the headache wasn't as bad. His body still hurt, but within a few minutes the pain began to lessen. For the first time in weeks, he could concentrate.

The first thing that came to mind was his enemy: Ryan Steele. If it hadn't been for that traitor, Decker's name would already be added to the history books. Generations from now, people would still know of his crime. His name would be the one that children feared in the middle of the night.

But Ryan had rescued his victim in the middle of the act. Not only had Decker been stopped, but he'd also been beaten, shot and humiliated. God, he could only imagine the memes that were circulating.

And then there was Ana. Lying, kid-withholding Ana. *I'm coming for you*, he thought.

And my son.

Decker tucked the med kit under his arm and stood. His stomach grumbled, and his mouth was dry. But his bones no longer ached. His flesh no longer itched.

He didn't know how many more doses he might need to overcome his cravings. But now, maybe he'd be able to make it to Mexico. Then, he'd retrieve his phone. He'd deal with Ana. Oh, yes. He'd make sure she knew what it felt like to lose a child. She'd feel the same pain he had when she disappeared, leaving nothing behind. And it had been because she was pregnant? The fact that she didn't want him to be a father hurt worse than the rejection.

Once he had his son, Decker would rebuild his reputation. He'd go from being the butt of jokes to the most terrifying person who ever lived.

Eva hung in the space between dreams and wakefulness. Her head hurt. Her back ached. Her shoulder was sore. Her eyes were swollen, and her tongue was thick.

She felt as if she were submerged, swimming deep in the waters of the Gulf of Mexico. An icy hand was keeping her underwater. She wanted to breathe but couldn't.

From the shore, someone called her name.

She tried to answer, but water filled her mouth. She started to cough.

Then a set of strong hands pulled her from the depths, and she opened her eyes. A man knelt next to her. The sun shone on him from behind, hiding his features in the shadows. And still, he was familiar. She screwed her eyes shut.

"Eva," the man said. She recognized his voice. He was the one who'd been calling to her from the beach. "Can you hear me?"

She tried to speak, but all that came out was a moan.

"Are you hurt? You took quite a fall."

How could she have fallen? Just a minute ago, she was in the ocean.

Then, she remembered everything. The helicopter crash. The storms. Taking refuge in a cave. Decker Newcombe, sick with withdrawal symptoms. He'd thrown her over a cliff.

And finally, she remembered him.

"Brett," she whispered. "Where am I?"

"You hit a ledge on your way down. Lucky for you. The rest of the fall..." His words trailed off. "Well, let's just say that falling all the way to the bottom of the ravine would've been bad. Very bad."

Honestly, everything ached. She wiggled her toes. Bent

her knees. Lifted both arms. There were no sharp pains. "I think I'm okay."

"Can you sit?"

"Help me up."

Brett placed one hand on her shoulder and the other on her elbow. He pushed from the back and pulled from the front. "I'll help. Let me know if it's too much, and we'll stop." His touch was soothing, his words reassuring.

She engaged her core and lifted her head and shoulders. Reaching for her bent knees, she pulled herself to sitting. The exertion left her winded. She wheezed, "I'm okay."

"Take your time." Brett rubbed her shoulder. "Decker has the med kit. He's not coming back for us."

She nodded. "I just want to get out of here."

"Do you think you can stand? We need to climb that thing." He nodded toward a sheer rock wall that was almost a dozen feet high. She tried to swallow, but a hard knot was stuck in her throat. "And then, there's still miles of walking to find the interstate."

Thank goodness she'd put back on her air cast when she woke to take over the watch in the middle of the night. At that time, she redressed in her flight suit, as well. Putting on the boot had been an afterthought. Now, she was thankful she'd taken the time. Still, if finding civilization seemed difficult yesterday, today it felt impossible.

She just didn't have any other options.

Chapter Fifteen

Eva stood. A bolt of pain shot through her ankle and wrapped around her leg. Her eyes watered. She cursed and stumbled. God, it felt good to be in his arms.

Brett caught her around the waist and kept her from toppling over. "What is it?" he asked.

"It's my damned ankle." Her jaw was tight, her teeth clenched.

"Is it the same one that was injured yesterday?"

"Yeah, but now it's about one hundred times worse." She inhaled and exhaled, thinking only of her breath. The pain in her foot dulled to an ache. "Maybe it was just stiff," she said, although she knew she was truly injured. How was she supposed to hike to the highway now? "I'm going to try to stand on it again."

Brett loosened his grip on her waist. "I'm still here to keep you safe."

She liked the idea of having him next to her. But really, she didn't have the bandwidth to worry about her love life—or lack thereof. Not now, at least. She placed her foot on the ground, putting weight into the leg. Pain, like a poker shoved through her bone, left her breathless. "Dammit," she cursed.

"It's okay," he said, "I've got you."

"How am I supposed to walk to the interstate now?" Even she heard the despair in her voice. "I can barely stand."

Brett touched her chin with a finger, lifting her gaze to meet his. "I don't know what we'll do once we make it off of this ledge, but I do know that we can't stay here."

Eva stared at the wall of rock. It would be a hard climb under the best circumstances. And frankly, she wasn't at her best. "How?"

Brett exhaled—a sure sign that he was thinking. "I want you to hold on to my shoulders. With you on my back, I'll climb to the top. Then, we'll go to the cave where we were this morning. It's dry and will stay cool once it gets really hot. Plus, the food's still there—and the cell phones. Maybe we'll get lucky and have a signal."

"What if we don't?" Until now, Eva had been able to face each problem as it arose. Maybe it was the constant pain in her foot. Or maybe it was coming face-to-face with a killer. Or maybe it was the fact that she'd been thrown over a cliff. But now, the metallic taste of panic coated her tongue.

"I don't know." Brett shrugged. "I'm just as lost as you. Honestly, I'm making all this up as I go along."

"You're right," she said, surrendering. "But listen…"

"No, you listen," said Brett.

Was he really going to start a fight now? "Excuse me?"

"Do you hear that?"

Eva stood still. There was nothing, not even the sound of the wind running along the spine of the mountain. "I don't hear anything," she began.

But that wasn't true. There was a faint *whomp*, *whomp*, *whomp*.

Her breath caught. "Is that a helicopter?"

"I think it is," said Brett, looking up at the sky. "I can't figure out where it's coming from, though."

Shading her eyes with her hand, she scanned the horizon. "There it is." She pointed at a black dot. "See?"

"Thank God." Brett waved his arm above his head. "Hey!" he yelled. "Over here!"

She doubted that the crew could hear them, but it didn't matter. Hope and excitement filled her chest until she thought she might burst. Waving her arms, she yelled, "Over here! Look this way, we're over here!"

The helicopter stayed on the horizon, never coming close. Finally, it disappeared from view, until even the noise of the rotors was too faint to hear.

Her eyes burned. Her throat was raw. Her ankle hurt worse than before. It would've been better if she'd never seen the helicopter and had the audacity to hope. "They didn't have a clue we were here."

"True," said Brett. "But they're searching for us, and they're close. I have no doubt they've laid out a grid and are going over each sector." He gave another exhale as he thought. "It's important that we get to the top. We'll be easier to spot in the open." His gaze traveled up the side of the hill. "You've got to hold on to my shoulders. I'm going to climb and pull us both out."

She'd seen every inch of his body. He was toned, muscular and fully male. But still, she would be a lot of weight to carry. "Are you sure? Maybe you could climb up and wave down the helicopter when it comes back."

"I'm not leaving you here."

"I'm not letting you kill yourself on my behalf."

He bent his elbow, tightening his biceps. The muscle was visible even under the sleeve of his flight suit. "You don't think I'm strong enough?"

"It's not a question of strength," she said. "It's a problem of balance. My weight is going to pull us both back and over."

"Everything's impossible until someone does it." He paused. "I'm willing to try. But if you aren't, then we'll think of something else."

She definitely wasn't convinced that this was the best plan.

But she didn't know of any other options. "Okay," she said. "We'll do it."

Brett turned so she could grab on to his back. "Hold on," he said. "Don't lean back and don't let go."

After wrapping her arms around Brett's chest, she lifted her thighs up to his waist. "How's that?"

"Good," he said, wiping his hands on his legs. "Let's go." Brett reached up and worked both sets of fingers into a crack in the rock. He pulled up, using his legs to walk along the wall.

They rose from the ground one foot and then another. He rested his feet on a rock ledge. "That wasn't so hard," he said, his breath ragged.

"Keep your strength," Eva warned. "No talking."

"Got it," he said. Looking over his shoulder, he gave her a wide smile. Despite the circumstances and the pain in her ankle, a fluttering started in her middle.

He stopped on a ledge large enough for them to both stand. She unwrapped her legs and stood on the narrow outcropping. Leaning on the solid rock wall, she kept all her weight on her right foot. For a moment, she shook her hand and arms, which had gone numb from her tight hold. Blood rushed to her hands, filling her fingertips with sharp pinpricks. But it was a good pain.

"How are you holding up?" she asked.

Using the sleeve of his flight suit, Brett wiped sweat from his brow. "I figure I don't have any choice but to get us to the top now. We're too far up to go back. Let me know when you're ready."

The ledge offered them safety, but that was only temporary. "If you want to do the final climb, we can go now."

He turned so she could grab his shoulders, and she wrapped her legs once more around his waist. Once she was settled, Brett began the ascent.

They just had to make it to the top. A helicopter would

spot them. Then, they'd be rescued. It was all so simple, it had to work.

At the same time, she knew each step was filled with risks and success wasn't guaranteed. But deep down in her gut, she knew that they'd make it. It was all because Brett was so damned optimistic. It was like his positive attitude was contagious and she'd caught the sunny disposition strain of the flu.

It was no wonder that she'd picked up something from him. From their first night together, when she couldn't wait to take him as her lover, they had definitely been much more than close. Or last night, where she needed the reassurance of his touch.

She held him tighter, resting her cheek on his back. With her cheek on his ribs, she could hear his breathing and the constant thumping of his heart. Both sounds were reassuring.

Yeah, the past few days had been a mess. But while holding on to Brett, she knew that there was no other person she wanted with her right now.

Too bad that by getting rescued, which was what she wanted, their time together would be over.

The muscles in Brett's arms burned with exertion. His hands were scraped, raw and aching. He wasn't sure if his back would ever be the same, but somehow, he'd done it. He'd scaled the cliff with Eva on his back.

She rolled off him, and he army-crawled forward, well away from the edge. For a moment, he lay on the dirt, breathing hard.

"You're amazing," she said. "I can't believe you pulled us all the way up that wall."

To be honest, he couldn't believe he had, either. Although quitting had never been an option. "What would you say if I told you that I never once reached the top of the rope in PE class?"

"I wouldn't believe you," she said. "And even if that's true, I think you deserve an A plus now."

He laughed. The muscles in his stomach contracted, and he groaned. Climbing up the cliff wall might have been the easy part. They still needed to traverse miles in this hostile climate, and Decker might still be lurking nearby.

Maybe he'd moved on by now, given that Decker had the med kit and no weapon. But Brett didn't put it past him to find creative ways to try to kill the only two witnesses who could report that he was alive.

The possibility that Brett might have to face the killer for a second time brought a chill to his soul.

"I'm just going to lie here for a minute," he said, "and catch my breath."

"Take all the time you need," said Eva. "You deserve a rest." She lay at his side and rested her head on his shoulder. "You did it." He turned his head to watch her. God, she was perfect. Beautiful. Smart. Brave. Dedicated and strong. Placing his lips on the top of her head, he whispered. "We did it together."

She rose up, resting on her elbow. "We make a pretty good team."

He ran his finger over her bottom lip. "We do."

She kissed the heel of his hand. His flesh was scraped and raw. "How are you?"

Honestly, every part of him hurt—especially his shoulder. "If my collarbone didn't burn with each breath, I'd almost forget that Decker shot me."

"It's the adrenaline," she said. "It numbs the pain for a while. I see it all the time in the emergency department. Too bad Decker took all our medical supplies." She smiled. It was better than seeing a sunrise after a stormy night. "I can kiss you and make it better."

"You think that'll work?" he asked, smiling at her in return.

"There's only one way to find out."

She bent to him, placing her lips on hers. Brett gripped the back of her head, pulling her to him, winding his fingers through her hair. He slipped his tongue into her mouth. This kiss was different from all the ones they'd shared before. He was no longer exploring her. Now, he knew Eva and this kiss was like coming home.

As much as he wanted to lay with her and hold her, staying here wasn't a good idea. He sat up, ending the embrace. They'd already survived a lot, but if they were really going to get home, they needed to take advantage of the cooler morning air.

Brett's pulse still raced. He could hear his heartbeat as it thumped. But wait. The sound didn't match the cadence of his pulse.

He pushed himself up to sitting and listened. There was nothing to hear. Had he been mistaken?

"What is it?" Eva brows were drawn together in concern. "Are you okay?"

"I thought I heard..." he didn't want to say what he thought it might be—what he hoped it was "...something," he concluded, noncommittal.

Shading her eyes with her hand, she glanced at the sky, then slowly stood and dusted the seat of her pants with her hands. "I don't see anything."

Disappointment, cold and heavy, dropped into his chest. Sure, he'd gotten Eva off the cliff's ledge, despite her wounded leg. Even he knew that the feat was damn near impossible. But could he rely on luck and fortitude to get them back to civilization?

Without a rescue helicopter, neither of them would survive. Had he somehow created the sound that he most wanted to hear? The sweet, passionate kiss might have conjured it out of his determination to get her to safety. "Maybe I imagined it."

"I don't think so." She pointed to the horizon. "Listen."

He strained to hear, then stood, his abs and legs screaming in protest, and gazed at the sky.

And then he heard it again. The very faint whir of a chopper.

Suddenly, a black speck marred the cloudless blue sky. Even

from where he stood, he knew it was a helicopter. All his aches and pains were forgotten.

"That's them." Excitement sent his pulse racing. "We have to get their attention."

"How are we supposed to do that?" she asked.

"We need something metal."

"Metal?" she repeated.

"Or something that's reflective."

"I know what we can use." She unzipped a breast pocket on her flight suit and pulled out her hospital ID. "It's not ideal." She held up the laminated ID. "But someone told me it does catch the light."

"None of this is ideal." Brett took the card, letting his fingertips linger on the back of her hand. "Let's hope this is enough."

Farrah had piloted too many search-and-rescue missions to count. Some had a happy outcome, but too many ended in heartbreak. So in moments like these, while she flew slowly over the ground, looking for survivors, she always tried to focus on those positive moments.

Holding the control stick of the Robinson R44 steady, she flew over the grid of coordinates that had been entered into her flight plan. It was a tedious task for sure, but the best way to conduct a thorough search.

Her aircraft had seating for four people: a single pilot and three passengers. Jason, the supervisory special agent, sat next to her. Two other FBI agents, one female and one male, sat in the back.

This mission was a bit of a cluster, and honestly, she wasn't sure what would happen if Decker Newcombe was found in the desert. But since all her passengers were FBI agents, she supposed that she wouldn't have to make any decisions about an apprehension.

In reality, they were searching for the nurse and the pilot.

Farrah hadn't met Brett personally. Still, the piloting community in San Antonio was small, and she'd heard his name more than once. He had a reputation for being a solid person and a good pilot.

"Do you see anything out there?" she asked into her mic.

"Nothing yet." It was impossible to miss the frustration in Jason's tone.

Then again, they'd been flying for hours. She was tired and frustrated, too. If they didn't find someone—anyone—soon, they were going to have to turn back and get more fuel.

"What are the chances that this isn't where the cell phone is located at all and what we picked up was a mixed signal?" Jason asked. "Or that Newcombe took the phone and dumped it? He just wanted to send us on a goose chase."

Farrah wasn't sure if it was a rhetorical question or even if she should answer. Still, she knew a little bit about tech. "It's not like there are hundreds of towers for the phone to ping off of," she said. "But I can't guess about the man who's at large." She didn't even want to say his name. "You've studied him more than I have. What's your gut tell you?"

"The probability that the pilot and nurse survived the crash is pretty small. And even if they did survive, I'm not sure how far they'd make it with Decker on the loose," he admitted. "But while there's a chance they're out there, I'll do everything in my power to find them. How much longer can we stay in the air?"

She checked the fuel gauge. They didn't have a lot of gas in the tank, but it was enough to stay in the air a little while longer "The chopper can handle another pass before we'll have to refuel."

Staring out the windscreen, she softened her gaze. That was when she saw it, a wink of light coming from the ground. "Holy crap. Did you see that?"

Jason leaned forward in his seat until the webbing in his harness pulled tight. "See what?"

"There's something down there reflecting light." She turned the chopper's nose to the right. "On the top of that hill."

"There is?" Jason asked. "I don't see anything."

Had it all been in her mind? After all, she'd been flying for hours.

It came again. Just a wink, like the flash of a camera.

"You have to tell me you saw it that time," she said to the federal agent.

"I did. Is that them? I can't tell…"

Farrah pushed the throttle forward, and the Robinson shot through the sky. From a quarter of a mile out, she could see two figures standing on the top of the ridge and waving.

Using the chopper's radio, she placed a call to the sat phone.

"Marshal Reyes," said Farrah. "We have some people you need to come and pick up."

Chapter Sixteen

Brett loved to fly. He liked helicopters more than he liked most people—his family notwithstanding. But he'd never felt as much joy as he did when the rescue helicopter banked to the right and started flying toward them.

Eva still wrapped her arms around his neck and leaned into him for support. He liked the feeling of her arms around his shoulders. Her body fitted perfectly next to his. How her breath washed over his ear. He wrapped an arm tighter around her waist.

"They do see us, right?" she asked.

The pilot of the aircraft dipped the aircraft from side to side. A pilot's way of saying hello. Waving with his free hand, Brett couldn't help but smile. "They see us all right."

The helicopter hovered over where they stood, the rotors sending a dust cloud rising from the ground. Eva tucked her head into his chest. He wrapped his arms around her, sheltering with his body. Nothing in the world had ever felt so right.

Shading his eyes from the dust, he studied the helicopter. Typically, Robinsons were rented by executives trying to avoid metropolitan traffic or tour companies taking sightseers over destinations, like the Grand Canyon.

But this one belonged to the Texas Rangers and was probably used for surveillance.

The pilot actuated the loudspeaker system. It was hard to hear her over the wind and the roar from the engine. But Brett could make out her words clearly enough.

"There's no place for me to land," she said. "A rescue party has been given your coordinates and will be to you within an hour. If anyone in your party needs medical attention, I can pull them up. But I'm low on fuel and don't have enough gas for much more airtime."

"You should go," Brett yelled in Eva's ear.

"I'm not leaving without you," she said. "We're a team, remember?"

He was tempted to let her stay with him. But her welfare was more important than what he wanted—which was to be with Eva.

"I'll be right behind you," he said. "Besides, you'll have to walk."

She shook her head. "I'm not going anywhere. Not when Decker is still out there. What if he comes back while we're gone and before the search party reaches you?"

"When Decker took the med kit, he got what he wanted. He's not coming back for me," Brett said, though he didn't exactly believe his own words.

"No way am I leaving you," she said.

The pilot was expecting some kind of response. He waved, a sure signal that they were okay.

The helicopter banked hard to the right and flew out over the mountain. The downdraft washed over them, trapping them in a storm of dirt and grit.

Closing his eyes, he held tight to Eva. Soon, he'd have to let her go.

"You wait here," he said. "I'll go back to the cave and grab the food and whatever else was left behind. It won't take me long."

"Absolutely not." Eva fingers dug into his shoulder. "No way are you leaving me here alone. We're safer together."

How did she not understand that keeping her safe was the only thing that mattered to him? He'd survive and find help if only because it meant that he could send someone to help her. There was no way he could tell her that, not after she'd made it clear what she wanted—and didn't—from him. "But your foot," he began. Sure, it was an excuse, but it was also true. Eva had been injured.

"I'll be slow, but I'm coming with you."

"All right then." He wrapped his arm around her waist. "Don't be shy about leaning on me for support."

Slowly, they made their way back to the cave. The food and phones were just where they'd been left the night before. Eva dropped to the sandy floor.

"How do you feel?" Brett asked.

"Very relieved. It seems so strange to know that help is on the way. Soon, we'll be out of here and all of this will be over."

He knew how she felt. "I wasn't sure how we were going to survive this whole mess."

"I thought you were the optimistic one."

Honestly, he wasn't sure if she were teasing—or not. But he didn't have the emotional depth to make jokes. Holding out his hand, he said, "I'll help you up."

She placed her palm in his. He pulled her to standing. For a moment, they just stood there, her hand in his. Her breasts pressed against his chest, and their hearts beat in sync. She lifted her eyes to his face. Their gazes met and held.

There was so much he wanted to tell her. That she was perfect for him in every way. That he admired her determination and strength even more than he admired her curves and beautiful blue eyes.

Now wasn't the time. Hell, maybe he never would find the right occasion. He squeezed her palm. "Can you stand?"

After letting her hand slip from his grasp, she said, "I can manage on my own."

For some reason, Brett knew she wasn't just talking about her injuries. He picked up the phones and the box of food. "We should probably head back to that ridge, just so the search-and-rescue team knows where to find us."

Eva just nodded and slowly walked out of the cave.

The sun had climbed in the sky. The air was warm, and the day promised to be dangerously hot. They took only a few steps when a male voice cut through the silence.

He couldn't make out the words, but he heard the tone and a pattern of speech. Was it Decker? Why would he come back if he had the medical kit? Then again, they had collected the rations. If the killer was going to survive, he needed food.

Until he knew who was out there, and what they wanted, they needed to stay quiet. The blood in Brett's veins turned to ice despite the heat. He stopped Eva with a hand on her arm.

She stood without moving. Obviously, she'd heard the voice as well, and they both shared a single question.

Was there any chance to face down the killer twice and survive?

Brett didn't have time to think about what to do next, when three people—a female and two males—crested the hill.

For a moment, nobody spoke. Then one of the men, who had a dark suntan said, "You must be Brett and Eva. I can't tell you how happy we are to have found you. I'm Ryan Steele. This is my boss at Texas Law, Isaac Patton. The lovely woman here is United States Marshal Maria Reyes."

"Stow the compliments, Ryan," said the marshal as she crossed the distance that separated them. "There will be plenty of time to debrief you both, but I figured you probably want these." She held out two plastic bottles filled with water. "I have a first aid kit as well. Looks like you both could use a little tending."

Without comment, Brett took the bottles of water. He

handed one to Eva before unscrewing the cap of his own bottle. He drank, draining half the bottle in a single swallow. "How the hell did you find us?"

"That's a long story," said Ryan. "But we've got a bit of a hike ahead to get back to the command center, so there's plenty of time to tell it."

The marshal took over, bandaging the surface wound on Brett's shoulder and giving both he and Eva some OTC pain meds. Eva was also given a set of collapsible hiking poles, which would help her to walk the miles back to their command post.

"Before we go," said the marshal as they prepared to leave, "I gotta ask about the prisoner. Did you see Decker Newcombe? Do you have any idea where he's gone?"

"We saw him all right," said Brett. "And as far as where he went, well, I couldn't really say."

She nodded. He could tell from the way she pressed her lips together until they lost their color that she wasn't satisfied with his answer. Still, the marshal knew she'd been told the truth. "Let's get going," she said.

And just like that, they were safe—or safer—and everything really had worked out.

Funny that in the moment, Brett was filled with regret. He should have told Eva how he felt about her. It seemed that he truly had lost his chance. Now, he doubted that he'd get another.

The hike back to the command center, which was actually at the initial crash site, was easier than Eva anticipated. There, another helicopter was waiting.

It took them directly to the hospital in Encantador. She'd been in the facility many times as a child and knew it well. There was an emergency clinic on the ground floor. On the second floor was a hospital with beds for two dozen patients. Most of them came from the clinic for acute care. Patients with any planned medical procedures traveled to a larger metropolitan area.

Eva and Brett had been sent to the emergency clinic. They'd been placed in separate rooms in triage and were awaiting medical evaluation. Although to call it a room implied things that the space didn't have. It was more of a narrow cubicle, with room for a single hospital bed, a chair and not much more, with curtains for walls.

Eva had been given a set of scrubs to wear. The air cast removed, her leg was surrounded in ice packs and propped up on a pillow. She'd been given ibuprofen and hooked up to an IV of fluid to fight dehydration.

"How're you doing over there?" Brett's voice came from the opposite side of the thin cloth wall.

It was a loaded question, and she took a moment before answering. Overall, she was great—fabulous, really. Yesterday, she was certain she was going to die in the Texas desert—either of exposure to the elements or as another victim of a serial killer.

But while she'd rather be in the hospital than hiding in a cave, Eva wasn't completely pleased that they'd been saved. She just wasn't sure why.

Her grandmother—the whole reason she was part of the flight crew to begin with—was just one floor above her. It was torturous to be so close and still separated.

And she hadn't even begun to process the crash or the aftermath.

So…how was she doing?

"Physically, I'm okay," she said. "Emotionally…" Her words trailed off, not just because the fabric walls only gave the briefest nod to privacy but because, honestly, she wasn't sure how she felt.

"Knock, knock." The curtain between the two rooms fluttered for a moment before it parted, and Brett's face appeared.

"I figured I'd come over and see how you're really doing. Want some company?"

"Sure." Her cheeks warmed. "How are you?"

Crossing into her room, Brett held on to the metal pole of an IV stand. A clear plastic bag hung from a loop. Tubing tethered him to the bag. "Hydration," he said, nodding toward the pole. "I feel fine, but the nurse insisted. They cleaned the wound on my shoulder. I was lucky, the bullet didn't hit the bone. The doctor put in a few stitches and told me to keep it covered for a few days. I have a prescription for an antibiotic. But I was lucky it wasn't worse, and no other serious injuries." He chuckled. "Guess I'll have a good story for the next pool party."

His face turned pale.

She realized his mistake the minute he spoke. There might be more pool parties in Brett's future. But none of them would include Wade. Or Lin. Or Stacy.

Her chest ached for him. She wanted to take his pain and make it her own. The thought left her breathless. When did she come to care so deeply and personally for Brett?

She thought she'd left his bed that morning because of Baba. But maybe she'd also come to fear the heartache that came after loving someone so completely that they became an extension of her soul. Not worrying about the joy but just fearful of the pain when they left.

Jeez, what a time to have an epiphany.

Then again, she supposed there was always going to be a clarity that came with facing death as many times as she had in the past forty-eight hours.

She couldn't say any of that, not now. Lines of sorrow were etched into Brett's forehead. So, she asked, "Do you want to talk?"

He worked his jaw back and forth. "Naw," he said, his voice hoarse. "I'm all right."

She doubted that was true. Still, she wouldn't press him

to say anything he wasn't ready to talk about. "If you ever need anyone…"

"Yeah, yeah. I get it. Thanks." He dropped into a chair next to her bed. "How's the leg?"

It was fine with her if he wanted to focus on something that was less consequential that the death of his entire crew. She said, "Right now, it's cold and numb—which is a good thing."

Together, they'd survived a helicopter crash, being lost in the desert for the past day and an assault by a serial killer. Yet now, there was nothing for them to talk about other than the mundane.

Since she didn't have anything better to say, she added, "They're going to do an X-ray to make sure nothing's broken. Assuming it's not, then I'll have to see how it heals. Not a lot can be done for a sprain. But if I pulled or tore ligaments, I might need surgery. I'll get an MRI soon to check for head injuries. Any more sophisticated scans will have to wait until I'm at a larger medical facility."

He nodded. "And how are you?" he asked, his voice low. "Really?"

"It all seems surreal," she said. "I'm sure that eventually everything we've been through will hit me. But for now, the last twenty-four hours feels like a dream. Or maybe this is the dream, and we're still out in the desert somewhere."

He scooted the chair closer, the legs scraping across the floor like nails on a chalkboard. He reached for her hand. "Are you going to be okay?"

"I'm not sure what being okay means anymore." She lifted the corners of her mouth, even though she didn't feel like smiling. "But I'll be all right." After all, she didn't have any other choice. Ready to change the topic, she asked again, "How are you?"

"Me? I'm fine. I don't even think I'm all that dehydrated."

"And emotionally?" she coaxed.

"I haven't even had time to think since the crash—only

do what needed to be done to survive." His voice was hoarse, caught on emotion. He coughed. "I don't know what to do next, you know. Once we get out of here, I'll go back to San Antonio. But I'm not sure how I'm supposed to go back to work. I can't just get back in the air with a different crew—not right now, at least."

"What will you do?" she asked.

"Honestly, I don't know." He exhaled. "How about you?"

Her heart ached for Brett. They'd lived through the same harrowing day, but for him it was worse. He'd lost his coworkers and friends.

But she knew exactly what she was going to do next. "As soon as I get out of this bed," she said, "I'm going to go up to the second floor to see my grandmother. After I give her a big hug, I'll probably stay in town for a few days. I can stay with my sister and her family."

"Sounds nice," said Brett.

"I don't know that I'll get a lot of rest. Besides Katya and Jorje, I have two nephews and a niece. They're all adorable, but the kids have a lot of energy."

"I know how it goes. My sister has twin daughters. They're cute and all, but after a few hours of playtime—especially when I'm giving nonstop horsey rides—Uncle Brett needs a nap."

She smiled. "I bet you're a good uncle."

"I try." He gave her hand a squeeze. "Speaking of naps, I should let you rest. Drop me a line now and then."

She was reluctant to let him go and tightened her grip on his fingers. "Thanks for everything, Brett. I wouldn't have survived without you."

He opened his mouth, ready to say something. Then he shook his head, seeming to change his mind. "You take care of yourself."

Before Eva could say anything, the curtain next to the hall

parted. It was US Marshal Marcia Reyes. "Hey, I hope I'm not interrupting anything."

Eva let go of Brett's hand. "Of course not," she said.

Maria stepped into the small cubicle, and three men followed. Eva recognized the duo from Texas Law—Ryan and Isaac—at once. The third man was tall with close-cropped blond hair. "We need to chat with you both about what happened out there." Maria nodded toward the blond man. "This is Jason Jones. He's with the FBI." She paused a beat. "He's got some questions."

Just like that first drop of a roller coaster, Eva's stomach plummeted and left her with a sick feeling. Were the authorities going to claim that somehow, as the two survivors of the crash, she and Brett were responsible? The chaotic moments right before the chopper went down flashed through her mind. It was all a jumble. Had she made a mistake? "The FBI? We didn't do anything wrong."

"I'm not accusing you of anything," said Jason. "But you understand that when a helicopter crashes, there's an inquiry. And when a serial killer gets loose, there's a full investigation."

His words did little to provide any comfort. "Okay."

Jason continued, "I also hate to tell you that this might drag on for weeks or even months. But for now, what I need is anything you might know about Decker Newcombe."

"What kind of things do you want to know?" Brett asked.

"Honestly, anything at all. What kind of interaction did you have with Decker? We assume he took Marshal Herrera's gun and his cash. Is he still armed? Do you have any idea where he might go?"

Brett spent a few minutes outlining the storm and the debacle in the back of the helicopter. He ended with the standoff this morning that ended with Decker armed and on the run and Eva being thrown over the side of a cliff. She added details when needed.

"I'm not surprised he pitched you into a ravine," said Isaac.

"That's part of Decker's MO to escape. He threw my girlfriend out of a car just so I'd quit chasing him."

Ryan lifted his hand. "Same. He stabbed mine to distract her from continuing her investigation into his crimes. She still has nightmares."

Great. So not only did she have a long investigation to look forward to, but PTSD, as well. "It's good to know I'm not alone."

Isaac said, "I could arrange for you to talk to either Clare or Kathryn, if you want."

It would be a strange sisterhood—those who had survived Decker Newcombe. Still, "It might be helpful to talk to them," Eva said.

Isaac nodded. "I'll get you their numbers."

"Back to Decker," said Jason. "Is there anything important that you remember?"

Eva began to shake her head but stopped. "He wanted the med kit."

"Med kit?" Marcia repeated. "Was he injured?"

"In a way," said Eva. "He was having withdrawals from pain meds."

"And did the kit have the type of medications he wanted?"

Brett said, "We don't carry any controlled substances on the aircraft."

"I did tell him about naloxone."

They all stared at her.

"It helps with the physical symptoms of withdrawals," she said. "It's especially beneficial with opiates."

"That doesn't make sense." Ryan rubbed the back of his neck. "Decker never used drugs before."

"He blamed the hospital." Eva tried to remember everything he said. "He told me that he was addicted to 'the crap—'" she hooked air quotes around the words "—that the nurse had given him. He was never my patient, but I heard some news that mentioned his injuries when he was captured. All his wounds sounded severe. The protocol would be to give him something for the pain. There was probably a plan in place to ween him from his current dosage, but the helicopter crash derailed that treatment."

Ryan shrugged. "I guess it's no surprise that he's having issues, then."

"It's not," Eva agreed.

"Let's get back to the time you spent with Decker," said Jason. "Did he mention anything about where he might go or what he might do next? Even if it doesn't seem important to you, it could be a clue."

Eva drew in a single breath and exhaled slowly. Before, her memories had been a jumble. Now she had space to think. Still, nothing came to mind. She shook her head. "Sorry, I can't think of anything."

Jason held out a white business card with the FBI's seal. "If anything comes to mind," he said, setting it on the end of her bed, "reach out."

The curtains parted again. A female aide pushed a wheelchair into the cubicle. She had a small diamond stud in her nose, and the tips of her white-blond hair had been dyed pink. An ID lanyard around her neck read Andrea Carlson, Certified Nurse's Aide.

"Wow," said Andrea. "It's really crowded in here. But doctor's orders, the patient has to go for an X-ray. So you all will have to excuse me," she said before backing out and making room for everyone to leave.

"I'd appreciate it if you didn't speak to anyone about your encounter with Decker," said Jason. "Not now, at least."

"Is that an order?" Eva asked, bristling.

"More like a friendly request," he said.

Then, the quartet of law enforcement filed out of the room, leaving only Eva and Brett.

He pressed his lips to the top of her head. "You take care of yourself," he repeated.

Before Eva could say anything, Andrea returned with the wheelchair. "We're ready for your scans. First the X-ray and then the MRI." The other woman continued. "Of course you know all of this, but we don't have a lot of the fancy equipment you do at San Antonio Medical Center. Depending on what's wrong with your ankle, you might be transported to a larger hospital."

She recognized that the small hospital in Encantador didn't have the funding or the patient population that a medical behemoth like SAMC did. But she wasn't about to be taken out of the area until she saw her grandmother—a request she was certain Andrea would grant.

But Brett was another matter altogether.

Eva swung her legs over the side of the bed. Andrea held on to her elbow and guided Eva into the wheelchair. She turned her gaze to where Brett stood.

He parted the curtains between their cubicles and lifted his hand, giving her a wave. Then, he slipped between the seams and was gone.

Her eyes burned and her throat was tight. After everything she'd endured it'd be foolish to cry now. Two days ago she hadn't even known Brett. But she wouldn't have survived without him. That meant he was more than a temporary lover. He was also the man who saved her life.

Eva didn't know if he'd still be in the hospital by the time she was finished with her scans. Was this their final farewell?

Chapter Seventeen

It didn't take long to get an X-ray of Eva's leg and an MRI of her skull. Back in the radiology department, Andrea was waiting with the wheelchair. As Eva eased back into the chair, she said, "My grandmother, Gladys Tamke, is a patient at this hospital. Is there any way I can see her?"

Andrea started pushing the wheelchair down a long hallway. "Because of the feds, the doctor gave strict orders that you can't have visitors until you're released. It really shouldn't be much longer. Once the scans are read, you'll be free to go."

She brought Eva back to the same triage room she'd occupied earlier. "Do you know if Brett is still here?" Eva asked.

"I think so." Andrea helped her back into the bed. "Do you want me to check?"

"Since the walls are cloth," said Brett, "I can hear you."

The curtain parted, and he appeared. He was no longer tethered to a pole with a bag of fluids.

"What happened to your IV?" Eva asked.

"They told me I'm free to go once I get the discharge papers," he said. "What about you? Is your foot broken?"

"Don't know yet."

"I'll check on those orders for you." Andrea slipped a pillow under Eva's foot. "Be right back."

Finally, they were alone. "I'm glad that you're still here," Eva said. "It was so rushed before that I didn't get to say good-bye properly."

"Obviously," he said, "I won't forget you."

She laughed. "Yeah, I guess not. How are you getting back to San Antonio?"

"I really haven't figured that out yet. I'm hoping I can catch a ride with someone, or the hospital will send somebody to get me. Once I get my phone, I'll call my folks in Dallas. I'm sure they'd come and get me, but it'd take them the rest of the day just to get here." He exhaled. "Maybe it's best if I just rent a car." He glanced in her direction. Eva's pulse quickened, just like always. "You can rent a car in Encantador, right?"

"I think there's a place about a mile out of town that rents cars," she said. Or maybe they only rented moving vans. "I've never had to do that here, so I don't know."

The curtains parted again, and a tall man with a sparse mustache entered the room. "Hi, I'm Dr. Flores. I looked over your X-rays and didn't see any broken bones. There might be other damage, like torn ligaments, so I'd like for you to check in with an orthopedist and also get a full-body MRI when you get back to San Antonio. Until you get to see a doctor, I'm going to refit you with another air cast for support. But I want you stay off that foot as much as possible. Other than that, all your labs look fine, and you're free to go." He held out a stack of papers in each hand, one for Eva and the other for Brett. "Both of you are free to go," he corrected himself.

With perfect timing, Andrea returned with an air cast.

Once the cast was in place, Eva swung her legs to the side of the bed and lowered herself slowly to the ground.

"How's that feel?" Brett asked, his hand under her elbow.

"Not bad."

Andrea removed Eva's IV. "Looks like you're all set. If you want to go to the second floor and check in with your family, I think there are a lot of people who'd like to see you."

Eva's chest filled with love for her family. "Thanks a million."

With a single wave, Andrea left the room. And once again, Eva was alone with Brett.

"Well, I guess this time," he said, "it really will be good-bye."

"I guess so." Her heart clenched. After such a short time, he'd become a mainstay in her life. What was more, she didn't want him to go. She reached for his arm. She wasn't ready for goodbye. Her fingers touched his wrist, and the fluttering in her middle returned. A flush crept up from her chest to her cheeks. When was the last time she'd had this kind of reaction to a man? Well, at least she knew that answer to that question. Brett really was one of a kind. "You take care of yourself. Send me a text now and then and let me know how you're doing."

"You aren't even going back to San Antonio? What about your job or your apartment?"

"My San Antonio apartment is a furnished rental, and the lease is almost up anyway," she said. Hell, the dishes weren't even hers. "All I need to pack up are my belongings, that won't take long. The job?" That was a little more complicated—although she didn't plan to be employed by SAMC by the end of the month. "After everything that happened over the past twenty-four hours, well, I need some time off."

"Maybe that's what I should do, too." He let out a long and loud exhale, a sure sign he was making a plan. Funny how after just a few days, she'd learned how to read Brett. In a lot of ways, she knew him better than almost anyone else—aside from her family, that is. "I might start looking for a new job. Maybe even relocate." He shook his head. "I don't know how I'm supposed to work at San Antonio Med without my crew. The ghosts of Wade and Stacey and Lin will always be in the flight facility." He held up a hand. "Like, I don't mean that they'll actually be haunting the place. It's just that I won't ever be able to walk through the door and not miss them like hell."

He studied the floor, as if the answers to the universe were written on the tiles.

She couldn't leave him alone, not when he was so glum. At the same time, the pull to be with her family was like iron to a magnet. "Before you go," she said, "would you like to meet my grandmother? She's upstairs. The nurse said my whole family is waiting."

"Your whole family?" He shook his head. "Oh no. I can't. I mean, I'd love to meet them all, but they're here for you."

"If it wasn't for *you*, I wouldn't be here for them to see." She gave his hand a squeeze. "C'mon, I'm sure they'll want to meet the man who helped get me here alive."

He shook his head again. For a moment, she was sure that he would refuse once and for all. Her chest ached. She knew it was best to ignore the feeling and whatever else it might imply.

"All right," he said at last. "I'd love to meet your family."

The flight suit, her shattered phone and her one remaining shoe had been stowed in a plastic bag with a drawstring closure. She picked up the bag and looped the string around her wrist. Brett picked up a similar bag from the foot of his bed.

"Baba's room is on the second floor," Eva said, exiting the triage cubicle.

"Baba? That's a cute nickname." Brett followed her into the corridor. On either side were curtained rooms.

This hospital was nothing like San Antonio Medical Center, with its top-notch treatment centers, state-of-the art equipment and world-class medical professionals. Would she really be able to leave all the hustle and bustle of a major hospital behind to work in a rural setting? She ignored the twisting in her gut.

"Baba is Ukrainian for grandmother."

"I like how it respects your heritage."

"If you like that," she said as they walked down the hallway, "then you'll love pierogis."

"Oh, I already love pierogis," he said. They'd reached the elevator. Stopping in front of the doors, he pushed the call button. "I know a place in San Antonio that serves the best pierogis."

"Until you've had my grandmother's pierogis, you haven't had pierogi. Trust me."

The elevator doors slid open, and they stepped inside. "I do trust you," he said with a smile.

She pressed the button for the second floor, and the elevator rose slowly. They stood side by side, his arm brushing her shoulder. Her skin warmed with the contact.

She wanted him to touch her more. To kiss her. To hold her. To beg her to come back to San Antonio and stay with him forever.

Then again, if he did, what would she say? Or do?

No, it was better that they part ways soon. She shouldn't have invited him to meet her family, but there was no turning him away now.

A *ding* sounded as the elevator staggered to a stop. The doors slid open, and without a word, Eva stepped into the hallway.

The scent of antiseptic and coffee and the sweetly rotting stench of illness hung in the air. It was the same olfactory miasma that permeated the corridors of San Antonio Medical Center. Hallways went off in four directions with a circular desk at the intersection, just like the nurse's station in SAMC's emergency department.

Then again, nursing was the same all over the world. There were people who needed care. It was a nurse's job to provide it. All the rest was just window dressing. Maybe she'd be okay working in Encantador, after all.

"They'll know my grandmother's room number," she said, inclining her head to the nurse's station.

A male nurse with dark hair and a name tag that read Dennis Wang looked up as they approached. "May I help you?"

"I'm Eva Tamke," she said. "My grandmother, Gladys Tamke, is on this floor."

From personal experience, she knew that gossip traveled fast in a hospital. That meant that Dennis was familiar with what had happened to both Brett and Eva. But he was a true professional and didn't mention anything about the ordeal. He glanced down at a clipboard. "Looks like your grandmother is West-11." He pointed down a hallway. "Second door from the end on the left."

She thanked him before turning down the corridor. Her boot clunked against the tile floor, matching the pulse that thundered in her ears. Soon, she was deaf to everything other than a single word she repeated over and over in her mind. *Family. Family. Family.*

The door didn't quite meet the jamb and sounds leaked out into the corridor. At once, she recognized her sister's alto voice and her laugh that was like music. Baba's voice was deep and gravelly—a side effect from age and a smoking habit she'd dropped decades earlier. There were giggles of children—so her nieces and nephews were at the hospital, as well.

She knocked, and the door swung open. The first person she saw was Katya, sitting with her back to the door. A toddler, her niece Abby, was cuddled on her shoulder. Abby looked up, smiling brightly, and squealed.

Katya turned in her seat and saw Eva. Jumping up, she ran across the small room. The sisters embraced like that hadn't spoken in years—not just days.

Eva's eyes stung, and her throat was tight. "It's good to see you."

Tears ran down Katya's cheeks. "We've been waiting for news. But the hospital takes patient privacy very seriously." She hugged Eva tighter. "I can't tell you how worried we've been."

Eva kissed her niece on the cheek as Jorje approached. "Hey, I'm glad to see you up and about."

She gave her brother-in-law a quick hug. Then, she hugged each of her nephews.

Finally, on the bed near the window, was her grandmother. When had she gotten so frail-looking?

"Hey, Baba," she said.

Her grandmother opened her arms. Like she was a little girl with a skinned knee or a broken heart, Eva ran to Baba.

"I was worried I'd never see you again," the older woman whispered. "What in the world were you doing on a helicopter in the first place? I thought you gave all of that up when you left the national guard."

It was Eva's turn to cry. She wiped her eyes with the back of her hand. "I was on the flight because it was coming here."

It seemed like a million years ago when she and Brett had been in the flight facility at San Antonio Medical Center. She turned toward the door. Brett still stood on the threshold.

"There's someone I'd like you to meet." Eva held out her hand, and he came to stand with her. "This is Brett Wilson, the medevac pilot. Without him, I never would've survived."

Brett gave her hand a squeeze. "I think she's giving me too much credit. Your granddaughter is an amazing woman. She would've done just fine without me."

Jorje held out his hand for Brett to shake. "It's nice to meet you. And thanks for taking care of Eva."

"She took care of me," Brett said as the two men shook hands.

"Sounds like you make a nice team," said Katya. "You were both fortunate to have each other."

Baba pushed a button on the side of her bed that lifted her to sitting. "Tell me—what happened? How did the helicopter go down?"

For a moment, Eva's memories dragged her to the helicopter's hold. Before the turbulence started, Decker lay in the bed, confused and in pain. He'd been mouthing words, most of which she couldn't hear.

But there was one thing she remembered.

Ana.

"I have to make a call," she said. "Does someone have a phone?"

Her sister held out a cell. "You can use mine."

She gave Katya's hand a squeeze as she took the device. Patting down the scrubs she wore, she checked for the business card that the FBI agent had placed on the end of her bed. She hadn't picked it up after all.

She wanted to curse.

"What's wrong?" Jorje asked.

"There's someone I need to call, but I can't find his business card."

"Who?" her brother-in-law asked.

"Jason." What was his last name? She turned to Brett. "You know, the FBI guy."

Slipping his hand into a pocket, Brett pulled out a small white rectangle of paper. "I got it right here." He held it out to her. "Why do you need it?"

"I just remembered something." Her heart was racing. "It might not be important, but it's not up to me to decide."

"You're calling an FBI agent?" Katya said. "What's going on?"

Eva hated to keep secrets from her family. But Jason had been clear—she shouldn't discuss Decker or his escape with anyone. "I'll tell you when I can." She needed privacy. Pressing the phone between both of her palms as if saying a prayer, she asked, "Can I bring this back to you in a minute?"

"Go," said Katya. "Make your call. We'll chat when you get back."

Eva stepped into the corridor, Brett right behind her. Every room was full. Nurses, aides and doctors roamed up and down the hallway. A janitor, pushing a bucket on wheels by a mop handle, walked past.

Brett placed his hand on her elbow, steering her toward a stairwell. "Let's try outside."

Their footfalls clanged on each step. The stairs ended at a heavy metal door that led outside. Brett pushed the door open and stepped onto a concrete pad. The South Texas sun beat down, shimmering in waves off the adjacent parking lot.

Cupping her hand over the phone screen so she could see, she entered the number for Jason's cellphone.

He answered after the second ring. "Agent Jones."

"This is Eva Tamke. You said to call if I remembered anything, and, well, I did remember something. I don't know if it's important or not."

"Eva, I'm with both Isaac Patton and Ryan Steele, and I've got you on speakerphone. Tell me what you remember. We'll figure out what it means on our end."

She glanced up at Brett. He gave her a nod of encouragement. "While we were flying, Decker was either in a state or talking in his sleep." She gave herself a moment to recall exactly what he'd said. "He asked, 'Ana, why did you go?' and also, 'Was it because of him?' I didn't know what he was talking about, but still you said to call."

"Ana?" Jason echoed. "That name doesn't ring a bell."

"Well, it does to me." She recognized Ryan's voice. "Years ago—God, it has to be more than a decade by now—he dated a woman named Anastasia Pierce. She just up and left him one day. Gave him a note that said something like, I can't do this anymore."

"We need to find out where Anastasia Pierce is now," said Isaac. "That way she'll know he's escaped, and even worse, he's thinking about her. Even if he was in a stupor, he might be thinking about going after her."

"Best I can recall," said Ryan, "is she was a grad student. She was studying biology or ecology or some such. She also worked at a coffee place part-time." He pulled a phone from his pocket and tapped on the screen. After a moment, he said, "That's weird."

The FBI agent drew his dark brows together. "What's weird?"

"She doesn't show up on a quick internet search," said Ryan, holding up his phone. Eva couldn't make out what was on the screen. "I mean, there's stuff about her. But old—there's an article she's mentioned in when she was in school. That's back when I knew her."

"That is strange," said Isaac. "Do you have any thoughts? You know her."

"Me?" asked Ryan. "I *used* to know Ana, but like I said, that was years ago. Maybe she's not real big on social media now that she's older."

"Or maybe she doesn't want to be found," said Isaac.

"Even if she isn't on social media," said Jason, "there are ways to find her."

Eva knew that eventually they'd find the woman—Anastasia Pierce. After all, one of them was with the FBI. The other two worked for some kind of private security firm. Still, she felt as if she were eavesdropping on their conversation. Besides, she wanted to get back to her family. "Well," she said, interrupting their brainstorming, "I hope that helps."

"It helps," said Jason. "If you remember anything else, let us know. Tell Brett to do the same."

She looked up from the phone and met his gaze. "I will."

The call ended, and she tucked the phone into the side pocket of her borrowed scrubs. She held out Jason's business card to Brett. "This is yours."

He waved it away. "You keep it. I didn't interact with Decker much, so there's not as much for me to remember."

He might be right. Still she said, "I have his number on my sister's phone. I can transfer it once I get a new phone for myself."

He took the card and shoved it into the front pocket of his

pants. For a moment, they stood in the oven-like heat. Neither spoke.

Finally, Brett said, "Well, I guess I better get going. Your family seems really nice. Tell them I enjoyed meeting them all."

"You're welcome to come back to the room." She wasn't ready to part ways and never see him again.

"I appreciate your offer," he said, his expression unreadable, "but I have to figure out how I'm getting home. Besides, your family wants to see you—not entertain some random stranger."

Brett was much more than a random guy. Still, she had no other choice.

Now, it really was goodbye.

Chapter Eighteen

Brett found a bench in front of the hospital and placed a call to his parents in Dallas. His mother wept when she heard his voice—the crash had made the news. His father, always stoic, said that he never doubted Brett's ability to survive. They promised to pass on the news to his sister, and he promised to come for a visit to Dallas soon. He knew his mother would be on the phone with Shannon as soon as they hung up.

But he didn't have any immediate plans to visit his family.

Looking over his shoulder at the hospital, he tried to figure out which window belonged to Eva's grandmother.

Brett's family had never been very emotive. He wondered what it would be like to have a boisterous and loving family like Eva's. Then again, he had other things to worry about beyond Eva and her kin. He had to get back to San Antonio, and honestly, he didn't know how he was going to make that happen.

Using his cell phone, he placed a call to Darla at SAMC's human resources.

The phone rang once. "This is Darla."

"Hey," he said, suddenly exhausted by the past twenty-four hours. "It's me. Brett."

"Omigod, Brett," she cried. "We've been worried sick about you and Eva. An FBI agent told us you'd been found and were being transported to the hospital in Encantador. How are you both?"

"Eva hurt her leg during the crash. She got an X-ray. Thankfully, nothing's broken. They don't have an MRI machine here, so she'll have to have more testing later. Other than that, she's okay."

"And how are you?"

"Me? I'm fine, physically, at least." Then again, he and Eva were the only two crew members to survive the crash. For the first time since going down, he thought of each of his friends in turn. Stacy, who was always serious. There was Wade, who loved to joke. Lin was forever cautious and careful. In fact, he'd warned against the flight. What would've happened if Brett had listened in the first place?

Suddenly, the sun became too bright. He closed them against the glare as tears leaked down the side of his face. He wiped his cheek with his shoulder.

"I'm so glad you're okay," Darla was saying. "We'd been told that there were fatalities. The feds are very hush-hush about what happened," she whispered. "But at least you're okay."

He wasn't sure if he'd describe himself as being okay. Still, he said, "I'm as good as can be expected." Exhaling, he started again, "I was calling because I'm not sure what happens next. I'll have to talk to the FAA and soon. Obviously, I can't fly my helicopter back to San Antonio, but I'm also not sure how to get back home."

Home. The word struck him in the chest. Would San Antonio ever feel like home again?

Darla said, "You let me worry about getting you back here. It might take some time. I'll reach out as soon as I have a plan," she said before ending the call.

He rose from the bench and walked toward the front doors

of the hospital. They opened with a *swish*. After being in the sun and the heat, the inside was cool and dark.

A sign indicated that the cafeteria was to the left. His stomach grumbled and clenched painfully. It had been more than twenty-four hours since he'd eaten a proper meal.

He followed a set of arrows, and soon, the scent of grease and fried meat hung in the air. The cafeteria reminded him of the lunchroom at his elementary school. A stack of trays sat at the end of a metal counter, along with a rack filled with cutlery. The food sat in warming pans behind a glass case. All the workers wore white aprons and hairnets or baseball caps.

He took a tray and a set of silverware, along with a stack of napkins.

"What can I get for you?" asked a man in a ball cap. The words Encantador Hospital Food Service had been screen printed on the front.

Brett scanned the selections. Mashed potatoes. Meat loaf. Sliced roast beef in gravy. Green beans swimming in a buttery sauce. Chicken parmesan and pasta with marinara. He smiled. All of it was comfort food—and exactly what he needed right now.

"I'll take the roast beef and gravy, potatoes and green beans."

"You want gravy on those potatoes?" the man asked, filling a plate.

"Is there any other way to eat mashed potatoes?"

The man laughed. "I guess not." He handed Brett his order. "Drinks are over there." He pointed to a soda machine, an iced tea dispenser and several coffee carafes lined up among stacks of paper cups, lids and straws. "You pay the cashier on your way out."

Brett filled a cup with ice and tea before setting a lemon wedge on top.

The cashier sat on a stool behind the register. "What've

you got?" she said, punching keys on the register. "That'll be seven dollars and eighty-two cents."

"That's it?" he asked. He couldn't buy a medium latte in San Antonio for less than eight bucks.

"That's it."

Somehow, Brett had kept his wallet through the entire ordeal. He found a ten-dollar bill and dropped the change into a wire basket with a handwritten paper sign that said Feeling Tipsy?

She smiled wider. "You have a nice day."

Only a handful of tables were filled. At one table, a family of four looked up as Brett came close. It was hard to miss the expectant expression on their faces. He figured they were waiting for news about a loved one.

Next to the window, a woman wearing a flight suit sat alone. Was that the pilot who'd spotted them from the air? So many people had worked hard during the search and rescue. He'd probably never get to thank them all. But at least he could tell the pilot how much she was appreciated.

Carrying his tray, he approached the table. "Pardon me," he said. "Can I join you?"

With a smile, she scooted a Styrofoam cup closer to her empty plate. "Have a seat."

"I'm Brett Wilson, by the way." He sat down.

"Farrah Kaufman," she said. "Nice to meet you." She paused. "I'm glad to see that you're up and around, by the way."

"So, you are the pilot who spotted us?"

"Guilty as charged."

"I want to say thank-you, but that doesn't seem like enough. Can I get you a dessert or something?"

"Ugh." She pressed her hand to her stomach. "I've eaten too much already. My girlfriend is into competitive bodybuilding, we eat a lot of lean protein and steamed veggies. I thought food like this would be a treat. It was while I was eating. Now?"

She pushed her plate away. "But you don't have to thank me. It's all part of the job, you know that."

"When you're the one on the ground hoping to be spotted by an aircraft, it feels pretty personal." He stirred the gravy into his potatoes and took a large bite. The potatoes had an earthy taste and a creamy texture. The gravy was savory and salty. Pointing to his food with his fork, he said, "Now that's good."

Farrah glanced over her shoulder before leaning forward. "Do you know anything?" she asked, "About Decker Newcombe, I mean."

As a fellow pilot, he felt he could talk to Farrah about the case. It was just that he didn't know much of anything. Brett shook his head. "Eva thinks he was suffering from withdrawals from all the pain meds he'd been given. It makes sense because he stole the medical kit and ran off."

"Any idea where he's headed?" she asked.

Brett took another bite and shook his head. "No idea." He didn't want to talk about the serial killer anymore. "So what's your story? How'd you become a pilot?"

"I flew in the navy for a few years. Got out and applied to work for the Texas Rangers. I was doing a sweep over the southern border when I got the call to come and look for you." She leaned back, stretching her shoulders over her chair. "In the past day, I've spent eleven hours in the air. I'm exhausted."

Regulations allowed for a pilot to spend only eight hours of flight time in a twenty-four-hour period. "Sounds like you've earned some time off."

"That I have," she said. "There's a little motel in town called the Saddle-Up Inn. I'm staying the night and then flying back to San Antonio in the morning. You're welcome to hitch a ride with me if you want."

Honestly, he wanted to get back before tomorrow. But he knew that waiting for Farrah might be his best option. "I'm supposed to hear back from the hospital soon. But if they can't get me back before tomorrow, I'll take a seat in your aircraft." He took a large bite of food.

"I'll be honest with you." Leaning forward, Farrah used a conspiratorial tone. "I don't like the idea of staying in Encantador. Not with Decker Newcombe on the loose, at least. He's as bad as they come, and I've met some real scumbags in my life."

He agreed with her but said nothing. Giving a slight nod, he kept eating.

Farrah continued, "What do you want to bet that he's headed our way? He seems to have something against this town—this place—and I don't want to be here when he comes back filled with vengeance."

If he were being honest, Brett felt that her fear was overblown. He wiped his lips with a paper napkin. "I don't think he'll make it here. Or anywhere else for that matter."

"Why's that?" Farrah asked.

"First of all, the odds are against anyone surviving in the desert for long," he said. "The last time I saw Decker, he was sick. He didn't have any food or water. Hell, he wasn't even wearing a shirt—just a windbreaker he stole from a US marshal he killed."

"Yeah," she said, interrupting. "That's exactly what I'm talking about. Despite everything you said, he still killed a guy. Plus, it was a marshal who was armed and trained to use his weapon."

She had a point. Brett shrugged and took another bite. "I assume there are still aerial searches for Decker going on now?"

"You know how that goes. It's hard to spot anything from the air. If he doesn't want to be seen, he can hide—nobody'd be the wiser." Farrah was right about that, too. "Plus, it's too damn hot to use FLIR."

A forward-looking infrared sensor mounted to the nose of an aircraft could pick up heat signatures on the ground. Then again, there had to be a temperature differential for the equipment to be effective. And right now, it was, as Farrah said, too damn hot.

"They can use that at night," he reasoned.

"I hate the idea of spending the night here," Farrah repeated. "I just want to get home to my girl and put all of this behind me." She leaned back in her seat. "Not that I regret finding you and your nurse friend."

Suddenly, he wasn't hungry anymore. The food in the hospital cafeteria really was delicious and leaving a single bite somehow felt like quitting. Still, he pushed his plate away and said, "Too bad I'm not able to fly your chopper. That way we could both get out of here today."

"You know." She tapped a fingernail on the table. "That's a good idea. I'd have to get approval first, and it could take hours to get. But it'd be less time than the twenty-four hours I'm required to wait. Sit tight while I make a couple of calls."

"Where else am I going to go?" he asked, taking a sip of tea.

Farrah pulled her cell from the sleeve pocket of her flight suit. "I hope this works," she said, "because I can feel it in my gut. Decker's heading this way."

"You have a feeling in your gut?" Brett joked. "I thought that was all the hospital food."

"Well, there's that, too," she said with a laugh. "Hang on for a minute. I'll be back."

As she left, Brett looked around the room. The other patrons had gone, and he was alone. In the silence, with nothing to do beyond listen to his own thoughts, he wondered about the missing killer.

Either Decker *was* hanging around—maybe to get rid of him and Eva for daring to thwart him—or he was on his way to wherever this Ana woman lived.

Neither was good.

Decker had gotten his craving for pain meds and the agony from withdrawals under control by taking a cocktail of naloxone and over-the-counter meds. Without the constant pain and nausea from before, he was able to think.

After killing a district attorney in Wyoming, Decker had lived off the grid around the border between the US and Mexico for over a year. He knew exactly where he was going.

It didn't take him long to find the dirt road and head south. He started to walk, every so often glancing over his shoulder. Too soon, he saw a cloud of dust billowing on the horizon. It was a vehicle heading his way.

If he was lucky, it was just someone using the little-known bypass. If it was someone with Homeland Security or people from another agency, well, then Decker's luck might've finally run out.

The gun hung from the back of his pants, hidden by the jacket. The cold metal dug into his spine. He had no problem shooting a cop. But by now whoever was on the road had spotted him and would notice if he reached for his weapon.

"Just play it cool," he said aloud.

As if answering, a hawk cried out as it circled overhead.

Dirt, caught in the breeze, wafted over him and he knew that the vehicle was close. He continued to walk. A moment later, he heard the sickly the cough of a motor. So, it wasn't law enforcement. If it was, the engine would be in tip-top shape.

His shoulders relaxed. His gait loosened. At times like this, he liked to think of himself as a lion on the Serengeti.

The cloud of dust surrounded him as an old truck rattled up to his side and stopped. The idling engine sounded like an old man with pneumonia.

He turned to the vehicle. A kid with dark hair and eyes leaned his elbow on the windowsill. Decker wasn't good at guessing the age of anyone—children especially. But he'd say the boy was either eight or nine years old. Behind the steering wheel was an old man with weathered skin and a straw cowboy hat. The man was a hundred years old if he was a day. Neither grandson nor grandfather were an immediate threat.

"You lost or something?" the kid asked.

"Since it's such a nice day, I'm just out for a walk."

The kid looked over his shoulder and translated for his grandfather. *"Como hace un día tan bonito, saldré a dar un paseo."*

The old man spit a long string of tobacco juice out the open driver's window. He grumbled, *"Idiota."*

Decker didn't need a translator to know what *that* meant.

The kid said, "My grandfather wants to know if you need a ride."

"Is that so?" he asked. "How far south are you going?"

"We'll cross the border, and then our ranch is another fifteen miles."

It wasn't as far as he needed to go. Yet he'd get there quicker by riding in the old truck than walking. It'd also keep him off the road and out of sight of any aircraft looking for him. Besides, he could always steal the truck later if he wanted.

"Much obliged," he said.

Decker opened the passenger door, and the kid slid to the middle of the bench seat. Settling in next to the boy, Decker pulled the door closed. The tires rolled forward, kicking up a rooster tail of dust.

The child studied Decker as the truck rumbled down the road.

After a moment, he glared at the boy. "What?"

"You a lawman?"

He choked out a laugh. "Me? Naw, kid. I'm no lawman."

"Why're you wearing that jacket, then?"

The child was clever, observant and maybe a little too shrewd for his own good. Decker was still wearing the marshal's windbreaker. "This?" He pulled on the collar. "It's a costume."

"It looks pretty legit to me."

Decker's temper flared. "Have you ever seen a real-life US marshal before?"

As if the kid had been scalded by Decker's anger, he scooted closer to his grandfather. "No."

"Besides, why would a US marshal be walking through the desert without any goddamn shirt? Answer me that if you're so brainy."

"I don't figure one would," said the little boy.

"I don't figure one would, either." Decker pulled the windbreaker across his chest and looked out the window. The color brown stretched out as far as he could see. Umber earth. Sienna rocks. Even the trees were withered and covered with dust, the leaves were more tan than green. An angry sun hung in an azure sky. Both seemed intent on baking the earth until there was nothing left but coffee-colored dust.

He could feel the kid's gaze on him like a tickle on his cheek. He glanced over at the child. "What now?"

The boy regarded him with large brown eyes, so dark they almost looked black. "If you aren't a lawman, are you a bad man?"

From the other side of the cabin, the grandfather regarded Decker, as well. He had the same eyes as the kid—just decades older. It seemed like the old man understood English better than he'd originally let on.

Decker looked back at the little boy and placed his hand on top of his head. "Am I a bad man?" he repeated with a smile. "I'm the worst man you ever met, and you should stop asking questions."

The boy's eyes went wide. Like his head was on a swivel, he turned to his grandfather. The old man held on to the steering wheel with both hands. His knuckles were white.

"Just keep driving." He kept his tone pleasant. "And we can all part ways as friends." He wasn't sure if it was a lie or not.

He really didn't like the idea of killing children—especially one who was so young.

But even a child could become a witness. And from here, Decker planned to vanish.

Chapter Nineteen

The old man and the boy dropped Decker off at the end of a long, narrow track. It was as far as he wanted to go. He'd considered killing them and taking their truck. But in a way, the kid reminded him of the son he didn't know. As he walked down the dirt road, he wondered if he'd made a mistake in letting them live. Then again, he never did care much for killing children. And given the way he'd been torn from his own son, he didn't want to do the same to this kid.

The lane ended at a small house with cinderblock walls, a tin roof and a plywood door. A sagging sofa sat next to the door in a sliver of shade thrown off by the house itself.

Each step crunched with the gravel underfoot, so he wasn't surprised to see the old woman, Juanita, appear at the door as he approached. Her once-black hair was now gray. She wore it in a long braid that dangled over her shoulder like the tail of a hangman's noose. She had on a housedress and plastic flip-flops. Her upper arms were fleshy, and her feet were covered in grime.

Parked in front of the house was a white sedan. It was the same vehicle he'd purchased for her years earlier. But that was when he was working regular and was flush with cash.

"What are *you* doing here?" Juanita asked.

The year that Decker had lived off the grid, he'd stayed in a similar house only miles from here. He'd chosen the location because it was close to the old woman. During that time, he'd paid her well to bring him food, water and information.

He didn't trust her, per se. But that was because Decker didn't trust anybody, not really. Yet Juanita had proved to be useful. She was willing to do almost anything if it meant that she got some cash.

Before kidnapping the undersheriff's daughter, he'd left a box of belongings with the old woman. He'd also paid her two hundred dollars to keep it all safe.

In the box was an extra set of clothes and new shoes, but what he really needed was his cell phone. To find out the truth about his kid, he had to talk to Seraphim. That phone was the only way he had to make contact.

Their relationship was purely transactional. And yet, he gave her a slow smile. "Is that any way to greet an old pal like me?"

"We aren't pals," she said. "I heard you killed a lot of people. The federales came to my house. I was questioned and detained for days."

The fact that the Mexican police had traced him to Juanita's door came as a surprise—and not a pleasant one. "What did you say?"

"I didn't say nothing. But they kept me in a stinking cell for days. I still have nightmares."

Her suffering wasn't his problem. He shrugged. Then he realized it *was*. If he didn't make her silence worth her while, she'd talk.

The woman continued, "I also heard you'd been taken to jail."

"Looks like I escaped." He sat on the old sofa. God, it felt good to sit down. He set the med kit on the ground next to him. "You got some water for me?"

"You got money?"

From the front pocket of his pants, he pulled out the cash he'd taken from the US marshal. He held up the folded bills before shoving them back in his pants pocket. "I got money."

She disappeared inside the house and returned with a plastic bottle of water. "For you."

He broke the seal and pulled the cap off. Then he lifted the bottle to his lips and drained it in a single swallow. The water hit his middle, and his gut cramped. Holding on to his side, he cursed. But the pain passed as quickly as it had come on. He held out the bottle to the old woman. "You got another one of these?"

She took the empty and folded her arms across her chest. "What do you want?"

"I need my stuff."

She held out her hand, palm up. "I need two hundred dollars."

His pulse spiked, and his heartbeat echoed at the base of his skull. "You what? I paid you when I dropped off the box."

"You paid me to keep the box," the woman said. "Not to give it back to you. I need money for that, too."

He pulled the cash out of his pocket and counted the bills. "Fifty-seven dollars. That's all I got." He opened the windbreaker, showing his bare chest. "Hell, I don't even have a shirt on my back to give to you. But you can have all my cash. Take it or leave it."

"Leave it," she said, flipping the braid over her shoulder.

"You're kidding, right? After all I gave you, you can't just turn your back on me."

She lifted a single brow. "I can't?" With that, she turned and walked back into her house. She slammed the door shut. From where he stood, he could hear the click as she engaged the lock.

Decker typically wasn't a generous man. But he'd paid the old woman well for the care she provided along with her loyalty. Now, it seemed like his money had been wasted. He was beyond angry. He was furious. And if she thought something as flimsy as a door lock was going to keep him out, she was sorely mistaken.

He stood. Striding to the front door, he removed the gun from the back of his pants. He struck the wood with the butt end of the firearm. "Open the damn door."

"Go away," she said. "I've got a gun. If you come inside, I'll shoot you dead."

Yeah? Well, Decker had a gun, too. "I don't like to be threatened." His jaw was tight. "And if you don't open this door, I'm coming in anyway, and then, you'll be sorry."

"I don't like to be threatened, either," she said. "Leave, or I will call the federales. Then, they'll come and get you and stick you in a cell. You're the devil."

He'd been called worse, so her words didn't bother him. But he'd done right by this woman for years. To have her betray him now was a blow he refused to ignore. He kicked the door handle. The lock held, but the wood splintered. He kicked it again, and the door swung open.

He doubted that she had a gun, but he wasn't going to risk getting shot. Dropping to one knee, he peered into the house. It was a single room with a bed in one corner, a small dresser at the end and a nightstand at the side. A round wooden table sat in the middle of the room, along with two mismatched chairs. A single bulb on a wire hung over the table. Against the far wall was a sink, a small stove and a refrigerator that was so old it could be considered an antique.

But the woman was gone.

Decker rose to his feet.

The door came at him, hitting him hard in the face.

For a moment, his eyes watered, and white dots floated in his vision.

The woman stepped out from behind the door. She held a rusty revolver that was as old as the fridge. She pointed the barrel at his chest. "I've shot men before," she said. "I might be old, but my aim is still good. Turn around and leave."

"I'm not going anywhere without my stuff." True, he didn't have money. But he did have medicine. Out here, where there were no luxuries and even necessities were hard to come by, the med kit might be worth something. "I got a medical kit from the air ambulance that was taking me to jail." He'd keep the remaining Naloxone for himself, but he didn't need the rest. "You can have it all. Save it. Sell it. I don't care. Just give me my belongings, and I'll be gone."

"I don't care if you gave me a million dollars. Leave now and don't ever come back."

Honestly, Decker was done with the woman. She might have a gun, but she hadn't pulled the trigger. From his experience, it meant that she wasn't going to shoot. Also, she hadn't told him that his box of stuff was gone. He figured it was still in the small house, somewhere. All he had to do was go inside and get it for himself.

He crossed the threshold.

"I told you to leave," she said, pulling back on the hammer with a *click*.

For a single moment, Decker was eight years old. His mother's latest loser boyfriend had come home drunk and mean. There'd been a fight. They always fought. It was hard to ignore the yelling and cursing since Decker didn't have his own room in the drafty trailer. He slept on the sofa.

The loser boyfriend had shoved a gun in his mother's face. Then, he'd pulled back the hammer. *Click.*

At eight years old, there wasn't much Decker could do except cry. Yet, in that moment, he swore he'd never be the victim again.

Without thought, he lifted his gun and fired.

The bullet punched a hole through her housedress, and the old woman's eyes went wide. The faded fabric turned red as blood bloomed across her chest. She stumbled to the floor. The gun fell from her hand and skittered away.

Decker came forward and looked down at her. She clutched her chest and gasped for breath. "You know," he said. "It didn't have to be this way."

"You are the devil," she said.

"Could be," he agreed. Although, he wasn't sure if she'd heard him. The woman was dead.

Juanita had shoved his belongings, as well as the box, under her bed. He changed his clothes and pulled out the phone. He pressed the power button. There was only ten percent battery left. But it was enough. He placed a call.

It was answered after the second ring.

"Yes?" The voice was electronically disguised. It reminded Decker how little he knew about Seraphim. Only communicating online, he'd never met the hacker in person. If they spoke via video, they wore a plague doctor mask and black leather gloves. The background was a black drape, and their voice was always altered to the same obnoxious squawk.

Decker didn't know the hacker's location, age, race or even their gender. Still, he said, "You know who this is."

"The last I heard you'd been captured and were going to jail."

"There was a change of plans," he said. And then, "I need all the information you have about Ana Pierce."

"There's not much about her on the internet. I've been looking for her and her son, but so far, I don't have much."

"He's my son, too." Or at least, that was what Decker intended to find out.

"I'll contact you if I need anything," he said, ready to end the call.

"Since you're free, what are your plans?"

"Me? I'm going to find my son. And you're going to help me." He found a slip of paper and a pen and wrote down Seraphim's phone number. Ripping off the sheet of paper, he shoved it into his pants pocket. Had Ana hooked up with a long string of loser boyfriends over the years? Was she married? Well, he was about to ruin whatever life she had—once the hacker found her, that is.

He took a few minutes to rummage through the old lady's kitchen. He found a case of bottled water, a box of cereal and a loaf of bread. It was enough food to get him where he needed to go. In a drawer of the small nightstand, he found the car keys.

Tucking everything in the box and picking up the med kit again, he left the house. Decker didn't bother closing the door. The sooner the wild reclaimed this house, the better.

As he drove down the narrow lane, he threw his old phone out the window. Decker was back, and nothing was going to stop him now.

It was 10:00 p.m. in London, England. Theo Fowler was still at his office on the fourth floor of the US embassy. He didn't mind being at work and not out at a pub like many of his coworkers. Hours earlier, he'd heard that the helicopter carrying Decker Newcombe had crashed in the Texas desert. Once again, the killer was at large.

He'd spent the last several weeks trying to unravel an online knot to find the elusive Seraphim, the hacker who'd helped Decker. So far, all he had to show for his efforts was a phone number that the hacker rarely used. But if Decker had the chance, he might place a call to that number.

Theo's computer pinged, and an automated message bubble appeared. You have one message.

He reread the message several times. Someone had called the hacker, after all.

From the NSA's database, it only took a few moments to locate the origin of the call—several miles south of the US/Mexico border. Reaching for his own phone, Theo placed a call.

It was answered after the first ring. "Special Agent Jones."

Theo had only been given the barest of briefings on Decker Newcombe, but he had a gut feeling that Jason Jones, the supervisory special agent out of San Antonio, would once again be the FBI's point man on the case. "Jason, this is Theo Fowler. I have a hit on a cell phone used by Seraphim. I found where the call originated." He read off the coordinates. "It looks like the call came from Mexico, not far south of the border."

"That might be our man," said Jason. "You're a lifesaver. Tell the NSA to be careful. I might steal you away and put you to work for the FBI."

Theo sighed. When people said things like that, he didn't know how to react. Was it a compliment? A threat? "Well," he said after an awkward pause, "we'll see."

Over the years, he'd learned that a neutral response usually made everyone happy.

"Thanks again for the tip," said Jason. "I'll be in touch."

Theo ended the call and rose from his desk. He liked living in Britain, the British people and their culture. But lately he'd been thinking about home. Was it time for Theo to move back to the US?

If he did, he wouldn't want to work for the FBI. Maybe there was something else he could do?

Brett still hadn't heard from either Darla or Farrah. Without a solid plan, he was in limbo, waiting in the hospital cafeteria. He refilled his iced tea at the dispenser and took a sip.

The air in the room changed, and he knew that Eva was close. Or maybe it was just his imagination because he wanted to see her so damn bad. He looked up.

As if she'd stepped out of a dream, she stood on the threshold.

He wanted to smile. He needed to play it cool. After taking another sip of tea, he said, "Hey."

It took everything in him not to pull her to him, wrap his

arms around her, feel her against him again. He'd missed her so much in the short time they'd been separated.

But she'd made her decision, and he had to respect that. Dammit.

"Hey, yourself," she said, and for a moment, there seemed to be something in her eyes. Like she was fighting her own feelings. Maybe that was wishful thinking, too. "I thought you were heading back to San Antonio."

"I was," he said. "I mean, I am. Or I will be, once a few things get straightened out. How's your grandmother?"

"Right now, she's sleeping. Katya and Jorje took the kids home."

"And you didn't go with them?"

Eva shook her head. "I'm going to stay here for a while, but I'm starving."

"I can vouch for the mashed potatoes." Then, he joked, "I mean, they aren't as good as my pancakes, but you know."

"I keep hearing that from you. Makes me think I missed out on something special."

He didn't know what to make of her comment. Was there more to her words, or was she just joking? He heard her place her order at the counter—"Hot roast beef, potatoes, gravy, green beans"—and he chuckled.

"What's so funny?" she asked, sitting back down with her food.

"That's exactly what I ordered."

"Oh yeah? Must be the meal of choice after being lost in the desert," she said. "Can you join me?"

Several pithy answers came to mind. He ignored them all and said, "I'd love to. What do you want to drink?"

"I'll take a caffeine-free soda."

Brett filled a paper cup with ice before filling it with ginger ale at the drink station. He set the cup next to her tray. "Here you go."

"Thanks." She reached for the cup and straw. "This all looks good."

"It's perfect comfort food," he said, sitting across from her.

After everything they'd been through together, it seemed like they should talk about something more than the quality of hospital food. Then again, maybe their relationship was over, and there was nothing more to say.

He waited as Eva ate her first few bites. Using her fork to point to her plate, she said, "This is really, really good."

"Agreed."

"I wonder what he wants." Still using her fork, she pointed to the door.

Brett turned to look.

Ryan Steele stood on the threshold and scanned the room until his gaze landed on Brett and Eva. He hustled across the floor to them. "Hey, man," Ryan said. "You know where Farrah went?"

"She's checking with her boss to see if they'll let me fly back to San Antonio."

"What do you mean," Ryan asked, "you're going to fly?"

He wasn't surprised that the security operative didn't know the FAA's rules. There was no reason. "A pilot can only be in the air eight out of every twenty-four hours. According to Farrah, she spent eleven hours in the cockpit and is grounded until tomorrow."

"But you can fly," Ryan clarified.

"I can."

Ryan narrowed his eyes. After a moment, he nodded his head, seeming to come to some sort of agreement with himself. "We've gotten some intel, and I need a pilot."

"What kind of intel?" Eva asked. She'd already eaten all the potatoes and gravy, along with half the roast beef. The green beans remained untouched.

"We think that Decker made a phone call about twenty-five

miles from here. If I can get you authorized to fly that helicopter, could you take it up in the air?"

Brett was on his feet before he realized that he'd stood. "If you get me authorization," he said, "I can."

Ryan slapped him on the shoulder. "Meet you at the helipad in ten minutes."

"I'll be there."

He waited until Ryan had left the cafeteria before speaking. "It'll be good to get into the air," he said. But there was more. Eventually, Eva was going to walk out of his life. He didn't know how long it would take to apprehend Decker— that was if they even found him. And by the time Brett made it back to the hospital, she'd likely be gone. "Well, I know we keep saying this, but I guess this time it really is goodbye."

She stood.

He opened his arms. "I hope this time I can get a hug."

"You don't need a hug," she said. "This isn't goodbye."

"It's not?"

"It's not," she echoed. "Because I'm coming with you."

Chapter Twenty

Eva left the cafeteria and walked quickly to the nearest elevator. As the car rose slowly, she had to ask herself a single question.

What was she doing?

The last time she'd been in the air, the helicopter crashed. After a day of being stranded in the desert, she'd been rescued. For that, she was truly lucky. So many things could've gone differently, and she wouldn't have made it home.

If all of that was true, then why had she volunteered for the mission?

Decker had been her patient before. Certainly, he wasn't her responsibility now. Or was he?

The car jerked to a stop with a *ding*.

It was true that Eva didn't understand her own motivations. But she did know what she needed if she was going to get in the air again. It started with getting her flight suit. It was still in the hospital bag, which was still in her grandmother's hospital room.

After pushing open the door, she peered inside. Her grandmother lay on the bed, her eyes closed.

The bag leaned drunkenly against the leg of a chair—the

same place she'd dropped it earlier. Without making a sound, she lifted the sack from the ground.

As she stood up straight, her grandmother's eyes were open.

"I didn't mean to wake you," Eva whispered.

"Oh, you didn't. It was Dennis. He's a nice man, but all day and all night, people are coming into the room. They want to take my blood pressure. My temperature. Look in my eyes with a blinding light. Who can sleep with a light like that shining in their eyes?" Baba gave a quiet chuckle. "You know, the doctor wanted me to stay in the hospital to get some rest. I've only taken cat naps since I got here. I'll need to go home just to get a full night's sleep."

It was a common enough complaint from patients. And Eva was happy that Baba had found some levity in a serious situation. Still, she didn't have much time to talk. "When I get back, we need to talk about plans for you."

"Oh no," Baba moaned. "Have you and Katya joined forces? Are you going to tell me that I need to move, too?"

"No, Baba. It's not that at all." She really didn't have time for this conversation and silently cursed that she'd brought up the subject in the first place. But she had, and there was no sense leaving her elderly grandmother with more worry. "I was thinking I could come here and live with you."

"What about your job? Your friends? Your apartment?"

They were all things that Eva had considered. Much as she'd told Brett, she said, "I can get out of the lease to my apartment with a month's notice. Obviously, I'd work here. And my friends in San Antonio will still be my friends. But you are family. You are who's important."

"I can't let you do that," said Baba. "You have a life already. Besides, you don't want to take care of an old lady."

Eva could feel the seconds slipping away with every beat of her heart. Reaching for her grandmother, Eva gave her hand a squeeze. "We can talk more when I get back. But right now, I have to scoot."

Baba tightened her grip, refusing to let go. "Where are you going?"

The FBI agent had warned against talking to anyone about Decker being on the loose. Then again, Baba wasn't just anyone. "I was on the medevac because we were transporting a patient." Glancing over her shoulder, she made sure nobody was standing next to the door. As far as she could tell, they were alone. Still, she lowered her voice. "The patient survived and is still out there. But the patient is…" she paused, trying to find the right word to describe the serial killer "…important."

"You had someone important on the air ambulance? Who?"

She really should follow the agent's orders, yet she found herself saying, "It was him, Baba. Decker Newcombe."

Baba sucked in a single breath, and her complexion paled. "He's back? Are you joking?"

"Honestly, I don't know much. The authorities think he made a phone call."

"But why you?" her grandmother asked, echoing Eva's own questions.

It was then that she understood her own mind and heart and soul. She was doing this all for Brett. It was more than the fact that they'd made love—in his home. In the cave. The two of them really had become a team. So, if he was going after Decker, she was, too.

How was she supposed to say any of that to her grandmother?

Baba's fingers dug into the back of Eva's hand. "I don't like that you'll be involved in looking for that fiend. But you're a strong, smart woman, an excellent nurse, and that gives me comfort. You do what you need to, but be careful. When you get back, we'll talk more."

Eva placed her lips on her grandmother's forehead. Her skin was thin and dry. Nobody knew what the next year or month or even day would hold. But for now, she knew what she needed to do Yet, her pulse raced. Was she really about to face down the killer again?

For an instant, Eva was a little girl, coming to her grand-mother for comfort and support. The thought of remaining with Baba came and went. But if Brett was going out again, so was she.

Walking across the room, Eva paused at the door. Baba lifted her hand, giving a final wave. Then the older woman settled into her pillow and closed her eyes.

Eva stepped into the corridor and retraced her steps to the elevator.

Dennis looked up as she passed the nurse's station. "How's your grandmother?" he asked.

"Good," said Eva. "She's resting now."

"I'll let her get some sleep before checking on her vitals again," he said. "Can I help you with anything else?"

She shook her head, ready to say no. Then again… "Do you have a well-stocked first aid kit I can take with me?" If she was going with Brett again, she should at least make herself useful. That meant being prepared.

"I can get you something," he said. "I probably shouldn't ask what's going on, should I?"

"The less I have to say, the better."

"Got it." Dennis moved out from behind the counter. "Be right back."

He returned a moment later with a medical kit much like the one she'd had on the medevac out of SAMC. Thanking him, she left the hospital.

The heliport was just a square of concrete with a pump for fueling aircraft. Next to the helipad was a small hangar with two rooms—a lounge with a sofa, chairs and a TV on a stand, and a gender-neutral restroom. The hospital in Encantador didn't have the funds to pay for its own aircraft or a crew. But being so far away from any major cities, often a medevac was the only way to get patients to larger facilities.

Quickly, Eva changed into her flight suit in the bathroom. Brett hadn't been given clearance to pilot the aircraft, yet he'd changed, as well. They waited next to a helicopter that sat on the helipad.

Four people approached—Ryan, Isaac, Jason from the FBI and a Black woman, who also wore a flight suit.

Jason said, "We've gotten clearance for you to take up the helicopter, Brett. Farrah is here to help with preflight."

Before Jason could say anything more, Brett said, "Eva's offered to come, and I think she should be onboard. Who knows what we'll find out there—what else might happen. That means we need someone with medical expertise. I can only take two more with me." He paused. Eva supposed the silence was to let the information sink in. "I'll let you all decide who gets the other seats. Farrah, let's get preflight done."

The trio of men circled into a tight knot. Eva assumed they were discussing who should go into the air and why.

Within minutes, the rotors started to spin.

Isaac and Ryan stepped away from Jason. "Looks like we're ready to go," said Isaac.

Eva ducked to avoid the downdraft as she slipped through the helicopter's open door. Brett was in the pilot's seat. Ryan sat next to him. Isaac was in the back seat. She settled into the empty seat and slipped on a headset.

"Buckle up," said Brett, his voice coming through the earphones.

She set the med kit on the floor, slid her arms into the five-point harness and gave Brett a thumbs-up. He turned toward the instrument panel and pushed the throttle forward. The helicopter rose from the ground. Soon, they were flying over Encantador.

At the edge of town, Eva found her grandmother's neighborhood and then her house. It didn't matter that she was a grown woman. There was something magical about seeing the familiar from the air. She wanted to say, *Everything down there is so small. All the houses and cars look like toys,* but kept the cliché to herself. Instead, she asked, "How do you know where to go?"

Ryan turned in his seat. "A call was made to an associate of Decker's. Since it originated in this area, it's just a hunch that he was the one who made it." He retrieved a tablet from the floorboard. "We have some satellite images of the area."

He showed her the screen, a picture of dirt, scrub brush and a small white house with a car parked next to the door. The resolution was good—almost the same as what she saw out the window.

"The place you work." She paused, not able to recall the name.

"Texas Law," Isaac offered.

Oh yeah, that was it. "How did Texas Law get that kind of picture? I mean, do you all control a satellite?"

Isaac chuckled. "We don't have anything that fancy. Hell, we don't even have our own helicopter—that's why we're hitching a ride."

"Maybe that should be the agency's next purchase," said Ryan.

"It's something to consider," said Isaac.

Eva wasn't going to be ignored that easily. She said, "But you do have that photograph."

"It's courtesy of the NSA via the FBI," said Isaac. "We work with other agencies on many of our cases. And finding and arresting Decker Newcombe is priority number one for a lot of them."

"One of the women he killed—the one whose murder was posted on the internet—lived next door to my grandmother." Eva wasn't sure why she shared that bit of information, but it seemed important.

"Is your grandma Gladys Tamke?" Ryan asked.

"She is."

"I know your grandmother then." Ryan powered down the tablet. "How's she doing?"

"Actually, she fell and is in the hospital."

"Tell me if she needs anything. I've done a few things around her house. My girlfriend, Kathryn Glass, lives across the street."

Baba had spoken about the handsome man who fixed her toilet and hung draperies. It must've been Ryan who'd helped all those times. It really was a small world, although she kept that cliché to herself, as well. So Ryan was the one who'd saved Kathryn's daughter from being killed during a live stream. It also meant he was the one who'd saved Decker from a burning building. "How's Kathryn's daughter? What's her name? Madison?"

"Morgan," said Ryan. "Physically, she recovered."

"Emotionally?" Eva asked.

Ryan shrugged. "She still has nightmares and refuses to be alone. She won't like that he's at large. I don't like it, either. She's been talking to a therapist, but it hasn't been long. Hopefully, she'll learn how to cope with what happened."

Brett said, "We'll be landing in one minute. There's no way to hide a helicopter out here, so whoever's in that house knows we're coming. Be ready for anything."

Eva's pulse climbed. Had she really volunteered to go looking for Decker Newcombe? Honestly, she shouldn't be here.

Then again, it was too late to change her mind.

During his time in the army, Brett had flown into and out of several active combat zones. Each time he felt much the same as he did now. Anxiety clawed at his gut—and yet, he was hyperfocused. His hearing was sharper. His vision was clearer. He was ready to act in an instant.

The skids touched the ground, and just like troops trained to storm a beachhead, Isaac and Ryan exited the aircraft. They ran toward the small white house with their weapons drawn.

Eva stayed in the back seat of the chopper.

Over the past few days, she had become the most important person in the world to him. It wasn't just because she was the lone survivor from his crew. His feelings for her were wholly personal.

It took only minutes for Isaac and Ryan to enter and re-emerge from the house. He could tell by the slump of their shoulders that they hadn't found what they were looking for. Ryan waved, and Brett powered down the engine. The rotors stopped spinning. He stripped off his headset and turned in his seat to look at Eva. The sun shone on her dark brown hair, bringing out the caramel color in some of her locks. Her skin was golden. She was so beautiful that his chest ached.

"We better go see what they want," she said.

"I guess so."

Brett opened the door and rounded the front of the helicopter. Together, they walked the short distance to where the security operatives waited.

"What's up?" Brett asked.

"There's a body inside," said Ryan. "Months ago, Decker mentioned that an older woman had been helping him live off the grid. The person inside looks to be older and female. It'd make sense that he came here. I can only guess why she ended up dead."

"Are you sure she's dead?" Eva asked.

"Positive," said Ryan. "There's a lot of blood around the body and no pulse."

Isaac picked up where Ryan left off. "We'll need to call this in and get crime-scene investigators here from both Mexico and the US. But for now, we need you to get back into the air and see if you can spot Decker."

Eva said, "I need to make sure she's actually deceased."

Brett assumed that her need to check was part of the oath she took as a nurse. Together, they walked into the small house.

The stench of meat left too long in the sun hung in the air. He swallowed down his rising nausea.

Like Ryan and Isaac had reported, a woman with her long gray hair in a braid lay on the floor. The front of her thin cotton dress was stained red. A pool of blood surrounded her body, making her look as if she floated on a lake of tar.

Eva donned a pair of surgical gloves before kneeling next to the body. She touched the woman's wrist, feeling for a pulse. With a shake of her head, she pronounced, "Blood loss, I'd say. Until someone gets a good look at her, my guess is that it's from the gunshot." She pointed to a blackened hole in the middle of the woman's chest.

He hadn't noticed the discolored or torn cloth because of all the blood. "I can use the helicopter's radio to call this in."

"Before you do that—" Isaac inclined his chin, nodding to the woman on the ground "—I have a few questions. How long do you think she's been gone?"

"Not long." Eva stood. "It's hot in here, which means rigor mortis will set in quicker. It hasn't started yet. So, she's been dead less than a few hours."

"Which means," said Ryan, "Decker hasn't gotten too far."

Brett knew that the helicopter was the best way to search. He also knew that in the satellite photo, a white sedan had been parked in front of the house. "I can look for that car," he said.

Ryan nodded. "Thanks, man. We need to stay here and look for clues as to where Decker might be headed next."

Already, Brett's blood buzzed with the need to be airborne. "Eva, are you coming with me?"

She looked at him and back to the body. "Maybe I should stay here," she said, "with her."

"There's nothing you can do for the woman now," said Isaac. "But you can help with the aerial search."

"All right, then," she said, walking toward the door. She handed the med kit to Ryan. "You might need this."

"I hope not," he said, tucking the plastic box under his arm. "But thank you."

Without speaking, Eva and Brett walked toward the aircraft. The shadow of the rotors stretched along the ground. He stopped.

Eva took a few more steps before looking over her shoulder. "Everything okay?" she asked.

Brett knew that the chapter of his life that he'd shared with Eva was close to the end. But he didn't want their story to be over. "I just want you to know..." he began.

His words trailed off. Maybe he was wasting his time by saying anything. After all, she had a life of her own. She'd also been clear that there wasn't space in her life for a relationship. But so much had happened since she sent him that text.

"You just want me to know what?" she coaxed.

If he was going to say something to her, this was his last shot. "I don't know what's going to happen next in either of our lives. But I do know that whatever it is, in the past few days—although, it seems like it's been a year—you've become the reason I've kept going on. I can't lose you now that I've found you. I just want to give us a chance to be, well, *us*." He paused. "The thing is, I've fallen in love with you."

"Brett," she said, smiling, her eyes shining. "Stop talking and kiss me."

Those were the best words he'd ever heard. Brett didn't have a crystal ball. He couldn't read the future. But really, he didn't need to be. He knew that their perfect first date was just the beginning of their happily ever after.

He didn't expect the flight plan of life to clear. He expected storms and turbulence. The thing was, he didn't want to take the trip with anyone but Eva.

It took Brett only a few minutes to start the engine and get the helicopter into the air once more. As Brett lifted off the ground, Eva sat at his side.

For a single moment, in the air with the woman he loved, life was perfect.

Epilogue

One week later

Eva sat on the sofa in the living room of her grandmother's house. Her ankle, still swollen and sore, was propped up on an ottoman with a pillow underneath. Two days earlier, she'd returned to SAMC and had been given an MRI. She had an appointment in a week to get the results. Until then, she'd been ordered to stay off her foot.

When she was at San Antonio, Eva spoke to Darla and put in her notice. She'd also told her landlord that she was moving out at the end of the month. Within weeks, the ties that connected her to her old life would be cut, and she'd be starting over.

From the kitchen came the sounds of banging pans and the salty scent of bacon frying.

"Are you sure I can't help with anything, Baba?" Eva had to yell to be heard over the din of cooking.

Her grandmother appeared at the doorway, spatula in hand. "You just rest." She flicked the spatula like a conductor with a baton. "I'll take care of everything."

"I'm supposed to be taking care of you. Remember?"

"Having you here is taking care of me and my soul."

Eva had mixed feelings about being waited on. First, she loved that her grandmother cared. Truly, having someone around seemed to lift Baba's spirits. On the other hand, Eva hated to feel helpless. Beyond that, she was bored with just sitting. Honestly, how many word searches could one person do in a week?

"I need to get back to breakfast. We're having company."

"Company?" Eva echoed. "Who's coming over?" Although, she really didn't have to ask. She could guess. "Is Brett coming over again?"

"Since he's doing the grocery shopping, I thought that making him breakfast was a nice gesture."

"You don't have to keep inviting him over just for my sake."

"I'm not doing any of this for you. It's all for me. Who wouldn't want a handsome pilot around?" Her grandmother winked to show that she was teasing before disappearing once more into the kitchen.

Truth be told, Eva liked having Brett visit often. He'd helped her with more than one word search. He'd taken her out in his truck, just so she could get out of the house. In the moments when the terror of the crash returned, he held her and told Eva that she was safe.

Since the day they were rescued, Brett had spent most of his time in Encantador. He'd taken a leave of absence from San Antonio Medical Center. For now, he was staying in a spare room of Ryan's apartment. It wasn't like Brett was in the way; Ryan spent most of his time with his girlfriend, the local undersheriff, Kathryn Glass. Who also happened to live across the street from Baba.

The sound of a car door slamming came from the street. Instinctively, she flinched. So far, Decker Newcombe was still at large. There was no reason to think that he'd return to Encantador or even Mercy, much less look for her specifically. But until he was in jail, she'd always be jumpy.

She pulled a curtain aside. Brett's truck was parked next to the curb. He carried a tinfoil and plastic to-go container and was already striding up the walk.

He saw her peering out of the window and gave her a short wave. She smiled and relaxed, letting the curtain fall closed. Reaching for her crutches, she rose from the sofa and hobbled to the front door.

Brett stood on the threshold, his hand lifted and ready to knock.

"You're up early," she said.

"And you're up period. Aren't you supposed to be resting?"

"I'm not putting any weight on my foot," she said, lifting her injured leg to prove her point. "What's in the dish?"

Brett lifted the lid. Fragrant steam, both sweet and yeasty, escaped. "I made pancakes." He lifted a flapjack out of the tin, perfectly round and golden brown. "You want to try one?"

She took a bite. It was light, fluffy and sweet. "You're right," she said. "Best pancake ever."

"It's perfect, right?"

"Better than perfect," she said, although she wasn't exactly talking about the food.

Across the street, Ryan emerged from Kathryn's house. He lifted his hand in greeting. "Hey, man," he called out to Brett. "I was just heading over to the apartment to chat with you. You got a minute?"

"Sure thing," said Brett. "What's up?"

Ryan jogged across the road and stopped at the end of the driveway. "This past week, Isaac and I figured something out. We can't find Decker using the resources we have right now. We bought an MD 600N. Or should I say that Texas Law purchased the helicopter. It's used, but in perfect shape. What we don't have is a pilot. That's where you come in." Ryan paused. "Basically, we want you on the team."

She watched Brett, trying to gauge his reaction. The thing

was, if he lived in Encantador, they could be together daily. Was he really willing to make such a big change?

Brett exhaled. "Can I have a day or two to think it over?"

"I'll have Isaac call you," Ryan said. "He can tell you everything about the job. Expectations. Salary. Benefits. I do know that you'd be stationed here."

"Thanks," Brett said, "it means a lot to me. Once I talk to Isaac, I'll let him know."

"Texas Law was a lifeline for me," said Ryan. "It could be the same for you." He gave a final wave and crossed to the other side of the street.

Once he was gone, Eva released a breath she didn't recall holding. "So?" she prompted, taking the last bite of the pancake. "What do you think?"

"I'll have to see the actual offer," he said. "But I'm curious about your thoughts."

She swallowed. "I want what's best for you."

He reached for her and took her hand in his. "But what's best for us?"

"Obviously, if you moved here, we would see each other every day."

"Is that what you want?"

Having Brett nearby would mean tearing down the wall Eva had built around her heart long ago. Sure, she'd created the barrier to keep her safe. But it had also kept her alone. Pulling him closer, she said, "I want you. I want us. I want to see what kind of future we can create together."

"Done," he said, placing his lips on hers.

As she melted into the embrace, Eva didn't know what the future held. But with Brett at her side, they could face anything.

* * * * *

Bodyguard Rancher

Kacy Cross

MILLS & BOON

USA TODAY bestselling author **Kacy Cross** writes romance novels starring swoonworthy heroes and smart heroines. She lives in Texas, where she's seen bobcats and beavers near her house but sadly not one cowboy. She's raising two mini-ninjas alongside the love of her life, who cooks while she writes, which is her definition of a true hero. Come for the romance, stay for the happily-ever-after. She promises her books "will make you laugh, cry and swoon—cross my heart."

Books by Kacy Cross

Harlequin Romantic Suspense

The Secrets of Hidden Creek Ranch

Undercover Cowboy Protector
Bodyguard Rancher

The Coltons of Owl Creek

Colton's Secret Past

The Coltons of New York

Colton's Yuletide Manhunt

Visit the Author Profile page
at millsandboon.com.au for more titles.

Dear Reader,

Welcome back to Hidden Creek Ranch! This is the second book in the series starring sisters who inherit their grandfather's former stud farm in east Texas, near Gun Barrel City (which is still the best name for a Western town ever). Charli and Sophia Lang are remaking the place into a resort where guests can pretend to be a cowboy for a day.

Except the ranch is overrun with lots of "ologists" as Charli calls them, all of whom are getting in the way. No one gets in Charli's way as much as Heath McKay, though. The former SEAL is her official bodyguard, and she lives to give him the slip...until he strikes a most unusual bet with her. The wager is designed to help Heath do his job, not put him in such close proximity to Charli that she starts to intrigue him. They definitely weren't supposed to fall in love, and the archaeologists weren't supposed to find solid gold statues worth millions of dollars hidden in the woods. How is Heath supposed to keep Charli safe when he's started to care about her, and the threats are coming at them from all sides?

Thank you for joining me on this adventure. I can't wait for you to dive into the pages and discover the allure of treasure hunting alongside Charli and Heath. Happy reading!

Kacy

PS: I love to connect with readers. Find me at kacycross.com.

To my firstborn—It means the world to me that you're still the most enthusiastic supporter of my books. This one is for you.

Chapter One

Charli could feel the ranch hand watching her. Not in the I'm-being-paid-to-keep-you-safe way, like she'd expect given the fact that he'd been employed to do exactly that. But in the way a man watched a woman when he wanted her to know he was interested.

Well, *she* wasn't interested.

She refused to so much as glance in his direction as she strolled from the back door of the house to the barn. Heath McKay was the opposite of easy on the eyes. The man was so hot he could burn a woman's retinas if she stared directly at him.

He knew it too. He was in that category of male who could charm a nun out of her habit. Who always had the next woman waiting in the wings—or maybe even right on stage at the same time as his current woman. How did Charli know? Because Heath McKay was Exactly Her Type in huge ten-foot-tall letters and she had crappy taste in men.

Her sister, Sophia, whom Charli secretly called Super Sophia, had hired him to make sure no one kidnapped any other Lang women from the ranch. After Sophia's harrowing experience of being taken from their home at gunpoint, she'd laid down some serious cash to ensure there were no repeats. Charli could have saved her the trouble. No one paid enough attention to The Other Lang Sister to bother kidnapping her.

She was about to change things, though. She had a plan. A good one. She was going to rise from the ashes of her old life and be the superhero of her new life. Maybe not Super Sophia, because her sister already had that locked. But someone else just as good, like Black Widow.

That was it. Charli could be Black Widow, eater of men, completely and utterly fearsome to the opposite sex. Black Widow was also awesome at her job and beautiful.

She could dye her hair red and buy some black outfits. It could work. She'd been telling herself to have a goal, hadn't she?

Now she just needed the right man to complete this picture.

"Paxton," she trilled as Heath's partner, the lean computer whiz, exited the new barn directly in her path. Lucky break. "Exactly who I was looking for."

Or rather, he was good enough.

"Me?" Paxton Pierce pointed at himself, a thin sheen of panic glazing his eyes that could be considered offensive if she let herself stop and think about it. "I was just…uh, Jonas is expecting me to move the horses from the south pasture with some of the other guys."

"You still have to do cowboy stuff even though you're technically doing security now?" she asked innocently, despite knowing that Paxton, Heath and Sophia's boyfriend, Ace Madden, were still working undercover as ranch hands. The fewer people who were aware of their real jobs, the better. "What if I have a security emergency? I might need you to subdue an intruder."

Heath was still watching her. She could feel his gaze between her shoulder blades, and it set off something inside that she could only describe as *delicious*. But she'd take that to her grave.

Charli let her fingertips graze Paxton's arm the way Black Widow might when she was being coy and flirty. It wasn't a chore. He was so cute with his clean looks and even cleaner Stetson, which looked like it had never hit the dirt. When she'd decided to move to the ranch and find a nice cowboy, Paxton Pierce was exactly what she'd pictured in her head.

Paxton could be the one to break her streak of cheating SOBs. He was clearly a great guy, one who called his mother every Sunday and had likely never seen the inside of a jail cell. Probably. This was her fantasy, and he could totally star in it.

Paxton's Adam's apple bobbed as he stepped just out of her reach. "If you have a security emergency, that's what McKay is for."

Yeah. Heath McKay was the problem, with his square jaw sporting a perpetual five o'clock shadow, and hooded gaze with even more shadows, and biceps that could make a woman drool. There was not one lick of *nice* anywhere in that man's body.

"Can't I switch babysitters midstream if I want to? Ask Ace to assign you to me instead?"

Man, there was an idea. Why hadn't she thought of that before now?

"Because—well, actually…" Poor guy swallowed so fast that he almost choked. "I'm what you call the brains. McKay is the brawn. Not that he's not smart, but his talents are definitely in the physical realm."

Oh, there was absolutely no question about the validity of that statement. But seriously. They'd caught the guy who had been terrorizing Sophia. The university people had squirreled away the gold coin she and Ace had found. What was there, really, to protect Charli from?

"I like a man with brains," she said with a little laugh.

Paxton did not seem bowled over by her charm. That was deflating. Maybe she should reel it back a little. Come at this from another angle. What would Black Widow do? She wouldn't sit around and wait for a man to figure out how awesome she was.

"Maybe you could find some time to ride with me out to the west pasture?" Charli fluttered her lashes. "I need to do a practice trail ride run before the guests start arriving next week."

That's when she'd start being taken seriously around the ranch. When people would see her as the other Ms. Lang instead of Charli, the screwup sister of the boss. As soon as she and Sophia welcomed the first guests, this place would stop being an inheritance and start being a dude ranch.

The Cowboy Experience. It had been her idea, one that she was secretly so proud of that she sometimes danced around in a circle of glee that Sophia had taken the suggestion.

Soon, she'd be able to forget she'd gotten fired from her last job at a pet store. A *pet store* for crying out loud. Where she'd been in charge of cleaning birdcages.

"Uh." Paxton glanced around feverishly. "I'd love to go on a trail ride but I, uh, I have to go do a thing with Jonas?"

"Are you sure? You don't sound sure."

Paxton edged away, pulling at his shirt collar as he practically tripped over his own two cowboy boots. "I'm sure. Ask McKay to ride with you on your trail ride, uh…thing."

She watched him go, the sun beating down on her back, vaguely disappointed Black Widow channeling had not gone well. But what did she expect? That she'd magically figure out in the course of two minutes how to not be a train wreck when it came to her love life? More practice needed, stat.

But when she turned around, Heath was standing a scant two feet away.

Not the sun on her back, then. *Him.* It was always him, right there, leaning against the fence, arms crossed in that insolent slouch that screamed Lock Up Your Daughters. His battered hat had seen more than its share of action, as had the very lived-in body underneath it. A scar ran along the base of his neck as if someone had tried to slice his throat but then abruptly stopped.

The man reeked of promise and next-level decadence.

Heath tipped his chin, his heated blue eyes tracking her with a lazy, practiced sweep. "Maybe you should try on someone your own size."

"Like who? You?"

She crossed her arms and stared him down in kind, but she had a feeling her own sweep of his cut torso and legs that went on forever had a lot more intensity in it than she'd like. It wasn't fair. No human should be that perfectly put together.

"Yeah. You could do worse."

"I have," she informed him sweetly. "That's how I know exactly what I'd find inside your box of chocolates. No interest in a repeat, thanks. You can toddle off and go do whatever undercover security agents do when they're pretending to be cowboys. I'm sure you're bored out of your mind watching me anyway."

"Bored is not the word I'd use."

Nonchalance rolled from him in waves, as if nothing bothered him, which pushed every single one of her buttons. A man this hot must have a volcano under his skin and she'd pay money to see it erupt. It would serve him right for harassing her.

"Well, when you think of the right word, don't come find me," she shot back and pivoted to walk away, speaking to him over her shoulder. "I'm going back to the house. Where I'll be doing very boring things that don't need your attention."

"Pierce is all wrong for you," he called, and she could almost hear his mouth tipping up in that amused smile that fooled no one. "You need someone you can't run roughshod over."

"I'll keep that in mind."

She escaped into the house, shutting the door of the blue Victorian behind her, then leaned on it, her lungs curiously unable to drag in air all at once. That man drove her bananas. But that didn't stop the frappé mode activating on her insides whenever he was around.

There had to be a cure for that. She'd tried going out with him once, just to see if she could burn off the attraction by feeding it. No dice. She'd spent the whole time with a heightened awareness that it wouldn't take Heath McKay more than about five minutes to break her heart. And she'd yet to patch it back together after the last loser had finished with it.

Careful to stay away from the windows in case *he* was peering through one, Charli skirted the kitchen island and dashed for the front door. Her babysitter was likely still stationed near the back door, his gaze trained on it in the event she made a reappearance.

Joke was on him. She lived to give him the slip.

No one put Charli in the corner. Well, except for the times she did it to herself. Which was most times. But that was the beauty of her brand-new plan. She was reinventing herself. No more screwing up. The time for that had long passed.

Skipping out the front door was a piece of cake. She had a lot of practice exiting a building without making a sound. She'd done it as a teenager plenty of times—it was easier to sneak out than it was to upset her single mother who was doing the best she could to raise three daughters after Charli's deadbeat dad had taken off.

Then there was the time she'd had to back up quickly after coming home to her apartment early to find Toby in bed with a very enthusiastic woman who was not Charli. Definitely not the time to hit a squeaky floor joist.

Better to stay off that subject before she forgot she was over Toby's cheating hide.

Back outside, Charli rounded the house near the long drive and headed for the woods. She really did have to scout the area for her trail ride, but she'd skip the horse this time. Too visible.

Heath would insist on coming along and she wasn't about to fall for that trap. The more time they spent together, the harder it would be to convince herself she wasn't attracted to him.

This circular path to the woods meant she had to veer close to the encampment where all the university people lived. They had said it would be temporary, but it was starting to feel like they'd never leave. Over two dozen tents lined the south pasture, most of them housing archaeologists or anthropologists or some other kinds of *ologists* with names that were largely unpronounceable by regular humans. There were some museum people thrown into the mix too, or at least that was her understanding, after they'd found the jade beads from some dead guy's tomb in Mexico. Pakal the Great.

Apparently, her deadbeat father had actually found some kind of treasure during his frequent jaunts to the Yucatan. The whole time he'd been busy ignoring his family, he'd scored some priceless artifacts and then buried them in various places around his father's ranch.

Grandpa Lang had died, then left the ranch to Sophia, Charli and their baby sister, Veronica, who had yet to check out her inheritance. Ergo, they now owned the treasure too, for whatever good that did when Sophia had unilaterally decided all the stuff should go back to Mexico.

As long as the *ologists* left before the guests got here, they could have the dead guy's tomb decorations.

And then Heath would be free to leave the ranch. No more laser beams between her shoulder blades. No more lying awake at night fantasizing about threading her fingers through his almost shoulder-length thick, curly hair, mussed from a day of hat-wearing, cowboy things.

"Hello, luv," a silky voice said from behind her.

Charli glanced over her shoulder to see one of the university guys with his eyes glued to her butt. He wore a Harvard

T-shirt and a smirk that he'd likely developed around the silver spoon in his mouth.

"Hey. My eyes are up here." She pointed with two fingers to her face. "And it's Ms. Lang."

"Ah. You're one of the sisters." His gaze traveled up her front to land on her face as instructed, but his attention still felt a tad...off. "I'm Trevor Longley. Which Ms. Lang are you, Sophia or Charlotte?"

"Neither one." Not that she owed him any sort of explanation, but she couldn't stand it when someone called her Charlotte. "I'm Charli. Charlotte is a spider or a princess, take your pick, but don't address me that way if you expect an answer."

"Charli, then," he adapted smoothly, catching her hand in his and bringing it to his mouth in some kind of weird eighteenth-century mannerism that she'd seen a dozen times on *Bridgerton*.

In real life, it wasn't so charming. It was kind of creepy. Plus, this guy wasn't British. He did have that moneyed New England look about him, though, so maybe he thought that counted for some reason?

"Well, see you around, Trevor," she said in hopes he would take the hint.

He didn't. He fell into step beside her, hooking their elbows together as if they were old pals and she'd invited him along on her trail ride scouting trip. This was getting a little tiresome and a lot out of hand.

She disentangled their arms and scowled at him, which obviously didn't mean the same thing to Harvard guys as it did to everyone else, since he just laughed.

"That's no way to be," he said with what felt like forced cheerfulness. "We're going to be good friends, I can tell."

"Because I'm giving you all sorts of come-on-to-me vibes?" she asked witheringly. "Maybe you need your vision checked."

Trevor's smile got a little less friendly and developed an edge she didn't like. "That's no way to speak to a guest."

No, it wasn't. Should she reel it back? Practice being a little more friendly? She kind of sucked at that. But there was something off about Trevor that tripped her radar.

"You're not a guest, Trevor," she emphasized. "You're a grad student who is quickly wearing out his welcome."

Where was everyone else? There were supposed to be approximately nine trillion dig nerds around here. Every time she left the house, she tripped over more than her share, yet there was no movement from the temporary campground. The woods behind her felt eerily quiet.

Why hadn't she thought to scout for a trail in the front part of ranch land where the grad students usually didn't go? Because she'd been thinking about Heath, not anything that mattered.

"You're going to want to watch your mouth, Charlotte," he said sharply and that's when he grabbed her.

His fingers bit into her arm as she yelped. What was this guy's problem?

She couldn't get free. No amount of yanking pulled her arm loose and the last tug wrenched her shoulder. "You're hurting me."

And if she didn't figure this out, he could do a lot more than that. Genuine fear coated her throat.

"Good," he snarled, all traces of his previous cheer gone. "I'm trying to be nice to you but you're obviously a bi—"

"Take your hand off Ms. Lang."

Heath. His voice saturated the tense atmosphere, flooding her with relief.

His expression as hard as his body, Heath materialized at her side, towering over her. And Trevor. Who didn't seem to be aware of the fact that Heath McKay stood a head taller and outweighed him by fifty pounds of muscle.

"Find your own amusement, friend," Trevor tossed out, his

fingernails cutting into her skin. Also known as not following orders.

Heath cracked his neck, his gaze lethally honed into Trevor's face. "Looks like I have."

Chapter Two

Heath didn't like most people. He liked them even less when they came with a big sign on their forehead that read *I'm Entitled*.

This Harvard guy was going for some kind of prize, though, with a how-fast-can-I-die vibe, putting his hands on Charli like he had every right to, even as she was telling him no. Freaking dig nerds. They'd scurried into every nook and cranny on the ranch, causing problems and creating security nightmares.

Now this.

"Looks like you have? What's that supposed to mean?" Harvard snarled. "You think I'm going to share?"

Heath leveled his gaze, boring straight into the dude, giving him a giant opportunity to do the right thing so everyone could walk away. "I think you're going to provide me with about fourteen seconds of very satisfying entertainment. And then I'm going to deposit you in the back of a squad car to face assault charges. Or you can reassess the situation and make your own course adjustment."

Harvard glanced at Charli and then back at Heath and laughed. *Laughed*, like Heath habitually walked around issuing empty threats.

Just because he'd made a vow to stop solving things with his fists didn't mean he couldn't take a brief hiatus from his new, calmer persona. In fact, it would be his pleasure.

No. No punching the idiot. That wasn't how this should go down. Heath wasn't that guy anymore.

Okay, deep breath. He could do this without resorting to violence. There were other ways to handle handsy jerkoffs. Even when Heath had a signed contract that said he was responsible for keeping Charli safe and had unwritten latitude to do that however he saw fit.

"You're going to want to take a step back, *friend*," Heath informed Harvard with as much venom in his voice as he could muster.

"Or what?"

That was the million-dollar question, wasn't it? Old Heath would have put this guy in traction and enjoyed every second of it. But Margo's exact words when she'd dumped him zinged through his head 24/7, leaving no room for his temper to make an appearance. If he wanted to prove to her that he wasn't the hothead brawler she'd labeled him as, he had to stop acting like one.

He *wanted* to stop. He wasn't a SEAL any longer. Reacting with a cooler head worked much better for civilian life.

Another deep breath didn't soothe the seething mass of anger simmering under Heath's skin. Dark edges crowded his vision.

And Harvard's hand was still clamped around Charli's arm. She didn't look quite as terrified as she had, but she was still in distress and Heath needed to fix that.

"Or I'll help you take a step back," Heath said silkily without specifying how he'd accomplish that. "How do you think your bosses would feel about you manhandling the owner of the ranch where you've been invited to dig?"

Harvard tossed his head. "My father's lawyers will handle any trouble you stir up."

Of course they would. His father probably paid a retainer fee specifically for this jerk-wad, much of which would have likely been spent erasing previous assault charges. It wouldn't shock him to discover Harvard had the rap sheet of a choir boy working on his Eagle Scout.

Now Heath was good and righteously pissed. Some trash deserved to be taken out, ex-girlfriends' opinions aside. "Then this is for both Charli and all the other women who have been standing in her shoes."

He popped the guy right in the nose. A good, hard, wholly satisfying jab that broke a lot of stuff that held his face together. The dark edges around Heath's vision dissolved. The dig nerd screamed and finally released Charli in favor of cupping his nose, which was currently pouring blood into his palm.

Nice. Heath took the opportunity to shuffle Charli behind him, where he could feel the heat of her warming his back. She clutched his arm, peering around it at her former assailant, clearly quite happy to have the wall of Heath between them.

It made him happy, too.

"I'll have you arrested for this!" Harvard announced, his bravado still in full force even after being treated to what amounted to the opening volley. "Do you know who my parents are?"

"Equally entitled brats?" he hazarded a guess, rolling up on the balls of his feet in case Harvard got some kind of idea that whatever dozen or so boxing classes he'd taken last semester would in fact help him here. This guy was the type who seemed incapable of taking a hint. Or a hit.

"My father—"

"Is not here," he finished for him. "And I would ask myself how hard it will be to dial him up after I break every single one of your fingers."

Finally, Harvard developed a slight glint of panic somewhere in the vast unreached places of his brain. "You can't do that."

"Well, let's deconstruct that, shall we?" Heath offered, crossing his arms lazily as if he had all the time in the world for a chat. Which he did, since Charli was his only job, but he'd already broken his vow once, and he'd rather not do it a second time. With his fists tucked away, it might be easier to remember to use his words instead. "If by 'can't' you mean I'm incapable, try me. Happy to give you a demonstration. If by 'can't', you mean you're going to stop me, thanks. I needed that laugh today. Or maybe you meant 'can't' as in it's a reprehensible thing to do and my moral fiber will prevent me from taking such a heinous step? Which is it?"

Harvard looked confused. Not a surprise. Most people didn't expect a guy they called the Enforcer in the Teams to have a vocabulary too. His ability to spit out twenty-dollar words was what had first won over Margo. She'd often told him how sexy the combo of muscles and a mouth was. Until he used the muscles. That, she wasn't so fond of.

"Heath, it's okay," Charli murmured from behind him, her palm still wrapped around his arm. "I'm fine. We can go."

"It's not okay," he growled, his gaze still boring into the dig nerd. "Because Harvard here isn't quite convinced that he should be taking a new path in life, one that leads him away from the wages of sin and toward the kingdom of righteousness where he respects women and fully understands the meaning of the word no."

He could practically hear Charli's eye roll. "I don't think you're going to convert him in the space of five minutes."

"I definitely won't if you don't let me continue."

Harvard tipped his head back, presumably to help with the blood flow issues his broken nose was causing him. "I need to go to the hospital."

Reluctantly, Heath nodded. "That you do. I'll let you live on one condition. That you swear never to touch another woman unless she asks you to. Square?"

"Whatever, dude. I'm walking away. Leave me alone."

"That is also up to you. I would be thrilled to never look at your face again," Heath informed him pleasantly. "You come near Charli, you get to find out what broken fingers feel like. You stay away from her, we never speak again. Your choice."

In what amounted to the smartest decision he'd made thus far, Harvard marched away, blood dripping from his fingers. Which left Heath with an even bigger problem—Charli. The thorn in his side. The Lang sister Madden had dubbed a loose cannon.

Heath just called her trouble. She even smelled like it, a infuriatingly indecipherable combo scent that was both feminine and dangerous at the same time. Probably because every time he caught wind of it, his body tensed for what followed: a punch of arousal to his gut and an unsettled certainty that she was about to piss him off.

"You're something else, McKay," Charli said, her voice a lot stronger now that Harvard wasn't around. "I thought you were going to talk him to death. Breaking his fingers would have been a lot more satisfying."

For him too. But he'd reeled it back, letting the dragon inside sleep. Maybe he could do this after all. Wouldn't it be something when he could show Margo that she'd called it wrong? That he was capable of being husband material.

But what would be more awesome—Charli not putting him in a position to have to break anyone's bones. He spun. "On that note, Ms. Lang, let's talk about why you went out the front door, like that was going to stop me from knowing you'd left the house?"

Charli had the grace to look embarrassed. "You have freakish stealth senses. It's infuriating."

"That's not an answer." He didn't uncross his arms, mostly because he hadn't lost the urge to break something and the only things around were a large rock or a tree, and he'd grown attached to the skin on his knuckles. "You can't give me the slip, so it's baffling to me that you keep trying. Maybe stop?"

"Maybe quit following me around?" she suggested sweetly, lifting her brown hair off her neck in an unpracticed way that would make a lesser man salivate.

Yeah, it was hot outside. Which was why he'd much rather be sitting in the shade doing surveillance with Charli safe in the house. "Talk to Sophia and Madden if you don't like it."

"Maybe I will. Paxton would be a much better choice to play bodyguard."

No. He wouldn't. Charli terrified him, which was amusing. But it was also not a good mix when trying to handle the difficult task of keeping her safe. Especially since she seemed determined to increase the complexity by refusing to cooperate.

"Good luck with that," he told her. "In the meantime, I need you to help me do my job. Go back to the house and stay there."

That way, he could circle back with their mutual friend Harvard and make sure the dude understood he'd made an ironclad promise that Heath would be helping him keep for the foreseeable future. It would be best if the dig nerd went back to New England and saved everyone some grief, but odds of that happening were slim, unless Heath encouraged him to further consider the idea.

"I have things to do." Charli's crossed arms mirrored his.

He fought the urge to uncross them for her. Touching her would open up a whole can of worms he'd rather leave sealed tight, and he'd already pushed the limits of his restraint by not breaking more of Harvard's face than he had.

"I'm a fan of things," he told her with feigned nonchalance that he wished would magically calm down all the stuff writhing to get out. "I can do things, too."

"I bet you can," she muttered. "I should have qualified that with *solo* things."

"There is no solo at Hidden Creek Ranch. Not for you." He

left off the implied bit, namely that she caused her own problems by not trusting him to do his job.

"I'll just sneak out again," she told him pertly. "So there's really no point in insisting that I go back to the house."

"Then I'll just come inside with you," he insisted through gritted teeth, willing his tone back into the realm of tranquil and collected. "You can't win this, Charli."

She stared at him, the air crackling between them with tension and a lot of other stuff that he'd refused to examine too hard. The whole point of New Heath was to show Margo what he was capable of in a relationship. Margo was it for him. He just needed to figure out how to get her back. He had zero interest in Charli Lang. The weird sparks between them didn't count.

"Fine. I'll go back to the house but only because I have a headache," she conceded. To her credit, she didn't protest nearly as much as he'd expected her to when he proceeded to escort her back the way she'd come, restricting herself to only a bit of jostling and thrown elbows.

Once he clicked the door shut—with her on the right side of it this time—he texted Madden to double up on rounds to ensure someone had eyes on all sides of the house while Heath made a short side trip to help the dig nerd pack up and leave.

Okay, and maybe to give himself some time to cool off. Because he was not cool. At all.

Replaying the scene in his head where the jerk-wad put his hands on Charli wasn't helping. Neither was reliving the feel of her standing behind him as he faced down the threat. He liked protecting those who couldn't do it for themselves. It was in his blood.

What he did not like was the sheer difficulty of stuffing his feelings into a tight container. It should be easier to handle a simple thing like reining in his temper. Granted, he'd made the vow to give up Old Heath before being assigned to watch over a champion button-pusher like Charli Lang.

But still. He'd done a lot of hard things in his life, not the least of which was earning his Trident after BUD/S training. Lots of guys rang out. But Heath had persevered, then spent a decade serving Uncle Sam overseas, ridding the world of filth one deployment at a time.

The loose-cannon Lang sister was not going to beat him.

Determined to ride off his anger, Heath saddled a horse and rode out to the university encampment. His mood didn't improve. Instead of tempting himself twice in one day, he found Harvard's project manager and had a civil word about reassigning the jerk-wad to another dig. The less people put him in a situation that required him to reel it back, the better.

Then he did a perimeter sweep along the east fence line at a full gallop that put enough endorphins in his bloodstream to take the edge off. Who knew that horseback riding would be the magic ticket to getting his sanity back?

Slowing to a walk to allow his mount—both of them, really—a chance to breathe, Heath focused on his surroundings, gradually aware of a prickle along the back of his neck. It was a warning sign he'd learned never to ignore, which was the reason he'd come home from Afghanistan alive.

Something wasn't right. What?

There. A circular patch of grass lay in the wrong direction from the surrounding area.

Heath cantered over to it, peering down at the green someone had stomped flat. No question it was a human, because in the center lay a couple of cigarette butts.

No ranch hand would have left behind something like that, not if they wanted to keep their job and their hide, because Jonas would have both if he caught one of his guys littering where the horses grazed. Not to mention how harmful a cigarette butt would be to a horse if one accidentally ingested it.

One of the university or museum people, then?

Or two of them… Heath homed in on the second circle, not as obvious as the first. It had been a meeting. One orchestrated outside of security camera range. For Heath's money, he'd say because one or both weren't supposed to be on site, or they would have just chatted anywhere on the property.

It was hard to tell from the evidence how long ago this meeting had taken place, but Heath recalled it had rained about a week ago, so probably since then. But the horses had been in this pasture two days ago, and several of them liked to eat the grass on the other side of the fence. Odds were, they would have trod all over these circles, destroying them.

So within the last two days. At least one, maybe even both these people weren't supposed to be here, which made them a threat to Charli and Sophia.

Oh, no. Not on his watch.

Adrenaline poured into his system, priming him for battle. A haze clouded his vision. He kicked the horse into gear, a warrior on the warpath.

Just as the horse hit a full gallop, he remembered. Forced a breath, like he'd been training himself to do. He wasn't the Enforcer anymore. He couldn't be. But then what did that make him? Who was this post-SEAL Heath McKay if he wasn't that guy?

Heath pulled the horse back into a trot and then stopped, rubbing the back of his neck as the sun baked his shirt into his sweat-soaked skin. What could New Heath do to handle this situation calmly and without violence?

Inform. Madden and Pierce needed to be updated on the situation.

Track. Heath could follow the trail and see where it led. Nothing more. And then he'd see what was what.

Chapter Three

"Earth to Charli."

Charli blinked and focused on Sophia's face across the desk that they were sharing for the moment. "Sorry. Did you say something?"

Sophia set her pen down on the pad that held her written to-do list, the one that she regularly vetted to see if the task would make it to the real to-do list on her phone. It was exhausting even thinking about having a tryout to-do list, as if one list wasn't good enough—the tasks actually had to *audition* for a spot.

"I said, is everything on track for the decorator to finish tomorrow?" her sister told her. "For the third time. I guess I don't have to ask what's taking all your attention after that big production Heath made to escort you into the house."

The wry twist of Sophia's lips set off a lick of guilt in Charli's gut and she glanced away, toward the wall of the office. "It's not what you think."

Nor did Charli think telling Sophia exactly what had happened with Trevor the Handsy Harvard grad student would be a great plan either. She'd just side with Heath and that would make it twice as hard for Charli to leave the house without her bodyguard in tow.

"I get it. I have a hard time concentrating sometimes too, when I know there's just a couple of walls between me and Ace." Sophia's voice took on this dreamy quality that she didn't have to explain at all.

Or rather, Charli would prefer that she didn't. Everyone knew Sophia and Ace were gaga over each other and they'd happily rub it in everyone's faces if given half a chance. It was both nauseating and jealousy-inducing.

"Yeah, you don't actually get it," she grumbled. "McKay is a pain in my butt, that's all."

"I thought you guys were dating."

There was a glint in Sophia's eye that Charli didn't like. It was part *I'm about to interfere* and part *what in the world is wrong with Ace's partner?*

"It didn't work out."

"Oh."

She could see Sophia trying to reason out in her head what the issue could have possibly been, and odds were high that telling her Heath was *exactly* Charli's type wouldn't actually explain anything. Neither did Charli feel like spelling out why Heath being her type wasn't a good thing. Sophia never made bad choices or screwed up anything.

This ranch—the Cowboy Experience—was Charli's chance to change her fate. Falling back into the same old same old traps wasn't happening. Except that meant she had to focus and stop making Sophia repeat herself.

More to the point, she had to stop daydreaming about Heath's biceps. And his unexpected chivalrous streak. Really, what woman could resist a man who *defended* her, and then threatened the loser who'd cornered her?

She'd never felt so feminine and important and protected in her life. Because of *Heath*.

It was messing with her.

Charli squared her shoulders. "The decorator will be done tomorrow. Guaranteed. I paid a little extra for a rush job."

"You did what?" Sophia set down the pen she'd just picked up. "Char, you can't do that without talking to me. We have a budget."

"Yeah, but I'm an equal partner," she argued, thrilled to have that leg to stand on. "I have to make decisions sometimes without consulting you due to time constraints. I'm trying to get a job done on schedule and did what I deemed best in that moment. Doing this together means you have to trust me."

Spoken like a true Black Widow in the making. Black Widow wouldn't flinch when faced with questions about her choices.

Sophia blew out a breath and nodded. "Okay. You're right."

She was? Charli stared at Sophia, convinced she'd misheard. "Okay? As in...okay? You're fine that I spent the extra money?"

This was a test. A trap. Something. Sophia never thought Charli was right about much of anything.

Shrugging, Sophia gave her a look. "I'm trying to do as suggested. Trust you. I don't like it, but I can't be in control of everything or there's no point in doing this together. So, yes. You're right."

Well. Charli crossed her arms and sank down a little bit in her chair as something light and fluttery beat at her heart. "That was a lovely apology."

Sophia rolled her eyes. "Don't get used to it. Switching gears after a lifetime of being a control freak isn't something I'm going to accomplish with a lot of grace."

A grin tugged at Charli's mouth. "I can give you a lot more chances to practice."

"Please—" Sophia cut off whatever she was about to say when someone knocked at the door.

Ace poked his head in without waiting for Sophia to call out to him, his trademark cowboy hat the color of beach sand set low on his forehead. "We have a situation."

Her sister's boyfriend had two modes: mushy in love with

Sophia and all business. This was definitely the latter. He bristled with authority, looking like he could handle anything thrown at him with efficiency and expertise. And he had. He'd gone searching for Sophia with righteous fury when she'd been kidnapped, yet still managed to give off the impression he'd invented cold calculation. He was attractive, if you liked the clean-cut all-American type.

In short, he was the opposite of his partners. An iceberg to Heath's volcano and Paxton's computer brain. Charli often wondered how in the world they'd become friends.

Sophia sat up straighter, her expression alert. "What's going on?"

Ace stepped inside the office, his hat automatically in his hand because he was that kind of guy. "McKay found evidence in the south pasture that we might have some unwelcome company on the property."

"There are a lot of people on the ranch who are unwelcome," Charli said with an arched brow. "You're going to have to be more specific."

Ace glanced at her. "It was a meeting between at least two people, conducted out of range of the security cameras. That means at least one of them isn't on the official roster of those authorized to be on site as part of the excavation team. In the digital age, we assume that a face-to-face conversation means someone didn't want their association tracked and also has a good handle on the ranch routine since they picked a time with low risk of being seen together by a staff member. All of that adds up to a problem."

Sophia's expression flattened. "An associate of Cortez?"

That was the name of the guy who had kidnapped her sister, but he was in jail with no chance of bail. Charli recalled that he'd given the authorities a very limited amount of information about his associates, but the one name he'd offered up had landed like a bomb: Karl Davenport. Her father's treasure hunting partner.

"It's possible," Ace admitted.

"Cortez only had one associate who matters." Sophia and Ace both looked at Charli. "It's true. I'm just saying it. It's Karl, right? That's who you think it is. Isn't that why Ace is here having this chat with us?"

The implications of that—she couldn't even wrap her brain around it. But she did know one thing. It meant there was a lot of Heath in her future unless she figured out something else superfast.

"My liaison at the sheriff's office confirmed that Karl Davenport is still at large, yes," Ace said. "And most certainly dangerous, given that he hired Cortez to rough up Sophia and scare her away from the ranch."

"Oh, man, this is not good." Sophia tapped her pen against her paper to-do list, her mind obviously on the hundreds of things that they still had to do to get the ranch ready to open its doors to guests in less than a week. What she did not look like was scared. Nothing scared Sophia. It was a skill Charli would like to learn.

"Maybe it's someone else," Charli suggested with a confidence she wasn't sure she felt.

This was the last thing they needed. The guests would be here soon, and it was already going to be hard enough to navigate around all the dig nerds. Throwing another threat into the mix didn't help.

Sophia stared at her. "Like who? Dad?"

"Well, maybe." That had honestly never occurred to her, but she latched onto the alternative with gusto. "Why isn't that possible? Just because we haven't seen him in years doesn't mean he won't make an appearance now that the university people are digging up his cache. Maybe he wants it back."

"That's also a possibility," Ace said with zero inflection, giving away nothing of what he was thinking. "Which doesn't mean David Lang isn't a threat to either of you. You'll forgive me if I wait to pass judgment on his paternal instincts until I have a reason to trust him."

"That's fair," Sophia said, and Charli nodded. "You'll certainly not get an argument from either of us on that front."

"Yeah, I'm happy to pass full judgment of his father skills right here and now," Charli said with a scowl. "David Lang is a name on my birth certificate. That's it."

Honestly, the idea of their father roaming around the ranch that he'd never bothered to claim as his birthright might sit worse with Charli than knowing it was Karl Davenport out there plotting harm to people she loved. David Lang was a parasite on humanity. The kind of man who dumped his responsibilities at the drop of a hat, who thought nothing of donating sperm and skipping town in favor of gold over his family.

"We're assuming nothing at this point," Ace told them. "Other than the fact that whoever it is doesn't intend to march up to us with identification and his hands raised. So we have a security issue that my team is handling. Needs to be allowed to handle."

And that was the real reason he was here. Charli could see it plastered all over his face. "You came to make sure I'm properly chastised about ditching my shadow earlier."

Sophia glared at her. "Charli. We talked about this. You can't roam around without Heath. That's the whole reason he's here. To keep you safe."

"I know," she grumbled as the reality crashed over her. If she wanted to cross the finish line with the Cowboy Experience, she had to give a little—and that meant agreeing to be babysat. "I hear everyone loud and clear. I solemnly swear I will drag McKay around with me everywhere I go, including the shower and to bed."

And that was precisely where she assumed he'd end up if given half an inch of latitude. She could see it now, the way he'd disarm her with the perfectly logical excuse that he could protect her much better if he never left her side and wouldn't it be handy to have someone to wash her hair while he was there and already naked?

Yeah. She could see it. Her brain seemed pretty set on looping that scene through her mind's eye over and over again. She nearly groaned as she pictured exactly how much of her bed Heath would take up.

Ace's expression, to his credit, didn't budge an inch. "The logistics of how he protects you are between you and him. I'm only asking that you don't leave the house unless you're in the company of the man tasked with ensuring you don't end up on the wrong end of a nine millimeter."

"Do you think we need to consider delaying the opening of the ranch?" Sophia asked Ace in all seriousness, like that was an option she was considering.

"Hold on," Charli protested as it felt an awful lot like the office floor had turned into quicksand. "I said I wouldn't go anywhere without Heath. You have Ace watching out for you. The guests will be fine. No one cares about them."

"Well, we don't know what these new intruders might want," Ace said, hesitating. "We can't be sure they aren't unknown threats with unknown motives. They could be after the treasure themselves, hoping to beat Davenport and the university people to the punch. Pierce ran a lot of analyses, but we don't have enough evidence to be certain about anything."

"We should consider delaying the opening, then," Sophia said with a nod, her mouth tight.

"No, we can't consider that." Charli pinched the bridge of her nose, as her plan started circling the drain. "Just give it a few days. Ace and his team will be stepping up surveillance and stuff, right?"

Ace confirmed that with a nod, tapping his hat against his wrist. "I'm hiring a couple of guys to start doing perimeter sweeps in rotation. We're not leaving anything to chance. The more information we can get, the better prepared we'll be to handle whoever these guys are."

"We don't have a couple of days," Sophia countered. "We have one day. If we're going to delay the opening, we have to give people enough notice to cancel flights and rebook."

Charli's temples started throbbing. "We're not telling people to cancel flights. The opening is happening."

Otherwise, her stake in this would slip away. This was the only thing she'd ever had in her life that she could point to and say, *This is mine. The Cowboy Experience is happening because of me.*

"Give it a day, Soph," Ace told her, and something passed between them that made Charli's throat hurt. They had something special that most people would never get to experience, herself included. Why couldn't she get interested in a straight arrow like Ace? Surely there were more guys like him out there.

Heath McKay wasn't one of them, though. That fact presented itself to her loud and clear when she texted him that she had to go to the store later, like a good girl who did what she was told.

She stepped out of the house and into the maelstrom of testosterone and biceps on her porch. "Punctual. I like that in a man."

Heath reset his hat on his head, the new angle highlighting his amazing cheekbones. "Agreeable. I like that in a woman."

She made a face at him. "Don't get used to it. As soon as you figure out who had the clandestine meeting in the south pasture, I'm back to inventing creative ways to frustrate you."

"Pretty sure that's still going on," he muttered as he opened the passenger door to his truck, an ancient flatbed that she'd always assumed he'd procured from somewhere as part of his cover. It didn't fit him in the slightest. A sleek Jaguar was more his speed, with a deep, throaty engine, ready to pounce or sprint away pending his mood.

"I'm here. In the truck with you," she pointed out when he

slid into the driver's seat, then nearly swallowed her tongue as the cab filled with Heath.

It was more than a physical presence. She could feel him along her skin even though both of his hands were on the wheel. Delicious. And then some. But she had no intention of feeding his ego by letting him see her reaction.

"You in here is what's frustrating," he commented mildly as he backed out of the circular drive in front of the main house. "What store are we going to?"

"Whatever one in town carries tampons," she said and grinned as he shot her a look. "What? You wanted to spend twenty-four seven following around a woman, congrats. This is part of life."

"Do you hate all men or am I just special?"

"Men are generally the spawn of Satan, but I will admit a particular pleasure at riling you specifically," she informed him with genuine cheer, a minor miracle given the way her day had gone thus far.

Heath rolled to a stop at a red light and turned his head to treat her to a once-over that wiped the smile right off her face. It was the first time she'd registered him really *looking* at her, and she suddenly had the worst feeling she'd turned to glass. As if he could see everything, even the things she didn't want him to.

"What?" she croaked out defensively. "Is my shirt backward?"

"Not all men are evil," he countered. "Though before too long, I'm going to be asking for the name of the one who left you with that impression."

Oh, man, he'd definitely walked right in and helped himself to a whole heap of Charli's vulnerabilities without her consent. That was not okay.

What would Black Widow do?

She'd kick the man on her way to the curb. "Beg to differ. You can ask for a name, but you're not going to get it. And for your information, more than one man has given me my set-in-stone viewpoint about the origins of the male species, so the odds of you changing my mind are zero."

"Wanna bet?"

Chapter Four

Wanna bet?

A throwaway phrase. One Heath hadn't necessarily meant for her to take literally. But Charli's brows lifted as she contemplated Heath, and dang if he didn't like being the subject of her perusal. Even if she was looking at him as though he'd started spouting sonnets. And yes, he did know what a sonnet was, but he wasn't planning on reciting any to her.

What had just instantly scrolled through his mind was way better.

"Do I want to bet what?" she asked.

"Whether I can change your mind. About men," he clarified because she was totally the type to misread this very specific offer, which definitely needed about a hundred guardrails to keep it from going south. "You've obviously got an ex in your rearview mirror who treated you like a disposable wipe. I'm saying I can prove to you that not all men are like that. I'm not like that."

Charli threw back her head and laughed, a silvery sound that shouldn't be coaxing ripples along his skin, especially not when he was reasonably sure he was the source of her amusement.

"It's not funny," he growled.

"It is on so many levels that I can't fully address each one fast enough." She held up a finger. "But really, I only need the one point. You have nothing I want, so there's nothing to bet."

Now she was talking his language. There was nothing on this earth Heath liked more than a challenge, and she'd just dropped one right in his lap. Never mind that he'd come up with this idea strictly because they had to spend every minute in each other's company. Why not be productive at the same time? Practice being New Heath a little.

Except she'd turned it on its head because that's what Charli did—disrupt things.

"Darling, you are such a liar. I have plenty you want," he drawled and grinned when a telltale flush rose up high on her cheekbones. "But I wasn't talking about that kind of bet. As much as I am thinking about some very interesting images you've kindly put into my head, I'm suggesting totally different stakes that I am positive even you will appreciate."

Heath kept his gaze trained on the road ahead, giving Charli plenty of space to work up a healthy curiosity. He could practically hear her teeth grinding from here, which put a nice little kick in his chest to know he'd managed to get her worked up. Finally, she crossed her arms.

"Spill it, McKay. You clearly have something up your sleeve. The sooner you lay it out, the sooner I can shoot it down."

"Shame signs."

The hard cross of her arms over her midsection went slack. "Go on."

"The bet is simple. If I don't change your mind about men, I'll wear a shame sign and post it to social media. You get to decide what it says. Heck, I'll even let you make the sign."

The exact moment when she got interested in this idea played out in a very subtle head tilt. A lesser man might have missed it, particularly one who paid a lot of attention to driving. But Heath had stayed alive in Afghanistan by honing his ability to read everything about his surroundings.

And she was frothing at the mouth to watch him lose. Game on.

"You're serious."

"As an undertaker at a hanging."

Her mouth twitched. "You're something else, my guy. I'm assuming that the reverse is true. If you somehow pull a rabbit out of that Stetson and hit whatever criteria I come up with that proves you've changed my mind about men, I have to wear your shame sign."

"Of course." He reset his hat on his head, already contemplating the sheer number of bunnies that he'd be forced to conjure before too long. Because she was going to say yes. He could feel it. "I already have the wording picked out. 'I was wrong, and Heath was right.'"

"You know my problem with men is that they're all horn dogs who can't keep their pants on around other women, right?"

Yeah, he wasn't confused. Trying not to be too stung by her tone, he glanced at her as he parked in the lot at the Walmart in Gun Barrel City. "What exactly happened with the former Mr. Charli that gave you the idea that's difficult?"

Her expression iced over. "There's no former Mr. Charli. And that's not part of the deal. No history lesson included. Take it or leave it. And note that my idea of faithful is extremely stringent. You'll get zero freebies like a random woman's number in your phone who's 'just a friend.'"

She accompanied this with exaggerated air quotes and a sneer that hooked him in a place he was pretty sure she hadn't been trying to reach. He stared at her, trying to figure out why the rock she'd stuck in her chest to replace her heart bothered him so much.

Charli meant nothing to him. What did he care if she'd been burned so badly by her crappy ex?

"For the record, I'm not a player," he murmured. That had

never been Margo's problem. "But I'm game for leaving our history out of the mix."

He was more than happy to keep his motivation for all this to himself, though he would have explained it if pressed. Probably. Maybe not all of it. Actually, he wasn't even sure he could fully express why this bet had become such a big deal so quickly, but it was.

Because if he could prove to Charli that he was different than her cheating ex-boyfriend, that he had what it took to treat a woman like a queen, then he could prove to Margo that he was husband material. Right? Charli would get to see a man who knew how to toe the line. One who could be more righteous than a choirboy on Easter Sunday with zero passionate outbursts to his name.

And Heath got a free pass to practice for the real thing. No one would get hurt. Everyone wins.

It was the most brilliant plan in the universe.

"How is this even going to work, McKay?" Charli asked, the thread of incredulity lifting the ends of her words past the point where it sounded like she was still on board. "To prove you're not a serial cheater, we'd have to get married and be together until the day we die. And you and I would probably kill each other before we hit our one-week anniversary."

He had to laugh because yeah. "That's what makes this such a great deal for you. You get the Heath McKay special and don't even have to worry about whether you can do your part long-term."

"Wait. What?" He had her attention now.

People streamed by his flatbed on their way into the store, but neither of them got out of the truck. With one hand draped over the steering wheel, he lifted a shoulder as if it was obvious. "This is a bet. You have to do something for me in exchange. This is not just a one-way street."

Though if this worked, he would get the most benefit. Old

Heath would be laid to rest forever. New Heath would emerge as a man worthy of an elegant, classy woman like Margo.

"You're saying you don't think I can do my part?" she ground out and then seemed to think better of doing her own digging in. "What are you even talking about? Is there more to this than you bringing me flowers or whatever passes in your head as a lame attempt to change my opinion about men?"

"Yeah. You have to give me a fair shot. Unlike the last time."

Clearly stymied by the direction of the conversation, Charli stared out the front windshield as if she hoped to glimpse whatever had captured his interest on the other side of the glass. Ha. Little did she know that every iota of his focus was on her. The shift of her leg against the seat. The way her index finger tapped against her elbow. A restless energy that his own recognized. It was part of what fascinated him about her, that she could be so magnetically alluring without a power suit or a pair of ice pick stilettos in sight.

And he didn't have any better handle on her this time than he had last time.

Nor had he realized that her previous rejection still prickled a little. Maybe that had snuck a few tendrils into the roots of this deal. She didn't have to know that.

"For your information, I gave you a fair shot last time," she informed him loftily.

Also known as the one and only time he'd tried to breach her defenses with the atrocious crime of taking her to dinner at the steak place one street over. He still wasn't sure what had spooked her, but since his heart belonged to Margo, the way it had ended—with her fleeing from his truck the moment he'd pulled up at the ranch—was for the best.

He'd only been trying to move on with the one woman who had sparked his interest in the months since Margo had kicked him to the curb. See if he did that again. This bet wasn't about that.

"We have different definitions of what constitutes a fair

shot," he countered mildly. "So different that I'm making it part of the terms of the bet. For this to work, you have to commit. Three weeks. No arguments. No weaseling out of it because you have a headache."

Suspicion narrowed her eyes as she swung her gaze to meet his. "What do you get out of this?"

The million-dollar question. Suddenly he wasn't so keen to lay all of his cards on the table, after all. "An opportunity to do my job without having to hunt you down for one. We have to spend time together, whether you like it or not. This at least gives us both a chance to relax a bit."

Truth. Or as much of it as he planned to give her.

Her chuckle caught him off guard. "You're the least relaxing person I've ever met and you're the liar if you don't say the same about me."

"I meant relax in the knowledge that we're stuck together," he shot back with a smirk. "You can't ditch me for three weeks. During that time, you treat it like we're in a relationship. I'm betting you can't do it."

Man, she was good. Not a muscle in her body twitched. He would know. He was so dialed into her that he might be able to detect if she so much as moved a hair. That's the only reason the slow smile that spread across her face punched him so hard in the gut.

"You're one more stipulation away from a straitjacket," she said and that's when he knew he had her. "Counter term. You have to take me on official dates. One a week for every single week of the three. You're paying. And no cop-outs. McDonald's doesn't count."

Shocked that she'd fallen right into his trap like that, he contemplated her, his own suspicions raising one of his brows. "You'd agree to that?"

She lifted her hands. "What, to letting a man turn himself inside out to impress me with his imaginative ability to conjure new and noteworthy date locales week after week? Yeah. I'd sign up for that in a heartbeat."

"Then we have a deal." He stuck out his hand, wondering if she even realized he'd already won.

Because whatever number her ex had done on her, the creep had done him a huge favor. Heath McKay knew how to treat a woman. Where she'd gotten the idea that he couldn't keep it in his pants, he had no clue, but commitment was his middle name.

Where he struggled was tamping back his tendency to be over the top with it. Margo wanted refinement—that's what he'd give her. After he spent the next three weeks getting his technique honed. New Heath had free rein from here on out. No letting his emotions off the leash. Should be easy. This was Charli after all.

Charli stuck her hand in his and the jolt sang up his arm. She'd felt it too, judging by the way she snatched her hand back and turned to look out the passenger window. "You're going to a lot of trouble just to get me to stop ditching you."

"I'm a workaholic. Sue me," he commented with a grin. "Besides, I like to win."

"Same goes."

Oh, he had no doubt. There was only a certain kind of woman who would take a deal like this one, and it wasn't the sort who looked forward to having a man pick up the check. Odds were, she'd go hard in the direction of trying to trip him up, stringing women across his path in hopes of goading him into violating the terms.

On that note—since he hadn't been born yesterday—they needed to put a few things in blood before he'd ever agree that he'd lost this bet at the end of the three weeks. Which he already knew she'd try to claim regardless. "When we get back to the ranch, we're each going to write down our criteria for how we judge who wins. It goes in a sealed envelope. Mine to Sophia, yours to Ace."

"What good is that going to do?" she complained, instantly dismissing it with a curt slice of her hand. "I'm just going to write down something that will stack the deck toward me, and you'll write down the same for you and we'll argue about it till the cows come home."

"I mean we'll write it down for each other. And then if it's sealed, no one can argue that the criteria wasn't met."

For who knew what reason, that was the thing that got a reaction from her. And it was the strangest mix of slightly dazzled and a whole lot unhappy about it. "You're a lot slicker than I give you credit for."

"I'll take that as a compliment."

And the bet as a challenge. In more ways than one. He certainly hadn't climbed into this truck with the intention of using Charli's shenanigans as a way to practice being New Heath. But if this was what it took to get Margo back, great. He could do his job keeping Charli safe at the same time. Brilliant.

That's when she slid out of the truck and sashayed into Walmart without so much as a by-your-leave, forcing him to scramble after her. As she walked, she tossed a smirk over her shoulder.

His chest iced over. She was planning something.

What, he had no idea. He'd missed that crucial point during the negotiations, too set on his own agenda to realize she had one of her own. Of course she did. No woman with the personality of a bottle rocket about to explode agreed to a bet that a mere man could change her opinion about much of anything, let alone whether he could change her mind about men as a whole.

Too late. She hadn't fallen into his trap. He'd fallen into hers.

Chapter Five

For better or worse, Charli had a new boyfriend. The best kind—one that would vanish in three weeks. Or sooner.

Not that she thought for a millisecond that any of this nonsense meant anything to Heath, which was most of the reason she'd agreed to the bet. Okay, maybe more like fifty percent, the other fifty percent being the absolute need to win. Not just because of the shame sign potential, though that had sweet bonus written all over it.

But because Heath McKay needed to be taken down a peg or twelve. He thought he could change her mind about *men*? Heath—who defined everything that was wrong with men and then tacked on a few more of his own unique surprises. That guy thought his moves would be smooth enough to make Charli forget that the whole time, he was trying to win a bet. And would do anything to get there.

That alone put her blood on boil.

Besides, Heath didn't know that Black Widow's superpowers lay in driving men away.

Nor did she have any plans to inform him. He had three weeks to do his best to resist her natural man repellent, but in the end, Charli would prevail. She always did.

Even her own father hadn't bothered sticking around.

Sometimes late at night, she relived that early childhood trauma of lying awake, straining for the sound of her dad coming back home. She'd wanted to be the first one to hear him, to realize that all her prayers had been answered. Eventually, she'd grown into an adult who'd gotten used to disappointments and a silent God.

This bet would be no different. She'd put Heath in his place and move on.

Except when she came out of her room, she practically tripped over her new boyfriend, who was waiting for her outside her door in a casual lean that made it seem like he was holding up the wall with his sheer physical presence, instead of the other way around.

Gah, how did he look so good in the morning? Any woman with naturally curly hair like his would have to spend hours taming it. Not Heath McKay. No, he stuck his chocolate brown hat over it and instantly turned into a cowboy supermodel, complete with the rugged five o'clock shadow that would make any breathing female wonder what it felt like against her skin.

"Do you ever shave?" she grumbled by way of greeting because pre-coffee, that was the best he was going to get. Better to get used to it now.

Heath rubbed his chin absently. "Only if I remember. Why, are you worried about beard burn when I kiss you?"

Gravity ceased to exist and nearly threw Charli to the ground, but of course, he was right there, grasping her arm the moment she faltered. Annoyed at his quick reflexes and even quicker grin, she scowled at him. "You never said anything about kissing."

"I never said anything about not kissing. Besides, if I have to be monogamous for the next three weeks, who else am I going to kiss?"

"A pig that flies by?" she suggested sweetly. "Because you'd have a better shot, frankly."

He just squeezed her arm with a slight thumb caress, which set off a flurry of tingles that she didn't hate. But she wasn't about to let Heath know that.

Only the look on his face shut down her throat, freezing it.

"Trust me, Charlotte," he murmured. "There will be kissing. We're supposed to be acting like we're in a relationship. It's a natural progression considering how much time we're going to be spending together. You're eventually going to realize you actually like me."

That was enough to get a laugh out of her icy throat. And make her forget to spit out a reminder at how much she hated being called Charlotte. "You keep right on dreaming, McKay. With an imagination like that, you should go work for Disney."

"Fine. No kissing. Unless you start it," he said, crossing his arms to show off his biceps, which she suspected he did to remind people that he could deadlift a half-grown horse if he had a mind to. "In the meantime, I have a job. Two jobs. Charli's babysitter and eventual Bet Winner. How smart of me to combine the two."

Yeah, she'd gotten the message yesterday. This whole bet was a scheme he'd cooked up to amuse himself while he did his job. That was another reason to lean into smearing him all over the pavement. Driving him into the arms of another woman would be oh-so-satisfying for a multitude of reasons.

Even though part of her wished it wouldn't be so easy. A small part. Tiny—way in the back.

Most of her just couldn't wait to shove his face in the fact that he'd done nothing but solidify her place in the world as a woman who had his number. It was zero. He had as much of a shot at changing her mind about men as she did of stumbling over one who could.

Which reminded her of the ground rules she'd come up with last night. She turned toward him to lay them out and misjudged the distance, smacking straight into his solid torso. His hands snaked around her waist instantly, holding her steady.

Holding her against the magnificence that lay under his shirt, which she'd thought she'd already cataloged pretty well visually. Oh, she so had not.

"Are we starting the kissing already?" he murmured, his smoky gaze locked on hers with enough intensity to steal her breath. "Or are you just demonstrating your willingness to stick by my side? I'll admit, I didn't think you'd be so into that aspect of this deal."

"I'm not." She lifted her hands and slapped them onto his chest, fully intending to shove him back a healthy step, but kind of got lost along the way when the feel of him fully permeated her fingers.

The good Lord had definitely been in a mood when He'd built this one. Then Heath had added additional texture, like the scar along the base of this throat, highlighted by the sun-bronzed skin around it. There was so much to see and do and explore that he should sell tickets to the wonderland of his torso. There might be drool in her future.

"Charli." She slid her gaze to his face, which was this delightful combo of leashed and struggling with it. "Unless you're planning to spend the next three weeks with me in your room with the door shut, you're going to want to stop looking at me like that."

That was enough to put a fire under her feet, propelling her backward.

And enough to allow her brain to jump-start itself.

Plus give Heath the opportunity to let a dangerous smile spread across his chiseled jaw. "Miz Lang, I do believe you've already moved on to third date territory."

"Oh, don't be ridiculous," she snapped, completely aware that she'd just handed him a lot of ammunition that she'd likely be sorry for later. "I never said I wasn't attracted to you. I'd have to be blind and maybe from another planet not to realize you look like a movie poster for a *Magic Mike/Yellowstone* crossover."

Instead of laughing like she'd expected—like any other man would have—Heath cocked his head and gave her another one of those deep perusals, as if her skin had vanished, leaving her thoughts and dreams exposed for him to read. "Why does it bother you so much? That you're attracted to me?"

"Because it makes it harder for me to win the bet. Duh." She tossed her hair, terrified he'd see right through her lie.

If he found out he was exactly her type, no telling what he'd do with that knowledge. Plus, she didn't *like* that she naturally drove men into the arms of other women. It hurt. And allowing herself to admit an attraction to him gave him the power to do that.

"Maybe instead of pushing me away, you should try sliding into this," he suggested. "It's a freebie. No harm, no foul. Practice being in a healthy, long-term relationship with no strings."

The concept was so mind-boggling she could only stare at him for a hot second. "What is this nonsense you're babbling about?"

He shrugged. "It only makes logical sense. If we're in this bet and I have to shadow you in the first place, why not drop all this animosity and just enjoy spending time with me? I'm not a monster. A lot of women find me a pretty good guy to have around."

"I just bet," she mumbled before realizing that she already had, which slammed a scowl onto her face. "You've proven how handy you are in a crunch. I get it. You're the bestest bodyguard in East Texas. What you are not is boyfriend material."

The temperature in the hall dropped twenty degrees, along with his expression. Ice cubes might start forming at any minute. "One of the stipulations of the bet is that you have to give me a chance. Which you've so far failed to do. You have no idea what I'm made of. That's the point of the bet, isn't it? Besides, you act like I'm planning on losing. Nothing could be further from the truth. This is your chance too, to be wined and dined within an inch of your life, doted on by a man who knows a thing or two about it."

With that impassioned speech hanging in the air between them, he spun and stalked toward the stairs.

Well. Mr. Temper Tantrum had a long three weeks ahead of him if he couldn't take a hit.

"I'll be downstairs," Heath called over his shoulder. "Not getting in your space. But you can't leave the house without me, so don't bother."

Charli had been on her way downstairs, but changed her mind, since broody cowboys with hooded expressions might be even more her type than the flirty, troublemaking kind. Her room sounded like a lot more fun.

But the moment she shut the door, the four walls mocked her. No, she hadn't given Heath a fair shot. Nor did she intend to. That would be a very quick way to lose the bet, especially if she forgot for a minute that none of this was for real. It would be easy to get caught up in it. Begin to believe some of his rhetoric.

How did she know? He'd gotten a pretty good head start during their one and only date.

The only way to handle the next three weeks and arrive on the other side unscathed was to stay in the zone. Show him that Charli on the offensive was a force to be reckoned with, the kind of hurricane that spit men out on her way to wreak more destruction.

Basically, standard operating procedure. Instead of Black Widow, she'd embrace Hurricane Charlotte. Best part—she already knew how to destroy everything.

Because that had gotten her exactly what she wanted in the past? Charli flopped onto the bed.

Her eyes squeezed shut automatically as the sight of Toby with that waitress from Applebee's spilled into her brain uninvited. It happened less and less now, but there was a time when the image sat front and center any time she was awake.

She'd recognized the waitress immediately because the tramp had flirted with Toby shamelessly, right in front of Charli. As if she hadn't been sitting there, or worse, provided absolutely zero threat to the woman's agenda.

It had messed with her head. She'd unleashed on him the moment they'd hit the threshold of their apartment, accusing him of exactly what she'd later walked in on. Only with distance had she started to question if he'd been unfaithful from the start—or if she'd driven him to it.

What if *she* was the problem? What if she turned men into cheaters, solely because they were looking for a scrap of affection and warmth, only to seek it elsewhere?

Ugh, no. She couldn't think like that. She was not the problem. *They* were.

And Heath McKay was exactly the man to prove it. All she had to do was exactly what he'd laid out—give him a fair shot.

Resolute, she stormed downstairs to find him, determined to get this bet rolling so she could win. As expected, he wasn't far away, standing in the kitchen chatting up Sophia, an easy smile on his face. Not the kind he ever gave Charli.

And the second he saw her at the entrance to the kitchen, underneath the arch that led to the dining room, his smile slipped into the self-satisfied smirk she'd long grown used to.

"Come to apologize?" he asked, crossing his arms, which she immediately realized was his way of putting a barrier between them.

He did that a lot.

Because he was always expecting Hurricane Charlotte to hit him full force in the chest?

Yeah, she needed to take a step back and reassess. Big-time.

Like Heath had said, this was her one and only golden ticket to see what might happen if she didn't act like a banshee on the loose in a relationship. What would better solidify to her that she wasn't the problem than to take him up on what he was offering? She could ease into this bet. See what it was like to be in a relationship where she already knew the score, with a clear end in sight. It could be like…training.

Besides, the moment she caught Heath's eye wandering, which it would, she'd win. She could smugly start doodling some signs and call him a dog, content in the knowledge that she'd been right all along. It wouldn't be her fault and she wouldn't be the one to blame for whatever happened.

And in the event she ever found a man somewhere who could actually be faithful, she'd have some intel to use. No one had to know she was using this fake relationship as a proving ground for what happened if she just relaxed and had fun while waiting for Heath's true colors to eventually show.

"Yeah, I did," she said with a nod, more convinced than ever that this was the right track—especially since it would knock him off his. "Come to apologize."

Heath's eyes goggled so hard that she almost laughed. Men were so easy. Sophia glanced between the two of them and shook her head.

"Not getting in the middle of this," she said and held up her hands, backing away slowly.

Neither Charli nor Heath watched her go. His gaze was locked firmly on her, slightly squinty, as if he couldn't quite figure out what had happened.

"Are you feeling all right?" he asked.

"You can cut the sarcasm," she said with less venom than normal and didn't even choke on it. "Especially since you know you hit the nail on the head. I had no intention of giving you a fair shot. And it occurs to me that you probably put that down as your criteria for what I need to do to win, so I'm essentially beating you at your own game by apologizing."

"Which you have yet to do," he reminded her, his smirk softening into enough of a smile that it didn't hurt nearly as much to return it as she'd have assumed.

"I'm getting there. I'm sorry I was so prickly earlier. I'm done. Where are you taking me on our first date?"

That's when someone banged on the back door hard enough to rattle the frame.

Heath's entire demeanor shifted from casual to red alert, his shoulders thrown back as he expertly slid in front of her, angling his body as a shield. Just like he'd done when putting himself between her and the dig nerd. He rippled with authority and promise, as if advertising to the world that nothing would get through him.

It was his Protect Charli mode, and it was so affecting that her mouth went dry.

"Stay behind me," he murmured, and she didn't mistake it for a request.

Besides, where would she go? She was exactly where she wanted to be. Well, almost. There was still a lot of space between them, and the heat pumping from his body would feel delicious against her skin, she had no doubt.

She followed him as he took two steps toward the door and opened it only a crack so she couldn't see who it was through the solid male torso blocking her view.

"I need Miss Lang," a male voice rang out, high-pitched with excitement and urgency. "We found something."

"Who are you?" Heath demanded as Charli tried to peer under his arm. "What do you need her for? I'll give her the message."

"Oh, I'm one of the grad students. Ben Fuentes. But that's not important. Dr. Low sent me to get Miss Lang. She needs to come to the Harvard trailer so we can show her."

He meant Sophia. But guess what? Charli's last name was Lang too and she was standing right here.

"Show me what?" Charli called out, muscling her way around Heath's growling form, pretty sure any grad student named Ben wasn't carrying a gun under his T-shirt.

Ben turned out to be a scrawny, earnest kid who might

outweigh her by five pounds. "The statue we found. It's solid gold. Dr. Low is conservatively estimating its worth at five million dollars."

Chapter Six

Chaos erupted at Hidden Creek Ranch after the Harvard find, and Heath wanted to punch whoever had unearthed the statue.

He shouldn't. But it was hard to remember why. None of the university people stood still long enough for him to wind up a fist anyway, another logistics nightmare that had become his reality in the four hours since Dr. Low's assistant had broken the news. Apparently, everyone on the ranch proper had heard about the artifact, and all of them wanted to see it.

Strangers milled around the Harvard trailer constantly, which wouldn't have normally hit his radar since Madden had made sure Heath knew Charli's safety was his number one priority, but the ranch operation had spiraled out of control more quickly than any of them could get a handle on.

No more undercover security. It was *all* out in the open now. Nice because Heath didn't have to help round up horses any longer, but that didn't make any of this easy.

With Charli safely in the house—for now—Heath tried to concentrate on his temporarily assigned task. There were too many people to account for. Anyone could slip into a crowd this size, and no one would know a threat had joined their ranks because they were all basically kids with academic degrees in stuff he could barely spell.

There should be lines. Check-ins. ID requirements.

That's why Heath was here. To instill order. Except the really smart ones were giving him a wide berth, clearly recognizing that the former SEAL with the glower might be the biggest threat around. The dumber ones stood in easy-to-pick-off circles, laughing and pushing up their glasses as they waited their turn to view the hunk of metal that had turned his life into a three-ring circus.

Madden stalked into his field of vision, likely from the house, but Heath wouldn't know because he'd completely lost his focus. And his cool.

"What?" Heath snapped. "Do you have a third job to hand me?"

Ace Madden, his oldest friend, didn't even blink at his tone, which was one of many reasons they jelled. "If I did, you'd handle it."

Yeah, like he was handling the first two so well? For all he knew, Charli had bolted out the front door like a prison escapee thirty seconds before the floodlights spilled into the yard. This would be the one and only time he'd be unable to follow her, which might account for at least half of the reason his skin felt so itchy.

The inability to punch something was the other fifty percent.

All he needed was an excuse, like another one of the dig nerds putting his hands on Charli. Of course, given Heath's current circumstances, someone could be dragging her off into the woods right now and he'd never know.

It was killing him.

And the longer he went without unleashing his frustration, the tighter his fists clenched.

"We need more guys, Madden," he muttered at about half the volume he'd like, but there were too many of the people they were here to keep safe milling around. And that was still his job, even if he didn't like the fact that he'd been temporarily reassigned.

"We do," Madden agreed. "Especially when Sophia is currently having a meltdown and I can't be there to provide the shoulder she needs."

Heath rolled his eyes. "Sure, and Sophia's version of a meltdown probably looks like a lesser woman having a bad hair day. I'm sure she's fine."

But Madden just gave him a look. "Let's have this conversation again when someone you love is kidnapped and held at gunpoint, which took about ten years off my life, by the way, then add in a complete monkey wrench like a priceless ancient artifact showing up at the ranch you're tasked with ensuring is secure while she's crying in the kitchen."

Aw, man. If it was anyone else, Heath wouldn't care how broken up about it the guy sounded, but it was Madden. He blew off some of his mad and breathed. Or tried to, anyway.

"Is Charli with her?" he asked. "Is she okay?"

"She's the one talking Sophia down right now." Clearly at his limit, Madden took off his hat and ran stiff fingers through his hair with the other hand. "I need these people in a line, McKay. I need to know everyone on this ranch at all times, where they are, what they're doing. How do I do that with a six-hundred acre ranch?"

Heath lifted his hands, mostly to cover the wash of relief that coursed through him to hear that Charli was still where he'd left her. "I'm the brawn. Shouldn't Pierce be running some numbers or something?"

"He is. He's holed up in Sophia's study throwing together a heat map that's supposed to cross-reference unique signatures with satellite imagery, but there are a lot of trees on the property, so it's taking a while for everything to do the whatever thing he calls it. Execute the code."

Heath nodded, focusing on breathing in hopes it would calm

him down. Everyone was doing their part, but it didn't help his state of mind to hear that Sophia was upset. Was Charli upset too? What if she was crying and Madden hadn't even realized because he was too worried about Sophia? No one was there to pay attention to the other Lang sister.

Since he was the only one who seemed to be concerned about that, the only way for him to get back to his real assignment would be to fix the mess in front of him. At least the part he could control. And *should*, because his friend needed him to.

"All right, everyone," Heath bellowed over the chatter to the entire field full of grad students. They all froze and looked at him. Excellent. "We're going to play a game called help me do my job. Line up if you want to see the jaguar head or whatever it is. If you don't want to stand in line, go back to your designated area. No exceptions."

"What if we've already seen it?" one of the dig nerds asked, with a nervous glance at Madden, as if trying to assess whether the two of them would enforce the rule. "Can't we hang out and discuss? I mean, this is *our* job."

"Oh, I'm sorry, you must have mistaken me for someone who cares," Heath shot back with saccharine sweetness. "That statue thing has been exactly the same for a thousand years, give or take. I'm pretty sure you can talk about it tomorrow without losing anything important in your analysis."

The dig nerd licked his lips, apparently contemplating whether arguing would get him anywhere, but finally nodded and slunk off, his cell phone already in hand to switch his commentary to text messaging, most likely.

A dozen or more people followed him, shooting Heath the kind of dirty looks normally reserved for authority figures who broke up keg parties. Fine. He'd take that. Though when he'd turned into the guy on the other side of that equation, he had no clue.

An eternity later, some semblance of a line had formed, and

Heath presided over it with his fists mostly by his side. There were a couple of dicey moments when a newcomer didn't realize how strictly enforceable "single file" was meant to be.

And he still didn't see any sort of opening that would allow him to peel off and check on Charli.

Madden had stalked off to oversee some other area of security that Heath didn't want to know about. Presumably to ride the back forty looking for intruders or possibly to check on Pierce's progress with his computer program. Not that Madden had any better of a shot at understanding that man's brain than anyone else did.

At seven o'clock, Heath's stomach had already started eating itself in protest for being so empty and the line had dwindled, so he cut it off, ordering everyone to go back to their campsites. He personally watched Dr. Low as she locked the jaguar head into the safe bolted to the trailer floor. Someone could drive off with the whole trailer, but it wasn't currently attached to a vehicle, and the ancillary security contractors they'd hired had showed up an hour ago to run perimeter sweeps overnight. Madden would probably put at least two of them on stationary sentry duty outside the trailer.

Word may have already gotten out to the world at large that the trailer held something worth five million dollars. It was Madden's job to make sure the quality of security matched the value. Heath had done his part. And now he needed to turn his focus to his slightly less relaxing second job—Charli. Assuming she'd stuck around this long.

An eternity later, he found her in the kitchen, leaning against the sink, phone in one hand and a beer in the other that she sipped absently. A couple of drops of condensation slid down the longneck, which meant it was cold, and he'd never seen anything he wanted more in his life.

Only he couldn't pick out whether it was the woman or the beer that had struck something inside him.

Until Charli glanced up, her gaze snapping onto his with…

something. Not animosity. Not her usual trouble. Something else, which he had no vocabulary to explain, but wanted to.

"Hey, stranger," she called. "You look like you need this way more than I do."

She crossed and pressed the bottle into his hand, which was indeed chilled enough to cool him down a few blessed degrees. Without hesitation, he guzzled the sweet nectar of a wheat beer he'd have never touched otherwise, but thoroughly enjoyed after a hard day of herding nerds.

Maybe because the glass against his lips had been against hers not moments before. He tried not to think about that too hard.

"Thanks," he rasped, wholly unsettled at this dynamic between them that didn't seem to be veering toward a knock-down-drag-out, which he'd been braced for.

"Have you eaten?" she asked, peering up at him critically as if she might glean the answer for herself.

"Not since a million years ago," he admitted, hard pressed to even recall the last time he'd put food in his mouth, especially since his gut was currently registering the intensity of Charli's gaze instead of its lack of food.

She shook her head, lips pursed, and snagged his wrist, leading him to the table. "Sit. I'll warm up some of the leftovers from dinner. It's hamburger helper, but with ground turkey, and it's not too bad if you don't think about it too much. Green beans or no?"

"Uh, yes, I guess?" Was there a right and wrong answer?

Charli's smile made him think there probably was, and he'd managed to find it. "You're a better man than Ace. He wouldn't touch a single green bean and Sophia threw one at him."

Before he could fully wrap his head around what was happening, she'd heated a plate of leftovers and slid it onto the table in front of him, adding a fork and a napkin. Then she plopped down on the bench seat next to him with a fresh bottle of beer, stuck her elbow on the table and leaned her face into her hand, her brown eyes huge and beautiful.

"What is going on here?" he blurted before realizing how accusatory it sounded.

But Charli's grin just widened. "If you have to ask, I must not be doing it right. Eat your dinner, McKay. You look like you're about to pass out."

From shock, yeah. "You're being nice to me. It's weird."

That made her laugh. "You've had a hard day handling university people. You deserve a break from Hurricane Charlotte. Don't get used to it."

No danger of that. No one had ever taken care of him, not like this. Well, maybe his mom back when he'd been a kid. But this was different. Completely. He took another sip of his beer that had previously been Charli's, unable to stop being dazzled by the entire scene.

Only he was too hungry to think about it too much. The hamburger helper wasn't terrible, even with the healthier option of ground turkey. As his arteries weren't getting any younger, it was a nice touch. The green beans crunched instead of turning to mush in his mouth, a surprise.

"Sophia is a good cook," he announced as he wolfed down the rest of it.

"I'd pass on your compliments, but I'm the one who made it," she countered wryly. "I can understand your confusion, though. Sophia reeks of the kind of woman who knows her way around a pot and a stove."

"It's definitely the best thing I've eaten in a while," he said and elbowed her. "Don't think I didn't notice that you kept your role as the chef a secret until you heard my opinion."

She made a face. "Not an accident. Tell me what's happening outside."

"You didn't poke your head out?" he asked. The hits, they kept on coming. "Frankly, I'm not even sure why you're still in the house. I expected you to be long gone."

The pause grew some teeth as she stared at him, and it took a lot to keep from fidgeting. Heath didn't fidget. But she'd always managed to get under his skin without much effort. Coupled with all the strange vibes running between them, he scarcely knew which end was up.

"This is me behaving," she finally said. "I told you I would. It's not your fault there's so much going on with the stupid statue."

This was such a revelation that Heath didn't bother to hide his reaction—which was caution and confusion and not a little disbelief. He put his fork down on the table and fully turned on the bench to peruse her without a barrier between them.

"I didn't believe you," he told her honestly. "Earlier, when I asked you to stay in the house and you said okay. I thought it was a throwaway line, one you'd immediately invalidate by climbing out the second-story window or something."

Her brief flash of a smile caught him in the gut. "It's too high. I broke my arm doing that when I was ten, by the way."

"Not a shock," he advised her and lifted his chin. "Madden said Sophia was crying earlier. It would be like him not to notice whether you were too. Are you okay?"

"Why, Heath McKay." She clutched a hand to her heart and gasped theatrically but not before he saw the emotional glint in her eyes that he suspected she was trying to cover. "Points for sincerity and since you went to the trouble to ask, I'll be honest. This jaguar head is a big problem. For more reasons than one. Let's just say I'm not a crier, but that doesn't make me okay."

Nodding, he didn't think. Just reached out and snagged her hand, squeezing it tight. Silently telling her that he got it. "If it makes you feel better, I'm not a crier either, but I almost made an exception when this one UT kid called me sir. Who did he think he was talking to? I'm barely old enough to be his…somewhat older brother."

That made her laugh and upped the emotion quotient in her eyes. Which he strangely liked a lot.

"You're being nice to me, too," she sniffed. "It's not as weird as I want it to be."

"I told you, most women think I'm a pretty good guy. It's not my fault you didn't believe me."

"Oh, I see." She did this thing where she rearranged their fingers in a fluid motion so they were interlaced. Like they were holding hands. On purpose. "This is you pretending we're in a relationship. I get it now."

Actually, he'd forgotten all about pretending. But he nodded anyway, as if she'd hit the nail on the head, and tried to conjure up an image of Margo. "Since you brought it up, I never did get around to setting a time for our first date."

She shot him a saucy grin that immediately drained Margo from his mind. "I hate to break it to you, but I think this is it."

Sharing a beer over the kitchen table while exhausted after a day of standing around in the sun? No. Not even a little bit. "This is *not* a date. Trust me, you'll know when it happens and it's going to be way better than this."

Tomorrow night. Maybe. If Madden could get all his security issues sorted by then. Actually, Heath would make sure he did. Because he suddenly didn't feel like waiting to flip this script and be the one to dazzle *her*.

Strictly for the bet. This time he'd remember it was practice.

Chapter Seven

Charli poured coffee into an extra-large Yeti cup she'd found in the back of the cupboard. It was probably meant for someone who had planned a long morning of riding clear out to the south end of the property, or maybe someone like Super Sophia, who needed the extra caffeine hit to mow through her gargantuan to-do list.

Well, Charli wasn't either of those, but she was a woman who couldn't get Heath McKay's blue eyes out of her head long enough to sleep. That counted. Especially when Sophia called a meeting at 8:00. In the morning! Like, who had meetings that early? Corporate weirdos and politicians probably. Not ranch owners.

Except this one, she thought. Her sister had no respect for how difficult it was to be an independent woman who didn't need a man but kind of wanted the one that had been dropped in her lap. Charli couldn't figure out how to admit that to herself, let alone out loud where it would become a quick path to losing the bet.

That was probably the most painful part—having to temper the stuff inside that Heath had stirred up last night with all his gentle consideration over how she was doing. This was what she got for agreeing to give him a fair shot. It was a quandary. Because, yes, she got it. He was actually not a bad guy. No news flash there. They *all* started out that way. They ended up the same, too—heartbreakers.

Charli eyed her coffee mug that suddenly didn't feel large enough to hold the amount of caffeine technically needed this morning. So, she gulped down a quarter of it, sticking her tongue out to cool it as she topped off the cup to the brim, then stirred in hazelnut creamer, the only way to fly.

Smug that she'd beaten Sophia to the office, she settled into the chair on the guest side of the desk, content to let her sister have the business side. Sure, they were equal partners, or at least Charli liked to think they both considered that the case, but that didn't change which Lang sister was good at organization and numbers and other stuff that crossed her eyes.

Sophia bustled in at eight o'clock on the dot, making it feel like a virtue to be precisely on time. And now Charli felt like an overeager golden retriever who couldn't wait for someone to play fetch with her.

"Good morning," Sophia said, her tone that of a well-rested woman who knew exactly her place in life. "I appreciate you being here bright and early. I know you're not a morning person."

"No one is a morning person," she grumbled. "Some people are just better at hiding it than others."

Sophia slid into her chair and set her own coffee mug, a regular-sized earthenware one with a blue rim, onto the desk, then steepled her fingers around it as if warming them. "I like mornings. Especially when it's quiet. I can actually think. Which is why I got up at five a.m. and sat on the porch."

The thought made Charli's head hurt. "What did you think about?"

"Whether we should start canceling bookings."

"What? No."

With that gauntlet thrown down, the meeting got serious.

Charli's spine stiffened, driving her to the edge of the chair. This was definitely not enough coffee.

"Char." Sophia rubbed at one eye and that's when Charli noticed that her sister didn't look all that well-rested and it was probably the ranch that had kept her up, not Ace. "We talked about this. The jaguar statue is the last straw. You saw what it took to keep everyone in some semblance of order yesterday."

So she'd peeked out the window a time or twelve to watch Heath corral all the dig nerds. So what? It wasn't a crime, and the scenery had a lot to recommend it.

"Heath handled it," she countered. "With style. And they hired all those other guys too."

Who had come heavily armed, she'd noted. Every single one of the new security guards carried a semiautomatic rifle along with an expression that suggested he would not appreciate being tangled with. The ranch was in good hands.

Sophia stared at her as if she'd just suggested that they coat the new security guys in honey and stake them on an anthill. "You think the guests will consider armed guards a good addition to the staff? Think again. We have to depend on word of mouth for the first six months to generate new business. I don't think 'they have people with really impressive guns' is the kind of review we're going for."

Slouching down in her seat, Charli stalled with a big show of drinking her coffee. Yeah, of course she'd thought of that. Kind of. It felt like a plus to have extra security on staff because that meant Heath would have the capacity to take her on a date sooner rather than later. Which she was looking forward to—strictly because he'd piqued her curiosity, no other reason.

What she should be focused on was the ranch. And the guests. Which she was, right now, and it totally counted. "I get the point. But they're moving the jaguar thingy at the end of the week. Dr. Low promised."

That news had been the one thing to get Sophia to stop crying yesterday. It had put a lump in Charli's throat to see her sister so upset, but it was just a minor setback. Everything would work out.

"You think that's the extent of what there is to find here?" Rubbing her eye again, Sophia blew out a breath and picked up her coffee mug but didn't drink it. "I'm afraid it's the tip of the iceberg. This place is going to be crawling with additional search teams and new experts. I don't think we have a choice but to cancel bookings and delay the opening of the ranch."

The fatigue in her sister's face poked at Charli. "This is because you think you have to do this by yourself."

"What, run the ranch?"

"Yeah." She rolled a hand in the general direction of the window. "And make decisions. You don't trust me with the really heavy lifting. Just the decorating and such."

"I'm not... Char, this is a conversation. A meeting. If I was going to make all the decisions, I would have done that at five thirty, when my brain got to the end of a very long list of pros and cons for delaying."

Sure. Her sister had every intention of listening to Charli's point of view. That's why she'd framed the whole thing as "we don't have a choice."

"Fine. Let's talk. Tell me when you think we can open if we delay."

"I don't know."

"Exactly. Because there's always going to be one more thing they might possibly find if we let the university people keep looking." This was where Charli could shine—laying down the law. "So we tell them they're done. Take your jaguar head and go. Don't come back. Your welcome is officially worn out."

"We can't—"

"This is *our* ranch, Soph. We can." Warming to her subject, Charli jumped to her feet, scarcely registering the slosh of coffee in her cup. "We don't have to cater to the university people. Maybe we introduce a treasure hunt element for guests. Like the diamond field in Arkansas where you can sift through sand yourself in search of one. I read that a woman found one worth millions of dollars not too long ago. We'll advertise that you too can find valuable stuff on our land if you just come pay us a lot of money."

This idea had huge profits written all over it. The publication of the jaguar head find would fuel that fire. It was free publicity. All they had to do was get everyone with university or museum affiliations gone—and boot the security detail—then work out the new plan.

No more Cowboy Experience. This was all about gold, baby.

But Sophia's dubious look sent her suddenly jubilant mood back down to earth.

"What?" Charli spread her hands. "You don't love this idea? It's perfect."

"We already have a ton of work into the first idea," Sophia said wryly. "Expensive graphics on our website. Signage. No plan for security when a guest finds the other five-million-dollar jaguar head, the female one."

Wait, what? Charli's mouth dropped open. "There's a female one? Why didn't you mention this earlier?"

"I've been trying to get there but you keep shooting off in another direction," Sophia supplied unhelpfully. "Dr. Low mentioned it when she came by last night. You were busy."

With Heath. And she wasn't even a little sorry. That scene in the kitchen last night had stirred up something inside her that she wasn't sure how to handle. But wanted to figure out.

It had felt like something real. How other people might interact in an adult relationship. She was starting to think she hadn't had one of those yet.

Sophia continued. "One of the people on her team authenticated the head they found as part of a cache of treasure cataloged in some cave drawings in Central Mexico. There are supposed to be two. Whoever hid the male head on the ranch property may not have possessed the second one. Or they might have and it's still here."

The weight of this information pulled at Charli's shoulders. Why did there have to be two? One priceless giant jaguar head couldn't be enough for the Pakal guy or whoever had commissioned the statues?

"That just means more publicity for us, right?" she suggested feebly, guessing that Sophia's implacable expression meant the treasure hunting idea wasn't happening. "Okay, fine. I get that we don't have the right kind of plan to manage a crap ton of people searching for something worth that much money. We stick with Cowboy Experience. But delaying the opening, dealing with cancellations, that's bad business, too."

Sophia was already shaking her head. "I'm trying to do the right thing here, Char. I don't want to screw up the Cowboy Experience before it starts. But we've got a lot of dominoes stacked up here that I don't know how to stop from falling and wiping us out permanently."

Yeah, that was the problem. Sophia didn't know. And that meant Charli couldn't know either. It didn't matter if she had four hundred and eighty-seven good ideas for how to manage these obstacles, no one in this room wanted to hear them.

She resisted crossing her arms and sinking down in her chair for a good long pout. Barely.

This was par for the course, though. Her sister didn't think she had a single thing to contribute, so that was that. They weren't opening the Cowboy Experience next week. Instead, they'd spend their time cleaning up after a bunch of grad students and wincing every time one of them scared the horses with their ridiculously loud videos they played on their phones, but never watched with earphones.

"I'm calling it," Sophia said. "Permanent delay of the opening."

"Compromise," Charli said and stood, willing it to come across as a position of power. "Delay the opening but set a deadline for the university people. Two weeks. If they don't find the female in that length of time, odds are it's not here. That'll have to be good enough."

Sophia blew out a breath. "Two weeks? That's so soon. Why not two months?"

Because that was too long. "Three weeks, final offer. And they have to publish the fact that the female head is lost forever on their way off our land."

Three weeks fit the terms of her bet with Heath, too. Then he could wear his shame sign and be gone from her life, taking all his confusing vibes with him.

Her sister nodded, but it didn't feel like a victory. "Okay."

Great. Three more weeks until Charli could point to the Cowboy Experience and say she'd done that. Until she could claim that she'd truly found her niche in the world. It was better than nothing, and meanwhile, she'd have Heath to entertain her.

Somehow, looking on the bright side hadn't fixed her frustration. Sophia had still driven a hard bargain and a compromise wasn't the same thing as trusting Charli. She had this. But her sister didn't have a single drop of faith.

Fuming and itching for a place to unleash her mood, she stalked out of Sophia's office. She found exactly who she was looking for outside, climbing from the driver's seat of one of the off-road UTVs that he and the other guys had started using in place of horses to ride the fence line.

"McKay," she called, and he swung around to face her, a grimace her reward for getting his attention.

Good. He was in a mood too. She could tell by the faint lines of annoyance around his mouth and eyes. Neither made him look happy to see her.

"You're not supposed to be outside," he said by way of greeting, his attention clearly split between her and whatever he'd been about to do when he'd arrived in the yard. "Go back to the house, Charli."

She crossed her arms. "You owe me a date. You can't keep using work as an excuse."

And here he thought she'd be the one trying to ditch their prescribed time together. But with the delay of the opening, everything was upside down and she did not do idle well at all.

No reason not to get this bet on the road. Especially since in her current state of mind, she'd be driving him away sooner rather than later. Men wisely steered clear of Hurricane Charlotte when she got a full head of steam.

Except Heath didn't cross his arms and glare at her in kind. He shut his eyes and sucked in a breath through his nose, then took off his hat to run a hand through his damp hair, which should look ridiculous after being squashed by a Stetson for hours. But nothing looked ridiculous on him. This might as well be a commercial for something masculine and expensive that no one could remember the name of but sold out instantly.

"I'm sorry," he murmured, his eyes locking onto hers, the glacial color in complete opposition to the warmth there.

She couldn't look away all at once. "You're not allowed to apologize. I'm mad."

His gaze bored through her, and the rest of the yard fell away. It could have been full of circus monkeys instead of grad students and she'd never hear a single chirp.

What did he see when he looked at her like that?

"Not at me, you're not," he countered mildly and then unexpectedly lifted two fingers to her face, sweeping hair from her eyes in what was obviously a clear ploy to touch her, but she didn't mind so much. His fingertips lingered, sliding down her cheek in a wholly delicious way. "It's okay, though. You can yell at me as long as you want. I can take it."

The man scrambled her brain. "You can't do that. You have to fight back."

His smile was nothing short of diabolical. "You can count on that. Later. Seven o'clock. Dinner. No excuses."

Mollified in more ways than she cared to admit, she cocked out a hip. "What if I'm busy tonight?"

"You're not." His gaze swept down to her toes, curling them without anything more than the heat he always generated. "Wear something pretty."

Oh, man. She'd have to raid Sophia's closet. The black Dolce & Gabbana Charli had been eyeing would do nicely. Sophia's shoes lacked even an ounce of personality, but that was fine. She'd pull out her red stilettos and maybe have a shot at being able to whisper in Heath's ear if the mood struck.

She blinked. Speaking of moods, Heath had completely changed hers. It was a neat trick that had certainly never been in the arsenal of any man she'd ever dated before. Er, any man she'd *wagered* with before. The more she reminded herself this wasn't real, the better.

That didn't stop her from thinking about their date the rest of the day.

Chapter Eight

The stairs in the Victorian house that had belonged to Charli's grandpa did not mix well with five-inch heels. Side note: halfway down the flight was not a good time to discover this.

Fingers digging into the handrail, she clomped down two more steps cautiously. If she ended up in a heap at the bottom, she'd be spending date night in the hospital instead of giving Heath grief over his choice of locales.

Because there was no way he'd come up with anything that would impress her. She'd lived in Dallas her whole life basically, and there was very little she didn't have access to from Cirque du Soleil to Taylor Swift to high-end restaurants to world-class shopping.

What she did not have was a lot of practice wearing these shoes on a ranch. Lesson learned for next time. There was no way on God's green earth she'd change now—this dress fit her like a glove and the in-your-face red of the shoes gave her confidence.

She'd need it to spend more than five minutes with a man like Heath who oozed masculinity and authority.

By the time she hit the ground floor, one ankle twinged, but she ignored it and strode across the hardwood like a supermodel, grateful all at once for the flat surface to practice. She was doing that a lot lately.

Practice. It shouldn't sound like such a bad thing. Was there a point in life when you got to stop practicing and start *doing*, though? That was the crux of why Sophia forcing the Cowboy Experience delay still stuck in her craw.

She wanted action. Hurricane Charlotte was in the house and that persona suited her to the ground, way better than Black Widow had. It was past time for her to move forward with the plan that would fix her life.

She made it to the kitchen without stumbling once. Small wins. Now she could get on with her practice date. The thought almost didn't curl her lip.

What did she want, though? A real date and a real chance with Heath? She'd had that. No, thank you. Practice was far better. She'd go into this with her eyes wide open, category five gale force winds ready to blow his cheating hide from here to eternity.

Except when she answered the back door at precisely seven o'clock, most of her brain function shut down.

Heath McKay knew how to clean up.

Hatless, he'd obviously washed his hair with angel's wings. Nothing earthly could make his curls look so soft and so perfectly tousled around his face. He wore a pair of khaki pants with an impressive crease likely courtesy of a dry cleaner, but the fact that he'd ranked her as worth both the cost and effort struck an odd nerve.

When had that become a bar that men couldn't hit? And how dare Heath be the one to leap over it with ease and grace?

"You're wearing date clothes," she said and yes, it sounded every bit as accusatory out loud as it did in her head. He'd worn jeans the one and only time they'd done this before.

"You're not," he growled, his gaze heating as he swept her from head to toe, lingering on the shoes. "You don't listen very well. That dress is the exact opposite of pretty."

She scowled to cover the wave of goose bumps rising on her skin along the path of his scorching sweeps. "What's wrong with this dress? It looks fantastic on me."

"That it does," he agreed, but he didn't sound pleased about it at all. Then he twirled a finger. "Go on and let's get the torture out of the way. Give me all of it. I'm pretty sure I can handle it."

"I'm not playing fashion model for your enjoyment," she said primly and almost crossed her arms over her chest but that would only highlight the V of the dress.

"Too late." His grin bordered on wolfish as he hustled her backward and shut the door, leaning against it. "You can't pretend you didn't wear that outfit for me. I already know you did. And Charli? I am enjoying the daylights out of it."

Well, that was something. The heated appreciation glimmering from his gaze worked its way beneath her skin and she almost shivered. Okay, he wasn't wrong. She had pictured his reaction a time or two as she'd gotten dressed. Was she really going to balk because he'd come out of the gate with an attitude?

It was Heath. Torture sounded like a good punishment for his dictatorial arrogance.

Good thing she'd practiced. Without the slightest wobble, she did a slow spin and relished the almost inaudible sound of him sucking in a breath. Ha. Take that.

Her spin screeched to a halt, courtesy of Heath's arms. Which he'd just hauled her into.

Breathless all at once, she lifted her gaze to his, registering all at once that the stilettos did indeed put her at a much different height that worked extremely well with his.

"I wasn't done with my pirouette," she grumbled even as her entire body sang with some otherworldly chorus that hopefully only she could hear.

"Yeah, you were."

His voice had gone hoarse and the catch in it prickled her

skin. She'd done that to him. She'd affected him. It was heady stuff. His hot hands at her waist didn't feel all that fake. Probably because the rest of her had made itself at home up against the hard planes of his body. Heath definitely didn't have an ounce of fat on him anywhere. Except maybe between his ears.

"You can unhand me," she informed him loftily, proud that their proximity hadn't affected *her* voice. "You'll wrinkle this dress and then I'll look like I just rolled out of bed for the rest of the evening."

Bad choice of words. Or good, pending how she was supposed to take the fact that his fingers spread across her back, nipping in deliciously. What he did not do was let her go.

"That happens to be my favorite look on a woman."

Of course it was. She nearly rolled her eyes. "If you're trying to lose the bet, you're well on your way."

"Funny, I don't see any other women around here," he countered. "Just you."

His gaze burned through her, and she had a bad moment when she realized she might have miscalculated with this dress. If her goal had been to keep all his attention on her, it would have been a brilliant move judging by his reaction thus far.

But that wasn't her goal, exactly. It didn't seem too likely that his eye would be wandering any time soon. In fact, he might not have peeled his gaze from her once from the moment she'd opened the door. It was…not a terrible feeling.

That's when it occurred to her that if she lost the bet, she might end up with a whole lot more than she'd bargained for. Because losing meant that he'd changed her mind. That she had to concede Heath wasn't like other men. It meant he was one of a kind. Special.

And she already knew that was true.

Her heart pounding, she stared up at him, terrified all at once that he'd read the things racing around in her heart. Dang it, even in the heels she hadn't gained enough of a height advantage to feel close to being on a level playing field. Which might have more to do with the vulnerabilities she'd only just started to uncover.

Being off-kilter pushed her into a dangerous mood.

"Seems like we're doing an awful lot of standing around on this date you promised me," she said snippily.

"I also promised you I'd fight back," he reminded her with a lethal grin. "How'm I doing?"

Oh.

She had to laugh, and it released a lot of the tension that had bunched her shoulders. This whole scene was a setup. He was practicing *and* making good on his promise from earlier.

"Better than I thought. You're a lot more diabolical than I'd bargained for."

"That's what happens when you make a deal with the devil."

That she had and she wasn't even a little sorry. Heath wasn't a simpering idiot like Toby. This whole thing wasn't real. How great was it that she could be completely herself, no holds barred, and Heath would just brush it off? He wasn't going anywhere, no matter what category strength Hurricane Charlotte reached.

Plus, he smelled divine.

Feeling a lot more solid, she made the mistake of relaxing, only to discover it nestled her deeper into his embrace, which he did not miss. The atmosphere around them fairly crackled and if there was ever a time in the history of the world for a first kiss, this was it.

Strictly in the name of practicing.

When her gaze dropped to his mouth, the corners lifted as if he knew exactly what she was thinking about. What she was considering.

Only odds were high he had no clue. Because what she was actually turning over in her head was how quickly they'd both dropped into this place where they were so easy with each other. It was slightly fascinating and wholly terrifying. But she didn't have the urge to flee. Not even a little bit.

"You're looking at me that way again," he murmured and lifted a lock of her hair away from her face. "I like your hair down."

"Yeah? I was going for a little less tomboy and a lot more 'I look like I belong on the arm of Heath McKay.' Did it work?"

"And then some."

He shoved his fingers through her loose hair, somehow making it feel like a caress. Suddenly dinner was the furthest thing from her mind. He'd given her all the latitude. He wouldn't kiss her—*she* had to make the move.

Would she? *Could* she?

That's when someone banged on the door behind Heath, startling them both.

He whirled instantly, reminiscent of the time when Ben the grad student had brought news of the jaguar statue. Charli's pulse tripled as everything warm and lovely and languid inside froze.

Heath bristled as he yanked open the door. "What?"

This time, she had five inches on her past self and could partially see around Heath's shoulder. It was Dr. Low and a couple of the higher up university people. No grad students in sight.

Foreboding settled into Charli's stomach. She knew before Dr. Low opened her mouth that her date was ruined.

"Someone broke into our research trailer," Dr. Low explained, her faint Southern accent more pronounced as she pushed her salt-and-pepper hair back from her ears.

"What?" Charli shoved at the steel shoulder blocking her way and it was only because Heath let her that she succeeded in ducking under his arm. "We have armed security agents guarding all the trailers. Is the jaguar head missing? How is that possible?"

The guys Ace had hired had all looked so formidable that Charli herself had tiptoed around them, and she was paying their salaries. If someone had gotten around *them*, none of this was going to work.

Dr. Low shook her head. "No, not the trailer with the safe. That's our admin trailer. I'm talking about the research trailer we moved to the east pasture where we found the head."

Pieces of Charli's vision started going gray, which didn't help her focus on the trailer under discussion. They had more than one trailer, she knew that, but she couldn't have told anyone the difference for a million dollars. And she vaguely recalled that the trailers used to be sitting at a right angle in the grassy area near the barn, but so many people had started milling around the yard in hopes of peeking at the gold statue, they'd moved one somewhere else. The south pasture apparently.

And she really needed a better handle on the things happening on her own property. This was her job now.

She squared her shoulders. "What happened? Was anything taken?"

One of the other PhDs spoke up, a man wearing a sport coat with elbow patches so ancient that they'd half worn away. "It doesn't seem like it. A lot of the equipment is destroyed, though. It was a very expensive break-in for nothing being taken."

"We'll call the police," Heath said, his jaw clenched so tight it was a wonder he hadn't cracked a few teeth. "Start cataloging what you can with pictures."

"We're already doing that for insurance purposes," Dr. Low said. "But this is unacceptable. This kind of thing can't happen again. It's set us back weeks."

The gray in Charli's vision went black as this uncontrollable urge to break something swelled through her fingers. "You make it sound like it's our fault. What exactly are you accusing *us* of?"

"Can you excuse us a moment?" Heath said and it wasn't a

question. He tugged Charli backward with a hand around her waist and shut the door in the faces of the university people.

And then he turned her in his arms and hauled her close. That's when she realized she was shaking. The solid lines of Heath soothed her instantly, though the gentle hand stroking the back of her head did wonders as well.

Her state of mind was in such a disarray that she decided to let him.

"This is a disaster," she said into his shirt, which was a lovely, crisp white button-down that smelled like a heavenly combo of laundry detergent and man.

"For them, yes," he murmured. "Not for you."

"How can you say that?" she wailed. "I literally just talked Sophia into opening the doors in three weeks, only to find out our security is useless, and people are breaking into the wrong trailer. They didn't take anything because the jaguar head wasn't in that trailer. Why are criminals so stupid? Can you hire more guys with guns? We need like ten more—"

"Charli." Heath's voice was so firm and sharp that she glanced up. "Breathe. I'm handling this. This is my job, not yours."

His eyes snapped with an emotion she couldn't name. Maybe because she'd never seen it before on any man in existence. Coupled with the strong arms that were literally holding her together at the moment, it felt an awful lot like he cared about her.

That wasn't right.

It was part of the act.

For some reason that calmed her down. Sucking in a deep breath, she tamped down on her swirling thoughts. This was practice for a real relationship. Sure, it was fun to be Hurricane Charlotte with no worries about scaring off the guy. But taking a step back and handling a crisis like a mature adult counted, too, and she frankly needed a lot more practice at that than anything else.

"Okay." She nodded and heaved another breath. "I'm okay. I trust you."

Instead of clutching his chest in a mock heart attack like she'd expected him to, he did the oddest thing. He leaned into their embrace—somehow, she'd ended up with her arms around him too—and brushed his lips across her temple.

"Good," he murmured. "Remember that."

And then he released her. His heat vanished from her skin, leaving her cold and feeling as if he'd taken a huge chunk of her with him.

"Stay in the house," he ordered as he swung open the door, disappearing through it without a backward glance.

The second the door shut, she locked it. Wrapping her arms around herself, she slammed her eyes closed and let her head thunk back against the wood. How was he so good at reading her? At calming her? At being so thoroughly exactly what she needed when she needed it?

I'm okay, she repeated as instructed. Best way to remember that was to keep it front and center.

But that wasn't the only thing that reverberated through her head.

I trust you.

That's what he'd meant for her to remember.

Chapter Nine

The bad feeling in Heath's gut got worse by morning.

The officers from Gun Barrel City personified small-town cops who rarely dealt with anything more serious than burglary, jaywalking and the occasional 911 call from a resident who had seen a shadow outside their window. Despite the connotations, the city's name had come from an early observation that the main road through town lay as straight as a gun barrel.

Heath knew that because Pierce had done a thorough dossier on the town, as well as law enforcement all the way up to the state level. Madden had looped in the Texas Rangers recently—the law enforcement agency, not the baseball team—as a courtesy due to the value of the jaguar head, but thus far, there'd been no need to lean on those resources.

Unfortunately, even this recent break-in hadn't changed that. No one else was impressed with Heath's bad feeling. Or his insistence that something bigger was going on than everyone was crediting.

After all, if Karl Davenport could hire someone to rough up Sophia, he could hire someone to distract everyone on the ranch with a petty crime that amounted to nothing more than misdirection.

These two cops who looked like they'd come from directing traffic near the church weren't going to crack the case of who had broken into the trailer. The patrol car that had rolled up in the yard had the city's motto—We Shoot Straight with You!—for crying out loud, painted on the side. That pretty much said it all.

No problem. Heath didn't need anyone's help to do his job.

Madden took point on giving the locals the rundown while Heath and Pierce stood off to the side of the clearing, running perimeter control. Which mostly looked like keeping the dig nerds out of the way. Easier said than done thanks to the fanfare.

Heath eyed the newest pair of sightseers, both grad students. He'd learned to tell based on how they dressed, which usually consisted of a dirty pair of worn jeans and an even dirtier T-shirt emblazoned with either the name of an indie rock band or a saying that they thought was funny but really, really wasn't.

The scrawny one didn't disappoint. His T-shirt read Pardon My Trench. The other one, Heath didn't like the look of at all. Not only did his shirt have nothing on it—which was its own kind of tell if, say, he didn't want to stand out—but he wasn't skinny. All archeology grad students were skin and bones, apparently, because they had no money and forgot to eat, or at least that's what one of the chattier ones had told him.

Eyes narrowed, Heath watched as the no-logo-shirt guy edged forward, obviously misunderstanding the role of the two former SEALs standing between him and the crime scene.

"Trailer's off-limits," Heath announced and crossed his arms. Usually that gave the dig nerds enough of a warning that they backed off.

Not this guy. He edged forward again, completely breaking free of the small crowd that had gathered to watch the police proceedings.

"Yeah, no, I get it, dude," No-Logo said with nod and took a couple of test steps in the direction of the no-fly zone. "It's just that I left the artifact I'm researching in there and I need to check on it."

"It's off-limits to everyone," Heath repeated as nicely as he could with clenched teeth. "Including you."

No-Logo nodded again. "I'm not going to stay or anything. I just need to check on it and make sure it's still in one piece. It's a bone fragment and—"

"Everything in the trailer is evidence. No exceptions."

"Oh. I see." The guy looked him up and down with an expression on his face that would have earned him some expensive dental work a year ago. "You don't have a degree in anything academic, obviously, or you'd understand the importance of my research."

The frisson at the base of Heath's spine shook loose something black and sharp as he set his heels. "Correct on all counts. My degrees are in black belts. Care to test out which are the most relevant in this situation?"

No-Logo had the gall to laugh and actually take a few more steps toward the trailer. "Is that supposed to scare me? What are you, like a glorified mall cop?"

Must not punch the idiot. Must not punch the idiot. The refrain did not stop Heath from wanting to do exactly that. But unlike earlier, when he'd clocked the dig nerd who had gotten handsy with Charli, he didn't have an excuse this time.

Pierce strolled over at that opportune moment looking an awful lot like Heath's savior. "Problem?"

"Yeah, this guy is not taking the hint," he growled as he shoved a thumb in the direction of the interloper, who had actually edged closer to the trailer, clearly working out in his head how to duck under the yellow police tape.

"You want me to talk to him?"

"No, I want you to rearrange his face," Heath spat.

If there was a way for Pierce to push up his metaphorical glasses, he would have. "I'm the brains. I don't hit people."

This from the guy Heath had watched dispatch three unlucky insurgents who had stumbled over him in what should have been a hard-to-find location in the top of a bell tower, where Pierce had hidden to operate a drone over hostile territory. If Heath hadn't been so far away, he'd have been there in a heartbeat to help, but it turned out Pierce hadn't needed it.

"But you could. You act like you sit in front of a computer for eighteen hours a day and have the complexion of bread dough."

"You're acting like you couldn't put him in traction with one hand tied behind your back." Pierce eyed him. "You feeling okay?"

"Fine," he snapped as No-Logo edged closer to the trailer. "I'm just…working on a new approach to how I handle situations like this. I'm not in the Teams any longer. Maybe it's time to hang up the Enforcer."

Pierce laughed and then broke it off abruptly when he caught sight of Heath's glower. "Oh, you were serious? What are you even talking about? That's who you are, man. You take care of things. I've never once thought that was a problem you should fix."

"Well, it is."

And he left it at that, even as Pierce shook his head. "Happy to have you in my corner no matter what. Meanwhile, your rabbit is itching to cross the finish line."

Heath glanced at the trailer and swore as No-Logo dropped to his knees and crawled right under the yellow police tape, then stood, heading straight for the door of the trailer. With no time to waste and a trailer full of CSI who would not be thrilled with an interruption they'd specifically asked Madden's team to help prevent, he stalked across the clearing in two seconds flat.

His temper boiled over faster than that.

He ducked under the police tape easily thanks to a rigorous morning routine that included squats, and halted No-Logo's forward progress like a record scratch when he snatched the back of his jeans. "Not so fast."

The grad student glared at Heath over his shoulder. "Let me go. You can't stop me."

"I can. I am," Heath countered, forcibly keeping his fist by his side as he dragged No-Logo in the opposite direction, which to the guy's credit wasn't as easy as it sounded.

He fought the entire way, digging in his heels and babbling threats, all of which Heath ignored. Instead he focused on breathing in hopes it would do something to reel back the black edges riding shotgun through his bloodstream.

With a loud rip, No-Logo's jeans came apart in his hand. Great.

Instead of squawking about it, the guy actually reversed course again, heading back toward the trailer without the force of Heath pulling him away. Why? Why did it always come down to this?

Rolling his eyes, Heath took off after the idiot and didn't bother to check his strength when he gave him a hard shove to the ground, then dug his knee into the back of the dig nerd's neck. The black edges softened and immediately stopped trying to hack through his veins.

But they didn't vanish completely. Heath tried to make his peace with that.

"I said the trailer was off-limits. Which supervisor am I speaking with about banning you from the premises?"

No-Logo sputtered and spat out a mouthful of dirt. "I'll have you fired for this."

Yeah, good luck with that, kid. "Since you're not being forthcoming with the details, I'll drop you with Dr. Low and she can sort out your transfer paperwork."

This threat did the trick. No-Logo stopped struggling and blanched. Bingo. Dr. Low probably wasn't his academic advisor since she was at the top of the food chain, but she wouldn't take kindly to a grad student who couldn't follow the rules.

A few minutes later, No-Logo sat with his head in his hands outside of Dr. Low's personal trailer, which she used as an office. His duty done, Heath slapped the dirt from his jeans and stalked back to the clearing to ensure no one else thought they were above the law.

Apparently, his little show of force had convinced everyone else to scatter. Only Pierce remained, his expression unreadable. "Guess you figured it out."

"Save it," Heath suggested, his mood veering back toward black.

It wasn't that he was mad at Pierce for pointing out the obvious flaw in Heath's plan to hang up the Enforcer while on a job that required him to be exactly that. What else would he contribute to the team if it wasn't the muscle? But why did his resolve constantly have to be tested? Couldn't the universe find a way to allow him to just stand around and *look* threatening?

When he got back to the house, Charli was in the kitchen looking for all intents and purposes as if she might be waiting for him. Good night, the woman shouldn't be such a sight for sore eyes, but he couldn't stop himself from drinking her in, letting his eyes feast on the way her leggings clung to her thighs and the enormous T-shirt she wore sat kicked off to one side, exposing a healthy slice of shoulder that he imagined would smell divine.

She was just as sexy in casual clothes as she had been last night wearing couture and stilettos.

That put him a worse mood. Because he shouldn't be thinking about her as much as he was.

"What do you want?" he snapped, crowding into her space in hopes of picking a fight, which did not improve things as the light scent of woman curled through his senses.

She stopped him with a well-placed palm on his chest but the way her fingers curved to nip in told him that she enjoyed touching him as much as he enjoyed letting her.

"Food," she advised him, her brown eyes missing nothing. "I thought you might be interested in taking me out to make up for our cancelled date from last night. So I haven't eaten yet."

Oh, yeah, he was interested all right. But that didn't magically transform his life into something more manageable. Why everything seemed to be conspiring against him lately, he had no clue.

"I can't." He slapped a hand over hers, searing her palm into his chest before she got the idea that she should step back. Because he really liked her where she was. "The place is crawling with cops who may need extra security help at any moment. The best I can offer you is leftovers while watching a movie upstairs."

One of the bad things about being so far from Gun Barrel City—you couldn't order food for delivery way out here. Which made date night far less spontaneous. But he'd work with what he could.

"Guess I put on the right outfit for that," she said sunnily.

That she had. Almost as if she'd read the room ahead of time and realized he couldn't actually leave the premises. Which begged the question of why she'd opened with the invitation to go into town for to dinner.

Warily, he swept her with a once-over that revealed exactly nothing of her motives. She had one, though. "What gives? You're being far too conciliatory."

"Now, that is a word I don't hear often in conversation with a hot cowboy." Her gaze burned with a thousand other things that she'd elected not to voice. "Would you like me to argue with you a little bit? Sock you on the arm to make a point?"

"It would make me a lot less suspicious, yeah."

She laughed and smoothed her thumb along the ridge of one rib as if she didn't mind that he'd captured her hand there the slightest bit. "I heard from Sophia that you've had a tough day. I figured you didn't need my crap heaped on top of it."

Really. "So you're fine with having a date night here at the house?"

"Oh, no, sport. Do not get ahead of yourself." She gave him the slip and waltzed out of reach to check out the contents of the refrigerator, presumably for the aforementioned leftovers. "This is not a date. You promised me something spectacular for our first date, so this doesn't count."

She was giving him a pass. That's what this was. Slightly dumbfounded, he scrubbed at his beard. "Then why would you take me up on the offer of warmed-up leftovers and a movie? You should go back to your room and do something you want to do."

"I am doing something I want to do."

The grin she shot him was full of mischief that he couldn't quite wrap his head around Charli's angle here. "Sure. You're volunteering to hang out with me but not insisting on counting it as one of the three dates you agreed to. And you're not giving me grief. What's your game, Charlotte?"

"You've cracked the code. I was totally trying to get you to full-name me," she said with a smirk that was so animated it almost came with its own soundtrack. "Don't bust a gut trying to figure it out. You're not the only one who can practice being in a relationship at a time when it's not strictly required."

That pronouncement whacked him upside the head so hard that it rendered him speechless. Heath didn't have a lot of relationship experience himself, but Margo had never once given him the impression she'd be fine with it if he suggested a movie at home. And as far as he knew, she didn't own a single T-shirt, nor would she be caught dead in leggings. Stilettos she had dozens of, but they were more arsenal than accessory. Most of what Margo owned could be considered as such.

Honestly, he'd describe Margo as high maintenance on a good day. Usually he hadn't minded that, but today it sounded…exhausting.

Practice sounded a whole lot less demanding. It loosened

his spine a notch. None of this counted. Not even toward their bet. He didn't have to do anything except eat and pretend to like whatever lame chick flick Charli threw on the TV.

There was zero pressure—from any direction—for the first time in ages. Heath rolled his neck and realized all the tension in his shoulders had eased off. He might even be able to describe himself as relaxed if this kept up.

Instead of standing there like a bump on a log, he helped Charli heat up the leftover tacos she'd found in the refrigerator, but she didn't put them on a plate. In a stroke of genius, she broke up the shells and dumped all the filling in a bowl with some shredded lettuce for an instant taco salad.

"I'm a fan of the way you practice being in a relationship," he mumbled around the first bite as they settled into the ancient couch on the second floor of the house.

This room had been deemed off-limits to future guests and would be for family use only once the ranch began operating as a hotel. That meant it had stayed comfortable instead of getting a makeover like the rest of the place.

"You haven't seen nothing yet," she advised him with an eyebrow wiggle. "Tell me about your terrible day. There was a guy giving you problems?"

Heath scowled at the mention of No-Logo. "Yeah, let's just leave it at that."

"I hope you broke his nose," she said so matter-of-factly that he blinked.

"I, uh...didn't. Not every problem should be solved with fists," he quoted without meaning to drag Margo into this conversation, but since her aversion to violence was to blame for his current sabbatical, it wasn't inappropriate.

Besides, he *should* be thinking about Margo. And how nice it was going to be when she smiled as he told her—showed her—that he'd changed.

"And sometimes it just feels good to watch cartilage

crunch," she countered darkly. "Like when you hit that guy who was bothering me. That was hot."

Since none of those words belonged in a sentence together, his immediate response was to stare at her. "Come again?"

She sighed dramatically. "You're going to make me say it, aren't you? It was one of the sexiest things a guy has ever done in my presence. And I mean that exactly the way it sounds. I'm not proud of it. But there you go. You're my hero and you can't make me stop thinking that way."

What way? As if it was perfectly fine in Charli's world if he flexed the muscles in his arms instead of just the ones in his head? As if she found him *more* attractive when he took care of things according to his natural inclination?

If that wasn't enough of a revelation, he spent the rest of the night wondering if this was Charli practicing a relationship, what did the real thing look like?

Chapter Ten

If Heath on the ground got Charli's motor humming, Heath on a horse should come with a surgeon general's warning—Caution: may cause heart palpitations, sudden swooning and temporary loss of feeling in your legs.

He also should have mentioned that he wasn't a slouch in the saddle, or she'd have totally brushed up on her equestrian skills. As it stood, they'd barely cantered out of the yard, and she'd already had to resituate herself twice. Though that might have more to do with the fact that she'd been watching him handle the reins and letting her mind connect a few dots about how well he'd grip other things in a wholly different scenario.

Which she should not be thinking about.

She and Heath were barely friends, let alone in a place where any *scenarios* would happen. There had been that almost-kiss, though…

"Thanks for coming with me on this practice trail ride," she said when they slowed their mounts to a walk once they cleared the split-rail fence enclosing the pasture the dig nerds had claimed for their campground. She was riding Ricky, a sorrel male and her favorite horse, while Heath rode the unimaginatively named Hershey, a brown gelding the color of chocolate.

"You say that like I had a choice in the matter," Heath said with a quirked-up mouth that made it seem like he wasn't too unhappy about it. "You're my primary job."

"And this is my job," she reminded him. "Or at least what will be my job in nine million years when we finally open the Cowboy Experience."

Assuming Sophia agreed to open it ever. The three-week delay seemed like a pipe dream at this point after the trailer break-in, but she'd been too heartsick to bother asking her sister for confirmation that the delay might be a lot more permanent now. The police had no leads, but that wasn't a surprise given Heath's professional opinion that Gun Barrel City's finest couldn't find their butt with a map and two hands.

"Honestly, you gave me an excuse to get out of Dodge," he admitted, and she nearly fell off her horse. Again.

"What is this?" she demanded. "You can't be okay with it when I make you follow me some place unpleasant to do your bodyguard duties."

"The sky is blue, the sun is warm. The horses are sprightly, and you needed to practice trail riding. What's not to like?" he asked nonchalantly. "If this is your definition of unpleasant, we need to have a serious conversation."

This was going to be a long ride if he was already this agreeable. Was this how he lulled her into a false sense of security and then pounced? It had been a while since he'd done that, but he still had the capacity to knock her totally off-balance if he wanted to. "Are you trying to get me back for the other night? The non-date?"

He grinned and it was the kind that lit up his whole face, making her sorry he was wearing sunglasses. She liked watching it when his eyes warmed up, turning a pretty color that reminded her of Nordic fjords.

"If by *get you back*, you mean practicing being in a relationship, it's only fair," he informed her. "I can't have you getting better at it than me."

That crossed her eyes a bit. "I didn't know we'd turned it into a contest. Don't we already have a bet going?"

He shrugged without jerking on the reins, and that was hot too. The man knew his way around a horse because of course he did. There was nothing that Heath McKay didn't excel at, including the ability to handle a horse. And Hurricane Charlotte. What was the point of pushing him if he just rose to the occasion and proved he could match her, time and time again? That's why she'd banked the Mach 5 storm surge and just relaxed.

Only it was totally not okay for him to do the same. What would they talk about if they weren't giving each other grief?

"Nothing like raising the stakes, I always say," he commented mildly. "I guess this doesn't count as a date either."

"It absolutely does not."

Though if someone had asked her to list out the qualities of a perfect date, this one had a lot of them: a gorgeous man in a battered Stetson and jeans that fit him so well that they might as well be painted on; an enormous blue sky stretching endlessly to the horizon; nowhere to be and all the time in the world to enjoy being outside with someone who made being with him easy.

Of all things. When had being with Heath become *easy*?

He was right—it was glorious to have an excuse to leave the ranch behind and forget all the mess, the continual cycle of a new crisis every five minutes. There was no one on earth she'd rather do that with than Heath. Practicing had started feeling like the only time she could be herself.

And she'd just keep that information to herself, thank you.

"Just checking," Heath drawled lazily. "At this rate, we'll never get to our first date."

"Nice try," she returned, even as she considered if maybe that might not be a bad thing—wouldn't a real date be sort of anticlimactic by now? "We're not canceling the bet. You'll get your shot at impressing me soon enough."

"I never said anything about canceling the bet."

It was implied, though, as if he'd perhaps caught the slightest hint that she'd started entertaining the idea way in the back of her mind that she might actually lose. Which she'd never admit to, even under threat of death.

So she spent a lot of time not thinking about how different Heath was from any man she'd ever met. And by not thinking about it, she meant obsessively turning it over in her head and then forcing the notion to vanish, only to have it reappear later when her guard was down.

They fell into a companionable silence as they rode abreast toward the back pasture, which stretched almost a mile away from the house, following the trail that skirted the woods. It was a pretty easy ride, which was the intent. This route would be the one she set for guests, assuming that most had never been on a horse before. It wasn't a short ride, though, and guests would feel it by the second hour.

Charli's mount, Ricky, skittered sideways out of nowhere.

"Easy, boy," she murmured and stroked his neck.

Then Hershey did a similar half prance to the side, yanking a few choice words out of Heath as he fought to get control.

Charli exchanged a glance with Heath as their horses continued to shy and spook, snorting loudly with eyes rolled back. He was enough at home in the saddle that he knew something was wrong too. She scanned the trail ahead, braced for literally anything to appear that might explain what had caused their mounts to freak out.

Only the ghastly sight that came into view around a bend eclipsed everything her brain had conjured—several skinned animal carcasses strewn haphazardly across the path. The bloody, flayed bodies of small animals lay in gruesome piles, buzzing with flies and other stuff she didn't want to think about.

She cut her eyes away, but the scene had burned itself into her mind's eyes. So, no sleeping tonight, then.

Ricky spun in frantic circles, fighting the bit. She struggled to calm the agitated animal while Heath dealt with his own panicked Hershey nearby. The stench of death and the visceral carnage was doing a number on her; she could only imagine what the horses were going through.

"I've got to get Ricky calmed down," Charli called over to Heath. "He might throw a shoe if he keeps this up."

"Probably a good idea to check out the scene anyway." His tone had a steel thread running through it that told her he wasn't unaffected. But Heath handled his disquiet a lot better than she did.

They both dismounted with extra care. The animals shifted nervously as Charli and Heath patted their noses. Heath slowly approached the horrific scene. Crouching down, he examined the torn flesh and trailing entrails of the skinned animals.

"What are they?" Charli whispered, not wanted to say out loud that without skins, it was really hard to identify the animal. Refusing to look at them played a factor in that too.

"Foxes and raccoons, mostly. A coyote." Heath's voice got steelier.

Anyone who could kneel down in that kind of horror for the time it must have taken to do this job had more than a couple of screws loose.

A shrill whinny snapped Charli's focus back. She turned just in time to see both horses rearing up in terror before pivoting and galloping full-tilt back down the trail.

"Ricky! Stop!" Charli cried out in vain.

Stupid horses. Except they were actually a lot smarter than the humans. Of the four, who was still standing around near the crime scene of a disturbed individual? Not the horses.

Now Charli and Heath were stranded deep in a remote part of the ranch. With zero weapons except the ones attached to Heath's shoulders.

"Do you think whoever did that is still around?" she whispered, hand to her mouth and nose to filter the stench.

"Nah." Heath wasn't speaking at a normal volume either, contradicting his denial. "The carcasses are not fresh. Probably closing in on six or eight hours old. Someone staged that scene, probably because they knew ranch personnel use this trail."

His meaning sank in. "Wait, you think someone did this on purpose?"

"No one skins a bunch of animals and accidentally leaves them spread over a trail." To his credit, he didn't add the *duh*, but it was implied.

"This is my first skinned animal crime scene," she shot back defensively. "It's a crime, right? You can't go around doing stuff like this on people's private property."

"Trespassing. At best," he practically spat. "You might could make animal cruelty stick and possibly harassment or some other minor intimidation charges. But this is unfortunately not going to be very high on local law enforcement's radar. Not with the break-in occupying most of their brain cells."

But coupled with the break-in, this was too much to be a coincidence in her mind. "This is sabotage."

Heath lifted his hands. "What? No one even knew you were going to be out here today. Why would someone sabotage your practice trail ride?"

"I don't know, but they did. Pretty effectively too. You said yourself that someone staged the scene here because they knew people used the trail. I'm people. I own the ranch too. Why not sabotage?"

Oh, goodness. What if she'd been leading an actual group of guests? This sort of horror would stick with a person, and they would definitely put it in their Yelp review. Her stomach squelched for a wholly different reason as she instantly became a fan of the delay in opening that Sophia had forced.

"I can't stand here a second longer," she announced as breakfast threatened to make a reappearance. "I guess we're walking."

Heath nodded. "I'll send some of the rookies out here to clean this up later."

A procedure she wanted to know nothing about. But as the ranch owner, probably she should? Maybe she'd ask him later. At the moment, she was full up on the subject.

As they started back toward the house, Charli pulled out her cell phone. No bars. Not that she was surprised. Reception was spotty at best, especially this far from the house. Sophia had installed a satellite dish for internet service, but the signal didn't extend out here.

They were in for a very long walk. In boots.

"You okay?" Heath asked, his arm bumping hers companionably.

Was she? A quick inventory gave her an answer she wasn't too happy with. "I'm pretty shaky."

"Given the circumstances, that's not too bad." Without a drop of fanfare, he slid his fingers through hers, lacing them tight as they walked. "I won't let anything happen to you."

"I'm aware," she said with a short laugh. "And I wasn't worried, for the record. It's just…a lot to process with the break-in and now this. It's like the whole universe is conspiring against me."

Not that her lack of success was anything new. If she thought about it too hard, she'd land on the conclusion that *she* was the problem. The Cowboy Experience would be fraught with issues for the whole of its existence solely because she'd touched it. After all, those animals had been carefully placed on the horse trail. The horses were *hers*.

"Don't talk about that, then," he said. "Tell me about what you did before you came to the ranch."

She shot him a sideways glance. "Small talk, McKay? Really?"

"Shh. It's a distraction."

His grin went a long way toward clearing out the squishiness inside, which left a lot of room for her to register complete awareness of the fact that they were holding hands as if they did it all the time, as if this stroll had all been planned from the get-go.

Practice. That's all this was. If she'd been his real girlfriend, he'd do something similar.

And honestly, a distraction sounded heavenly. Especially in the form of an endless conversation with the one person who made her feel like she was standing on solid ground.

"I worked at a pet store. Bird section mostly."

His eyebrows lifted. "A pet store? I expected you to say you came from corporate America. Man-eater division."

"Ha, that was Sophia." One hundred percent, designer clothes and everything. Maybe if Charli had stuck with college, she could have followed in her sister's footsteps, but Charli and school had not gotten along. "Birds paid the bills."

"Did you like it?"

"No," she responded instantly despite not ever having considered the question either way. "The birds were mean to me. They pecked my fingers any chance they got. I think they knew I wasn't really a pet person, deep in my heart. Can we find another distraction? Tell me about being in the service."

"That's not a subject for mixed company." He said it so shortly that she glanced at him. His jaw was clenched the way that usually indicated she'd vexed him in some way.

But this time, she hadn't been trying to. "I'm sorry. I didn't know it was off-limits."

His jaw relaxed a fraction. "It's not. It's just…a lot of stuff along the lines of the scene we left behind. Whatever romantic notions you might have about Special Forces, wipe them from your mind. It's bloody, thankless and soul-draining."

"Well, I'm thanking you," she announced pertly. "For your service. You did something difficult and special, and it means something."

Heath swallowed. And swallowed again. And she realized he was dealing with some emotions she had no idea how to help him through. Or that she'd desperately want to. So she just held his hand the way he'd held hers and they walked in silence.

If he could practice, so could she. And keep her mouth shut about how much she longed to feel like this for real, as if a man like Heath would always be there for her, exactly like this.

After a few minutes, he cleared his throat. "Sorry. That's a bit of a sore subject. I didn't mean to make you feel like you picked up a rock, only to find a rattlesnake under it."

"I didn't feel like that at all," she told him truthfully. "This is a safe space, Heath. No judgment. We won't speak of it again."

"The thing is," he said so carefully that she couldn't help but glance over at him. "Maybe I want to."

Chapter Eleven

This is a safe space.

The strange thing was that it felt like one. Not just because Charli had articulated it into being. He'd felt like that with her for a while now. As if he could be fully himself, no holds barred.

She certainly wasn't like any woman he'd ever met. He couldn't have come up with the name of one who would have stood in that grisly animal carcass dumping ground and kept their cool the way she had.

Margo would have screamed and thrown a hysterical fit, probably strictly for the attention and to ensure Heath spent a lot of time soothing her emotional distress. Not once would she have clued in on whether he had his own brand of emotional distress.

Charli had, though.

"I know we said no history lesson," he said, and she glanced at him, then back at the trail, which he appreciated. It was a lot harder to talk about some things than others, but she seemed to get that. Almost as if she knew that if she stared at him, he'd never get the words out.

"That was before," she said nonchalantly. "I don't know if you know this about me, but I like to break rules."

For whatever reason, that actually got a laugh out of him. Which he also appreciated. "I feel like you deserve to understand a few things. And since this isn't a date, I don't have to worry about impressing you."

"Oh, you manage to find ways regardless," she said in a singsong voice. "I don't know any men who excel at identifying skinless animals."

If that impressed her, he really wanted to know more about the ex who had done a number on her. But he wouldn't push—that was hers to share if and when she chose to. At the moment, his most important objective was getting the fifty-ton boulder off his chest. The one that had dropped into place when she'd asked him about being in the service.

"Job hazard, I guess. I learned a lot of things they don't teach you in school while in the navy. I loved being a SEAL," he murmured. "But there's a lot of other stuff wrapped up inside that package that I haven't processed well. It's taken me a while to unpack it, especially because there are complexities."

"That has a woman written all over it," she interjected so matter-of-factly that he did a double take.

"How did you guess that?"

She shrugged, a small smile gracing her face that had a glow from their walk in the sunshine. "No one can introduce complexities like an ex."

Now his need to know about hers had risen to an epic level. He shoved that back in favor of the bigger elephant in the room. "Her name is Margo."

Oddly, voicing the name of the ghost living in his chest lifted some of the weight. As if speaking her name had loosened something inside, something he'd only just become aware of—Margo Malloy had a hold over him that wasn't entirely healthy.

And little by little, he was picking his way through the obstacles Margo had strewn around him in all directions as far as the eye could see. Only here with Charli in this moment had he paused long enough to see the impediments for what they were—a field of land mines.

"I hate her already," Charli commented and stuck her tongue out. "She sounds exquisitely beautiful and probably speaks three languages. Does she compete in marathons too?"

Heath chuckled. "I think she speaks more like fourteen languages, but if she's ever run a day in her life, I'll keel over in shock. I don't even think she owns a pair of shoes that don't have four-inch heels."

"Oh, one of those." Nodding wisely, Charli squeezed his hand. "Is she like an interpreter or something?"

"What? Oh, you mean because she speaks so many languages. No, she's JSOC." And then Heath had to roll his eyes at himself because even now, he fell into acronyms to describe things that had been a part of his life for so long but weren't anymore. "Joint Special Operations Command. Margo is an SO intelligence analyst."

The face Charli made had him biting back another grin. Who would have thought she could get him to laugh in the midst of unloading all the crap Margo had piled up inside of him?

"Smart and beautiful. I definitely hate her."

"Jealousy might be my favorite look on you," he mused, earning a sock on the arm courtesy of Charli's non-hand-holding fist. "Y'all are completely different women, and trust me, that's a good thing."

She got quiet for a long minute. "Can I ask what happened with Margo?"

"Why wouldn't you be allowed to ask? I wouldn't have brought it up if I was just going to shut it all down."

They'd been walking long enough that the sun had shifted, throwing the shadows of tree branches across her face. "Because that gives you the right to ask me similar questions."

She didn't want him to. That much was clear. So he wouldn't, no matter what. "Safe space, Charli."

That's when she let her gaze slide toward his, locking in place. A wealth of things passed between them, and he found himself stroking her thumb in some kind of half-comfort, half-caress combo that felt so completely right that he couldn't fathom how he and Charli hadn't always been like this with each other. How he hadn't known instantly what *wrong* felt like—the same wrong he'd felt for so much of his life.

"Duh," she returned loftily. "Do you think I walk through scary woods possibly hiding serial animal killers with just anyone?"

Holding hands, to boot. But he didn't point that out in case she had a mind to change that part of the equation and he was not done touching her. Not by a long shot.

"Margo coordinated missions," he said, figuring it was better to get this part over with before he forgot the whole reason he'd brought up Margo. "Mine, a lot of times. We worked together. Pierce was her go-to guy since he did intelligence for our team, but we were often in the same meetings. One thing led to another and before long, I was dreaming up perfect proposal scenarios in my head. Spoiler alert. She wasn't rehearsing how to say yes."

"Ouch," was her only contribution to the conversation, a rarity. Usually, she had plenty of commentary or a smart-aleck comment. Or both.

Apparently, she was taking the safe space rules to heart. Despite the fact that they were wholly unspoken, they both seemed to know what they were. No grief. No giving each other a hard time. Not out here.

This wasn't *practice*. It was something else entirely.

"Margo hated my job," he said bluntly. "She's not a fan of violence."

Charli blinked. "Maybe she should have picked a different career. And a different boyfriend."

Yeah, the irony wasn't lost on him, but if his Trident had been her only problem, they'd still be together. "You have to understand that Spec Ops is nuanced. Sure, I did my share of cleaning out terrorist hidey-holes in godforsaken places, but a lot of warfare is strategy. That's what JSOC does. They're analyzing intercepted data. Making decisions about strike zones and drone range. Margo and her team fight our enemies from a war room. They're somewhat removed from the actual logistics."

"So?" Charli's scowl plucked at a string inside him that he didn't know was pulled so taut. "What's that got to do with the price of rice in China?"

"She didn't like that my fondness for getting physical is pretty much my default," he admitted, scrubbing at the back of his neck, which had grown hot enough to get itchy. From the sun. Probably. "Even when it's not strictly warranted."

Throwing up a hand, she waved it in a broad circle as if shooing away flies. "What in the Sam Hill is that supposed to mean? Last time I checked, you have a body that won't quit and a very good command of it. That's sexy, no two ways about it. Which part of getting physical did she have a problem with and are you sure she's smart? She doesn't sound smart."

Oh, yeah, the back of his neck was hot all right. Along with the rest of him. Charli hadn't meant all of that as a compliment—at least he didn't think so—but he *felt* complimented. And a little objectified. Which worked for him in *so* many ways.

"Not that kind of physical," he growled. Though now that the subject had been broached, he had to stop himself from the instant denial that had sprung to his lips. Because honestly, Margo hadn't appreciated his tendency to be touchy-feely. And he'd never thought about the correlation. "Okay, yeah, maybe that kind too. She mostly didn't like that I get into fights occasionally."

She'd called him a brawler at heart often enough and he knew *she* hadn't meant it as a compliment.

"Sounds like Margo needs to date one of her robot drones,"

Charli informed him with an animated fierceness that dug into his skin. "She picked a guy with one of the most physically demanding jobs on the planet. One who likes being in the moment, who gets a sense of satisfaction from protecting those who can't do it themselves and then tells you she doesn't like the thing that makes you who you are at your core. If I ever meet her, I'm going to punch her for you."

Heath stopped in the dead center of the trail, accidentally swinging Charli around to face him since their hands were still connected. But that was fine. He wanted to see her the way she saw him. Unlikely. Her skill at peeling back his layers was unparalleled.

"I do like being in the moment," he said, a sense of wonder coating the realization. "Do you really think about me like that? As someone who uses his fists to defend people?"

"Duh," she murmured. "Instead of stopping you, Margo the Idiot should have sat back and watched occasionally. You're like a poem in motion sometimes and it's so beautiful it hurts my chest."

She was looking at him again, the way she did sometimes, the way that made him think she had things on her mind that were best taken behind closed doors. He liked that look on her. Liked the way she made him feel.

Except the whole point of *practicing* with Charli had been to win Margo back. That's what he should've been focusing on, not the fact that Charli had called him beautiful with that catch in her throat.

"I'm sorry Margo did that to you," she murmured. "She made you think you needed to do something different."

"Yeah," he admitted readily, grasping at the threads of the conversation. At all his reasons for why Margo's opinion counted. "I need to become someone she could see herself marrying. Because she couldn't. Said I handled myself like a hormone-hopped-up teenager who wasn't husband material, whatever that means."

"I wondered why you'd make that bet with me," she said, her expression lightening with dawning certainty. "It didn't seem like there was anything in it for you. But I get it now. That's what you wanted to practice. Being husband material for Margo."

The reminder was a bucket of cold water.

With that, Charli stepped back and pulled her hand loose. His felt strange and empty without hers in it, which shouldn't be a thing. The moment was over, if there had ever even been a moment in the first place.

She dusted off her hands and smiled, clearly of the same mind. But her smile had an edge he didn't like.

"You should have said so from the beginning," she told him brightly, almost too much so. It felt a little forced. "I had no idea we were whipping you into shape so you could strut your husband-material stuff in Margo's face. That is a challenge I can get behind in a hurry. When we're done, she'll be asking you to marry *her*."

And then Charli set off toward the house again, the intimacy between them completely broken. What was he supposed to do, tell her she was wrong? She wasn't.

This whole bet had been strictly to get Margo back. That's all he'd wanted for ages. Charli was on board with helping him get there—and she'd provided the much-needed reminder that Margo was the goal, not cozying up to Charli. What wasn't to like about this plan?

Everything. And he had no idea when that had changed.

Chapter Twelve

Charli's relationship with Heath was *practice*. It always had been. No matter how real it had started to feel.

Thankfully, he'd reminded her before she'd done something totally stupid, like kiss him.

Heath was still in love with Margo. That much had been obvious from the way he talked about her. Good. *Great*. This was perfect. One more step toward winning the bet—after all, if he spent a lot of time pining after another woman while on a date with Charli, that totally violated the whole point of the bet. It was basically over before it started if he couldn't focus on Charli for more than five minutes.

Granted, they'd have to go on a date for that to be a factor. During which, she'd be totally aware the entire time that he was thinking about Margo as he practiced being the perfect mate on Charli.

She'd give him points for the excellent distraction. Not once on the walk home had she thought about the skinned animals.

When they got back to the ranch, she had to think about them, though. Heath called a meeting that he conducted at the kitchen table and for once, she wished she could bow out. Not only was the subject terrible, Ace sat next to Sophia and

Paxton took the very far end of the table, leaving Charli to sit next to Heath.

Her knee brushed his thigh as she slid onto the long bench seat that she'd never minded before, but not having her own chair meant that it was completely obvious that she'd opted to sit as far away from him as possible. He spared her a glance laden with meaning, but what was she supposed to do, sidle up to him and coo all over his manly muscles while he treated her to that megawatt smile that she'd started thinking he only gave to her?

Firming her mouth in a straight line, she stared at the table as Heath outlined what had happened, leaving out the grisly details, which she appreciated for both her sake and Sophia's. Her sister didn't need the image of all those animals in her head, the way they were in Charli's, and neither did she want to relive them.

"They were planted?" Ace asked, his tone razor-sharp.

Heath nodded once. "Very clearly. The carcasses were stacked in pyramids."

She hadn't noticed that detail. Not surprising since she'd studiously avoided looking at the scene with much care. But she had opinions none the less. "Whoever did this knew it was a trail for horseback riding. And was probably aware I was planning to do a practice trail ride today. So that means it's someone on the ranch."

Sophia looked like she'd been punched in the face. "Great. That means we only have a hundred and forty-seven suspects."

"It's okay," Ace said softly and gathered her closer with the arm he slung around her sister's waist. "This is what I'm here for. We'll handle it, Soph."

Soph. The cutesy nicknames and being there for each other with casual intimacy made Charli's eyes sting with jealousy and longing. Sure, she was happy for them, but she wanted a man to look at her the way Ace looked at Sophia. As if he *saw* her. As if he'd cut a swath through hell itself if it stood between him and her.

The way Heath talked about Margo. He was going to enormous lengths to get her back, obviously because he thought Margo was worth it.

And what did Charli have to look forward to? *Practice.*

She glanced over at Heath almost involuntarily. It was her default lately, to seek out his steady gaze, to let him settle her. Except he was already watching her, his expression hooded and stormy. Searching for something. An answer.

What did it mean that she knew exactly what he'd been trying to figure out?

Yeah, she'd been the one to put the distance between them. For a *reason*, one she didn't feel like explaining. Everything was standard operating procedure to him, and why wouldn't it be? Nothing had changed on his side.

He'd talked her into the bet for a very specific reason—to figure out how to be the man Margo wanted him to be—and Charli's job was to help him get there. *While* he treated her with the reverence and respect a man should treat a woman he planned to be in a long-term relationship with. Only Charli wasn't the actual woman he dreamed about at night.

Squaring her shoulders, she tapped on the table to get everyone's attention. "What's the next move, guys? How are you going to handle this?"

Preferably as quickly as possible. But she didn't say that. Honestly, she didn't have a lot of faith that it mattered. They still didn't know who had broken into the lab trailer and even if they caught both guys, it didn't mean nothing else bad would happen.

This ranch might as well be cursed.

And if the Cowboy Experience never got off the ground, she'd have nothing.

"We're going to report it to the police first," Ace said and nodded to Paxton. "Pierce will take point on analyzing all the video footage from the property. Our guy must have left a trail of some sort. We'll find it."

They talked logistics for another thirty minutes, complete with a warning that neither Lang sister should leave the house without an escort. Well, that's what was *said* but they really meant Charli shouldn't. Sophia wasn't the flight risk, apparently.

When the totally useless meeting ended, Charli stalked out of the kitchen, intent on a hot bath and a mindless book. But Heath caught up with her well before she hit the staircase.

"A word with you, Ms. Lang," he drawled, and she rolled her eyes at the firm hand on her elbow that told her it wasn't a request.

Back to that, were they? "I have a date, McKay, and it's not with you."

The volcano in his irises bubbled and frothed. "No dates with anyone other than me. Nonnegotiable."

Well, well, she'd struck a nerve. Looked like her plans for the evening might have changed slightly. He wanted to go a round? She cracked her neck.

This was where they'd find out what he was made of, per his own request. A husband test, so to speak, because she couldn't think of anything more on point than a knock-down drag-out fight that would prove he couldn't hang in there when a woman had righteous indignation on her side.

"Jealousy is *not* my favorite look on you," she lied with a totally straight smile while secretly reveling in the nip of his fingers against her skin. "Careful or I might get the impression you care who I go out with."

"In case it's slipped your mind, my job is to keep you from resembling one of the skinned animals we found in the woods," he shot back with an impressively saccharine tone. "That's my only priority and there is nowhere in my contract that states I have to do it while third-wheeling it with you and another man. Besides, that violates the terms of our bet."

"What in the world are you blathering on about?" she said, shoving her face in the direction of his but he hadn't gotten any shorter, so she only ended up with a nose full of Heath's woodsy-piney-clean-male scent that wafted from the V of his button-down shirt. "I never agreed I wouldn't date other men."

He showed his teeth. "You did. When you agreed to give me a fair shot. Allowing another man to romance you cannot be described in any way, shape or form as a fair shot. Look it up in the dictionary."

A fair shot? Yeah, she'd given him that. Enough of one that she forgot that it wasn't real. Enough of one that she'd fallen for his sorcery and had actually started to think they were being authentic with each other.

"Oh, I see," she sneered, one hand on her hip. "It's totally fine if you're sitting around mooning over Margo while holding hands with me, but the moment I start making eyes at someone else, that's off-limits. What was I thinking? Oh, that's right. That you're a two-timing misogynist who can't spell monogamy with three sets of Scrabble tiles."

Instead, Heath crowded into her space, his frame fairly vibrating with tension that she could feel through her thin shirt. Oh, he was in a mood. She liked it when he was in a mood, especially when it matched her own.

Let's go, McKay.

She slapped two hands on his chest to force distance between them. He was so finely crafted that she forgot for a minute that she wasn't supposed to touch the artwork and let the pads of her fingers slide into the grooves of his ribs.

That's when she made the mistake of meeting his gaze dead-on. The volcano erupted, blue flames engulfing her with heat that rippled across her skin. Oh, my, that was delicious.

"I'm not thinking about anyone but you, Charlotte," he growled, and it rumbled through her fingers. "It's not what I was expecting when I proposed this bet."

That lovely confession melted all over her, softening her ire as she stared up at him. "What were you expecting?"

"A way to make spending every waking second in each other's company tolerable." The brief flash in his gaze spoke volumes. "I may have gotten more than I bargained for."

Two for two. A man who could admit when he was wrong was dead sexy. It was enough to get her to take a step back, even as she recognized that he didn't mean he thought about her the way she thought about him.

"My date is with my bathtub and a book," she murmured but he was still close enough that she could feel the exact moment when his body released its coiled tension. "It wouldn't be entirely inaccurate to say I wasn't expecting to prefer that to going out with another man. As your punishment for assuming that's what I meant, I'll let you think about me in my bath outfit."

It was something she'd say to a boyfriend. Wasn't this practice? Two could play this game.

He made a strangled sound deep in his throat, his expression darkening. "You might have just become the proud owner of a bathing partner. What kind of bodyguard would I be if I didn't ensure your complete and utter safety in all situations?"

Okay, practicing had just gotten a quadrillion times more interesting. And dangerous. But first—interesting. She swept him with a cool, assessing glance. "I don't believe you'd actually fit in my bathtub."

"Wanna bet?"

The laugh that got out of her felt a lot like a palate cleanser. "I'm still in the middle of the last bet you bamboozled me into."

His smile warmed her immensely. "And doing a stellar job at it too, I might add, despite the big mistake I made dragging Margo into this equation. For that, I'm sorry."

The apology was so unexpected and so sincere, it nearly buckled her knees. What was this twist? How dare he change the rules midstream. *This* was the man his ex-girlfriend thought needed a major overhaul before she'd contemplate the idea of marriage?

Nothing inside her skin felt right. When she'd started this fight, she'd expected him to career off the rails, maybe land a few of his own verbal hits. Get back to that place where they barely tolerated each other, and everything made sense. They'd always sparred pretty well with nothing more than their vocal cords and a healthy amount of chemistry. Why would this be any different?

Except it was. Because something *had* changed. What, she couldn't put her finger on, but this was not Heath conducting business as usual. This was Heath being... Heath. Solid. Un-yielding, even when she pushed him. Matching her, toe to toe, giving as good as he got, and never, ever dropping the ball.

It was more than sexy. It was...something else she had no vocabulary for.

"I don't know how to have this conversation if you're going to fight dirty with the only thing guaranteed to render me speechless," she grumbled.

"And yet, you're still talking," he pointed out without a drop of irony. "But you still haven't told me what set you off in the woods. That was what I thought we'd be fighting about."

The volcano in his gaze had receded. Slightly. Actually, his eyes still burned pretty bright, but the energy didn't feel like it might lash out and burn her alive at any moment. It just felt... focused. On her. She didn't hate it.

But she did hate the question marks in his comment, and she was woman enough to admit she had played a part in the vibe going south between them.

"It's stupid. I just didn't like the idea of being your testing ground, only to have to give up my spoils to Miss Special Op-erations. I mean, she already won the interview question and probably the evening gown competition. Thanks to me, she's getting the husband of her dreams and all I get is the satisfaction of watching your shame sign video."

His lips quirked. "If you wanted to poke the bull, you picked the right way. That sounds a lot like you think you're winning our bet. Nothing could be further from the truth."

"Except the bet is that you'll change my mind about men," she reminded him, though why she had to was beyond her. "And here we are with another woman in the wings. The exact scenario I was expecting. Which means you lose."

Instead of immediately flaying her with his argument to the contrary, his gaze softened, drawing her in, settling around her like a soft blanket. Swallowing her whole before she could blink, wrapping her in something that felt a lot like gentleness.

That, she had no defense against.

"The difference here is that I'm being up-front with you," he murmured. "Isn't that the whole point? You're mad at men who keep secrets. Jerkoffs who tell you one thing and do another. Make you believe something that isn't true. I'm not hiding anything from you. Margo is the reason I made the bet and I've never given you one reason to think this is anything other than practice."

Oh geez. He wasn't wrong. That mean *Charli* was the other woman in this scenario.

And she had it totally backward. The more he practiced with Charli, the closer he'd come to winning. Because it wasn't real. Because the more he didn't put the moves on Charli, the more apparent it would become that he could, in fact, spend a great deal of time with another woman and not cheat on Margo.

Completely off-balance, she scowled. "You have a long way to go before you convince me you're different."

"How long? Tell me what I'm up against," he suggested with the gentleness that might be her undoing, but the point still stuck in her gut like a word spear that shouldn't hurt as much as a real one.

He'd been nothing but honest with her and she'd thus far refused to return the favor. How could she say she'd won the bet if she didn't tell him what was on the mind that he'd volunteered to change?

"His name is Toby."

"I hate him already," Heath ground out with gritted teeth in a parody of her comment about Margo, which oddly relaxed her spine. Unexpectedly.

"Not so much fun being on the other side, is it?" she commented with a tiny smile. "I'll make it worse by telling you *her* name is Mandy. Which I know because she came on to him right in front of me. Then I had the pleasure of realizing he'd taken her up on the blatant invitation later when I walked in on them."

Heath's hands had curled into fists by his side, the white knuckles giving her an unparalleled amount of joy. This was what someone having your back looked like.

"I hope you punched her."

"I didn't, no." Though now she was thinking she should have. It might have been a form of closure that she'd thus far been denied. "I turned around and walked out. It was easier. At least until I tried to get my stuff back and he refused to open the door. He was in there too. I could hear his phone buzzing when I called it."

"Please tell me he then gathered everything up and placed it carefully in a box for you to retrieve later."

She shook her head. "I've made my peace with the fact that I'll never get my stuff. He's probably dumped it in the trash by now."

Heath's glower could have singed the paint off an iron fence and she should probably be ashamed at how giddy his rage made her, but come on. No one in her life had ever been even slightly ticked off on her behalf. Heath didn't even know Toby and she had a feeling if they happened to be in the same place at the same time, Cheater McCheaterpants would not come out the better for it.

"Get your purse," he growled. "We're going to pay Toby a visit."

Chapter Thirteen

"You know you can't actually break any of Toby's bones, right?" Charli commented from the passenger seat of Heath's truck where she was sitting way too far away from him.

"Says who?" he snarled, aware that he'd done very little actual talking since she'd confessed the details of the raw deal her ex had treated her to.

Pieces of work like Toby needed a few broken bones. It wasn't quite the same as crushing his spirit the way he'd done to Charli, but it was a close second, and it was the only pain Heath had the capacity to inflict.

"Margo, apparently," she informed him with a smirk that did not improve his mood. "And since you've appointed me as the judge, jury and executioner of your Win Back campaign, I guess me too."

The face she made distracted him from his grim determination as his flatbed ate up the miles between Gun Barrel City and Dallas, where they were headed for the reckoning she'd been denied. He would fix that for her. Possibly with a few less fists than he'd set out to use.

But not because his temper had abated even one tiny iota. Because she wasn't wrong and that pissed him off even more.

"Your job is to keep an open mind about relationships and my role in one. Not tell me what to do."

Now he was snapping at her. Mostly because she was still too far away, and his fingertips ached to feel her skin against them. Just one little hit of Charli would soothe him, he was sure, but he refused to reach out. If he could power through without that fix, it meant he wasn't addicted, right?

Everything was fine. Just because he'd started craving Charli's brand of humor and her tendency to be 100 percent on his side no matter what didn't mean anything. They were spending a lot of time together. It stood to reason they'd start to appreciate things about each other.

"Beg to differ," she said mildly, not even the slightest bit cowed by his mood. "When you're on a mission to right a wrong on my behalf, the least I can do is make sure you're staying on the straight and narrow. It's what you asked for, McKay. If this was up to me, I'd pay extra to see Toby in traction."

"You're not paying me in the first place." But the sudden image of her jackhole ex in a full-body cast did cheer him up a bit. Instead of sitting here stewing in his own righteous fury, maybe he could lean into this unexpected fantasy she'd introduced. "What else would you like me to do to him? If it was up to you."

The look she shot him said she knew exactly why he'd asked. When she smiled, it was purely diabolical, and he had a very hard time tearing his gaze away from her in favor of focusing on the road to Dallas.

"Oh, I like this game," she announced with undisguised glee and clapped her hands. "You could break all his fingers. You threatened to do that to Trevor, and I have to admit it was a nice touch."

Heath lifted a brow, amused all at once. His knuckles gained some color as he eased off his grip on the steering wheel. "Trevor? That was the dig nerd's name? Precious."

"He introduced himself to me," she explained, distaste coating her tone. "Like we were at a club, and he was gracing me with his presence."

Now he wished he *had* broken all of Trevor's fingers, even though the university had kicked him off the project. Couldn't dig up many treasures if you couldn't hold a shovel, and surely he'd dialed up Daddy as quickly as he could to get a new assignment.

"What else?" Heath demanded. "And let's stick with Toby since he's the one who hasn't suffered yet."

"Well, let me think. It's not often I'm asked to get creative about how to torture someone who hurt me."

Charli shifted in her seat, angling toward him and lifting one knee onto the bench seat so that it grazed his thigh. She didn't pull away. It was a subtle move, but it was clearly not accidental, and it tore through him with unexpected fire.

Margo, Margo, Margo. It shouldn't be this hard to remember why he'd cared so much about her.

"Let your imagination run free," he insisted magnanimously, since this was all hypothetical anyway, and his mood had just mysteriously improved.

Toby might not even be home, which would be a shame. Heath wouldn't hesitate to break down the door to ensure Charli had a chance to search the entire apartment for any item she wished to retrieve—whether it originally belonged to her or not—but scaring the bejesus out of her ex would be the likely extent of his satisfaction given the warning he'd just received.

No, he couldn't punch Toby in the solar plexus like the jerk deserved. And wasn't that a kick to know that Charli had appointed herself his keeper?

"You know what would really set him off?" she mused thoughtfully. "If you kissed me in front of him."

The sudden image of doing exactly that flooded him and he had a hard time shutting off the accompanying heat for more reasons than one. But he did have enough brain cells left over to be impressed with her brutal brand of retribution, which so neatly fit the crime.

That didn't make it a good idea. "I'm not kissing you for the first time in front of Toby."

"Eliminate that as a factor, then. Pull over and kiss me now."

Heath nearly swerved off the road and it was only the steady drum of the rumble strips that jolted him into correcting course. Her smile held way too much satisfaction for his taste. Oh, she didn't even have the first clue how much he wanted to do exactly as instructed.

And how conflicted the whole thing made him.

"Let's keep thinking," he suggested darkly as she laughed.

"I'm only kidding, of course. I know your heart belongs to Margo." She waved a hand at him abracadabra style. "But it's not my fault that you have all of that going on along with a healthy side of Neanderthal. It's apparently working for me."

And it worked for him that she appreciated the full package. What was he supposed to do with all of this?

A road sign for Dallas flashed by, indicating they had another twenty minutes until the city limit, which wasn't nearly enough time to sort out the mixed messages his body was giving him. Guilt at the mention of Margo wasn't pairing well with the sizzle in his blood. Hyperawareness of Charli's knee against his thigh wasn't slowing down the sizzle any. And knowing that she'd be totally fine with it if he did rearrange Toby's face might be the best adrenaline high he'd ever had.

Scratch that. *Worst.*

It was the *worst* high. Adrenaline wasn't his friend. If he ever hoped to reel back the part of his personality that would always be the Enforcer, he had to stop enjoying it when Charli encouraged him to be himself. She wasn't the one he needed to be thinking about impressing.

But he couldn't stop himself from imagining how Charli would react if he did pull over and kiss her. That occupied him until she told him to take the next exit and soon, they'd pulled up to a nondescript beige apartment building in Richardson that refused to distinguish itself from the ninety others they'd passed on the way here.

"Far cry from a six-hundred-acre ranch and a three-story Victorian house," Charli commented, her voice flat enough for Heath to figure out that she had some emotions about this trip that she hadn't shared.

He didn't hesitate to lace their fingers together—strictly for her comfort, not because the contact skimmed through his blood quicker than lightning. "You're better off. Let's get your stuff back."

Logistically, it made sense for Charli to lead since he had no idea where they were going, but it chafed not to be the one in front. It hardly mattered. There wasn't a single thing in a hundred-mile radius that could get the drop on him, even if it had been months since he'd depended on his reflexes to keep himself and his team alive.

Some things would never change, though. As they mounted the stairs to the second-floor apartment near the parking lot, his senses cleared and the slight uptick in his pulse flooded him with crackling energy.

The fact that Charli had opted to keep their fingers laced had something to do with it too. And he didn't even mind that it had probably been for show. This arrangement benefited him as well for reasons he didn't want to spend a lot of time analyzing.

He did steal the task of announcing their presence from her, though. When Heath beat on the door, the sound reverberated through the wood with some oomph that gave Loverboy plenty of warning that answering it wasn't optional.

Unfortunately, Jackhole Toby was slightly smarter than he sounded and swung open the door, ruining Heath's plan to kick it in. He shuffled Charli behind him, just in case, but honestly, she could probably take Toby in a fair fight.

"You Toby?" he growled at the scrawny weakling who either

used a ridiculous amount of sunscreen or never went outside. Plus, he had *gel* in his hair that sculpted it into a fan over his forehead. It was literally the most nauseating hairstyle Heath had ever seen.

"Yeah. Who are you?" Toby gaze shifted to Heath's hat and then swept him with an assessing glance all the way down to his boots. Which took a minute since the guy was a head shorter than him.

Then he caught sight of Charli peeking out from behind Heath's arm.

"What are you doing here?" he said with a scowl.

"No. You don't talk to her." Heath snapped his fingers in Toby's face and reversed his index finger to point at himself. "You talk to me if you decide you have something to say. Meanwhile, you're going to stand aside while Charli spends as long as she likes gathering whatever from this residence she wishes to take. Got it?"

"What is with this guy?" Toby asked Charli, completely ignoring Heath and his very patient explanation of what was about to go down. "If you want to talk, I have a few min—"

Heath pushed open the door, effectively shoving Toby out of the way. "You listen about as well as you do relationships. Move aside and keep your filthy mouth away from Charli."

Then he crossed his arms and crowded Toby until he backed up defensively, trapping him against the wall of the entryway, which allowed Charli plenty of room to navigate behind him into the apartment. In another subtle move, she pressed her hand to Heath's back as she passed.

"It's okay. This won't take me very long," she said.

Her tone was off. The Charli he knew spit fire when she got riled and if there was ever a right time to be riled, this was it. But he hadn't imagined the warble in the last couple of syllables. Whatever it was about this situation that had made her feel vulnerable wasn't okay, and he had his guess about where to place the blame.

Heath eyed Toby, who was frowning at him as if he had a right to be annoyed or put out by this surprise visit.

"Problem?" Heath growled.

"Yeah. But it's between me and Charli. I don't know who you are—"

"The person who is going to break your face if you so much as look at her again," he informed Toby succinctly. "She doesn't owe you one second of her time. And you don't deserve a millisecond."

"Look, man, I don't know what she told you, but—"

"She didn't tell me anything. I just don't like the look of your face." Heath's fist ached to plow right into the jawline of Loverboy, to inflict more pain than this loser would have the ability to deal with. But he kept his arms crossed.

Because as his newly appointed Win Back campaign manager, Charli expected him to. And he didn't want to disappoint her.

He'd finally gotten his chance to stand around and look threatening instead of being forced into using his strength to make a point. Was he really going to waste it?

Toby scratched his neck, finally looking a little uneasy. "I didn't think she'd move on so fast."

Heath didn't bother to respond to that statement when the reason for that should be perfectly obvious—that's what a woman did when she found a real man. Except she hadn't moved on, not the way Jackhole thought she had. This was all for show. And wasn't that a shame?

Charli deserved to have a man treat her well, especially after the way this one had treated her. Yet, she'd have a pretty difficult time meeting one when Heath was the only man she was spending time with.

The thought should have him stepping aside. He shouldn't care who she went out with. But when she'd told him she had a date, a red haze had filled his vision. Kind of like what was happening now.

Imagine if he actually had to watch her go on a real date. And he would have to watch. His job would still be his job, even if Charli elected to give him a taste of his own medicine and find some other guy to take her to dinner since Heath couldn't seem to find the time to do it.

More to the point, a date with Charli still wouldn't be anything other than practice. It shouldn't bother him so much.

"Where did you meet Charli?" Toby asked, as if they were having a chat in his foyer and he had every right to ask questions. "She's never been into country music. I can't believe she went to a honky-tonk."

The sneer was implied. Amusing.

"She's my boss," Heath told him just for fun.

Technically it was true, though he doubted Charli had ever thought about it that way. Neither had he, honestly, and now he had a lovely fantasy about her sitting on a desk with her legs crossed primly as she bossed him around with that smart mouth of hers.

Charli reappeared from the back of the apartment, lugging a box filled haphazardly with stuff, including a hoodie slung across the top that hid the majority of the other contents.

"Hey, that's mine," Toby protested and actually took a step toward Charli like he planned to wrestle the hoodie from her fingertips.

"You gave it to me," she insisted.

She paused near the door, releasing the box, but grabbing the hoodie protectively in a way that made Heath's stomach clench. Maybe he'd misread some of her cryptic emotions from earlier. Did she miss this guy? Seriously? Was that why she hadn't found a replacement yet?

"To wear, not to keep," Toby informed her and reached out, as if he intended to grab the hoodie in a forcible take-back.

Heath stepped between them. "She gets the hoodie. You get the waitress. Everyone wins."

Toby glared at him. "I didn't think she told you about that.

You don't understand, it was a one-time thing. A mistake." Then, he actually tried to step around Heath to speak to Charli. "She meant nothing to me, I swear. I tried to call you, but—"

Heath stepped between them again, and this time, it was easier to keep his fists from clenching. This guy wasn't worth it. "Charli, go to the truck. I'll carry the box down. We're done here."

Thankfully, she did as ordered. Heath hefted the box into his arms and walked out of Loverboy's apartment, leaving him sputtering about the hoodie. The fact that he was more concerned about the sweatshirt than Charli pretty much summed up the entire altercation.

After stowing the box in the bed of the truck, Heath slid into the driver's seat. Charli was already in the passenger seat, buckled in, and uncharacteristically quiet as she sat there clutching the hoodie.

"I'm sorry," he offered since it was clear she still had big emotions seething around inside. He got it.

She glanced up at him, her gaze snapping. "For what? You're the only person in this equation who did the right thing. I should have been the one to smash a fist into his nose after he had the audacity to try to explain away his cheating."

Heath grinned. "I would have paid extra to see that."

The joke seemed to break the dam and Charli rewarded him with a watery laugh as she tossed the hoodie to the floorboard and stomped on it. "I cannot wait to get home and burn that thing."

"Oh, is that what you wanted it for?" he commented with far less glee than what was happening on the inside. What was wrong with him that he felt such a blinding sense of satisfaction that she wasn't pining over Loverboy?

"It certainly wasn't to wear," she shot back and then her eyes widened. "That's not what you thought, right?"

She smacked him in the arm, and he caught her hand, pulling her close with it until he could see the slight smattering of freckles over her nose. "Your decisions are your own. Wear it if you want to. But I would have a very hard time not ripping it off you."

Charli shuddered but he didn't mistake it for a temperature-related reaction when heat climbed through her expression simultaneously. "Well, that just sounds like a challenge."

They stared at each other as the atmosphere sizzled between them. "You're not supposed to be challenging me to get physical. It's the other way around."

"That's the thing, though, Heath," she murmured. "Everything you do makes me feel safe and protected. No one has ever stood up for me like that before. You're amazing and you did it without grinding Toby into the carpet. If you'd needed to, you would have. I trust your judgment because you know the difference between when to stand down and when you can't."

The clearest sense of awe flooded Heath's chest as Charli's lips tipped up in a small smile.

"Now I need you to trust yourself," she said.

Chapter Fourteen

Heath was waiting for Charli outside the door of her bedroom by the time she rolled out of the shower the next morning. Despite the door being closed, she knew he was there. She could feel his energy seeping through the walls. That was the problem with a man who had as much going on inside him as Heath McKay—he couldn't contain himself even if he tried.

Most of the time, she didn't mind just soaking him up. It was a guilty pleasure that she'd deny if asked. Thankfully, there was no enforcement agency questioning her motives when she allowed herself to bask in the way he made her feel. *Feminine. Heard. Understood.*

They might even be friends at this point.

Except she'd never had a friend who treated her like Heath did. Nor had she ever had a friend who set her blood on snap, crackle, pop mode with nothing more than a look.

That's why she couldn't face him today. Not after the way he'd handled Toby. Yeah, she'd heard every word of their exchange yesterday. The whole scene had settled into her bones—along with Heath. She didn't think she could dislodge him if she tried.

So that was a problem. This thing she'd developed for him, it had to go.

They called it a crush for a reason. It perfectly described what was going to happen to her sooner rather than later. Like the moment Heath realized he was already husband material times infinity.

And then he'd go back to Margo.

Miss Special Forces would take him back because of course she would. The woman had probably already cried herself dry over her idiocy at letting him go in the first place.

The broken heart in Charli's future was exactly what she'd been trying to avoid by not going out with him the first time around. The bet should have provided enough of a cushion to fall back on. But no. He had to be wonderful and strong and perfect at pretty much everything. Handling her ex had been the straw that squished the camel's heart.

How was she supposed to avoid Heath when she'd agreed to be joined at his hip? How was she supposed to stay away when all she wanted to do was throw open the door, drag him inside and start something he would never finish?

Or would he?

That was the other thing that was burning her up. If this was all practice, why did it seem like he wanted to kiss her for real sometimes? Why hadn't he taken the bait in the truck yesterday? Sure, she'd used her flirty I'm-not-really-serious voice when she'd dared him to pull over. No, she hadn't missed the way he'd said he didn't want to kiss her the *first* time in front of Toby. Like there'd be a second and third and fourth time.

There weren't going to be *any* times. She had zero desire to find out how principled he was. Because if he did kiss her, then he was even more of a dog than she'd pegged him to be. But if he didn't, she'd lose the bet. And know forever that he'd found a better woman, one he couldn't get over ever. Charli wasn't even a blip of temptation on his journey back to happily-ever-after with Margo.

It was killing her. That's why she'd slept a measly two hours last night. Why she was pacing in front of the door, glancing at the knob every forty seconds as she contemplated opening it and acting like everything was fine. Or not opening it and leaving Heath to cool his heels for a few hours while he guarded the pathway to her door, a grumbly bear who would gladly bite the head off anyone who tried to get to her.

That part might be the worst of all. It was becoming way too easy to believe he'd started to care about her the longer he defended her against all manner of evil in the world.

Before she drove herself to the brink, she grabbed her phone and pulled up a calendar. They still had two more weeks before the arbitrary deadline she and Sophia had agreed to. Two weeks to find the other jaguar head before word got out that it existed.

The university people had agreed to keep it a secret as much as they could, given that everyone involved had cell phones and social media accounts. Charli knew they'd focused almost all their dig nerds' efforts toward locating the hiding place of the other head—assuming it was also hidden somewhere on the ranch.

It was highly likely that the jaguar head was here somewhere. Charli's luck didn't work any other way.

And if she had a prayer of getting her life going, the stupid thing needed to be in that safe on its way to Fort Knox, or wherever university people kept ancient statues worth millions of dollars.

"I can hear you pacing, you know," Heath called through the door with barely concealed amusement.

"So?" she shot back. "This is my room. I'm allowed to pace if I feel like it."

"Fair. It just feels like restless pacing. Something on your mind?"

Trust Heath to correctly interpret the way she paced. She rolled her eyes. The man paid far too much attention to her, and she liked it far too much. "I have so many things on my mind I couldn't possibly describe them all to you."

"Do any of them have something to do with breakfast? I'm starving."

"I'm not hungry," she lied. "You can go on without me. I'm working on ranch plans."

That much was true. But if she didn't send him away, the temptation would still be out there in the hall, wearing jeans so worn they were practically a butter-soft second skin.

And the fact that she knew the texture of his jeans might be at least half the reason she'd had trouble sleeping. The other half could be the fact that she also knew the density of the powerful thighs encased in those jeans. The things you could catalog by firmly wedging your knee against a man's leg in a truck could not be overstated.

Heath wasn't leaving. His presence hadn't budged from the hall. "The day you're not hungry hasn't arrived. What's going on?"

This was the one time she wished he wasn't so dialed into her. Other times, it felt...nice to know that he'd started to figure out some of her tells. That was part of the problem. She enjoyed the way he paid attention to her. It was going to her head.

"Nothing," she responded brightly. "I'm just rearranging some of the stuff I got back."

Honestly, she hadn't bothered. The box of her belongings had been meager at best. The retrieval had been largely symbolic, and instrumental in bringing about her current mood.

Because it had solidified something for her. She'd never felt like her life had really started back in Dallas. Walking back into that apartment she'd shared with Toby had rung some of her bells the wrong way.

It had never felt like her place.

This ranch? *Home.* Just not *her* home. Not yet. Making her mark with the Cowboy Experience would go a long way toward fixing that. That's why she needed to focus on figuring out how to move forward. Sophia had all of her own tasks laid out in her millions of planners. Charli had never been one for making lists, but she had a running agenda in her head. That counted.

And the first item on her mental to-do was finding that jaguar head. It could lead to clearing out the entire place of dig nerds because why would they stay after that? Even the single jaguar head was the find of the century. Once they had the other one, it was all over. They couldn't possibly justify hanging out in hopes of hitting a third jackpot. Right?

So that meant Charli had a vested interest in being the one to locate the head.

"You're still pacing," Heath called.

"You're still not eating," she pointed out. "I'm fine. Go eat."

Just to throw him off, she scampered to the box and pulled out the handful of paperbacks she'd never gotten around to reading but liked the look of on her bookshelf. It made her feel like she could be the kind of person who read for fun. Eventually. If things settled down enough and she found some downtime, she could totally be a reader.

Carefully, she placed the books on the dresser since this bedroom she'd chosen didn't have actual bookshelves. Which was fine since she didn't have an actual library. The four slim volumes of classics fell over immediately.

"What was that?"

"A noise," she informed Heath grumpily. "One you wouldn't have heard if you'd gone to the kitchen like I told you to. My books fell over."

"You have books?"

"I can have books," she returned defensively, hoping he didn't ask her the titles because obviously he was the type who did actually read, and he'd probably read all of these multiple times. She'd fail the quiz and then he'd ask her why she didn't have bookends.

And the answer was that she'd never had bookends because

she'd leaned the books up against the end of the bookcase, but she didn't have a bookcase anymore so that was a logistical issue she hadn't solved yet. The whole thing was giving her a headache and all she wanted was for Heath to leave her alone so she didn't have to spend 24/7 trying to figure out how he'd gotten under her skin.

"Do you want some help putting your stuff away?"

Oh, he'd like that, wouldn't he? An invitation into Charli's room where his Heathness would spill over into all the empty spaces, including the ones inside her, and warm up everything, reminding her how bleak and horrible it felt to be in here alone.

She hugged her abdomen with both arms, wondering if it was actually possible for a person's guts to spill out strictly from longing.

"That's okay. Thanks," she called as an afterthought.

"Now I know something is wrong," he said with an edge to his voice. "You never say thank-you."

"That's not true, I say it all the time." Didn't she?

"Not to me," he commented. "I'm starting to get a complex about it."

She rolled her eyes again. "Thank you, Heath. You're the best, Heath. I don't know what I would do without you, Heath."

"Never mind," he muttered. "I definitely didn't have a lack of your sarcasm in my life."

Now he sounded vaguely...something. She frowned. That was one thing she couldn't do with the door closed—read what was going on in his eyes. So maybe she *was* a reader. Huh.

When she flung open the door, against her better judgment, mind you, he was leaning against the wall with that loose, lazy pose that screamed exactly how comfortable in his body he was, one booted foot crossed over the other. That hat pulled down low over his face that he hadn't bothered to shave. Again. Even the scar near his collarbone screamed *too hot to handle*.

He was so delicious that her skin actually reacted, a swath

of goose bumps racing across it, chasing the flush of heat that accompanied her first visual smorgasbord of the day.

Then she met his gaze and what she saw there set her back a step.

"Did I hurt your feelings?" she whispered as something flickered in his depths.

She had. She'd stumbled somehow while wallowing in her own crap.

"Men don't have feelings." His voice was oddly flat. "We have urges. Mine is usually to break something."

She suspected he hadn't meant to answer the question, but he actually had. "I'm sorry. I'm not in my right head yet. Thank you for taking me to get my stuff yesterday. It was implied, but that's not good enough for the effort. It was really amazing."

Heath's arms were still crossed but they relaxed a fraction as he tipped his head in acknowledgement.

"I'm fine," she told him. "I also appreciate that you're concerned. No one else pays enough attention to me to figure out if I'm anything, let alone not okay. Thank you for that too."

He eyed her suspiciously. "That sounds like a lead-in if I've ever heard one."

What was wrong with her that the one person who spent the most time in her company accused her of never saying thank-you and of having an ulterior motive when she did?

No wonder he preferred Margo. Charli was a hot mess who destroyed stuff simply by breathing on it. She had to do better. That's what this bet was about, after all. Practice. On both sides. If she'd never had an adult relationship before, one where each of them treated the other with respect, how could she expect to get it right unless she started figuring it out right now?

Despite knowing it would set off a chain reaction of butterflies in her stomach, she reached out and placed a hand on his arm. "No agenda. Just…thank you."

Without a lot of fanfare, he covered her hand with his. "You're welcome."

Something passed between them, and it was so light and bright that it filled her chest so fully that she couldn't breathe.

She yanked her hand free. "I'm really not hungry. Go. I'm going to finish putting my stuff away."

Thankfully, he nodded, his gaze searching hers, but he didn't seem to find whatever he was looking for. "I'll be back later to catch up with you on your plans for the day."

Since she didn't have any, other than making doubly sure she avoided Heath the rest of the day, that wouldn't take long. "Have a good breakfast."

The moment his bootsteps faded from the stairs, she bolted back into her room and slathered on some sunscreen, then changed into old clothes, shoving a baseball cap over her hair. Giant sunglasses hid her face and with any luck, she'd pass for a dig nerd if none of them looked at her too hard.

Hiking boots in hand—no reason to alert anyone to the fact that she was creeping down the stairs—she made it to the front porch without anyone seeing her. Sophia would have ratted her out in a heartbeat and Ace probably would have too, but thankfully they were nowhere to be found.

She had to get out of this house. Out of the sphere of Heath's influence before she lost her mind. She needed fresh air, stat.

Taking a horse would be too obvious, so she laced up her boots and put her legs to good use, vanishing into the trees as quickly as possible, her back on fire as she braced to be stopped with a solid hand attached to Heath's body.

Nothing happened. Somehow, she'd legit managed to give her bodyguard the slip.

Now she could breathe again. And find that jaguar head.

Chapter Fifteen

Clear air. Yes, that definitely should have topped Charli's list a lot sooner. This was her ranch, and she should be spending a lot more time on it—all of it. She'd headed in the opposite direction of the university people's camp, not that it mattered. They'd spread like ants over the entire property.

No problem. She could avoid the dig nerds if she tried hard enough.

The ranch property opened up into a number of pastures just down the hill from the new barn. Sophia had filled her in on how the old barn had collapsed, which had happened before Charli had gotten her head wrapped around the concept of being named as one of the new owners.

Inheritance. It was one of those words that you heard applied to other people. Not to yourself. It hadn't meant much to Charli at the time, for sure. Some money maybe. But Sophia hadn't wanted to sell. Veronica, their younger sister, emphatically insisted they shouldn't keep the ranch.

Charli had been caught in the middle, totally unsure which side she should pick. Story of her life. The money from the sale would have been nice, but she knew herself. It would have slipped through her fingers with little to show for it other than a new car and some expensive shoes. The rest would have gone unaccounted for.

Veronica would have used the money to do something smart like start her own business or invest it. Sophia would have stuck it in a savings account and kept on being Super Sophia at whatever corporation she'd elected to tame next. The only one who would have kept drifting was Charli.

Because she was the most like their father.

It was an ugly truth she'd always known in the part of her heart way in the back. That's why it had been so important for her to put a stake in the ground at the ranch. To make it a home. Her home.

Being out here in the midst of it—*alone*—did wonders for her state of mind. This was hers. All of it. Sure, technically she owned one third of it, but there wasn't a way to divide it up like a pie chart. She liked to think of it as all three of them owning the entire ranch. As if their shares sat on top of each other instead of side by side.

This was what she'd expected to feel during the horseback ride. A sense of pride. Ownership. *That's my tree. This stretch of grass? Mine. That fence post belongs to me.*

Instead, she'd spent the entire day engrossed in her riding companion, even after they'd found the animals. That's what Heath did to her—took her brain hostage—and if she was being honest, he commanded the attention of most of the rest of her too.

That's why this break from him had been so sorely needed. She could think about important ranch things and forget about Heath. He certainly didn't think about her when he wasn't in her presence. All his mental energy went toward Margo.

This part of the ranch contained remarkably few people. Most of the nerds had focused their dig sites in the woods, which stretched along the east side of the property. That's where the creek ran, but you had to know where to look for it. She remembered that from the few times she'd visited her grandparents. It was a bit of an inside joke for Sophia to have named the place Hidden Creek Ranch, but Charli appreciated it.

Since she'd wanted to avoid the university people, she'd veered toward the pastureland. Plus, if the dig nerds spent all their time in the woods, odds were high they'd find the jaguar head…or they wouldn't because it wasn't hidden there. No reason for Charli to duplicate their efforts.

No one was in this far-south pasture. Jonas, the ranch manager, kept the horses closer to the house in deference to all the treasure hunt activity. It was more work to feed them, but it eliminated a lot of hassle and prevented the university people spooking them. Which just proved the urgency of finding the female head—the sooner they got these extra people out of here, the sooner the ranch could return to normal. And the sooner they could get the Cowboy Experience up and running.

And finally, Charli would have a place to belong.

No more Tobys. No more pet stores with the pecky birds. No more running from real life, her default. *That* was the inheritance she'd gotten from David Lang. That was what she was up against—the DNA her father had infused into her blood. She could consciously put that behind her and *belong*.

Charli's boots crunched through the tall grass as she trudged across the neglected pastureland. A slight breeze blew against the long grasses, rifling through the split ends for acres upon acres. It would take forever to search every square inch, especially without tools, which she'd forgotten about in her haste to give Heath the slip.

Well, this wasn't wasted effort. She could still enjoy the breeze and feeling her own earth beneath her feet.

The breeze picked up, flattening the grass and then releasing it to gently bob. There was one place where the grass seemed shorter, as if it had been trampled or mowed recently. Except that would be really weird, considering the horses hadn't been in this area for weeks.

Curiosity piqued, Charli set off for the cleared-out area because, why not investigate? As she got closer, she could see the outline of a circular something, overgrown with weeds and vines.

She pulled one of the vines away and saw that it clung to stone covered in moss. What was this, some kind of grave marker? She knelt down, wishing she'd worn gloves, and yanked another vine free, a long one that curled over the top of the circle. A lizard darted away from her hand, and she yelped, jumping a solid four inches.

Oh, thank god. One of the little green ones. Those she didn't mind but there were probably other ones—and maybe snakes too—that she did not want to come across.

She shuddered. Well, too late to worry about that now. If she cared about snakes, traipsing around in a big field full of things they liked to eat was not the way to avoid them.

Another yank and she had partially uncovered the circle. It was a hole in the ground ringed by stones, so deep that she couldn't see the bottom. A well. Right? What else would be out here in a pasture meant to hold animals who would need to drink a lot of water?

More to the point, it was a deep hole in the ground that would be a great hiding place for stuff. Like a gold jaguar head worth a lot of money. Best of all, probably no one else had found it yet since it was out here in the middle of a field the university teams cared nothing about.

Enthused by her find, Charli leaned closer to inspect the well. The ancient stones creaked beneath her weight. Wow, this thing might be older than she'd first assumed. She shone her phone's flashlight down into the darkness, cursing her lack of foresight in bringing a real flashlight.

There were still a few stupid vines stretching over the opening, casting too many shadows. She pulled at a couple with her left hand. The earth shifted and she lost her balance. And her grip on her phone, which tumbled into the hole.

That had *not* just happened. Charli cursed.

Her phone's flashlight was still shining, and she hadn't heard a splash. That was a good sign, right? But geez, it was so far down the hole. She could barely see it, even if she angled herself right over the opening.

The stones of the well's edge crumbled under her weight. With a *crack*, the whole edge collapsed. Flailing, she grasped at thin air as she fell into darkness.

The fall was quick and brutal. Her wrist absorbed most of the impact, sending a searing pain through her arm. Her hip glanced against something hard. Maybe her phone. Or the well floor.

Her lungs on fire, she struggled to catch her breath, heaving great gasps of air. The opening above her let in a bit of light but not nearly enough. Given her luck, she'd landed on her phone and killed it, which had also effectively eliminated her one light source.

It was dark. She was in a hole. No one knew where she was. She was *so* screwed.

Panic edged in faster than she could check it. A scream clawed its way out of her throat, which did zero good and got the rest of her body in on the panic. She started to shake as pain forked up her arm, sharp and agonizing.

Okay, this was probably the worst thing that had ever happened to her, but just like anything else, there was no one to rescue her. She had to figure this out on her own. What would Black Widow Hurricane do?

Climb.

Sucking back the panic, she crawled to her hands and knees, whimpering as she accidentally put some weight on her wrist.

So that was a problem. Broken probably.

Well, she'd just have to use it anyway. This well wasn't going to lift her out via a magic carpet. She felt around for some crevices in the well wall. It seemed to be made of the same stone as the part above ground. If her arm didn't hurt so badly, she might have a second to appreciate the construction quality of this well. How had they gotten the stones all the way down here?

And where was all the water? Had this well dried up at some point—or was it not a well at all?

Honestly, she didn't care enough to spend a second more of her precious brain power wondering about the creation and maintenance of whatever this hole in the ground was. Tentatively, she reached up to search for a niche or a ledge to hoist herself up, the fingers of her good hand scrabbling for purchase. Finally she got a solid enough grip to try to pull.

Okay, good. This was working. She levered herself up, slamming her feet into tiny cracks between stones, gasping as one boot slipped off the weatherworn stone. Barely managing to avoid sliding back to the floor, she froze, locking her fingers in place.

Somehow, she kept her position. But she had to *move*.

Now came the hard part. She stretched her left hand high, wincing as pain radiated from her wrist, but she didn't have the luxury of being a baby about this. Her fingertips found the next ledge about a foot higher than the stone she clung to with her right hand.

The second she put her weight on her injured wrist, a lightning bolt sailed down her arm and lit up her entire body with agony. It was so bad that she lost her grip and fell back to the floor in a heap, a torrent of angry tears cascading into the dirt beneath her cheek.

She felt sorry for herself for exactly thirty seconds, during which she cursed Heath for not realizing she'd given him the slip and then following her on this ill-advised adventure, Sophia for telling the university people they could look for more Maya crap, and David Lang for giving her not only a tendency to drift but a healthy amount of curiosity and zero fear.

Except for right this minute. She had a lot of fear. It was suffocating her.

But she couldn't give up. Something was poking her hip and that needed to stop. She felt around and her fingers slid over a smooth flat object. Her phone. She nipped her fingertips around the edges and when she tilted it, the screen lit up. Glory be. She'd been sure she'd smashed it in the fall. Somehow, she'd managed to switch off the flashlight with her hip. Bet she'd never be able to do that twice.

No bars. Not that she'd thought for a second cell service would pop up on the screen. She'd had to check, though. At least she had light for as long as the battery lasted. This was a positive. *Focus on that.*

Rolling—carefully—she sat up and fumbled with her phone, shining it around the bottom of the well. Or whatever it was. Because it didn't really seem like it had ever held water. Wouldn't it have mold or something along the edges? And it was kind of wider at the bottom, like a...cave. Sort of similar to the ones closer to Austin in the Hill Country, where the water table had carved out the limestone.

She ran the light along the edges until she couldn't swivel any further, then scooched around until she could sweep behind her. Oh, man. There was a wide passageway from the main area, which would have been super handy if it had still been another exit point, but it looked like it had caved in on itself several feet back.

And there was something over there. A few piles of what looked like old fabric.

Charli blinked and held the phone up higher. Had someone used this area for storage at one point? That seemed so unlikely. Wouldn't it have flooded when it rained?

But if there used to be a different entrance, anything might be possible.

She climbed to her feet, wincing as her abused body let her know that she'd fallen twice in the last few minutes, and limped toward the piles. She nudged the one closest to her with her foot, expecting the fabric to disintegrate, but whatever was under it was pretty solid.

Kneeling gingerly, she used her good hand to pull on the fabric, but it was wrapped tight. One good push up allowed her to free the dusty covering, which reminded her of the stuff that covered patio chairs with the rough texture, and then the wrapping came loose.

She yanked it free and gasped. Never, never again could she claim she had anything but pure, blind dumb luck because holy ancient Maya gods, she held the other jaguar head.

The statue gleamed in the light from her phone, unmistakable even though she hadn't studied the other one at length. This one had the same burnish to it, as if it needed to be polished, the black markings of the jaguar's spots fading into the gold along the edges. The flat, black eyes stared at her.

This one, which surely was the female, had a similar round, collar-type thing ringing the base of the head, like the other one. That's what the statue stood on and the collar was covered in what looked almost like cartoons, but she was pretty sure it was the Mayan language, which kind of resembled Egyptian hieroglyphs but not really.

Oh, man. She definitely couldn't climb out of here with *that* tucked under her arm, even if she felt stronger in an hour or so. Which wasn't likely with no food and water.

Okay, think. Could she dig out where the tunnel had collapsed? She stumbled over to the giant pile of dirt, rock and a few tree branches, but she couldn't budge even the very top layer.

Frustrated, she stepped back and kicked one of the other piles of fabric, the ones she had forgotten about instantly. Boy, she was some kind of adventurer. What if she'd hit the mother lode of Maya treasure and all she could think about was escape? Wasn't there some saying about one jaguar head in the hand meant there were two more in the bush?

She poked at the pile of fabric, but this one wasn't solid like the other one. Plus, it was a lot longer and thinner. Running her light up the length, she got a funny squiggle in her gut that the pile of fabric looked like…pants. That led to a shirt. And a face. Or what was left of it.

Not a Maya treasure. But a body. A dead one. And she was trapped with it.

Chapter Sixteen

Heath shoved his hat back further on his head and jammed his finger in the direction of the pastures.

"Spread out," he barked. They'd been messing around in the woods too long and had almost lost the light. "Do not miss a single inch of ground. You shoot a flare if you find so much as a piece of thread that might be from Charli's clothes. Got it?"

The group of dig nerds nodded solemnly, and the leader held up his flare gun, the one Heath had painstakingly showed him how to use. Meanwhile, he was counting down the seconds with his thundering pulse because it was yet another delay in getting to Charli.

The woman was going to kill him. Only fair. He was pretty sure he was going to return the favor. As soon as they found her. *Assuming* they found her, which given their lack of success over the last eight hours wasn't a given.

"Move," he instructed the dig nerd team, who'd volunteered to take the front section of pastureland. They meekly complied, trotting off like a herd of lazy buffalo.

Heath, Pierce and Madden were leading a second team including Sophia and a few of the ranch hands. Their objective: combing the back section of pasture along with the dogs, where they obviously should have started instead of wasting time in the woods. The dogs strained on their leashes, and Jonas spoke to them in the same soothing voice he would use with a spooked horse. They were itching to get going and so was Heath.

Pierce settled a hand on Heath's shoulder, his expression calm. "We're going to find her."

If only faith worked in these situations. Heath bit back a testy reply because they'd all been at this for eons already. He wasn't the only one who was hot, tired and terrified. Sophia hadn't stopped pacing on the porch, even though she'd personally walked the entire front half of the fence line with Madden earlier this morning. This was after she'd called every single person she could think of who knew Charli or had spoken to her recently.

Nada. Just like everything else they'd tried. Charli was missing. Like, full tilt, dropped off the face of the earth, no note, car in the half-circle driveway, purse and wallet still in her room, missing. Just…gone.

He'd do a repeat call to everyone in the county if he could do that and ride a horse at the same time, but so far, he'd been wildly unsuccessful dialing while at a full gallop.

Madden crossed the yard and shoved a sandwich into Heath's hand, obviously sensing it was the opportune moment since this was the first time in over eight hours that he'd been in the same spot for more than five minutes.

"Passing out from lack of protein isn't going to help anyone, McKay, least of all you," Madden murmured and jerked his head. "Sophia called her mom. She's on the way."

Oh, God. If Sophia had finally given in and called Mrs. Lang, that meant she didn't have a lot of hope for a positive outcome. Well, he wasn't giving up. Period. Guess he hadn't lost his blind faith after all.

After all, Heath had extracted a high-profile Taliban prisoner from a compound hidden in the extensive cave system of the Spin Ghar Mountains. In the dark. He could find Charli.

He'd been standing here immobile during their regroup session for too long, that was the problem. It made his mind spiral, worrying that she'd been kidnapped by one of the unsavory characters lurking in the shadows of this long-drawn-out assignment.

And that was the rub, right? He had no clue who he was up against, if so.

What if they'd taken her somewhere off the ranch? He'd never find her. And he was way past the point where he'd deny caring if asked. This went beyond an assignment, and it wouldn't surprise him if everyone had guessed that already. Madden and Pierce had wisely kept their cracks about it to themselves, which he appreciated, because he did not want to break his vow of nonviolence by knocking out the teeth of one of his friends.

But that didn't mean he planned to spend a lot of time examining the curl of panic in his gut or why it was making his throat hurt. Why everything inside screamed at him to move, to find her. What if she was hurt? What if she was lost? She needed him and he was failing her.

Plus, this whole situation had smacked him in the face with the fact that he needed her too.

Sophia paused midwhirl and buried her head in her hands, scrubbing at her eyes. "If she just took off for a spa day and didn't bother telling anyone, I'm going to disown her."

"She didn't just take off," Heath said for the millionth time. The worst part was that he almost wished she had. That would be better than the alternative. "If she had, she'd be back by now. Or she'd have called."

Anyone with a cell phone had been tasked with trying to call her but she never picked up. So that eliminated any possibility that she was ducking Heath or Sophia's calls. They'd even tried getting Veronica to call her. She had nothing to do with the ranch, so even if Charli had descended into some sort of temper tantrum over Heath's method of personal security, she wouldn't have suspected her younger sister of wanting to locate her.

And honestly, Charli had stopped causing him problems a while back. They'd been on the same page lately. She wouldn't do this to him deliberately.

This was a bad situation. He could feel it in his gut. And it was getting worse. Statistically speaking, the odds of finding Charli went down exponentially with each hour that ticked by.

They'd crisscrossed the woods twice already, working in teams since he couldn't physically search an entire six-hundred-acre ranch himself, not in a few hours. If something didn't break soon, he had a feeling he would be personally going over every inch with a flashlight before too long.

Shoving the last of his sandwich into his mouth, he chewed and swallowed, wordlessly taking the bottled water Pierce had pressed into his hand. He checked his walkie-talkie—again— as the others did the same.

"Let's go," Madden said and led the charge, but only because Heath's knees had gone a little weak. From lack of food combined with physical exertion. Probably.

Was it worse to admit he was out of practice at executing an operation with stone-cold reflexes or that the mission itself had personal undertones that were messing him up?

Stalking ahead, he ignored everything but the terrain beneath his feet.

They were walking this time, at Heath's insistence. He'd been so sure they'd find Charli in the woods and in his arrogance, he'd also made the wrong call of being on horseback. Better to cover a lot of ground, in his mind. Wrong. They'd do this section on foot and that's what was going to make a difference. It had to.

"Cut the dogs loose," he instructed Jonas, who had maneuvered the hounds to the search party's twelve o'clock position.

Another necessary shift in strategy that he'd felt in his gut. Jonas unsnapped the leashes, still stone-faced as always.

Madden glanced at Heath as Pierce caught up to them both, but it was a testament to their partnership that neither of them questioned his directive. These guys had his back no matter what. It was nice.

Shrugging, Heath kept his gaze on the ground, scanning for visual clues as he explained anyway. "We tried following the dogs in the woods, hoping they would lead us to her. That didn't work. We don't have time for that now."

The sun had started to set. Charli had been missing since nine twenty this morning, when he'd realized she wasn't refusing to answer the door for some mysterious reason, but because she wasn't actually in her room. After an hour of assuming she'd reappear, he'd known in his soul that she was in trouble.

The dogs seemed to sense that they were the stars of the show, eagerly pushing their noses along the ground despite not being trained bloodhounds. Putting his faith in them might be another problem, but Heath had few options.

If this had been Afghanistan, he'd have military-grade equipment at his disposal, complete with infrared scanners, drones and night vision goggles. In East Texas, he had his eyes, his brain and some dogs Charli petted occasionally.

The breeze from the north fluttered the split-seeded tips of the overgrowth in this pasture. Another problem. Under normal ranch operations, Jonas would be rotating the horses through these pastures, which would have naturally mowed down the grasses as they grazed.

Instead, the search party got to contend with acres and acres of tall foliage that would easily hide a small woman who might be passed out cold from who knew what.

Heath bit back an order to hurry. The dogs needed to be thorough, not rushed.

As he scanned the field to the left, the breeze ruffled the grass differently in one particular section. He shaded his eyes against the glow of the setting sun. It definitely looked like the grass was flattened in that area in comparison to the rest. It might be Charli.

Without a word, he shifted his trajectory to head in that direction. Pierce automatically split off from the group and followed him. Madden stayed on the group's course with Sophia, but he'd redirect everyone in a heartbeat if Heath called him on his walkie-talkie.

The flat grass area was a hole in the ground. An old well by the looks of it, but the stones around the edges were crumbled in on the edges closest to the center. It looked fresh.

"Charli?" he called, and his heart stumbled as he heard scrabbling inside.

"I'm here."

The sound of her voice emanating from the hole unleashed a slew of sensations that swept through Heath's body and not one of them he could name. Except mad. That he knew he was plenty of.

"Why don't you climb out now," he instructed as calmly as he could, given the adrenaline levels currently flooding his veins. "I'll grab you when you get close to the top."

"As fine an idea as that is, McKay, don't you think I would have already done that if I could?" she shot back with far less sarcasm than he would have expected.

She sounded so weak. It was alarming. "Is the shaft blocked or something?"

After a long pause, he heard her response drift up to him. "I broke my wrist when I fell. I can't put any weight on it."

"Call the others," he instructed Pierce over his shoulder. "Have them bring a rope."

Then he wasted no more time, slinging a leg over the edge of the hole. He couldn't wait for proper gear, not if Charli was hurt. If he'd known he would be descending into the pits of hell with nothing more than his best ninja skills, he'd have worn something other than cowboy boots, but he'd done worse in far more desperate circumstances.

Never with someone he cared about deep in a hole in the ground, though.

Calf muscles screaming, he braced both legs against the outer walls, pushing out to keep from sliding. Gymnast he was not, but he could brute-force his way down in a controlled descent with the best of them. As he shimmied down the stones one agonizing inch at a time, the flashlight and walkie-talkie clipped to his belt loops slapped his hips with each jerky movement.

That was going to leave a mark.

"Are you practicing to be Spider-Man for Halloween?" Charli called up the shaft wryly. "Because you're nailing it."

His chest heaved from the exertion. Man, he was out of shape. Something like this wouldn't have even winded him a year ago. "If you want to be rescued, save the small talk."

Finally, he hit the dirt floor and shook out his aching biceps, then resituated his hat, which he hadn't lost in the descent, so he'd count that as a plus. It was pretty dark down in the depths, but he could sense Charli just off to the right. His fingers yearned to reach out, just to assure himself she was safe. The rest of him just wanted to fold her into his embrace and never let go.

He crossed his arms. "Not the locale I would have picked for a date."

"Good thing this isn't a date. How did you find me?"

Heath switched on the flashlight. The glow lit up her face, highlighting the smears of dirt across her cheeks. She had a twig in her hair, and she cradled her right wrist against her body. The sight of Charli injured put him in a dangerous mood.

"Well, it was simple really. I read the note you left and decided to let you suffer for your sins, then went to a bar to live it up since you so magnanimously gave me the day off." The edge in his voice echoed off the worn, dingy stone surrounding them. "How do you think I found you? I kept looking until I did. Eight hours we've been at this, Charli. Everyone. The entire ranch. Your mom says hi, by the way."

Charli's mouth tightened. "I didn't ask you to come after me. I didn't leave a note for specifically that reason."

His laugh sounded as forced as it felt. "You're so welcome, Charli. I'm glad you appreciate the effort. No, no, I refuse to leave you here despite your very compelling arguments to the contrary."

"Don't be a jerk," she returned and shifted her arm, wincing.

"Let me look at that."

The mulish look she shot him didn't do his mood any favors, but he wasn't here to make friends. Setting the flashlight down, he pulled her closer by the shoulders and took her hand, gently turning the wrist over. When she cried out, his stomach clenched.

"Yeah, it's broken," he said gruffly.

"Thanks, Sherlock, I am thrilled to hear expert medical opinion comes along with your manly muscles. Whatever would I have done without you?"

Her exhausted expression pulled at some other parts of his chest that he'd rather remain unaffected, but that ship had sailed a long time ago. He sighed.

"Let's not do this, okay?"

"Do what? Practice being a couple?" she practically sneered. "Guess what? The bet was your idea, and this is what people in a relationship do. Fight. Especially when one of them is being horrible to the other one."

Heath checked his eye roll because yeah. She wasn't wrong. "I'm tired. It's been a long day."

"Back atcha," she said with one hip jutted out like a supermodel on the catwalk with plenty of lip and attitude that convicted him for that crappy non-apology. "You didn't ask, so I have zero motivation to tell you, but we're not alone down here."

Instantly, his spine stiffened, and he hustled her behind him, his feet spread and arms poised to take apart any threat that tried to get to her. They'd have to come through him and hope he let whoever had threatened her keep their limbs attached.

"Relax, Rambo," she huffed on a half laugh, half snort. "It's of the not-currently-alive variety. And I don't mind telling you that being stuck down here with a corpse has scarred me for life."

"A...did you say a corpse?" Heath swept the well area beyond where he stood with Charli and saw the body in question that was decaying enough to have him cover his mouth with his shirt.

"You get used to it," Charli commented with a wrinkled nose. "But that pales in comparison to what else I found."

She pulled something shiny out from under a tarp and he blinked. "Is that the other jaguar head?"

Dumb question. It matched the first almost exactly and what else would anyone expect to find in the hiding place of a five-million-dollar statue but a dead body—which he'd lay odds had not ended up that way accidentally. But why kill whoever the unfortunate soul was, only to leave the ancient statue behind?

"The one and only." Her grin came out as a half grimace. "I quit feeling lucky about three hours ago when I started accepting the fact that there would be two corpses in here before too long. I...well, I had a lot of time to reflect on how dumb it was to ditch you. I shouldn't have. If you promise not to look at me while I do it, I'm going to admit I was wrong and say I'm sorry."

The catch in her voice undid him. Flat unwound everything that held his heart, his lungs—his soul—together, all of it uncoiling in the depths of his stomach. He muttered a curse and yanked her into his arms, tucking her deep into the place that she'd just emptied out.

Charli snuffled against his shirt, her bad arm hanging at

her side, but the other one clung to his waist and she felt like heaven against his body.

"I'm sorry too," he murmured into her hair as she filled him up again to the brim, with heat and light and pure bliss. Whatever he'd been furious about blew away in an instant and he forgot everything but this woman, here, now. "You scared me."

"I'm sorry," she whispered again against his shirt and repeated it mournfully. "All I could think about was you. That I'd never see you again and how mad you must be. I thought I was going to die and the last memory you'd have of me is how crappy a practice girlfriend I am."

"This is not practice, Charlotte," he growled. "Safe space. Take a time-out for a minute."

Just as she drew back, her gaze searching his, a rope hit the ground behind him. He looked up to see a dark head leaning over the edge of the well.

"You guys ready to get out of there?" Pierce called.

Chapter Seventeen

Charli's brand-new cast sucked. All she wanted to do was sleep when they finally got home from the emergency clinic in Gun Barrel City, but the skin under the plaster itched and everything hurt. Especially her throat. From holding back the screams, most likely.

Predictably, Heath followed her up the stairs to her room, his hand at the small of her back like he was afraid she might pitch backward down the stairs if he wasn't there to catch her.

Well, that made two of them afraid of that, dang it. She had plenty of other things to worry about too, like blubbering gratitude for his heroic efforts to make sure she didn't die. And maybe some other stupid feelings churning around in the mix that felt an awful lot like fodder for losing the bet.

He *was* different. He'd proven that over and over again. What he was not? *Hers.* The time-out at the bottom of the well notwithstanding.

Whatever that had been about. A time-out from what? The bet? Practicing? That wasn't a thing, not in her world.

Heath paused at her door, dropping his hand. "Want me to help you get ready for bed?"

"You'd like that, wouldn't you?" she said with a smirk,

desperate to get back to a place where she understood the dynamic between them. Understood why her chest hurt when she looked at him.

"Yeah, a woman with a broken arm is my kind of hot date," he muttered, his eyes on the ceiling in what looked like a not-so-veiled attempt to keep his temper in check. "But sure, try to take your clothes off with one arm. I'll wait."

"I can call Sophia."

"The same sister who walked all over half this ranch today and is currently about to slide into a bubble bath drawn by her equally exhausted boyfriend?" Heath crossed his arms and leaned on the doorjamb. "That sister?"

Yeah, she hadn't thought that through. She sighed.

The man would not stop showing up for her and she was sick and tired of pushing back the tendrils he'd snaked around her heart. Especially when he said confusing things like *this is not practice*.

Was he saying it didn't feel like practice because she'd messed it up or because he'd truly been worried about her? As a friend. Right? And why didn't she know? Because she didn't want to ask. Didn't want to have it clarified so she knew for sure it had been a friendly hug that had felt anything but.

As soon as his partners had lifted them out of the hole via the sturdy rope they'd thrown down, Heath had driven her into town to have her wrist checked out with Sophia and Ace in tow. Sophia because she'd refused to let Charli out of her sight and Ace because he'd refused to let Sophia out of his. Heath had stayed glued to her side because he was Heath.

Paxton had stayed behind to call in the body they'd found, then planned to assist the local police with securing the scene. No one knew about the jaguar head except the five of them, per Sophia's directive. Which Charli appreciated. Tomorrow morning, they'd figure out how to manage what would surely become a forty-seven-ring circus combined with a petting

zoo and a rave once word got out that they'd located the second head.

There better not be any jaguar babies or extended family
statues out there somewhere or she'd punch something.

"I'm running on fumes, McKay," she said as it all hit her
like a ton of bricks. "I can't do this now. Please just let me be
for tonight and I promise, tomorrow you can go back to being
your domineering, confounding, hotter than asphalt self and
I'll be in a much better place to take you down a few pegs.
Deal?"

Heath nodded once, though his expression could give a
mule a run for its money. He didn't argue thankfully, and it
felt like a small win as she shut the door in his face. Until she
tried to wrench her shirt off with her good hand and wound
up smacking herself in the face.

Cursing, she eased off her hiking boots and jeans, which
went easier, then padded into the en suite bathroom. Dear God,
was that her face? It was practically unrecognizable under a
layer of dust and some black streaks of who knew what. Bat
poop probably.

It took four million years to scrub her face clean with one
hand, only to find some of the black was bruising—nice—
and another four to get a brush through the bird's nest on top
of her head. An actual twig fell out, so that was lovely.

Exhausted all over again, she opted to get into bed with her
shirt still on. She could surely wash sheets with one hand after
she'd slept for twelve hours. But her brain would not shut off
long enough to sleep. For one, she was still filthy, and she had
a hard time not thinking about what kind of ick she might be
spreading around in her bed.

She eased off the mattress and trudged back into the bathroom to wet a washcloth, then ran it all over her body, only to
realize as she collapsed back into bed that she'd just splatted
right in the middle of the dirt she'd transferred there earlier.

Another futile struggle with her shirt later, she sank to the floor and slumped against the wooded rail of her bed frame, cradling her cast. Angry tears pricked at her eyelids. For what? Because she was in pain, emotionally overwhelmed, and weak from not eating but not hungry enough to actually put something in her stomach.

And her throat still hurt.

Maybe a glass of water would help. She stumbled to the door and flung it open, nearly tripping over the cowboy spread out on the wooden floor of the hall with his back to the door-frame, which had to be uncomfortable.

"What are you doing out here?" she grumbled, annoyed that her McKay-dar seemed to be busted. How had she not realized he'd made himself at home outside her door?

He rolled and climbed to his feet with a grace that shouldn't seem so effortless on a body with so much bulk. Even boot-less, Heath towered over her, his hair adorably rumpled and untamed without his hat. Good gravy. This version of him might be even more delicious than the put-together one.

"Dancing the cha-cha, obviously." His voice sounded like he'd gargled gravel and the lines of exhaustion around his eyes aged him instantly.

Nope, no feeling sorry for him. She clamped down on the wash of emotions, especially the tender ones. Coupled with the precarious vibe between them, she had no choice but to go on the defensive until she knew how to manage the things zinging around in her heart. Preferably without giving him an advantage that would crush her, at least until she understood what he meant by *this isn't practice*.

"I wasn't going to ditch you again," she told him. "At least not tonight."

Heath's gaze flickered. "That wasn't my concern."

It took her a second to figure out what he meant. Because they'd found a body. And a jaguar head. He'd been worried about someone trying to get to her in the middle of the night, and instead of scaring her, he'd elected to forgo his own comfortable bed.

Her heart stopped zinging and started tumbling.

"I didn't ask you to do this. I can take care of myself," she returned hotly.

"Yeah, I can see that," he said without a drop of irony as he eyed her dirt-streaked shirt. "Meanwhile, I'll sleep better knowing that you're inside your room, safe and sound."

Sleep better on the floor? Sure. The warmth of his stupid self-righteous hero complex would definitely lull him into a peaceful slumber. "This is not one of those times I'm going to say thank-you."

"I wasn't confused."

Her eyelids fluttered shut. Could he be any more unflappable at midnight? Or anytime? They were standing in a semi-dark hallway, the house hushed for the night, and all she could think about was this man spider-crawling his way down a well shaft to get to her. There was no reason for him to have done that. He could have told her to hang on while he went to fetch the rope or waited for the others to get it, then lowered himself down.

But he hadn't.

She ached to ask why. She wanted to hear him confess that hearing her voice after spending a very long stretch of time convinced he never would again had opened up a place inside him that he'd had no clue existed. That's what had happened to her. She'd basically given up hope and then her name had floated down from heaven on the lips of Heath McKay and everything had shifted.

And she'd thought her feelings for him had been jumbled *before* she'd fallen into the well. Add the ghost of Margo into the mix and she had no clue how to be in her own skin.

The angry tears resurfaced. One splashed down on her cheek and she swiped it away, but not before Heath noticed. His expression caved and he muttered an expletive, drawing her into his arms without explanation. Since that was exactly where she wanted to be, why would she argue?

"Don't cry, slugger," he murmured into her hair, which quite frankly might be her favorite way for him to speak to her. "Let's reel it all back for a while and just…"

"Stop practicing?" she suggested as he walked her into her bedroom, leaving it open.

"I was going to say sleep."

Apparently, only he could call a time-out. She clamped her mouth shut as Heath gently spun her around and peeled her shirt from her sore body. It wasn't the slightest bit sexual. It was worse. Tender and intimate, as if they'd done this so many times that the ritual had become as familiar as her own skin.

With only two false starts, Heath found the drawer in her dresser with the oversize T-shirts she slept in and expertly drew one over her head, settling it on her shoulders as he threaded her arms through the holes. Who knew a man *dressing* you could be so…actually she had no idea what this feeling was.

Wordlessly, Heath led her to the bed, settling her into the correct side of the mattress without asking because of course he would be observant like that, then nodded once.

"I'll be in the hall if you need anything."

She needed *him*. How pathetic was that, to yearn for a man she couldn't have? "You can't sleep on the floor. It's ridiculously uncomfortable."

Hands shoved in his back pockets, he shrugged. "I've done worse."

"Not after spending all day searching for me without stopping," she correctly him crossly. "Get in the bed and don't argue with me. It's big enough for two adults who have a tenuous friendship and one of them is in love with someone else besides."

He hesitated long enough that she almost called his name, worried that bringing Margo into the mix had been a mistake.

But she'd wanted him to know that she got it. He'd never pick Charli. It was fine.

"I won't maul you in your sleep," she said, the scowl on face hurting the bruised places. "And think how much better you'll be able to take out an intruder if you're well rested."

That seemed to be the deciding factor since he shed his clothes without a word and slid beneath the covers.

Oh, my. When she'd offered, she'd sort of expected him to stay dressed. Every drop of moisture fled her mouth. She lay there, senses on such full alert, so painfully aware of Heath that her teeth hurt.

She'd promised not to maul him in his sleep, but she'd never said a word about what she might do while he was awake. All that Heath-ness was right there in touching distance, and she wanted to reach out more than she wanted to breathe. But she wanted to be shut down far less.

Plus, she wasn't that woman. His heart belonged to someone else. She could not in good conscience go after a man who was committed. Even as a part of her knew deep down that she didn't have a prayer of dislodging Margo in the first place.

"The sound of you not sleeping is so loud, I can hear it way over here, you know," he murmured, flipping to face her and that was so much worse.

She rolled away, facing the wall. "I'm overtired. It's not a big deal."

"Yeah, same," he admitted, sounding as weary as advertised.

Her fault. She'd led him on an exhausting search and rescue mission that shouldn't have happened. Finding the other head via her pure, dumb luck remained the only good thing that had come out of it.

She owed him. She rolled back. "Turn over."

"What? Why?"

"Just do it, McKay." She didn't even have the strength to snap at him but he did it anyway. Probably too tired to argue.

When she threaded her hand through his hair and started massaging his head, he let out a husky moan that nearly undid her.

If he kept that up, she'd forget all her principles in under point-zero seconds. Because now all she could think about was getting a repeat of that sound, but in wholly different circumstances.

"How did you know that's exactly what I needed?" he murmured.

Her eyelids slammed shut. His rich, decadent voice in the dark did sinful things to her body, things that she hurt too much to enjoy. And she really, really wanted to savor all the sensations Heath caused, even if he didn't mean to do it. Even if all of this wasn't real.

"Oh, you know me. Always practicing," she said lightly, reveling in the feel of his hair against her fingertips since this was the perfect excuse to touch it. "Since there's no time-outs tonight."

He fell silent for a beat. "Is that what we're doing? Practicing?"

"Sure. You're exhausted thanks to me. This is what I would do for you if we were together for real. Take care of you. Isn't that what an adult relationship is all about? Seeing that the person you love needs something and doing it."

"Your arm is in a cast," he pointed out needlessly since it currently lay wedged against her leg, probably adding to her bruise count.

But she wouldn't move for a million dollars. His masculine, clean scent had drifted over her, winnowing down into her blood. "So? My other arm is fine."

"I should be taking care of you," he grumbled and suddenly rolled to face her so unexpectedly that she didn't have time to fully prepare.

Who was the genius who had decided to switch off the lights? She was missing out on a whole experience here of seeing his beautiful cheekbones up close and personal, plus the chance to memorize what he looked like in her bed so she could conjure up the image later.

"My turn," he told her. "Roll over."

Oh, that was an unexpected twist. She couldn't comply fast enough.

But he didn't rub her head or even stroke her hair, which would have felt nice. Instead, he gathered her in his arms and spooned her against his delicious heat.

Instantly, she relaxed despite her previous conviction that having a hot cowboy in her bed would produce the exact opposite reaction. But this was something else. Something she'd craved without knowing it would be the glue that fixed broken places inside.

She'd never been this warm and this content in the whole of her life.

"Just to be clear," she murmured against his well-defined arm muscle that shouldn't be such an excellent pillow. "I do not sleep with men on a first date."

She could feel his lips turn up against her cheek. "This is not a date, Charlotte."

"Why don't I hate it when you call me that?" The claws came out when anyone else full-named her.

He was silent for a beat. "Because you know I only use it when we're being genuine with each other."

How could she be anything but genuine? She'd never succeed at being anything else with him. "I generally only think of myself that way when I'm at my worst. Hurricane Charlotte, at your service."

His thumb brushed against hers. "But that's when you are your truest self."

The certainty of that settled inside of her, not feeling as foreign as she would have expected. Neither was the hard press of his legs against the backs of hers. All of it overwhelmed her, beating against her rib cage to escape. "What are we doing, Heath?"

His thumb stilled. "Practicing?"

With a question mark and an implied *duh*. Because what else would it be? That's what he meant by being genuine—he genuinely didn't feel anything for her. Fine. That was perfect. It allowed her to stuff everything back in the box, where it should be.

"Yep," she agreed brightly. Too brightly for the middle of the night. "I've never slept like this with anyone, so we'll have to see how it goes. I might be terrible at it. It's a good thing—"

"Shh," he said into her hair and his breath floated over her. "You're still not sleeping. That was the point of this. So we can both rest."

And he needed to. He'd more than earned the right to rest, to have a respite from her. She could read between the lines. What she could not do was sleep, not with all the stuff churning through her head and her heart.

She was falling for him.

She could feel it happening, powerless to stop it. This man could break her. Shatter her into a billion unrecoverable shards.

It was exactly what she deserved for putting herself in this position, for pining after another woman's man. For letting him scoop her up into this wholly improper, wholly delicious embrace under the guise of *practicing*.

None of this felt like practicing. Worse, whatever she learned here would go to waste because she couldn't imagine being like this with any other man.

Apparently, Heath could also market himself as a sleeping pill because the next thing she knew, it was morning, and she woke draped over him. He slept flat on his back, and she'd wiggled her way into the crook of his arm, one leg thrown over his.

Shameful.

But when she tried to work herself free without waking him, his arm tightened, clamping her in place. And then Heath opened his eyes, still heavy with sleep, and the bottomless abyss of blue scored her on the inside where a man should never have been able to touch.

Which scared her more than anything else that had happened to her in the last twenty-four hours and that was saying something.

"Hi, good morning," she said with fake cheer. "I need food and ibuprofen stat."

Prying herself loose only worked because he let her and then she fled.

Chapter Eighteen

When Heath came back to the house after taking a shower in the ranch hand's quarters where he normally slept, Charli was right where he'd left her, sitting at the breakfast table sipping coffee like he'd asked her to.

He paused before announcing his presence to just...take a minute. Man, she was so much stronger than any woman he'd ever met. Not only had she survived a fall into a well, she'd found the jaguar head and a human body, and somehow resisted curling up in a ball in the corner after finding herself trapped with a corpse.

She was something else. Someone he'd never have said he'd be attracted to, but here they were. His skin still tingled from the feel of her against his fingertips.

Nothing in his head or his chest lined up quite right when he looked at Charli. She'd destroyed him and then knit him back together with nothing more than her fingers in his hair. Tending to him. Because that's what a woman did for someone she cared about in Charli's world.

Not in his. He'd never even dreamed that someone could pay that kind of attention to him. Or would. Especially after a day that included her being trapped in a well and breaking an arm.

What was he supposed to do with her?

Charli wasn't alone in the kitchen. An older woman who must be her mother sat with her, both of them glancing up when he made a noise to let them know he was here before his silent reckoning got creepy. Yep. They had the same eyes.

Mrs. Lang insisted that Heath call her Patricia, taking his hand and warmly thanking him for saving her daughter. Which was a totally legit thing to be grateful for, but geez. What was it about mothers that made him want to duck his head and get a haircut?

Maybe it was because he and Charli had crossed some kind of line last night. What line, he didn't know, but everything had changed and yet nothing had. It had always felt like they were entangled in ways that were difficult to explain.

Nor was anyone asking him to, least of all Charli. She couldn't leave the bed they'd slept in together last night fast enough. He got it. Everything had turned upside down and it was big and strange. He should probably check in with her.

But the security company that bore his name had multiple things going on today and he owed it to his partners to show up. Despite the fact that all of them needed some downtime after the long darkness of the day before, no one was going to get it.

Before the craziness started, he planned to dump copious amounts of caffeine down his throat. As he pulled a mug out of the cupboard above the coffee maker, Charli joined him, sliding right into his space as if they'd always stood here together in a scene straight out of the domestic bliss playbook. She even smelled perfect, like vanilla and woman.

"Let me," she murmured and took the mug from his hand. "I owe you this, plus about a million other things."

Speechless, he watched as she grabbed the carafe and poured the coffee, then dumped two spoonfuls of sugar into it, stirred, then added the exact right amount of creamer. She'd even done it in the same order as he always did, which he'd honestly never even thought about as a routine, but she'd somehow learned his coffee preferences expertly as if she'd memorized the steps.

"What is all of this?" he asked suspiciously.

"Do I need a reason?" When she glanced over her shoulder, she must have realized the answer to that was *duh*. She rolled her eyes. "I like being able to take care of something for you. You run around being all capable and stuff. Makes it hard for me to reciprocate. Deal with it."

She handed him the mug and he sipped, biting back a moan as the first rich taste hit his system. "How did you know how to make this for me?"

She flashed him a guilty grin. "I can't tell you on the grounds that it might incriminate me."

"You have a spy camera set up in here?" he guessed and glanced around for show despite being 100 percent aware there was no such thing thanks to Pierce's careful sweeps for any foreign equipment.

"Which part of *I can't tell you* wasn't clear?" She hip-checked him and winced, instantly sobering the vibe between them. "I guess I fell on that one."

That hip and a lot of other places that he'd personally cataloged while helping her change into her T-shirt last night. She'd heal but the rage that had built in his chest as he'd noted the marks on her skin roared right back. There wasn't anything he could break that would fix it for her. That was the problem. She hurt and he couldn't do anything about that or his urge to plow a fist through something.

"I'm sorry," he murmured. "Want me to kiss it and make it better?"

She glanced at her mother, still seated at the table on the other side of the kitchen and turned her back to the table deliberately, leaning in to whisper. "Heath McKay, are you flirting with me?"

That teased a smile out of him, because of course Charli

would have the power to amuse him even in the midst of his physical response to her pain. "Yes. Strictly for practice, of course."

Her expression instantly flattened as she nodded. "Of course. I knew that. The coffee is practice too."

That was the same voice she'd used last night, after she'd asked what they were doing and he'd answered the question with a question because he had no idea. He loved Margo or at least that's what he'd been trying to tell himself for quite some time. But at this point, he didn't have a lot of confidence he'd be able to pick love out of a lineup.

Margo had never done anything like rub his head or make his coffee. What did that mean? He was driving himself nuts with questions that shouldn't be so hard to answer.

Heath tipped up Charli's chin with his thumb so she could see his sincerity. "The coffee was a nice touch. I'd like to stand here and flirt some more, but I'm afraid today is going to be a nightmare. For both of us."

Which started almost immediately when Madden, Sophia and Pierce rolled into the kitchen, business faces on. Everyone took a spot at the table.

Beneath it, Charli slipped her hand into his, warming him in places he hadn't realized were cold. He suspected she'd needed the connection to settle something inside.

At least he could do that for her. And would, as much as she wanted. It worked out that it settled something inside him too. Who knew secret hand-holding would be so affecting?

"Logistics meeting," Madden announced.

Sophia touched her mother's shoulder. "Mom, this is going to be so boring. You're welcome to stay if you would like but Ace is going to be talking about some of the security changes that have to happen now that we've located another jaguar head."

And a dead body. But Heath kept that to himself. Everyone

was enough on edge without the added fear that there might be a killer on the loose. Though it had to be on Madden's mind.

"*Another* head?" Charli stressed. "You mean *the other* head. Right? The only one. Say that's what you meant."

Sophia glanced over at Charli, her expression grim. "I talked to Dr. Low about that. She's pulling in some other experts from the museum in Mexico who might be able to verify if there are more."

Charli groaned and tried to rub her forehead with the arm encased in the cast and nearly hit herself in the eye. "No more heads. We need these people to leave, not bring more experts to the ranch. We might as well move the opening date of the Cowboy Experience to next year at this rate."

"Actually," Madden interjected. "That's not a bad idea."

If Heath hadn't been holding her hand, he might have missed how agitated that statement made Charli. He stroked a thumb down hers, but her spine didn't loosen, and he needed it to.

"Can we table that conversation for the moment?" Heath wasn't asking, though, and plowed ahead. "We need double the number of armed guards pronto."

That did the trick. She relaxed, letting her shoulder graze his arm in a way that set off sparks in places that needed to stop sparking ASAP. This game required his head in it with no distractions, and all he wanted to do was wrap himself and Charli back up in the cocoon of darkness where they could keep pretending the real world didn't exist, that they hadn't made the stupid bet, and he'd never let Margo get her hooks into him in the first place.

"Already on it," Madden confirmed with a nod. "They'll be here by noon."

"No one leaves the house without one of the three of us," Heath continued, wagging a finger between himself, Madden and Pierce. "I'm thinking it wouldn't be out of place for us all to renew our acquaintance with our friends Smith & Wesson."

Sophia glanced at Madden and the look they exchanged

carried a lot of unspoken language meant to leave everyone else out of the conversation. Normally Heath would be the one Madden shared his concerns with, but things had subtly shifted with the introduction of his friend's relationship with Sophia. It should bother him more, but given the vibe between him and Charli, and the ways they'd been learning to read each other, he got it all at once.

This was what a relationship looked like. It was mind-blowing how wrong he'd gotten it with Margo. How right it felt with Charli. Did she feel it too?

"Everyone should make that decision for themselves," Madden said quietly.

"Can I have a gun then?" Charli wanted to know.

"No," Sophia and Heath answered at the same time. Charli looked so crestfallen he rushed to amend that with, "At least not until I teach you how to use one."

That got him a smile and a head bop on the arm, which seemed to raise her spirits. Until there was a knock at the front door and Sophia left to answer it, then returned in seconds with the sheriff in tow. His badge gleamed against his sedate brown uniform, both ominous this early in the morning.

"I'm glad you're all here," the sheriff announced gravely, his hat in his hand. "Thought I would come by personally to tell you some difficult news. We've positively identified the deceased as David Lang."

Forget a pin—you could have heard a feather drop in the room.

Heath immediately removed his hat in kind, wishing he hadn't seen that bombshell coming a mile away. Charli sucked in a breath, her grip on his hand tightening, but otherwise, she accepted the news stoically.

Sophia, not so much. She started crying and Madden folded her into his embrace, murmuring to her while he stroked her back. Which Heath totally would have done for Charli if she'd seemed like she needed it, but in her typical fashion, she met this challenge head-on.

"Are you sure?" she demanded of the sheriff. "No question?"

The sheriff nodded. "We used two corroboration methods to verify."

Because of the level of decomposition, no doubt. The sheriff was being discreet by leaving out the details, but most likely the police had access to Lang's dental records and possibly existing DNA samples since he'd grown up here at the ranch, likely utilizing still-existing medical services in town.

Mrs. Lang, who had returned to the room with the arrival of the sheriff, stepped forward, her face frozen. "Do you know how long he's been dead?"

The sheriff met her halfway and extended his hand to shake hers. "You must be Mrs. Lang. I am very sorry for your loss and to be meeting you under these circumstances. I'm afraid I can't give you specifics yet. We've ordered an autopsy, which will help us determine cause of death as well as the date. Rest assured we'll open an investigation immediately if foul play was involved."

Mrs. Lang murmured her thanks and put a comforting hand on each of her daughters' shoulders. Heath's skin got tight and started feeling like it was on backward, so he bowed out, catching Madden's eye and jerking his head toward the door.

Figuring it was better to let the Lang women grieve without an audience, he hightailed it to Charli's bedroom to wait it out. Man, that was a rough scene. He didn't do grief well in the first place. It was one of the few things that couldn't be pounded out of his system, and it hurt to watch other people hurting.

Especially Charli. And wasn't that a kicker to find out that he could bleed just as easily when someone else took the hit.

Some forty-five minutes later, Charli wandered through the door, not seeming overly shocked to find him lounging on her bed, boots kicked off and hat on the floor next to them. Which he'd done strictly to show her that he was here and present for as long as she wanted him there.

"Heath," she croaked, looking as if she might faint at any second. Before he could spring out of the bed to catch her, she held up a finger. "Time-out. No questions."

He nodded. As if he'd have denied her anything.

Without a word, she crawled onto the bed and right on top of him, collapsing against his chest. Automatically, his arms came around her, cradling her close. She was shaking.

"Hey," he murmured, inhaling her scent, which inexplicably calmed him. "I've got you. Breathe with me."

She did, falling into the rhythm that he set. He stroked her hair, pausing occasionally to circle her temples soothingly. After an eternity of his heart feeling like she'd seared it with a hot knife, the trembling eased off, finally stopping entirely.

"Good girl," he whispered and lifted her face with his thumbs. Then wished he hadn't.

Charli's expression was ravaged. Coupled with everything else, it put his body on simmer, the edges of his vision going black. Not a good thing, especially when there wasn't a target for him to punch. But this was where he would temper his tendencies, pull it all back. For her. Because she needed him to.

"What can I do?" he almost bit out and course-corrected quickly, leveling his voice on the last syllables.

"You're already doing it."

Her accompanying sigh reverberated through his chest, the sentiment likewise spreading through him like warm honey, soothing him in the same vein as he'd tried to do for her. Who knew that they'd be so good like this? That they could pull each other off the roller coaster at a time when they both so desperately needed it?

She sat back on the bedspread, her legs under her, taking all her heat and light and vanilla-y scent with her. But she threaded her fingers through his and it was enough. They clung to each other as they each processed their own very different emotions.

"It doesn't feel like enough," he muttered. "I hate seeing you so upset."

Charli shook her head. "The terrible part is that I'm not upset that he's dead. It's fine, he's basically been the equivalent of dead for a long time anyway. But now it's like…final. We can't ever have a conversation where I tell him what a lousy piece of filth he is for leaving us."

"And what if you find out he's been dead for years?" he added because he got it. It was a lot to take in.

"Exactly. It changes things. It changes how I think about myself." She eyed him. "Why are you here? You left the kitchen and I thought I'd find out you'd galloped off on a horse or something."

He scowled. What kind of man did she take him for? "And leave you to deal with all of this by yourself?"

To be fair, he had actually left her in the kitchen, but he had good reasons for that. She'd needed to be with her family, not a bunch of onlookers.

She stared at him, and he had the distinct impression she wasn't at all sure what to make of what she saw. That made two of them. "I don't get any of this, Heath. Why the bet? Why frame all of this as practice? Because it doesn't feel like you need much."

Oh, he definitely did. Whatever had just happened between them, whatever you called it, he could do that a hundred more times and still not feel like he'd mastered it—but more to the point, no other woman had ever made him want to try. Or afforded him the opportunity to.

This bet with Charli was 100 percent practice, but not for the reasons he'd originally laid out. Not anymore.

He forced a chuckle. "If it makes you feel any better, this is not the kind of thing I've ever done before."

Disbelief climbed its way up Charli's expression. "What?

Show up for me? That's what you do, Heath. It's like you can read my mind and know exactly what I need from you."

"Took me way too long to find you yesterday," he muttered as everything inside revolted against what she was telling him. That he was good at this relationship business when in reality, he was stumbling around blindfolded, depending on his senses to guide him. "I meant I've never done *this* before. Whatever *this* is."

He waved his hand in a circle to encompass the two of them, punctuating the point.

"It's practice. Isn't it?" She stared at him, her eyes huge and damp and full of something he couldn't look away from. "That's what we agreed to. The bet is almost an afterthought now. Because somewhere along the way, I realized how much I want to get it right."

He let himself fall into the possibilities that she meant she felt the way he did, that it had stopped feeling like rehearsal a long time ago. That this might be the realest real deal there was.

"I want to get it right too," he murmured.

"Of course you do," she said and squeezed her eyes shut. "For Margo. It's a lot easier for you because you have her in mind when we're practicing. I'm turning myself inside out for some nameless, faceless dude I haven't met yet. He's going to be different. What if getting it right with you is wrong with him?"

White-hot rage stole his vision as he processed the idea that for one, he and Charli were not in fact on the same page with what was happening between them and two, at some point she'd move on. Into someone else's arms. Who was not Heath.

He wanted to destroy that nameless, faceless dude.

Just as the black edges bled into the field of white, she squeezed his hand. It centered him. Brought him back from the edge in a blink.

"Thank you for introducing the concept of a time-out," she

told him. "Our friendship means a lot to me. In a lot of ways, that's practice for a relationship too. Because this matters to me in a way a romantic relationship wouldn't. I can tell you things I would never say to someone I was dating for real."

So…that's what all of this was to her? Them becoming *friends*?

The tiny sound he heard inside could quite possibly be his heart breaking a little. But honestly, it was the best scenario. He did love Margo. Probably. And did want to impress her with his new personality, the one that could come back from the brink of hulk-smashing drywall with nothing more than a squeeze of someone's hand.

"That's what I'm here for," he said weakly but meant it.

This was how it should be. If he got back together with Margo, she'd become better too, simply by virtue of seeing what lengths Heath had gone to in order to win her back. That's how it worked with Charli. They both tried, they both gave, they both course-corrected when needed.

Like he needed to do now. Charli expected him to act like a friend—that's what he'd be.

Feeling as if he still wasn't quite on the track he'd expected to be, he ran his thumb over Charli's, gratified she'd never released his hand. "We're both learning how to have an adult relationship without the risk of screwing it up."

Her expression grew thoughtful. "I'm realizing I've never had one. An adult relationship. You see what my model for relationships is. My dad ending up at the bottom of a well, leaving all of us to believe he abandoned us. My ability to take things at face value is broken. It scares me. Maybe I'll do all this practicing and screw it up when it comes to the real thing. Maybe I'm broken."

The utter bravery it took for her to admit that she was scared crushed him.

"I want you to hear that you're getting it right," he said

fiercely. "Safe space, Charli. I wouldn't lie to you. You're not broken."

If there was ever a moment in their history when he wished he could call a time-out, it was this one. No one else existed in the world except her. A time-out would allow him to do exactly as he wished, and if he had that latitude, it would be to kiss her. To explore the way she made him feel, as if they were embarking on something new and wonderful together.

That wasn't what they were doing here, though. The romance part of their relationship didn't exist. But naming it and claiming it did nothing to lessen the tide of Charli in his blood.

Neither did the look on her face, as if she'd found something precious and could hardly believe her luck. He wanted it to mean something other than what it did.

"You heard me, didn't you?" he said, his voice huskier than it should be given the circumstances. "All this practice is not for nothing. You're this close to winning the bet."

He held up his finger and thumb with zero space between them and a smile curving his lips that he almost didn't have to fake.

Tipping her face up, she caught his gaze. "Does this mean you're finally going to take me on a date?"

Chapter Nineteen

Straightening things out with Charli should have worked to clear Heath's head. He shouldn't be so distracted. But the fact of the matter was that he couldn't concentrate on the security issues that should be his sole focus. Instead, the entire breadth of his mental capacity was going toward planning a perfect first date.

She deserved that. After learning to make his coffee and giving him a fair shot and a dozen other things that signified her commitment to their practice relationship, he needed to step up his game.

"Would it be totally cliché to just make reservations at a nice restaurant in Dallas?" he asked Pierce as they walked across the yard to debrief the new security guards their third-party company had sent.

Pierce rolled his eyes. "Yes, McKay. It would. Try again."

"A picnic?"

"Let's keep thinking," Pierce suggested, as if he could claim the title of Most Romantic Man Alive without breaking a sweat and Heath was merely a bothersome novice.

"If you're so smart, what would you do?" he shot back.

"I don't know Charli very well, so I can't tell you. That's for you to figure out. It's supposed to show her that she's worth the effort to take five minutes and plan something that is meaningful to *her*," he stressed. "What does she like?"

"To antagonize me," he muttered with a double take at Pierce's eyebrow lift. "What? It's her favorite hobby."

To be fair, he poked at her in kind pretty frequently. Maybe he even started it on occasion. But when she faced him down with that snap in her gaze—she was the most beautiful woman in the world.

The times they reeled it back…those were the best and came far too infrequently. Was it at all in the realm of possibility to call a time-out for an entire date?

Except that pretty much negated the experiment. Plus, he liked sparring with her as much as she seemed to. That's why this was such a strange, wonderful relationship—and yes, they had one. A friendship. Officially. It was new, and difficult to quantify, but real to him.

And so different in a good way than any relationship he'd ever had before. They were *friends*. It wasn't as terrible as it sounded. Plus, it was what he had to work with.

Pierce was right, but Heath had no plans to admit it out loud. Charli warranted whatever it took for him to find the perfect first date and he'd think on it until the idea unfolded naturally. It wasn't like he could spring for the time off tonight, not with all the additional security logistics.

The gun tucked into the holster at his hip was a part of that, a necessary one. That was the beauty of a place like Texas with open carry laws, and Heath had wasted no time getting the additional license to complement his concealed carry license the moment he'd arrived.

He just hadn't expected to use it in quite such an obvious way. Anyone in a half-mile radius—or further, pending their surveillance equipment—hopefully had zero question about his willingness to use his weapon to keep the peace.

Or destroy it if someone came after Charli. With or without his firearm.

He and Pierce got the new guys organized, showed them the extra beds in the bunkhouse where they would sleep during their off hours. They were running armed guards around the clock, three on the trailer where the jaguar heads lived in the safe bolted to the floor and two making rounds between the house and the woods, with unscheduled loops around both.

The hope was that this would be temporary, just until the university people rolled out with their treasure and took the chaos with them.

"If we're set here, I'm going to spend a few hours on my drone code," Pierce announced once they were able to leave the guards to their jobs. "The quality of the thermals is not where I'd like it to be given the circumstances. I got some new sensors that should solve the issue with the denser brush near the creek too."

Since all of that sounded like as much fun as learning Swahili, Heath waved him off to go do his geek things in solitude. That's why God made people like Paxton Pierce, so the Heaths of the world didn't have to think about the finer points of sensors and whatever nonsense went along with increasing the quality of thermal imaging.

All this tension and attention to the hardware of the surveillance *and* personal protection variety was making him antsy. They'd found the other head. Well, Charli had, by accident, but it still counted. This whole cuckoo environment should be easing up but he felt more on edge today than he ever had before.

But with Charli in the house and everything Madden had asked Heath to do completed, maybe he could spend some time googling date ideas. Nail something down. He wanted to show Charli that he was invested, that he could get this right too. In the name of practice, of course.

Internet reception was better closer to the house, so he

headed in that direction, his phone already in his hand as he
went with the "on the nose" option and googled "perfect first
dates."

That's why he didn't notice the woman standing near the
back door until she called out, "Hello, Heath," in that cultured
voice that he used to hear in his dreams.

Margo's voice.

It was all wrong in this setting. Margo's voice didn't go
with East Texas or the dirt in the yard. Neither did it sit right
in his chest.

He glanced up, straight into Margo's stunning hazel eyes
that could turn the color of molten silver or iced tea or a moss-
covered log pending what she was wearing. Today, the armor
of choice was a sleek black jumpsuit with wide legs and a
crystal-encrusted belt around her minuscule waist. Barbie pink
stilettos, of course, and a pink jacket thrown over her shoulder
completed the look that he had no doubt she'd spent a fortune
in time and money to pull together.

Her face had a flawless complexion thanks to the trifecta
of genetics, expensive skincare routines and a deal with the
devil, probably.

Good God, she was still an uncommonly beautiful woman,
and he felt absolutely nothing when he looked at her. What
was *happening*?

"What are you doing here?" he demanded, so floored that
he couldn't have found his manners with a military-grade
GPS receiver.

She laughed, the trilling, slightly amused one that used to
make him smile, but now only confused his already beleaguered senses.

"No hug for someone who used to pick up your favorite
Chinese food?" she asked sweetly, holding up her hands.

Heath's muscles jumped to do exactly as bid in some kind
of Pavlovian response before he could check them. Shocking
how easily she could *still* evoke a response in him. But then,

she'd been doing that for a long time, and he'd always had zero resistance when it came to her.

She folded herself into his embrace, bringing with her a cloud of spicy perfume she regularly restocked from a store in Morocco, which he knew because he'd given her the first bottle for Christmas an eon ago.

Nothing had changed with Margo, apparently, even after she'd given him the boot.

It threw him off-kilter and he'd never quite been on-kilter with her in the first place.

He pulled away and crossed his arms, focusing his attention front and center on facts, not his own stupid hang-ups when it came to this woman. "I can't say a hug is how I thought you'd want to be greeted the first time we saw each other after... what happened."

It's not me, it's you.

That's what she'd said when she dumped him. It still stung, honestly. Not only the smug, sarcastic phrasing, but the whole concept.

What *was* wrong with him, exactly? That he liked being physical? That it made him feel good to protect people and make sure other people knew they couldn't threaten or bully their way through life?

That was Charli's voice in his head. He shouldn't be thinking about her or how much better he liked her narrative.

"Oh, Heath, let's leave the past in the past, shall we?" she murmured, her stilettos inching closer to him as she swept him with an appreciative once-over. "I'm a fan of how you're flourishing in this environment."

His eyebrows shot up so high that they nearly hit the brim of his Stetson. "You hate it when I don't shave, and I've never once heard you say a positive thing about boots."

It was so weird, but he'd sworn he would react differently the next time he came in contact with Margo. He'd planned it all out in his head, how he'd sweep her off her feet with his new, improved, much calmer persona. But here and now, with the real reunion happening, his temper had already started swirling twice in thirty seconds.

Was it possible that Margo *herself* had been the one to constantly provoke him into being such a hothead?

Margo folded her jacket over her arm, contemplating him. "Maybe I've come to appreciate things about you now that I've had time and distance to contemplate our relationship."

That was closer to the conversation he'd hoped to have, but very far from the one he'd expected. "So that's why you're here? You want to apologize to me and start over?"

"As happy as I am to see you again," she said, "I'm actually here on official business."

When Margo's smile gained a strange edge, every nerve in his body blipped into high alert. "JSOC is getting into the Maya treasure business?"

Margo lifted one shoulder delicately. "When the treasure in question is tied to the funding of a sleeper cell out of Iraq, I'm afraid the answer is yes."

His arms were crossed so tightly that his muscles started to ache. "And you naturally requested this assignment when you saw my name come across your desk."

The incredulity dripped from his voice but really, he shouldn't be so shocked. Word had gotten out all right. And brought with it a slew of new challenges that he couldn't have anticipated even with the aid of a crystal ball.

"Life has so few coincidences." She smiled and he didn't miss the glint in her gaze.

This wasn't just a job. Or just a drive-by reunion. It was both. And felt exceptionally mercenary all at once.

His knees actually went weak as he absorbed this blindside. How like the universe to throw this enormous monkey wrench in his path the second he'd set up a practice run with Charli—which he wasn't done with, not by a long shot. He was supposed to be figuring out how to be in a relationship by spending time with her, not by shepherding Spec Ops representatives around who came with history that suddenly weighed more than an albatross.

The complications, they were legion.

If Margo wanted him back, great. He should *want* to spend time with her. He owed it to himself—and Charli—to try out his new husband material persona on his ex-girlfriend. It was what he'd been practicing for. Why was he being so weird about it?

Heath pinched the bridge of his nose. "How is this going to work, then?"

She smiled and it was the one she used when she wanted something. "I was hoping you'd be my ace in the hole. For old times' sake."

She *would* liken this to a poker match. Heath shook his head. "The jaguar heads are in a biometrically accessed safe and I'm not one of the people with the keys to the kingdom. You'll have to go through the bigwigs at Harvard for that, if they even decide to let you near them. And they don't have to listen to me on that, by the way."

Nor would he advise them to. He wouldn't get near that conversation with a ten-foot pole.

"Well, this is a dilemma," she said smoothly. "What can we do to facilitate my investigation? I don't want to pull in local law enforcement. I thought that by coming to you first, we could avoid all of that."

Yeah, dilemma was the word all right. As not-so-veiled threats went, this one landed a pretty hard punch. If he kept digging in his heels, she'd circumvent him and his partners, then blast onto the property with the blessing of Gun Barrel City's finest. He'd be completely cut out of the picture. That did not sit well, especially not when he still didn't understand what was happening here.

For the first time, he had the luxury of seeing Margo without blinders on. It was quite possible that she'd always used her connection to him in ways he'd never examined fully.

He'd have to play along. At least until he got a clearer picture what in the blazes this was all about. Because he didn't for a second believe JSOC cared about jaguar heads, nor that someone had magically unearthed a connection to terrorists half a world away.

He couldn't discount a sense of edginess since Charli had discovered the body of her father and there were too many other unknown elements in the mix. They didn't have a blessed clue about what kind of buddies David Lang might have picked up along the way. They didn't know how he'd died. The trailer break-in hadn't been resolved, not fully. And there were still too dang many people on this ranch coming and going as they pleased.

Margo was the last straw. How was he supposed to separate his win-back campaign from *his* job, especially when she insisted on combining the two? Funny how that had never been an issue with Charli.

"Fine, I'll be your liaison," he told her, painting a smile on his face that he hoped came across as genuine.

Margo practically purred as she sidled up next to him, heels boosting her into his space in a way that used to feel comfortable. Welcome, even. It was neither all at once.

"We should spend some time debriefing," she suggested silkily. "Maybe over a brandy."

His gag reflex nearly created a soundtrack of his opinion about that plan. Who actually drank brandy on purpose? She never had before. Oddly, that anomaly tripped his radar the hardest. "Sure. Give me an hour to take care of some things. I *am* working."

"Oh, right. Your new job." She said it as if naming a previously unknown virus and hooked her arm through his. "I'm sure I don't have to remind you that the brass at Fort Bragg don't like to be kept waiting. The sooner we can get this pesky terrorist funding issue dismissed, the better."

Was that her goal? To eliminate suspicion cast on this treasure? Somehow, he didn't believe that was her actual assignment. But the only mechanism to figure out what she wasn't telling him lay in playing her game for as long as it took to unwind all the layers of deception going on around here. Neither did he think she was the only one with an agenda.

"Thirty minutes," he amended, silently cursing the satisfied smile she flashed him.

"Great. We can catch up at the same time," she suggested with a heated once-over that had all the subtlety of a warhead.

"Great," he echoed.

Suddenly, he had a very bad feeling he'd been practicing all wrong.

Chapter Twenty

Charli felt really good about establishing the friendship boundary around her practice relationship with Heath. Sure, it smacked of self-preservation, but he didn't have to know that she'd thrown up as many walls as she could to keep herself on the straight and narrow.

It was far too easy for her to forget that when he took her hand, he was thinking about Margo, not Charli. Then she remembered and it burned through her as if she'd swallowed a quart of battery acid.

He deserved to be happy, to get what he'd been working so hard for without the additional burden of Charli's ridiculous and misplaced feelings.

She hadn't quite figured out what she deserved. To be alone for a while probably. Spend some time working on the Cowboy Experience and then see whether the Heath-shaped place in her heart had shrunk at all.

Ace had taken Sophia and Patricia into Gun Barrel City to talk to the sheriff. They needed to find out how long the autopsy and investigation would take, then drop by a couple of possible venues for a memorial service.

Charli had begged off with the excuse of sticking around the ranch so she could work on the guest menu for meals they'd serve once they were able to open. Sophia intended to hire a full-time chef who would probably have some ideas as well, but given their lack of income thus far, the pay range wouldn't attract top-tier talent at first, so Charli had volunteered to do some research.

That lasted all of fifteen minutes, the longest she'd ever sat in Sophia's desk chair, and it felt like fourteen minutes too long. How did her sister sit in this thing for hours on end?

Fresh air needed, stat. Charli pushed back from the desk and wandered outside. Maybe she could quiz some of the hands about their favorite dishes and call the menu Rustic Ranch Fare.

The moment she stepped outside, the entire ranch panorama fell off the face of the map. All Charli could see was a svelte blonde viper wrapped around Heath, a solid dose of possessiveness dripping from her fingers. There was practically a pop-up bubble above her head with *mine* in capital letters and flashing lights.

Heath's chin swiveled and he locked gazes with Charli. His expression flattened as if he'd snapped a cable supplying all his emotional energy. She barely recognized him, as if she'd stumbled over a doppelganger who definitely looked like Heath McKay but had actually been born in Argentina and didn't even speak English.

"Ms. Lang," he called, his voice a match for his expression.

Since she was the only Ms. Lang around thanks to her ill-timed bailout from the memorial service, she crossed her arms so neither he nor the viper could see how her hands shook to hear Heath address her so formally.

"What's up, McKay?" she said.

Heath walked toward her. Viper on the other hand, no. The woman strode across the yard as if she owned it and everything around her, including the town and possibly the whole state. If this woman had ever suffered from lack of confidence, Charli would eat Heath's hat.

"We were just coming to the door," Heath said flatly. "So I could introduce you."

"You must be Charlotte Lang," Viper said and even her voice had been specially crafted to be mesmerizing.

There was no reason to hate her. But Charli did. Instantly.

"It's Charli," she corrected. "No one calls me Charlotte."

Except Heath. But if he recalled their conversation about what it meant when he Charlotte-ed her, his expression sure didn't show it. His current one resembled granite.

Charli stuck out her hand, figuring it was her job to be civil to someone who was a guest on the property. Surely the practice would come in handy for when real guests came, because odds were high she wouldn't like everyone who paid to enjoy the Cowboy Experience.

"This is Margo," Heath added almost as an afterthought.

Charli's hand turned to lead and dropped to her side.

The name rocketed through Charli's soul like a throwing star ricocheting inside her, its cutting points drawing blood with each tender surface it hit. The viper was *Margo*. She had every right to wrap herself around Heath, and he had every right to enjoy it as much as he could.

"Oh," she croaked. "That's, um, nice. It's nice to meet you, I mean. Margo. Hello."

Margo ignored the fact that Charli stood there like a wax statue and extended her hand with enough grace to convince anyone that if her mother was a viper, her father had been a gazelle. "Margo Malloy. Intelligence analyst with JSOC. I'm happy to meet you. I'm here to investigate the recent discoveries on the ranch."

Woodenly, Charli clasped the viper—Margo's—hand and released it immediately.

"Investigate?" Apparently, Charli's ability to use her brain had been sucked out of her by the force of Margo's presence. "I don't understand. You're here to investigate something?"

Like, whether Heath still belonged to her? That was a quick one, requiring no intelligence whatsoever. There hadn't been a whole lot of pushing her away on Heath's part, after all, and the woman had practically been climbing him like a tree.

"Yes, the recent discoveries," Margo repeated without a drop of frustration, as if she had no clue she was speaking to an idiot who hadn't gotten her wits about her yet. "The Maya jaguar heads. JSOC has an interest in delving further into this situation."

Oh. *Those* recent discoveries. Charli blinked. Margo was here because of the stupid gold heads? If she didn't have an audience, Charli would scream. Actually, she might anyway. It wasn't like she could pale in comparison to Margo any further.

"Investigate away, then," she muttered. "Don't let me stop you."

Margo glanced between Charli and Heath, who'd turned into a mute bump on a log. Probably because he wished he could be done with his bodyguard duties so he could have a proper reunion with Vip—Margo.

"I'm told you're the best person to assist?" Margo said with a lilt on the end as if not sure her intel was correct.

Assist? Was that military speak for getting Margo coffee? "I own the ranch. Is that the skill set you're looking for?"

The joke fell flat. But it wasn't much of a joke.

Not only did Margo not laugh, she cocked her head, studying Charli curiously. "I just need someone in charge. If that's you, great. I hope we can work together so I can get out of your hair as soon possible. My goal is to make this investigation fast and painless, especially for you since I've descended on you with no warning. The more you cooperate, the quicker I can leave."

Well, that sounded fantastic. Anything that would get the

viper off the ranch and hopefully take Heath with her worked for Charli and then some.

The idea didn't relax her an iota. "Happy to help. What are you investigating exactly?"

Margo brightened, a feat since she'd walked into this conversation with a great deal of animation, as if she didn't have an off switch. "I'm so glad you asked. Most of the details are classified but the basics I can share. We intercepted some intelligence that suggests the jaguar heads you found might be linked to an organization we have eyes on. We think the treasure was intended to help fund their activities."

An organization? Like the government of a foreign country or the Boy Scouts? Charli had a feeling if she asked, Margo would say that information was classified, which was a handy way of never having to admit to anything. "What will you do if you can prove it?"

Margo smiled. "Shut them down. They can't operate without money."

But the treasure wasn't in their possession. It was in the hands of the Harvard people and heavily guarded besides. If Charli hadn't come into this conversation already intimidated, she might have a better handle on how to ask the right questions, but as it stood, she didn't want to stand here jabbering with Special Ops Barbie any longer than she had to, so she bit back her questions.

Probably she just didn't understand how any of this worked.

Heath picked that moment to join the conversation. "Margo will be here for a couple of days. She'll be combing through the sites where the two heads were found. I'll run point on security, to ensure she can come and go at will."

That made even less sense. After all this time, what possible clues did Margo expect to find?

"Great," Charli forced a smile. "Let me know what I can do to help."

"You can speak to the head of the dig," Margo suggested

immediately as if she'd been waiting for that exact offer. "I'll need full access to the treasure so I can catalog it as evidence. Also, if this isn't too delicate of a request, I would really appreciate some assistance navigating your father's finances. We'd like to look for transactions that may tie him to the organization under investigation."

Follow the money. That part Charli got. But that didn't make it any easier to comply. "Sorry, I have no idea who could help with that. My father didn't live here or, like, communicate with us too much."

Or at all. Though it wouldn't shock Charli to find out her father had gotten killed by some nefarious "organization" out of the Middle East that he'd tried to sell his treasure to.

Margo nodded. "Okay, that's completely fine. We'll work with what we have."

That was not the first time she'd made reference to a *we*. "Do you have a team arriving?"

"Just me." The woman's smile hadn't slipped once, which was starting to grate on Charli. "Though I do plan to borrow Heath as frequently as I can."

"Heath?" His name on Margo's lips dumped a bucket of ice water on Charli's head. And she'd been off-balance in the first place.

Every scrap of Charli's spare energy funneled into pretending she hadn't just realized Margo's presence meant the end of practicing with Heath. Which didn't leave a lot left over to keep her on her feet. She might even be weaving.

This morning, Heath would have caught her. Not now. She was on her own.

Margo leaned in, tilting her head as if imparting a secret. "I'm sure I don't have to tell you how handy he is in the field. We used to work together. He was the kind of operative you could count on to get the job done."

The thread running through the other woman's voice carried more than a hint of longing. And familiarity. Neither did

Charli think the phrasing was accidental—she'd totally meant it as a double entendre.

It put Charli's back up. "Yeah, he told me. Along with the rest of your history."

That got a rise out of the ice princess, who had thus far maintained a completely even keel. Challenge flittered through her hazel eyes as she evaluated Charli. "Then you know we were more than colleagues."

"That's not relevant, Margo," Heath interjected, his voice still oddly flat.

"I'm fairly certain that it is." Her gaze narrowed a flick. "I hope we can all be professional about working together, Ms. Lang. I've been looking forward to renewing my acquaintance with Heath."

Yeah, and Charli looked forward to acquainting Margo with a pile of horse dung, but she painted a smile on her face anyway, one that carried its own challenge. Whatever Margo thought she'd picked up on, it didn't exist. But Charli knew what a threatened woman looked like, and this was it.

Margo thought Charli represented some type of *competition*, here. Which was hilarious. But inexplicably put Charli in a much better mood.

She showed her teeth. "I can take you out to the site where I found the second head. Hope you brought horseback riding clothes."

"Horseback?" Margo blinked. "Can we use the ATV I saw around the corner?"

"That belongs to the university people." Charli crossed her arms, leaving out the part where they let anyone use it who asked. She shot Heath a glance, but he didn't correct her.

"Oh, all right," Margo conceded with a faint voice. "Let me see what I have with me."

And like that, Charli was dismissed. "We'll be here when you're ready," she called after the rapidly disappearing Margo.

* * *

Charli double-timed it to the house so she could beat the viper back to the yard. And not be near Heath.

"Charli, stop walking away," Heath called and followed her up the stairs.

She liked it better when he called her Charlotte. At least then she knew nothing had changed. "I'm not walking. I'm stomping. There's a very clear difference."

She hit the last stair extra hard to prove her point.

The svelte viper was *Margo*. Of course she was. A living, breathing Barbie doll, with the perfect accessories and a sexy job, plus the preemptive claim on Heath's heart. No mystery any longer why Heath had framed the bet as practice. The real thing was leagues better than his practice field.

"Then stop stomping," he ground out as she strode into her room. "And talk to me."

"I have to change clothes to take your girlfriend out to the well."

She slammed the door in Heath's face, which helped her mood a little. It slid right back into a black place when he slung the door open, crashing it into the back wall, then stormed into her room as if he had every right to be there.

"Acting childish is not going to work," he said.

"Back at you. Go away."

This was her sanctuary and he'd invaded it. Of course, he'd done a thorough job of that the night they'd slept together. She could still smell him on her sheets, which she should have washed and hadn't, like a big Loser McLoserpants who could only score the faint scent of a man. The real Heath belonged to the viper.

She made a big show of vanishing into her closet in search of riding jeans and her boots, so she didn't have to look at his stupid face, which was not disappearing into the hall as she'd instructed him.

"Stop pushing me away," he told her, and the door opened wider.

He crowded into the space that a real estate agent would have called a walk-in closet with plenty of room for clothes and two people, but really, really wasn't big enough for all of the stuff in her chest plus Heath.

"I'm not," she countered sweetly, clamping down the keening sound desperate to get out as every cell in her body sucked in Heath's essence, so close, but so far away. "Why would I do that? We're done practicing. The bet is over. Now we can move on. What's not to like?"

Heath stood there, his eyes the color of thunderclouds, hat in hand as he ran stiff fingers through his hair. "What is going on with you? I want to talk to you and you're being..."

"Hurricane Charlotte?" she supplied and shoved at his chest.

Big mistake. Huge. She'd only meant to get him out of her closet so she could switch her pants for jeans, but the wall of Heath didn't budge an inch. Her fingertips had amnesia and forgot that they weren't supposed to be enjoying the rock-hard feel of him.

"Yeah," he growled, smacking a hand over hers and lacing their fingers together. "I thought we were friends."

The tic at the corner of her eye picked that moment to flare up as she stared at him, all her ire leaking out of her pores, leaving her feeling deflated and like a crappy, jealous witch who couldn't get out of her own head long enough to see that Heath needed her to get this right.

"We are," she said with completely fake cheer. "So that's Margo."

"Yeah. That's her." His voice had lost none of its edge. "I didn't invite her here if that's what you're thinking."

No, that hadn't been what she'd thought at all. "Why didn't you? It's totally fine if you did. It's Margo. The pot of gold at the end of the rainbow. The prize in your Cracker Jack box. A—"

"I get it," Heath snarled. "What I don't get is why everything went sideways between us."

"Really? You don't?" Charli squeezed her eyes shut. "You were the one being weird. You could barely look at me out there. I felt like—"

My soul had been crushed.

She couldn't say that out loud. He hadn't done anything wrong. Just like he'd told her a long time ago, Heath had been nothing but honest with her.

Charli was the one who had fallen headfirst into their practice relationship and done the one thing she shouldn't have.

"Charli." She could hear him scrubbing at his beard in frustration. "Look at me. Please."

Ha, he'd like that, wouldn't he? Because then she'd start crying and she never cried. Except for the six or eight times he'd been so supportive and strong and beautiful that he wrenched that vulnerability right out of her, and she was not in the mood for a repeat, not under these circumstances.

She had to reel it back. Be the friend he expected.

She opened her eyes. The storm had passed in Heath's gaze, leaving behind a few choppy waves and darkness in the distance, but mostly calm. And a thread running through it all that she couldn't help but cling to.

This was the Heath she'd fallen in love with.

"This is so not what I planned," Heath murmured. "I was looking for perfect first date ideas when she showed up."

Well, this situation was not much better than when they were sniping at each other. "Good thing she did. It was time. You don't need any more practice."

Charli didn't either. She was done. There was no way she could step back into her role as his proving ground, knowing that's all she'd ever be. Knowing she was the other woman and Margo would be the one hurt by it. If she knew.

Charli wondered all at once if Heath would tell Margo that he'd practiced his skills with another woman. That it was

Charli he'd spider-crawled down a well to rescue and cuddled later that night when she couldn't sleep. That he'd held Charli's hand while she navigated skinned animals and her father's death.

"Charli." He sucked in a breath and exhaled it on a broken note. "This is not—I'm having a hard time figuring out what to say."

She threw up a hand, stopping the flow of words that she already knew had the power to eviscerate her. "There's nothing to say. Margo is a lovely woman. Clearly gracious, and well, she's obviously not ever going to need rescuing. She probably spends her Saturdays volunteering at the animal shelter and befriending every person she's ever met."

"Yeah, no," Heath drawled with his eyes rolling heavenward. "If that's the impression you got from her, you need your eyes checked. She spends Saturdays eating navy SEALs for breakfast when they don't perform operations to her exacting standards."

"Then on Sunday, she'll spend it with you, marveling over how much you've changed." Forcing the words out of her mouth was getting a little easier the longer she did it. Practicing paid off. Who would have thought?

"That makes one of us who is sure."

Oh, man. He was adorably scared that his practicing *hadn't* paid off. That Margo wouldn't recognize the lengths he'd gone to in order to win her back. Her heart cracked.

"You've been working hard on yourself, Heath," she told him earnestly and squeezed his hands. "Safe space. I wouldn't lie to you. She'd going to be so wowed by you. You deserve to be happy. With Margo. Nothing else matters but that."

His expression flattened and he nodded. "You're right, of course. Nothing else matters."

Except the fact that Charli might possibly be in love with him herself. If Margo hadn't shown up, there'd been a lovely scenario running through her head where she told him and he smiled, his own heart in his eyes as he kissed her sense-less and told her he'd been working up to a similar confession.

Obviously that wasn't happening.

"This is your chance," she said and bopped him on the arm. "You're one hundred percent grade A husband material now. Through and through. Margo showing up here now is the uni-verse's way of rewarding you. The timing is too good to be a coincidence. Go get her and show her how much she means to you. She'll honor all the effort you went to."

I would.

Her chest caved in, and she struggled to breathe. Impossible when these tight bands had constricted so hard that it hurt to try to get a deep enough breath.

Heath's eyelids dropped as his mouth firmed into a line and he nodded once. "Yeah, okay. We've already jumped out of the helicopter. It would be ridiculous not to pull the para-chute's rip cord now."

She gave him a watery smile. "I'm sure Margo would love to hear you compare her to a parachute. You should tell her that one."

Heath rolled his eyes. "She would love four dozen Dendro-bium orchids in an heirloom vase."

"Then you should get her some," she insisted, refusing to think about how *she'd* have been thrilled to be presented a wildflower he'd picked in the fallow horse pasture.

"This is not how I thought this conversation was going to go," he muttered. "I thought you were mad about Margo."

Mad? No. Heartbroken might be closer to the truth, but she'd choke on it before she let even an inkling show. He didn't need her emotional crap piled on top of his reunion with Margo. It would make her seem pathetic and petty, especially since he'd always been very clear with Charli about the bet. And that this was practice.

"Oh, well." She ducked her head and warbled out a laugh that nearly made her wince. "I mean, she's beautiful and could give Blake Lively lessons on accessorizing. Who wouldn't be jealous, right?"

"She has nothing on you," he murmured, his eyes burning with intensity all at once.

She has you. "You don't have to say stuff like that to make me feel better. I have my own brand of awesomeness."

"That you do," Heath conceded and stepped back. "If you're sure there's not more to talk about?"

Like what? How it felt as if her insides had been scooped out with a shovel? Smiling brightly, she shooed him away so she could change. "We're totally good. I'm over my hissy fit about how unfair it is that she can prance around a horse ranch in heels and not trip. Do you think she'd tell me where she got those shoes?"

Chapter Twenty-One

"I hate her," Charli muttered as Sophia slid into the chair behind her desk, coffee in hand.

"Who, Margo Malloy?" her sister asked with an eye roll. "She is something all right."

Something Heath preferred. And as much as Charli would like to deny it, she could totally see how any red-blooded man would find himself slavering after her. The woman was gorgeous and cultured and orchestrated a lot of secret military stuff, particularly with Heath, once upon a time. Whom she clearly wasn't over.

His campaign to win her back was a cinch.

"Yeah." Charli sipped her own coffee glumly, her second cup on what was already a very long morning. "I thought I had her with the offer to take her out to the old well on horseback, but it turns out she can stay on a horse. And that she packed six-hundred-dollar jeans that she didn't mind getting dirty."

Plus a pair of riding boots of the English variety meant for fashion, not form, but Margo made it work with a laugh, telling Charli that she'd never expected to actually be on a horse in those boots. Joke was on Charli, then.

Plus, she'd had to watch Heath ride next to Margo, his stoic face back in place, uncharacteristically quiet.

No, that's how he'd been back at the beginning. All the time. They rarely spoke to each other after their one botched date, the only real one they'd ever been on. And then something had happened. Changed. They'd talked all the time after that.

She missed it. She missed *him*.

Heath had left early this morning to take Margo out to the site where they'd found the male head. They'd been gone for over an hour already. Not that she was watching the clock, but with each minute that ticked by, the jumpier she got.

Why, she didn't know.

It was the perfect opportunity for Heath to make a move. They were going to be alone in the woods. Why wouldn't he take advantage of it, spring a well-timed kiss on the woman he dreamed of getting back into his arms?

Good thing Charli hadn't eaten any breakfast, or it would be threatening to make a repeat appearance.

The doorbell chimed and Charli held up a hand to stop Sophia from standing. "I'll get it. I need the distraction."

She started to swing open the door and heard Heath's voice in her head warning her to be cautious, especially when he wasn't around. Good grief, the man had infiltrated even her conscience. But it wasn't bad advice, so she peeked through the peephole to spy her younger sister standing on the porch.

Veronica.

Oh, man. Not who she'd been expecting. Despite Sophia informing her that Veronica was coming down from Dallas for their father's memorial service, Charli hadn't realized she'd be here today. Or sporting a new haircut that put the *sever* in *severe*.

Charli flung the door open to admit her sister to the house, meeting her at the threshold for an enthusiastic hug. It had been way too long since they'd seen each other.

"Hey, what's all this?" Charli called and riffled her fingers through the extremely short razor-cut ends of her sister's hair. "This is rocking."

Veronica touched her dark brown hair almost self-consciously. "Time for a change."

Oh, geez. Every woman on the planet knew that a man had to be at the root of that sentiment. "Did you and Jeremy break up?"

"Yeah, but right after Christmas," Veronica said vaguely and waved that off. "It's not a big deal."

Charli bit back the slew of questions that her sister clearly didn't want her to ask, meanwhile calculating how she was just now hearing about this. Hadn't she texted Veronica a couple of months ago to check in? Maybe it had been closer to three months. With everything that had been going on in her own life, she and her younger sister hadn't talked in far too long.

That was on Charli.

"Want some coffee?" Charli offered. "Sophia and I were just going over some business stuff. You can hang out with us if you want."

"Sure, that would be great."

Okay, now Veronica was scaring her. "I was expecting you to say no," she countered with a laugh. "You don't care about the ranch business. You were the one who was heavily in favor of selling, remember?"

"I remember."

Something was really off with her sister, and it wasn't just the breakup with her boyfriend of four years. There were fine stress lines around her brown eyes that aged her. Also, Veronica had never met a situation she didn't want to talk to death, usually with well-researched bullet points and a multimedia presentation.

"Everything okay at work?" Charli asked as her sister followed her into the kitchen.

Veronica laughed, a short brittle sound that didn't sound the slightest bit amused. "I have no idea. I quit."

Charli practically dropped the carafe in her left hand, which she'd been forced to use more often thanks to the cast on her other arm. "Oh. Are congrats in order? Did you get a better offer from a bigger law firm?"

There was a strange shadow in her sister's gaze, and it definitely didn't have a lot of better-job-more-pay type vibes. "No, I quit-quit. As in I'm not employed. It's still new and I'm still processing."

Carefully, Charli slid the carafe back into the coffee maker, wishing not for the first time that she had the money to spring for a Keurig. But all of the ranch's cash flow was tied up in renovations, and of course no guests meant no income.

No guests also meant Charli would have plenty of downtime to be there for Veronica. Something was clearly going on, but the fact that her sister hadn't immediately spilled all her secrets told her that it was more than a run-of-the-mill adulting dilemma.

She handed Veronica the coffee mug and tilted her head at the silver canisters full of creamer and sugar. "Help yourself. By the way, I know a little something about quitting your job and showing up at the ranch because you have no place else to go. So does Sophia. If you wanted to talk about it."

"I'm fine," Veronica said shortly and ran fingers through her hair with a jerky motion that maybe meant she still wasn't used to the new length. "I mean, I'm not here because I quit my job. I'm just here for the memorial service. Then I'm going to figure out the rest of my life."

She and Sophia knew a thing or two about that as well, but Charli kept that to herself since Veronica didn't seem to be in too much of a chatty mood. "Okay. I'm glad you came. It's going to be a little weird to have a memorial for someone who's been dead to us for years already."

Their mother had been the one to request that her daughters attend and insisted that everyone treat the service like a normal one, even though the forensic pathologist hadn't determined the cause of death yet, so the body hadn't been released to the family. Neither did Charli think she should point out that none of them had many fond memories of their father.

Veronica nodded, looking relieved at the subject change, and she followed Charli out of the kitchen, trailing her to Sophia's office. Sophia wasn't behind her desk, though. She was standing at the window, watching something out in the yard as she drank her coffee.

Curious, Charli joined her. Veronica took a second to give Sophia a hug and then did a double take as she caught sight of what had so thoroughly captured Sophia's attention. Not shockingly, her sister's boyfriend stood on the slope between the house and the barn, a small semicircle of ranch hands intently listening to whatever Ace was saying. Paxton stood directly to his right, listening with crossed arms.

"Who is *that*?" Veronica asked.

"That's Ace," Sophia said with a small smile. "Isn't he gorgeous?"

"Yes, I've seen nine hundred and forty-seven pictures of him on your Instagram," Veronica said dryly. "I meant the other one. The only one not wearing a hat."

"Paxton," Charli supplied helpfully. "He's cute, no?"

The three of them shifted their attention to the third partner in Heath's security firm, the one Charli had once thought might break her bad luck in the man department. Paxton was objectively handsome, but he couldn't hold a candle to Heath's sheer, rugged male beauty. Plus, it was entirely possible that she might be a little too much for someone with Paxton's mild demeanor. He kept to himself and caused zero waves, choosing to fade into the background when possible.

Heath was totally it for her. He'd ruined her for other men, and she couldn't even be mad at him over it.

Veronica on the other hand clearly appreciated the view. "He's definitely easy on the eyes. How do you get any work done around here if that's what's going on right outside your window?"

"Oh, it's easy," Charli replied with an eye roll. "We don't do any work. We sit around and wait for one of the *ologists* to show up with more bad news."

As if giving voice to that thought conjured the woman herself, Dr. Low exited the trailer perched at the edge of the wide space near the barn, closing the door behind her and locking it. One of the armed guards let her clear the short staircase and then took up a new position in front of the door, his semi-automatic rifle crossed over his chest. The scene was straight out of a movie full of special effects and actors with chiseled jaws, but this was Charli's real life and it kind of sucked.

Veronica watched with unveiled interest, the shadows Charli had seen in her eyes earlier completely banked. Maybe she'd imagined her sister's disquiet. But she didn't think so.

"Are we safe here?" Veronica asked, sounding more like her lawyer self than she had since she'd walked into the house. "When you said there were armed guards on the property, I guess I pictured it a little differently, like maybe they were doing rounds at the fence line and staying out of sight. But this is quite a bit more in your face than I was expecting."

Sophia sipped her coffee and nodded. "I'd trust Ace with my life and have, more than once. Heath is keeping up with Charli, no small feat, but I think he's the right man for that job."

"Hey," Charli protested without a lot of heat. But only because that wasn't wrong. "I have to do my share of keeping up with him too."

Ugh, she hadn't thought too much about what *that* would look like. On purpose. The bet had been designed to keep Heath entertained while he protected Charli, but at the end of the day, he still had a job—as Charli's bodyguard. Could her life get any worse?

The university people needed to clear out *soon*.

Veronica glanced at her with an eyebrow quirked, her gaze sharp as she took in Charli's expression, apparently seeing something there. "Sounds like a story there. Spill all the tea, Char."

A tight band snapped tight around her lungs all at once.

"There's no tea," she mumbled and drew in a breath. It didn't help.

Sophia bumped her with an elbow. "Oh, there's tea. It was a little hard to miss that he slept in your room the other night instead of the bunkhouse."

"Oooh," Veronica trilled and settled, her posture expectant, into the love seat Sophia had pushed against the far wall. "Tell, tell. This is a big development, yes?"

"Not even a little bit." It hit her all at once. Margo. The bet. How far she'd taken *practicing*. "It's not like that, not like you think. We're just friends."

Veronica and Sophia glanced at each other, but it was Sophia who spoke. "I've seen you two together. You could light firewood from ten paces. I know you said it wasn't working out after that one date you went on, but I thought...well, I mean, couples fight and make up all the time. I kind of assumed you were figuring it out."

"Yeah, we were," she responded glumly, slumping to the floor to lean against the wall under the window so her eyes would quit flicking to the horizon to see if Heath had come back from his jaunt with Margo yet. "Figuring out how to get him back together with Margo."

Sophia visibly flinched. "What? What is that supposed to mean?"

She told her sisters about the bet and how Heath had flipped it on its head by introducing the idea of practicing. It sounded ridiculous out loud. Even to her, and she'd been the one to blow it way out of proportion.

"That's..." Veronica blinked a bunch. "Fascinating. I didn't think people did stuff like that in real life."

Yeah, well, she didn't need her sister's hypercritical tone to feel stupid. And now she wished she'd kept her mouth shut.

"Judgmental much?" Charli shot back and set aside the coffee that had turned to mud in her mouth. "I just wanted to win. I wasn't expecting to fall—"

Abort, her brain screamed, and she clamped her mouth shut. Too late.

Sophia brightened and clapped like she'd just descended the stairs on Christmas morning to find Santa had dropped half of a Tiffany's store under the tree. "I knew it! I knew you guys were falling for each other. Ace owes me ten bucks."

Ace had bet against Heath falling in love with Charli? The bands around her lungs became knives instantly. "That was a sucker's bet, Soph. He knows Heath is still in love with Margo. And it's fine. There's nothing between us."

Rubbing her forehead, Sophia sank into her desk chair, fiddling with her coffee mug, contemplating Charli with an unreadable expression. "If that's what you want to believe, okay. But I don't think that's even a little true. I've seen you together. There's a mirror on the wall behind the kitchen table, or did you forget? Every time y'all sit together, he's holding your hand on the down-low. You're constantly on his mind, whether it's to make sure you're being taken care of when he can't be around or talking about you to Ace."

This was news she hadn't heard. "He talks about me?"

Sophia rolled her eyes. "If I'd known any of this was in question, I'd have clued you in a long time ago, but yeah. Ace thinks it's entertaining, so of course he mentions it to me."

"Then why did Ace bet against me?" she couldn't help but ask. "Because he knows Heath is still in love with Margo. Like I said. They've been friends a long time."

The question was rhetorical, but Sophia treated the answer like she'd wagered everything on final Jeopardy. "I don't know why he took the bet. Ace never said anything of the sort, plus how would he know that? Men never talk about important stuff, just sports and firearms."

That didn't mean Ace hadn't figured it out. Her sister's boyfriend was sharp and intuitive, which made him good at his job, plus he'd worked with Margo too.

"I think the most important question is whether you've told Heath you're in love with him," Veronica said in her opposing counsel voice.

"What?" Charli croaked. "Why would I tell him that? It's not true. I would—"

"You're lying," Veronica interjected simply. "I have a very expensive degree in psychology and another one that says I can practice law, plus a dozen cases in my rearview mirror that every partner at my law firm said were unwinnable. I win because I pay attention to what people don't say. You're in love with him. It wasn't practice for you. Does he know?"

"No," she said flatly, figuring it was better to come clean instead of throwing even more kindling on the fire of her sister's argument. "And no one in this room is going to say a word. He's in love with Margo and that's that."

Honestly, his commitment to his ex-girlfriend spoke volumes about his character. Ironic that his most attractive feature meant that he'd never be hers. And that she'd lost the bet.

"Oh, honey." Sophia clucked. "Did he tell you that? He's a moron."

"He didn't have to say it," she insisted, letting her head thunk against the wall. "I saw them together. Plus, he's been really clear since always that he wanted to get back together with her."

"Sometimes people's feelings change," Veronica muttered, sounding as if she might have a lot more to say about that, but opted not to.

"And sometimes they don't," she countered.

"Sometimes they don't," Sophia agreed and pointed at herself. "And that's a good thing. I had to tell Ace how I really felt, or I might have lost him. Now we're talking about the kind of forever I didn't think was possible."

"Yeah, exactly," Charli said with her brows raised. "We

don't have a lot of positive relationships to look at for inspiration. What if I do tell him and we ride off into the sunset? There's always a sunrise and those don't always bring good things. His feelings might change about *me* at some point. That's a running theme here."

Men *never* picked her. Not the way Sophia was talking about. It was too big a risk to lay it all out there, only to be left once again, either by cheating or abandonment. Same end. It was so much better to step back than to invest her entire soul in someone who would ultimately wind up shedding their relationship one way or another.

"Besides, it doesn't matter," she said and pushed away from the wall, done with this subject. Past done. "We have a lot of other things to worry about with everything going on around the ranch."

That's where her attention should be, with the treasure still on site, plus the unanswered questions about the trailer break-in and their father's cause of death.

Veronica seemed to realize it was time for a subject change and smiled slyly. "Does that mean I get my own personal bodyguard? Because I can do math and there's one left who doesn't seem to be otherwise occupied."

"Yeah," Sophia said, her mouth flattening out as she considered the point. "I wasn't thinking that would be necessary since you're only here temporarily. But it wouldn't be a bad idea to ask Paxton to keep an eye out for you and Mom while you're in town."

Veronica cleared her throat, her expression decidedly wry. "I was thinking more about the *personal* part of the equation, not the danger."

When Sophia gave her sister a strange look, Charli translated for her. "She and Jeremy broke up. I think we are witnessing a rebirth of her interest in jumping back into the dating pool. Perhaps we could ask one of the auxiliary guys to watch after Mom and arrange for Paxton to be directly assigned to Veronica."

"Oh." Sophia flashed a broad smile. "I will see what I can do as the employer of Madden, McKay and Pierce's services. No promises. Keep in mind that the danger is real, though. You can't treat him like his protection is optional, which some people seem to forget occasionally."

Charli shot Sophia a withering look. "Most of the bad stuff happened around the house or in the woods. Nothing exciting has ever happened in the horse pastures."

"Except for you falling in a well and breaking your arm," Sophia pointed out with a nod toward the cast on Charli's arm. "Fortunately, Heath has stellar tracking abilities, or you might still be down there."

"Wait, what bad stuff happened in the woods?" Veronica wanted to know.

"Charli and Heath ran across some dead animals that appeared to have been planted," Sophia supplied.

"Rather not relive that," Charli said with a shudder. "Let's just say I've never more strongly considered being a vegetarian than I did in that moment."

"So one of the trailers was broken into, someone planted dead animals, and Dad was found dead under mysterious circumstances." Veronica ticked off the points on her fingers. "Did I miss anything?"

Charli and Sophia glanced at each other and shook their heads, Sophia speaking for them both. "I don't think so. I mean, there was the incident when I was kidnapped and I guess before that, the same guy broke into the house. But Cortez is in jail. Why?"

Veronica stood and paced, looking every bit like a high-powered criminal defense attorney addressing the jury. "The animals and the trailer break-in are recent, and Dad's death is likely several years old, which means they're probably not related. It would be highly unusual for a murderer to return to the scene of the crime so much later and terrorize the victim's family."

"The statues alone are worth ten million dollars," Charli reminded her. "That means all bets are off. It's too much money to assume anyone is doing anything rationally. Plus, we already know that Karl Davenport is an associate of the guy who kidnapped Sophia."

And they knew that Karl was their father's treasure hunting partner. Anything their father may have been involved with, Karl would know about. The mystery of their father's death might be years old, but they'd just found his body recently. It didn't feel like a coincidence. Or unrelated.

"That's true," Veronica said and turned to pace in the other direction. "But why murder Dad and then leave the extremely valuable statue you killed him for with the body?"

No one had a response to that, least of all Charli, who had actually asked herself that same question during the hours she'd been alone with both her father's body and the statue. But if the recent threats weren't related to their father's murder, that meant they were dealing with two different people, not one.

And the danger quotient might be even higher than they'd assumed. That was the important thing to focus on right now, not all her confusing feelings for Heath.

Chapter Twenty-Two

The jaguar heads were gone. *Stolen.*

Heath stared at the open—empty—safe, his heart doing a tango and his stomach threatening to squeeze out through his throat. Outside the trailer, people shouted and milled about, crossing in front of the large picture window above the desk like panicked ants as their mound collapsed in around them.

"How are the statues gone?" he repeated for the fourth time as Dr. Low wrung her hands uselessly, the same thing she'd been doing since she'd reported that the safe had been broken into. One of the guards had grabbed him as he'd crossed the yard on his way to the house.

"I don't know," she mumbled, which was the petite academic's equivalent to a wail. She'd remained largely composed in the scant few minutes since chaos had erupted. "I came back from a meeting with Dr. McDaniel in her trailer and found this."

She gestured to the empty safe, her face etched with disbelief. The thief had carefully dismantled the silent alarm in a feat worthy of someone with Pierce's level of skill. They were dealing with a professional, obviously.

His eyes darted around the small, dimly lit space, taking in

Dr. Low's undisturbed laptop, several labeled artifacts standing intact on a shelf near her desk, and her personal items, including a phone and an expensive-looking handbag. Nothing else had been so much as touched.

Just the safe.

Heath cursed as blue and red lights flashed against the far wall announcing the arrival of the local law enforcement. At this rate, they should get a room in the house and stick around. Save time on their commute out to the ranch.

Of course, there wasn't much left to protect.

The three guards who had been on duty at the time of the theft stood behind him, silently accepting their complete failure. They weren't the type to wear their emotions on their sleeves, but he could feel their nerves as they exchanged glances.

"Outside," he snapped to the guards, who immediately did as bid, likely aware that their employment contract with Madden, McKay and Pierce was not going to end with a favorable review.

He followed them so the police would have room to start cataloging the disaster, and then stopped where the three guards stood in a defensive clump. Nothing would save them from his wrath, but before he destroyed them, he needed answers. "What happened? How did the thief get past you?"

One of the guards, a burly man named Murray who had twenty years at the St. Louis PD in his rearview, shook his head. "You know as much as we do. Dr. Low went to her meeting. I saw her lock the door. Wilson took up position in front of the door like he usually does when she leaves, and Jones and I took perimeter. She came back and rushed out to announce the safe was open. I grabbed you. End of story."

Not end of story. This was not happening. Not on his watch. "There has to be something you can remember. Some detail. Thieves do not wave wands and magically appear inside a locked trailer."

The trailer was in view of the house and the barn, deliberately. The clearing had fifty feet of visibility from all sides. Only a ghost could have accomplished this feat.

Then there was the interesting timing, given that they'd only recently discovered the second head—and David Lang's body. Someone could have broken in and stolen the single head, especially since there was a period of time when the security hadn't been as strong, well before they'd found the second one.

Had someone been lurking in the wings, waiting for them to find the second head? Someone who knew there were two? Like Karl Davenport, David Lang's former partner, who topped the list as the likely suspect. And fit the profile of a ghost quite well since no one had actually seen him in the flesh.

Had he been one of the two people who had met at the fence line near the cigarette pile Heath had found?

Heath pinched the bridge of his nose as Murray, Jones and Wilson shifted restlessly. Finally, Jones offered, "That intelligence lady was asking questions yesterday. About the safe."

Of course. That was her job. "I'm sure she asked a lot of questions about everything."

Murray nodded. "That she did. For about an hour. I think she spent at least two with Dr. Low."

And two with Heath this morning. Margo was nothing if not thorough. He'd walked her to her car and as far as he knew, she'd left to fly home, since she'd finished the on-site investigation. She'd mentioned that she would be subpoenaing David Lang's financial records, but that would take weeks to be granted.

The rest of her investigation could take place at Fort Bragg. Such as it was. She'd invited him to stay at her place for an extended visit when he finished his assignment here, heavily alluding to an enthusiastic kiss-and-make-up session in the future. Until the theft had been reported, he'd thought of nothing else except why the idea of taking her up on it made his skin crawl.

Eventually, he'd have to let Margo know the statues had been stolen. But the trail was fresh at the moment and daylight would only last another four and a half hours. Madden was occupied with the local police, acting as their liaison while they did their initial pass on the crime scene, while Pierce had holed up with his surveillance footage looking for a shot of the thief.

That left Heath to do the legwork.

"You three," he said to the guards and pointed at the knot of locals who looked to be a mix of badges and possibly CSI, probably borrowed from a bigger city's department. "Give your statements to whoever is handling that, then park somewhere. Don't leave. You'll be dismissed when I say you are."

Satisfied that they would do as ordered, Heath set himself the task of looking for clues. With everyone else occupied, including the police who were good at taking statements and not much else, someone had to get the jaguar heads back.

The thief had entered the trailer some way and he wanted to know how. Pierce might turn up something in the recorded footage, but that would take hours, and Heath needed to be doing something now.

Preferably something that would burn off the adrenaline pumping through his blood and ease the black edges crowding his vision.

Except he'd taken no more than a half a step toward the trailer when Charli burst from the woods behind him. Alarm flared in her eyes, widening them, and her hair fell around her face in a disarray that sent his pulse into the stratosphere.

"What's wrong?" he demanded.

She bent at the waist, breathless, but finally wheezed out, "Heath, someone's breaking into your truck! I saw him from the house and had to go out the front door, then double back—"

"Get behind me," he ordered, his brain already connecting dots. "Stay close."

It was the thief. Trying to escape with everyone's attention stuck on the crime scene. Clever.

But the filth hadn't counted on Charli still being in the house, likely with her gaze glued to the window since he'd explicitly told her to stay inside with her mother and sisters. He'd yell at her later for disobeying him.

Or maybe not, if her quick action helped him catch the thief.

He dashed toward the truck, his boots pounding on the ground. There was no time to ensure Charli could keep up, but he couldn't protect her if he opened a gap between them. Instinctively, he matched her pace, and automatically took her hand to pull her along.

The thief would not get away. Not from Heath.

But when he rounded the corner and his truck came into view, the figure crouched near the truck's wheel well was not stealing Heath's truck. He was vandalizing it.

And his name wasn't Karl.

"Harvard," Heath snarled as the kid jerked his head, dropping the can of spray paint in his hand.

It rolled under Heath's truck, right beneath the expletive marching across the door in three-foot letters.

The guy who had manhandled Charli leaped to his feet but didn't run like Heath had expected him to do. Instead, Harvard stood his ground in some misguided show of bravado. As if Heath wouldn't tear him apart in seconds with zero provocation.

Blackness edged through his vision, tempting him to act, pushing him to destroy.

"What do you think you're doing?" Heath barked and the kid had the audacity to sneer.

"Payback," he said with a cocky grin.

He'd gotten his nose fixed. It would look much better broken again and Heath's fist ached to repeat their first encounter. But there was so much more at stake here.

"Is that why you stole the jaguar heads?" It would explain a lot. Who else would have enough knowledge of the university's equipment and procedures to bypass security but an insider?

"Jaguar heads?" A glint of confusion flitted through Harvard's gaze as he glanced at Charli, who hovered at Heath's elbow, thankfully staying out of the line of fire. "Is that redneck slang for something, cowboy?"

Yeah, for the reason Heath was about to turn the kid into hamburger meat. He reeled it back. This was one of the times when he needed to use caution instead of letting his temper boil. Charli's trust in his ability to figure that out settled into his bones and he let that ride for a long minute.

"Where did you hide the heads?" Heath asked him, his voice evening out as the strangest sense of calm soothed his raised hackles.

Harvard edged back an inch, clearly confused by this new, less violent Heath. "Man, I don't know what you're talking about."

Sure. It was a total coincidence that this kid had showed up at the exact time of the theft so he could deface Heath's truck. Maybe Harvard hadn't intended to steal the vehicle since he likely had another ride stashed somewhere. The vandalism represented an ultimate Screw You as Harvard rode off with his ten-million-dollar bounty.

"That's fine," Heath returned pleasantly. "The police can sort this out. Good thing they're already on site collecting evidence from your other crime. I'm sure they'll be quite thrilled I'm able to provide them a suspect to match the fingerprints taken from the scene. It'll cut down the investigation time exponentially."

"Wait. What?" Alarm flitted through Harvard's gaze as Heath watched calculations scroll through the kid's head. "You can't take fingerprints from skinned animals. You won't pin any of that on me."

Oh for the love of Pete. Heath bit back a curse. Pieces clicked into place instantly. The skinned animals had been *this* guy's calling card? Along with the vandalism, it fit. Random, petty acts of a desperately immature grad student who had suffered humiliation at the hands of someone twice his size with twice the intellect.

"Oh, we can and will," Heath promised him. "Plus the theft of the ancient, priceless artifacts that are currently missing. I'm sure everyone will appreciate it if you just return them."

Harvard sputtered. "I didn't take anything. I may have trashed some of the other students' research, but it's all garbage. They're analyzing bone fragments and sifting through beads like all that crap matters."

Bone fragments. A hint of a memory darted through Heath's head. That's what No-Logo had mentioned he was researching outside the ransacked trailer. Harvard wasn't confessing to have broken into the guarded trailer containing the safe, but the research trailer. Intending to cause havoc. Not to steal anything.

That would explain why the kid didn't seem to have a clue what Heath was trying to goad him into confessing. Was that really the case? Harvard wasn't the thief? Then who was?

The entire world had gone off its axis.

"All right," Heath said dismissively. "We'll let the cops straighten this out."

With no warning—and thus no chance for Harvard to make a break for it—Heath grabbed him by the arm and hustled him back the way he and Charli had come. Straight to Gun Barrel City's finest, where he deposited his protesting detainee. Given that Heath had a measure of authority at the ranch, none of the police officers batted an eye when he told them to arrest the kid and throw theft charges at him.

They wouldn't stick. Harvard had convinced Heath that he wasn't the mastermind of the statue theft, but that left so many open questions, it wouldn't help to mention them to the local authorities.

"You know he didn't take the jaguar heads. Right?" Charli suggested as she dogged Heath's steps away from the general chaos of the police taking statements and attempting to organize the scene.

Heath had plenty enough of that experience to want to avoid being the keeper of the peace at a crime scene on this ranch.

"Yeah, I know," he told her with an eye roll. "It was meant to keep everyone busy."

"You think it was Karl." Charli chewed her lip. "And that he killed my father too."

This was so not the conversation he wanted to be having with her right now. Or ever. She was wearing a T-shirt that was too large for her, so it sat off to one side, exposing a bit of shoulder that he couldn't peel his eyes from all at once.

What kind of dog was he that he couldn't think of her as a friend? Margo should be the woman on his mind, but he couldn't force that, even if he wanted to. There was no comparison between the two—and he couldn't envision starting things back up with Margo at this point. It felt...wrong.

And Charli didn't seem to be at all interested in his feelings on the matter. He'd even tried to broach the subject before Margo had showed up. And after, forget it. Charli couldn't have pushed him away fast enough.

He got it. Heath was fine for practice but not for real. It was never real, not on her side. Not even the times when it had seemed like they were so in sync that they were practically reading each other's thoughts.

Heath was just her bodyguard.

"Go back to the house and I'll be in later," he mumbled, aware that the situation was indeed an indictment on his abilities to do his job. After all, the name of the security company employed by the ranch had his name on it.

"Yes, sir, Mr. Babysitter, sir."

She saluted and wheeled to do his bidding, but not before he caught a glint in her eye that sat funny in his gut. As if her smart-aleck response might have more to it than just Charli giving him regular grief.

Great. Had he hurt her feelings? There was no scenario where he had the time to chase after her and yank an explanation out of her as to what was wrong. That part of their relationship was over.

Groaning, he rounded the trailer, avoiding everyone with a uniform, as well as Madden, who was still riding point with all the locals.

Heath needed to end this thing. Now, not later. Not by sitting on his hands while less invested people took up the mantle. He still hadn't answered his own question about how the thief had gotten into the trailer, who was likely Karl, as Charli had surmised. Nothing Harvard had said pointed at him as the thief.

But Karl could be anywhere with those heads by now.

Careful not to disturb anything that might yield fingerprints, he checked the entire perimeter of the trailer for handholds that might allow someone with a bit of skill to scale the fiberglass siding and roll onto the roof.

There were a couple of spots that might be viable. The thief had surely worn gloves, but just in case, he opted not to press his own fingers into the crevices to check if they'd hold a man's weight.

Besides, going in through the roof would be like asking to be spotted. Especially in daylight. A niggle in his gut shifted his gaze. If he'd been doing this job, he'd never pick *up* over *down*.

He dropped to the ground and peered at the undercarriage. It took him a while to find what he was looking for, but eventually he spied the cleverly hidden square in the floor of the trailer. Just as he suspected. The thief had cut a hole in the floor. Just like Heath had done in an operation near Kandahar to extract a briefcase from a locked room.

Likely the thief had created the hole last night under cover of darkness, then accessed the brand-new entry point today. That's why none of the guards had seen the thief. Wouldn't shock him if the timing turned out to overlap with shift change.

The hole wasn't large either, which could explain Dr. Low not noticing the cut from the interior. He'd never seen a picture of Karl Davenport but if he measured in at an average male height and weight, Karl wouldn't fit through this hole. Neither would Heath, for that matter, a fact he knew for certain because the first time he'd practiced cutting a hole for Kandahar, it had been too small.

Margo had laughed at his poor judgment as she'd cataloged his progress on the mission, asking if he'd planned to invite her along to push *her* through the hole.

His pulse kicked up a notch due to the narrative forming in his head. The one where the thief wasn't Karl but someone with a much smaller stature. Someone who had established a perfectly legit reason to visit the trailer and spend as much time cataloging it as she wished to.

Margo.

She'd likely walked up and asked the guards when their shift change happened and they'd blithely told her, blinded by her smile and considerable charm as she stole the jaguar heads out from underneath them.

Heath let that wash over him as the truth burned a hole in his chest.

She'd played him. She hadn't taken this assignment to cozy up to him in hopes of rekindling something between them. She'd taken it to *distract* him.

And she had. He hadn't followed up on his suspicions about her orders from JSOC. Which likely didn't even exist. In retrospect, he should have asked a lot more questions about why Spec Ops would care about some Maya treasure.

What an idiot he was. Shame and not a little embarrassment coated his skin like shellac.

What he did not feel was heartbroken.

That told him everything he needed to know about why the whole scene with Margo had felt…off. He wasn't in love with her anymore. If he ever had been in the first place.

She'd reevaluated during their time apart—so had he. With distance, he could see their relationship was dysfunctional at best. At worst, toxic. And she wasn't as pretty as he'd remembered. She wore entirely too much makeup, and you could feed a small village for what her diamond earrings cost.

Now he knew what it was like to be with a woman who not only encouraged him to be himself, but seemed to *like* him, too. As if Heath McKay unfiltered and unaltered worked for her in a million different ways.

It was heady, especially in comparison. A relief. He should have realized all this a long time ago, saved everyone a lot of grief, especially Charli. What if instead of trying to give Margo the benefit of the doubt, he'd just told Charli how he felt about her? Would she have thought about it and realized how good they were together?

He had to find out. As soon as possible.

Unfortunately, that had to come *after* he fixed this other mess. If Margo was the thief, he was the only one with a prayer of finding her. He was the only one with the skill set. The score he had to settle with her for stealing from the Langs and making a mockery of him? That was just a bonus.

Chapter Twenty-Three

Heath texted Charli again at a rest stop and waited for a reply. Nada. Just like the last three times.

Her lack of response sat in his gut like a cocklebur, sharp and uncomfortable. And worrisome. Things between them were still strained, that much he knew, but come on. He'd gone out of his way to make sure they were okay, that Margo hadn't changed anything between them.

If nothing else, he and Charli were still friends.

Which he'd do everything in his power to change eventually. As soon as he could.

But no response could mean Charli had fallen down another well.

She better not have. He'd specifically instructed Pierce to stick to Charli like white on rice and he'd trusted his partner with his life on many occasions, so smart money said it was something else.

Was she ignoring him? He'd explained that he'd had to go in all three text messages, that he'd fill in the gaps as soon as he could. But he couldn't risk tipping off Margo, just in case she'd set up a tap on everything Lang-related. It would be her style.

With no time to waste, he pushed on, cranking the air conditioner in the SUV he'd rented. His truck was still at the body shop getting a new paint job to erase Harvard's artwork on the door panels. Too bad he couldn't have arranged a flight, or he'd have done it. His contacts in the military were suspect at this point, though—all the people he knew also knew Margo and there was no telling how many others had been turned.

Not to mention the fact that he wasn't 100 percent convinced he'd find Margo at her father's lake house in Austin. It was a gamble, but a good one given that she'd often spent time there when she'd had vacation from work.

If she wasn't there, he faced a long few days of trying to track her with a cold trail. He was trying not to think about that—but unfortunately his thoughts drifted to Charli the moment he let his guard down. The distraction alone made that a bad idea.

But he couldn't help it.

He missed her. Not for the first time, he wished he'd had the latitude to invite her along. She'd have made this trip a thousand times more interesting. It would have been a good chance to spend time together. Learn some things. Talk about their favorite movies. Whatever. He craved that kind of normalcy. He'd never had that before and wanted it desperately.

The roads in this area of Texas stretched for miles, long and winding and treacherous for someone who had been on the road for three hours already. He had to find Margo, had to confront her about the stolen jaguar heads and the lies.

The weight of her duplicity bore down on him. Who had turned her? And why? What was her end game?

When he finally reached the lake house after only one wrong turn, a chill washed over him. The structure itself stood up on a hill, a dark silhouette now that the sun had set. He parked the SUV a short distance from the house, rolling it into the heavy brush to avoid drawing attention.

As he exited the SUV, gravel crunched beneath his boots, ringing out in the still air. Heath froze. After a beat, he heel-toed it to the tree line, hoping there'd be enough ground cover to mask his steps.

The night air was heavy with humidity and the scent of sage from the bushes growing wild along the road. Hills rose behind the house, a majestic backdrop that he wished he had time to explore. It would be a lot more fun to have made this trip with the intent to hike. With Charli.

Was she thinking about him? Did she miss him?

That was one thing about being with someone like Margo. She was pretty self-sufficient, and she'd never once expressed a single personal thought about Heath being gone all the time when he'd been with the navy. She'd only cared whether he'd completed his missions or not and whether the team had been successful.

Honestly, sometimes he'd wondered if she'd have even missed him if he didn't come home. And not for the first time since he'd found the hole cut in the floor, he cross-examined himself on why he'd wanted her back so badly.

Pride. Probably. Which pretty much drove him now too.

With each step, his senses heightened. Crickets chirped, insects buzzed, and moonlight reflected off the giant picture windows overlooking the lake.

Slipping through the shadows, gratified that he hadn't lost his stealth skills, he crept through the row of hedges landscaped to the hilt, peering into the first window from a hidden vantage point. It was dark inside, but the front room led to a hallway and a single light shone from the back of the house.

Could be a security light programmed to switch on after dark. Or it could be Margo.

Heath circled the house, keeping to the darkest pockets as surely Mr. Malloy had cameras around this property and possibly pressure sensors to warn of intruders. But he couldn't take the time to study the security logistics. Especially given that he planned to get inside in a matter of seconds.

At a window approximately three-quarters of the distance

to the back of the house, he surveyed what he could see from this vantage point. There were fewer shadows here thanks to the floodlight affixed to the highest peak of the roofline, but as he tilted his head, he saw her.

Margo. She moved through the room with purpose, clearly outlined by the overhead lights. It was a bathroom of enormous size, with an ocean of white tile. Fortunately, he had zero qualms about spying on his former girlfriend while she took a bath.

Not that he'd stick around to enjoy the show. It would simply be a good distraction for her while he figured out his entrance logistics.

She didn't stay in the bathroom, though. In typical Margo fashion, she checked out her appearance in the full-length cheval mirror, straightening the straps of the black tank top she wore. Then she exited the room, flicking off the lights with her index finger.

Heath waited a millisecond to ensure she didn't backtrack, then quickly scouted for a good way inside. A lucky break— several of the windows were open on the second floor to let in the cooler night air. Which also meant Margo wasn't expecting him.

He couldn't wait to see her face when she realized he'd figured out her game so quickly.

A trellis near the screened-in porch made an excellent ladder, though it wasn't so easy to push the ropy vines aside with his boots. He made it to the roof of the porch after a minor brush with a startled lizard. With agonizing caution, he crept across the porch roof to one of the open windows, an old-fashioned kind with a turn handle. Margo had cranked it just enough that he could get his arm up through the crack and lever it open wide enough for an entire former SEAL to slip through.

Glad he hadn't lost his touch, he toed off his boots and stowed them in a shadowy corner in case Margo passed by this room. The downside of being out of the Teams—he had boots, not stealth footwear, and had never envisioned a scenario where running security on a ranch in Texas would require anything different.

Granted, none of this had anything to do with the ranch. Charli and her sisters were just the unlucky owners caught in the middle of whatever game this was.

Heath slid across the threshold of the bedroom and into the hall. A light shone at the far end. Margo stood underneath it, hands clasped in front of her. Waiting for him.

The hall light glinted off a long kitchen knife between her palms.

"Hello, darling," she purred. "So nice of you to join me."

Adrenaline coursed through his veins, cutting off his self-congratulatory spiel. She'd set this up. It was a trap, and he'd fallen right into it, a blind lion scenting fresh meat, then limping his way right into the lair of the hunter.

"It was good of you to leave such an easy trail to follow," he returned, schooling the expression on his face, though it was likely a lost cause. She knew she'd bested him. This was her gloating face.

She lifted a manicured brow. "Honestly, I expected you much earlier. Couldn't find a ride?"

"Obviously I can trust no one," he said with a shrug. "Plus, there was a little matter of a vandal I had to ensure the police arrested. I can do two jobs at once. Can you?"

She had no reason to answer him, but she didn't hesitate. "Quite well, apparently. It's amazing how much information comes across my computer screen that presents interesting opportunities. Only a fool wouldn't see the potential to profit."

"That's what this was? A paycheck?"

Margo lifted her shoulders. "What isn't about a paycheck? That's what we work for, isn't it?"

Maybe *she* did. But he worked with Madden and Pierce because they meant something to him. Because they believed in each other. They all cared about their clients and about ensuring people who couldn't protect themselves had someone in their corner who could. At least that had always been the case before.

Charli had been different from the first. Who knew the perfect woman for him preferred jeans and horses over couture and superficiality?

But he couldn't think about her. Not now. This situation needed his full attention, particularly given the hardware involved.

Did Margo know he'd tucked his gun into the waistband of his jeans? Or did she truly intend to stab an unarmed man?

"I need the heads back, Margo," he told her with far more calm than he'd expected. Than the situation called for.

She clued in on it, too, cocking her head and surveying him with a puzzled sweep. "Who are you and what did you do with Heath McKay? Did you take a Valium in the car?"

There was nothing funny about this showdown, but he couldn't help laugh at her question anyway. "I didn't have to. I'm a reformed hothead. Sorry I didn't send you an announcement."

"That's an egregious oversight." She tsked and brandished the knife. "I'm overdressed for the occasion, then. I was expecting a knockdown, drag-out fight."

He lifted a brow. "You against me? I've never been *that* much of a hothead."

"Well, that's debatable," she said delicately and sniffed. "And I didn't want to find out what your limits were."

That stuck him in the gut far deeper than any piece of steel could. She thought he might lose control one day and...what? Actually hit her? The thought made him green all the way to his toes.

Thankfully, Charli hadn't flinched at being front and center with Heath. Present in a way that he'd never had before. Or realized he'd want so deeply.

"That's okay," he said with a tiny smile. "Someone else helped me figure out what my limits are."

Granted, a lot of that had come about because Charli had tested them. But it still counted.

"Oh, yes, your country bumpkin." Margo nodded sagely. "I could tell something was going on between you. That'll last about another two seconds, until you get bored and start spoiling for a fight. She does know that you're not overly fond of roots, right?"

"My relationship with Charli is none of your concern," he told her with zero heat and enjoyed every second of it. Holding out his hand, he flipped his fingers in a gimme motion. "The heads, Margo. They belong to the people of Mexico, not your highest bidder."

She laughed. "I'm not selling them on the open market, are you insane? I'm the delivery girl. Half up-front, half upon transfer. You don't know the guy."

"Try me." He showed his teeth.

"Silver hair? About yay tall?" Margo made a shelf out of her hand at about the six-foot mark. "Name's George."

"George." Heath rolled his eyes. "Because that doesn't sound fake. We're not having a conversation here, Margo. This is my job and I'm not leaving without the statues. Don't get in my way or you will find out what I'm capable of."

She raised the knife, malice churning through her eyes. "Come and take them, Navy Boy. I've never been one to stay behind a desk. Might be a harder job than you anticipated."

Flashing her a smile that she didn't know what to do with— judging by the confusion floating around—he used the scant few seconds to catalog the hall, noting the window behind her, the staircase winding to the ground floor.

One second he was standing there, the next, he'd leaped forward, rolling into a crouch, then swept one leg in an arc to take out Margo's from underneath her.

She went down with a cry, but contorted midair and drove the knife downward. Straight into his leg.

White-hot agony lanced through his calf. He bit back a scream and rolled with the wave of nausea for a second. But he had to move. Couldn't just lie there and bleed.

Margo leaped to her feet, not the slightest bit dazed. They both glanced at the knife that had clattered to the wood floor near the wall. As she dove for it, Heath twisted and pulled the gun from his waistband, aiming it at her heart.

"Back away slowly," he rasped, and she threw up her hands. Good. She wasn't going to be stupid.

Fighting through the pain, Heath climbed to his feet, careful not to put weight on his sliced leg, and palmed the knife. Blood seeped into the fabric of his jeans, but he didn't have time to check how deep the cut was.

"Take me to the heads," he ordered her and jerked the barrel of the gun to the left as he held the knife in her general direction. Hopefully she got the hint that he'd gladly use either on her.

"Not even if you shoot me," she said with a defiant toss of her hair and crossed her arms. "You can't fathom how much money I'm being paid to deliver these statues to my client."

"Is it worth the gamble that you might die in the process?" he asked her quietly, struck all at once that he'd imagined himself in love with this woman not that long ago. And she'd waltzed back into his life as an enemy—one who didn't seem that unhappy about the lot she'd chosen.

And she certainly didn't want him back. It was a relief to finally be shed of this woman forever.

She scoffed. "Please, you wouldn't kill me."

No, he wouldn't, not unless he had to defend Charli. Or himself. That was the thing she failed to realize. She'd meant something to him once, and still did, but not the way she seemed to assume. "I was talking about your client. Once he has the statues, there's no reason to keep you alive. And

if you're dead, he doesn't have to pay you the second install-
ment. You're dealing with criminals, Margo. They don't have
to honor the rules of engagement."

Not that she was doing that either, but there was still a
part of him who didn't want to see her suffer for the terrible
choices she'd made.

"What would you have me do, darling?" she purred. "Hand
them over to you in hopes my client will see the error of his
ways? I don't think so."

Heath nodded. "Okay. We'll do this the hard way, then."

While they'd chatted about her descent into darkness, he'd
maneuvered close enough to the side table near the stairs to
pull the long runner free. Before Margo could formulate an
escape plan, he flung the knife to the other end of the hall,
out of reach, then snagged her wrist, twisting it behind her
with his free hand.

Shoving the gun against her ribs, he forced her to walk.
"Move. Heads. Now. Or you will have a bullet wound through
multiple internal organs. Your choice."

Margo hesitated for so long, he started formulating plan B.
Then she spat out a curse, testing his strength with a surprisingly strong yank against his grip on her wrist.

He'd been braced for that since moment one. So it didn't
work. He jammed the gun deeper into her ribs. "Try again. See
where that gets you. Or cooperate. Then this is over faster."

Finally, her spine relaxed a fraction. Which in turn allowed
him to breathe a tad easier.

He held the runner with his teeth as she stalked down the
stairs. It was dicey trying to keep up with her and not let on
that the pain piercing his leg with each step nearly stole his
breath. The trail of blood he left on the floor should probably
concern him more, but unless he passed out, it couldn't be a
factor.

Once they hit the ground floor, he'd lost enough blood that
he needed to make things easier on himself, so he tied her

wrists together with the runner instead of using it as a tourniquet, which had been his first plan.

"Keep going," he advised her as she shot him a black look.

Snarling low-level threats that amounted to nothing more than grumbling, she led him to into a well-appointed office. Behind an oil painting of a ship, she revealed a safe.

"Good luck with that," she taunted. "I'm not going to tell you how to open it."

Heath's head swam from stress and blood loss. There was no guarantee that she'd even put the statues in the safe, but he had a feeling she'd wanted to see him sweat over this additional complexity or she wouldn't have led him to this room in the first place.

"You don't have to tell me," he informed her and unplugged a lamp from a side table next to a leather chair, then force-sat her in the chair, tying the cord around her legs with a sailor's knot that she no doubt recognized.

She could still likely get loose if he gave her long enough, so he scuttled from the room as quickly as he could in search of towels and water to clean up his leg. Losing more blood wouldn't help this situation.

In seconds, he'd found a bathroom and cleaned up the worst of the wound. It wasn't as deep as he'd feared and the knife hadn't cut anything critical other than his skin, so he tied a fluffy guest towel with the monogram AAM around his calf.

As he exited the bathroom, he spied Margo's handbag sitting on the island in the kitchen. Not one to look a gift horse in the mouth, he took precious seconds to go through it. She'd slid her phone into the front pocket, which he didn't dare hope he could get into unless she'd enabled facial recognition. No one in Special Ops would ever do that since an enemy could easily use it to gain access to important data, even if you were dead.

Something fluttered to the floor as he pulled out her phone.

A slip of paper. Crouching, he picked it up, his eyes widening as he took in the sequence of numbers. They sure looked an awful lot like exactly what he was looking for. But really? Surely Margo hadn't *written down* the combination to the safe.

But this was her father's house. Not hers. There was no reason for her to know the combination. And no reason for him not to try it. Worst-case scenario, it didn't work and he moved on to plan C.

"Found it," he said as he clomped back into the home office and flicked the paper up between two fingers to show her.

Something flashed across her face, informing him instantly that it *was* the combination. He shut his eyes in disbelief. If she hadn't stabbed him, he'd never have pulled his gun and none of this would have unfolded. She might have run, and he might have chased her, never realizing the statues were in the house all along.

Within seconds, the safe popped open. Gold gleamed from its dark interior. The jaguar heads.

He scooped them out and shut the safe. "Nice doing business with you, Ms. Malloy. I hope I never see you again."

Heath exited the room, Margo muttering slurs on his character that got more inventive the further he trudged. The trip to the second floor to retrieve his boots nearly killed him but an eternity later, he had everything he'd come for. Once he got out of the house, he called the local police to come pick up Margo, and explained—very patiently—that they needed to coordinate with the Texas Rangers and Gun Barrel City PD.

Not his problem any longer. He'd spent far too long thinking he wasn't good enough for Margo, that he needed to change to make her happy, but the truth was that she wasn't good enough for him. The missing element in his life wasn't the ability for him to manage his temper, but the acceptance of it. Of him. Wholly and unaltered. He only needed Charli to be happy.

And she still hadn't responded to any of his text messages.

Chapter Twenty-Four

Charli liked being babysat by Paxton even less than when Heath had been her shadow. Actually, it wasn't the same at all. With Heath, she'd felt like they were spending time together while he protected her from harm. Like they were connecting.

It was only when Paxton had materialized at her side and mumbled something about Heath asking him to fill in that she'd understood that Heath was gone. *He'd left.* As in flat out just walked out the door with Margo.

Well, of course he had. That's what she'd encouraged him to do. His commitment to Margo remained steadfast, ironically one of his best features.

But was it too much to have wished he'd said goodbye? That Charli had meant enough to him to take two minutes to call a time-out and pull her into his arms for the last time?

Clearly that wasn't a thing. Then he'd *texted* her.

Heath: I'm sorry, but I have to leave

Heath: Are you okay? I'm worried about you

Heath: I'll explain later. I just can't right now

Of course she'd ignored him. Oh, she'd read all the text messages, but what was there to say? To explain?

She'd known this was coming. What she hadn't anticipated was Heath still trying to maintain contact, like everything between them hadn't been torn up at the roots like a tree in a hurricane.

The missing jaguar heads provided an almost welcome distraction, tossing her into the middle of a mess that she and Sophia, along with Ace and Paxton, had to temper without Heath's help. Charli was just now coming to realize how much order he'd brought to the chaos. And not just on the ranch. He settled *her* in ways she hadn't honored nearly enough.

The local police had no leads but insisted on going over every inch of the ranch a second time. Keeping the dig nerds out of the way proved nearly impossible and Dr. Low kept trying to talk to Charli about insurance claims. By dinnertime, she just wanted Heath. And a bath. And to sleep for a million years.

None of those were going to happen.

Finally, she managed to roll into bed at midnight, exhausted but unable to sleep. Stupid cast. She couldn't get comfortable, and Heath wasn't here to soothe her with his heat and magical touch.

Fine. That was fine. She didn't need him.

The crunch of gravel outside made her bolt up and she dashed to the window to see a nondescript SUV rolling into the circular drive at the front of the house, then continue to the back. Just as she grabbed her phone to text Paxton that they had unwelcome company, Heath swung out of the driver's seat.

Heath.

Alone. Without Margo.

Oh, dear heavens. What was he doing here?

She watched him walk toward the kitchen door instead of the bunkhouse, hatless, his gait a funny one-two step. Was something wrong with one his boots?

More to the point, he had a lot of nerve showing back up here after not even bothering to say goodbye. Really, she should have realized that he'd come back to finish his assignment since his security company still had a contract with Sophia.

But still. She had a piece of her mind to give him.

She marched down the stairs without a single consideration for her Hello Kitty pajamas, meeting him at the door of the kitchen, arms crossed so she didn't reach out to touch him, just to assure herself that he was here and whole and real. This man didn't belong to her and for all she knew, Margo was waiting for him at a hotel somewhere while he picked up some of his things that he'd left behind.

"Look what the cat dragged in," she said.

The kitchen light threw his features in harsh relief, highlighting fatigue and stress. "I can't fight with you right now, Charli."

"I thought we were friends," she stressed, not because that's what she'd wanted them to be to each other, but she'd thought that part of their relationship was sacred.

He clomped past her into the room with that same one-two step. That's when she noticed the rust-colored stains caking the leg of his jeans, which had been sliced open to the knee. Her pulse shuddered to a halt in milliseconds.

"What's wrong with your leg?" she quavered as she forgot all the things she'd meant to lambast him with and rushed to his side to help maneuver him onto the bench seat at the table.

He didn't protest when she helped him ease off his boots. When she saw the row of uneven stitches, the sound that came out of her mouth wasn't even human.

Not rust stains. Blood. *Heath's* blood and a lot of it.

"What happened?" she demanded and sucked in a hot breath, then asked a second time, but a little more calmly.

"I got the statues back."

Heath slumped without warning, nearly sliding to the floor,

which left her with no choice but to slide over to him, cradling his head against her shoulder as best she could with the stupid cast.

"Of course you did," she murmured, smoothing his hair back from his forehead. Then what he'd said registered. "Wait. What?"

"The statues. I opened the safe. There they were."

He was slurring his words, which would have been alarming enough without his eyelashes sweeping up and down in exaggerated blinking motions, as if he couldn't quite focus on her.

"You went after the statues?" she repeated in the world's biggest duh moment. "Not Margo?"

"Both," Heath corrected, and his eyes closed for so long, she thought he'd gone to sleep, but then he pried his eyelids open with what appeared to be considerable effort. "Margo took them. Had to get them back. My leg hurts."

So many things crowded into Charli's chest she could scarcely breathe. "Margo took the statues. She stole them? From the safe?"

Heath nodded. "And then she stabbed me."

Charli's eyes widened so far that they started to ache. Nothing he was saying made any sense, but she did know one thing. He was scaring her. "I'm guessing you've lost a lot of blood."

"So much blood." His words slurred again.

Okay, two things. He needed to sleep for like twelve hours. And she needed to know that he was safe and that Margo couldn't touch him. There was a slight possibility that he'd mixed some things up, but she'd take Margo in the role of villain any day and twice on Sunday.

"We'll pick up this conversation later," she advised him and hefted one of his arms around her shoulders, trying to stand with Heath's dead weight leaning on her. "Okay, this is not going to work unless you help me. Let's get up, Heath. Come on now."

After three tries, he did it and then somehow, they managed to get up the stairs to her room with only one false start and a quick breather midway up. And they didn't wake anyone. A miracle.

As soon as he saw her bed, he whumped onto it and fell back crossways over the comforter.

"Not so fast." She crawled in after him and roused him enough to get him to scooch sideways so his head lay on the pillow. She'd sort out later what a colossally bad idea it was for him to be there.

Geez, he was so beautiful, even ashen-faced. The flutter low in her belly came hard and fast and she shoved it away. This was no time or place to be thinking like that, when Heath was practically catatonic. And still technically off-limits, at least until she heard the full story about Margo and the stitches. Probably not then either, dang it.

There was still too much unsaid between them.

It was harder to tear her gaze away from him than she'd like to admit, though.

What had happened? Never in five million years would she have guessed that Heath would be lying in her bed tonight. That was yet another miracle, one she didn't trust. At all.

The blanks in recent events were enough to get her moving—away from the temptation to forget all the questions and whatever unnamable things had started spreading through her chest, warm but confusing. Just as she started to roll from the bed, figuring it was better to let him sleep alone, he pulled her against his side, settling her in next to him with a soft sigh.

Oh, well, gee. Nothing she could do about it now. She snuggled into his body, careful of her cast and his stitches. The tide in her breastbone settled instantly and she might have melted into a puddle of Charli-goo.

Why had she done such a moronic thing as to fall in love with him?

"Missed you," Heath said into her hair, his breath stirring against her skin. "I texted you all those times. Is your phone broken?"

"Yep," she lied, figuring it was better to let him think that than to get into why she couldn't have responded. To make up for it, she drew little circles against his skin, wherever she could reach, hoping it would soothe him to sleep.

He shouldn't be talking. Not now, not ever. Especially if he was going to say sweet things that she immediately got busy misinterpreting.

"I'm not in love with Margo," he slurred and let that bomb-shell sit there between them as her fingers froze.

"Maybe we can talk about that in the morning too," she advised him. Man, he must have lost more blood than she'd realized. He was practically hallucinating now.

"Wanted to tell you as soon as possible. Drove very fast and far to get here."

With that pronouncement, he fell into the deepest slumber, leaving her to lie there replaying *not in love with Margo* over and over in her head until it lulled her to sleep.

In the morning, she opened her eyes to the sight of Heath's blue ones trained on her. They were much clearer than last night but still strained, with fine fatigue lines around them. Something else flitted through them that stole her breath.

And terrified her more than anything else ever had in her life.

"Hey," he murmured. "I don't know how I got here. Do I have a lot to apologize for or just a little?"

"You don't remember much of last night," she said. It wasn't a question because of course he didn't.

That would require him to recall the things he'd said without a reminder and her life didn't work like that.

"You don't have a single thing to apologize for. You basically passed out the second your head hit the pillow." She rolled from the bed despite it being the absolute last thing she wanted to do.

"Stop running away, Charli."

Heath's voice had gained a lot of strength too. That was the only reason she didn't flee to the bathroom after gathering up her clothes. Plus, she didn't like it when he read her mind. Or that he'd called it correctly.

She wasn't a coward and to prove it, she turned and stuck her non-cast hand on her hip. "For your information, you need a shower, and I was going to go downstairs to make you breakfast while you washed off all the blood and other...stuff."

Like Margo's fingerprints.

But saying that would require finishing their conversation from last night and she'd rather not. His presence here had so many land mines associated with it that she scarcely even knew how to talk to him.

If Margo had taken the statues and he wasn't in love with her any longer, what did that mean? That was the question she wanted to ask. Which was why making breakfast appealed so much more, because it was downstairs. Away from Heath. Who hadn't stopped watching her with that mixture of pure, unadulterated affection and slight exasperation.

"I can't take a shower with stitches," he informed her calmly. "Only a bath so I don't get them wet. And you're right, that's what I need, along with you in charge of the soap, washing the places I can't reach."

The implied intimacy in that nearly caught her hair on fire and she'd literally never wanted to do anything more in the history of time.

So instead, she made a face at him. "You'd like that, wouldn't you? To have me attending to your every need. Should I find a French maid uniform?"

Heath contemplated her. "What do you think is happening here, Charli?"

Oh, man, the million-dollar question. She sat on the very

edge of the comforter, but only because her knees had buck-led. "I don't know. You were here and then you left. Margo was gone too, so naturally I assumed you left together and that was that. I spent all day yesterday making my peace with that, and then…*this* happened."

She waved at the bed to encompass the enormity of his big body in it. The implications were clear. He'd come back to her once he didn't have any other options.

"Considering the fact that Margo's responsible for these stitches, I think it's safe to say she's no longer a factor in my life." The bed shrank as he locked her in his sights, his gaze heated and bubbling over. "I came home, which I should have realized much sooner was wherever you are."

"No." She sliced her hand at the air, blinking. "That's all wrong. You're in love with Margo and everything between us was just practice."

"It's not, Charli. It never felt like practice to me."

It had never felt like practice to her either. But hearing him say that, confirming that he'd been feeling the same way all along—it wrecked her. Last night, he'd said he wasn't in love with Margo. She desperately wanted to take that at face value.

But she couldn't. "And yet you still chose her. Not me."

The mournful last note made her sound pathetic. Heath re-acted instantly, though, climbing to his knees and crawling to her. He was too close, and she didn't want him to sense how truly torn apart she felt inside. It was a lost cause, obviously, because he just tipped her chin up and drank in whatever he'd found in her expression.

"I'm sorry," he murmured. "It was a mistake from the first moment. I never should have put her between us."

Well, if there was anything sexier than a man who apolo-gized and admitted he'd screwed up in the same breath, she'd never run across it. It weakened her and she didn't want to be weak. Not about this. "That's… I appreciate that, but it doesn't change the fact that whatever you think there is between us is only the result of the bet."

Heath shook his head, his mouth tightening. "We should have canceled the bet a long time ago."

"What?" She dragged out the word with exaggerated flourish to hide her genuine shock. "What is this thing you're saying to me?"

"There's no bet," he said with exaggerated enunciation, as if to make it perfectly clear he knew exactly what he was telling her. "Not anymore."

His thumbs came to rest on each side of her jaw and stars exploded against her skin where he touched her. Deeper down. Behind her eyes. In her heart. With no bet and no Margo, what was she supposed to hide behind to ensure he didn't destroy her?

"You can't quit now. You're winning," she muttered, instantly sorry she'd blurted that out, but he'd beleaguered her senses from day one. Why should this be any different? "I don't know how to navigate all of this, Heath."

"What is there to know?" he asked, his thumb brushing across her cheek. "I'm here, you're here. Let's figure it out together."

She wanted that more than anything. Wanted to sink into him and know that it was real this time. But that would require her to take a step toward him too. To make herself vulnerable.

And she didn't know how to do that and survive if he left her again—if he didn't come back.

"Heath?" His thumb stilled. "It doesn't feel like practice to me either. I can't understand how that happened. How to trust this is real when it was never supposed to be."

"We came into this all wrong." He heaved a sigh. "But that doesn't seem to have made much of a difference in how I feel about you."

Her heart missed a few beats. "What way is that?"

"Like I stumbled into a wolverine–honey badger cage match honestly."

That almost made her smile. "Fair. I'm still mad at you."

Heath leaned into her, resting his forehead against hers. "Also fair. But I didn't know I had a choice, Charli. Be honest with me. With yourself. Did you give me one?"

"That's not the point," she protested and pushed back on his chest, a thread of panic chilling her. She wrapped her arms around herself for warmth. Protection. "It was always Margo for you. Until she turned out to be the bad guy. And then it was all Charli, all the way. I want to be picked first. I want to know that there's a man out there who sees my worth from the first and is like, *I want that*. No holds barred. No question."

To his credit, Heath didn't touch her again but the expression on his face sure did. It reached inside and squeezed her heart.

"Let me tell you what I thought was going to happen with Margo," he said, opting to slide off the bed in favor of pacing, though it was more of a one-two shuffle, as he ticked off his points. "I wanted to be different, the opposite of a man who is a self-confessed hothead. I thought if I did that, she'd see it and meet me in the middle. She'd be inspired to be different too. But I didn't know how to be that guy. I thought it was a failure on my part that I couldn't stop using my fists. Then you came along. You flipped that script on its head."

"Because it's stupid to want you to be someone different, Heath," she informed him crossly. "You're already perfect."

His quick grin faded. "That's exactly right. I'm perfect for you. Not Margo."

"But that's who you wanted the whole time," she countered, though his words were weaving a spell she feared she might not be able to break. "You never wanted it to be real. Every time things got a little intense, you threw down how it was practice."

"You jumped in to agree with that every time!" He sucked in a hot breath and exhaled, staring at her. "What in the blazes did you think the time-outs were for? Because I wanted it to be real, but I also didn't want you to accuse me of cheating. It's a fine line. One I wanted to honor and I did, but not solely because it was important to you, but it was important to me too. I needed to give my pride a chance with Margo, but that's all it ever was. Pride. A way to make myself feel better that she couldn't love me the way I am."

The sentiments winnowed underneath her skin, loosening her resolve. Dissolving her arguments.

He must have sensed he had the advantage, because he crossed back to the bed, halting directly in front of her so she couldn't look away, and pushed a finger to her chest. "You taught me that a relationship should make you better, not just different. You make me want to be the best version of myself. I'm only husband material when I'm with you."

Okay, that was going way, way too far. What was he saying, that he wanted to *marry* her? Panic licked through her blood as she slapped his finger away. "That's ridiculous. You're you, no matter what. What in the world could possibly be different with me that you can't—"

"Because I'm in love with you, Charli," he practically shouted.

Everything inside her exploded in a shower of confetti and fireworks as she stared at him. The moment shrank down, heavy with anticipation and meaning and a billion other things she couldn't sort fast enough. "Say that again."

"I'm in love with you." He squeezed his eyes shut for a blink. "Though this is not the way I would have liked to announce that."

Well, this was absolutely the way she would have liked to learn that. It changed everything.

Boosting herself up on her knees, she took his beautiful face between her palms, wholly unable to be anything other than honest in that moment. "I'm in love with you too. It's making me bananas."

Snorting, he pushed his cheek into her palm, his scraggly beard rough against her skin. "Obviously that's going around."

"Did I ruin this?" she asked in a small voice. "I don't know if you know this about me, but I'm neurotic and I tend to pull the trigger first, then ask questions later."

Heath's lips tilted. "I thought I was the one ruining it with my late declarations and ridiculous temper. Though it is par for the course with us to get around to saying how we really feel during a fight."

"I like fighting with you," she murmured, gratified when he nodded his agreement. "You're my safe place. The only person I can trust when I'm Hurricane Charlotte."

And he hadn't given up, moving on to easier, greener pastures. Even when she pushed him away. He wasn't like Toby. Or her father, for that matter. *She* was the one like her father, running from the best thing that had ever happened to her.

This man was everything. So much more than husband material. So much more than a man tasked with keeping her safe.

He was her match.

The only man who could stick with her through everything she could throw at him. Whether he considered it practice or the cold, hard reality of being hit in the face with the brute force of Hurricane Charlotte, he took it all. And kept on ticking.

She couldn't fight this any longer.

"Heath," she murmured and nuzzled his face with hers, which turned into a kiss in the space of a heartbeat.

Their lips fused together, the sensation of finally, finally falling into this moment sliding through her with so much silk that she sighed. This wasn't the heightened, electric kiss she'd expected. It was far sweeter, far deeper, as if every thread in the universe coalesced into this meeting of souls. The way their bodies fit together felt like reuniting missing pieces.

His fingers threaded through her hair as he cupped the back of her head, tilting her neck to deepen the kiss and she let herself go, let herself open to the experience of being wholly consumed by Heath McKay.

This was not a kiss. It was a surrender. On both sides. He held nothing back, pouring himself into the kiss, stamping his signature over every cell in her body, and she accepted everything he was giving her eagerly.

He quite literally overwhelmed her. She loved him so much.

"There's no bet." He slid his lips into her palm, kissing it as he hooked her with his stormy gaze that was now full of something else, something hot and hungry. "No Margo. This is not practice. It's the real thing, no excuses. If you're scared, that's fine. There's a lot of that going around too. But talk to me instead of running. Or pushing. From now on."

She *was* scared. It was unreal how he could read her, how he continually made everything better by virtue of just being Heath. He had the power to destroy her, but she trusted that he wouldn't. That he'd be there for her always. "That's a deal. Now tell me again."

"That I'm questioning my sanity? Done." His smile lit her up inside. "But despite all of that, I love you, Charlotte."

"You know what this means, right?" She brushed a finger over his lips. "You won the bet."

"Oh no, my darling. We both won."

Epilogue

The day of the memorial service brought with it a cold front that required Charli to pull out her fall jacket to guard against the brisk wind. She buttoned up and joined Heath, gripping his hand tightly as they took their seats next to Sophia and Ace.

Veronica sat on Sophia's other side, Paxton next to her. Probably in his role as her newly appointed bodyguard, though—please God—there soon wouldn't be much to threaten any of the Lang sisters. The university people had their stupid jaguar heads back and as far as she knew, they'd found no evidence that Pakal had commissioned baby jaguar statues.

Their mother, Patricia, sat ramrod straight, dry-eyed, next to an empty seat. Symbolic? She'd lost her husband years ago when he'd abandoned them all in search of treasure. Thankfully, Charli had figured out that she didn't have nearly the same sense of wanderlust as her father. And that nothing could compare to the love of a good man.

Heath spread his arm behind her, his fingers warm on her shoulder.

The service began, a pastor Charli had never met walking up to speak about her father. The guy had never met David Lang either, opting to make benign comments about his work and the discoveries he'd made that contributed to the world's knowledge of Maya history and culture. But she knew there was so much more to him than that, layers upon layers she and her sisters had no opportunity to uncover now that he was dead.

She'd almost missed how like her father she was. She'd been so busy trying to paint Heath with the wrong brush that she'd never realized how David Lang's abandonment had shaped his family into people who could easily repeat his mistakes.

But she wasn't going to. Heath deserved 110 percent and she would give it to him as long as he would accept it.

As the pastor invited anyone who wished to share memories to come up, Veronica was the only one to stand. Ironic since she couldn't possibly remember their father too well. He'd left when she'd still been pretty young. Her bold, brilliant sister had the knack for words, though. That's how she'd won all those cases, not because of her fancy degrees.

Paxton watched her sister with careful attention, but he did that with everything. Charli hoped he would provide a lovely distraction for Veronica while she was in town, but the odds of lightning striking three times for the Lang sisters didn't seem very high. Especially not since Veronica still seemed to have unresolved feelings for Jeremy—otherwise, she would have blown off their breakup a long time ago.

The pastor closed the service soon after, leaving the family to receive the condolences of David's acquaintances from when he'd lived at the ranch and probably some people who had known Charli's grandpa.

Heath leaned down to kiss her temple, pulling her tighter into his side via the arm he'd kept slung around her waist the entire time. "You doing okay?"

She nodded. "I'll be a lot better when you can put your hat back on. It's weird to see you without it."

Grinning, he ran his free hand through the ridiculous curls at his neck. "You love my hair."

She did. It was her favorite thing to wake up with her fingers tangled up in his hair. He had a new scar on his leg, a near match to the one near his throat that he'd earned during an operation in Kandahar, but she got to fall asleep against his very lived-in body every night. She liked to think that the sheer force of her love had gone a long way toward healing all the hurts inside him.

He'd certainly made up for lost time loving her hurts away.

Some two hours later, Charli got sick of playing hostess. There were only so many times you could smile and nod when people talked about a man you'd never known. She retreated to Sophia's office, which was apparently her office too since her sister had bought her a desk and her own chair. Charli half sat, half fell into it, a different kind of chair than the one Sophia used, and it wasn't too bad. More comfortable for sure.

Veronica followed her into the office and Sophia poked her head in a moment later.

"Is this where we're hanging out to avoid all the mourners?" Sophia asked and slipped inside, shutting the door to lean against it. "Man, I love Mom, but she owes us for this."

"It's been interesting seeing how many people had good things to say about Dad after all this time," Charli allowed and jerked her chin in Veronica's direction. "At least we got to spend some quality time together. Have you decided what you're doing next?"

Her younger sister shrugged. "I don't know. I was thinking I might stick around for a little while, if you don't think I'll be in the way."

"No, not at all," Sophia said at the same time Charli said, "Yes, you'll absolutely be in the way."

But then she grinned. "I'm just kidding. We all know 'stick around' is code for 'I'd like to make kissy faces with Paxton.'"

Veronica didn't laugh. "I'm not sure that's going anywhere. I was thinking about writing a book, though. About the treasure and Dad's role in finding it. I was really inspired by what the pastor said at the service. And I don't remember him at all. It feels like a nice way to connect with him."

Biting back the negative comments instantly forming, Charli just raised her brows. "That sounds great."

Sophia's phone pinged and she glanced at it, then up at Charli, her expression puzzled. "Uh, Ace says you should go to the window."

What in the world? Charli jumped to her feet and strode over to the big picture window that overlooked the yard, Veronica and Sophia scarcely a half inch behind her. Heath stood there, obviously waiting for her. And wearing his battered Stetson, which he pointed to and flashed her a thumbs-up.

What an adorable goof. She nearly opened the window to yell out something about how it would be more of an improvement if he'd turn around so she could appreciate the rear view, when Paxton appeared with something wide and white in his hand. He handed it to Heath, who turned the card to the window.

It said:

This is my shame sign video.

Paxton pulled out his phone to start recording it, which felt silly when Charli was standing here watching the whole thing, but the fact that he'd held himself to the letter of their bet put a strange lump in her throat.

That alone propelled her toward the latch. She threw up the sash and called out, "We already established that we both won. What are you doing?"

He held his fingers to his lips and pulled the lead card away from the stack to shuffle it to the back. The second one read:

I made a bet with Charli Lang that I could change her mind about men. Except she changed my mind about everything.

The third one read:

The bet was never about winning but about Charli putting me through my paces so I could become husband material.

Oh, man, he was going to make her cry. She shoved a palm against her lips as Sophia grabbed her arm and held on.

The fourth one read:

Charli told me I didn't need the practice, but that's only because she makes it easy to love her.

The fifth one read:

And honestly, I never dreamed about being anyone's husband but hers. Charlotte Lang, will you marry me?

Aw, dang it. That broke the dam, and she laughed through her tears as he got down on one knee and held up a ring box. She didn't bother to go around, just vaulted through the open window to the yard, and sprinted to the man she loved. Who caught her easily when she flung herself into his arms, despite being off-center.

"I like the way you do shame videos," she told him and held on to the brim of his hat as she kissed him with every ounce of the gale force winds inside her.

"Is that a yes?" he asked between kisses. "Because I have to send this video to my mom and she's going to want to know the answer."

"I don't know. Maybe we should practice some more so we can be sure I'm wife material."

"I already know," he growled. "You're everything I want and then some."

A few more tears fell to her cheeks as she nodded and held

up her finger so he could slide on the ring. "You know a wedding counts as a date, right?"

And then they were both laughing, though Heath had a shiny glint in his eyes as well.

The Cowboy Experience represented a chance to change her fate, to find a place to belong, and that's exactly what had happened, just not the way she'd imagined it. Thank God. She'd found Heath. A cowboy who definitely had to be experienced to be believed. He was exactly what she'd needed but never dreamed would be possible.

* * * * *

Romantic Suspense

Danger. Passion. Drama.

Available Next Month

Colton's Last Resort Amber Leigh Williams
Arctic Pursuit Anna J. Stewart

Mistaken Identities Tara Taylor Quinn
Kind Her Katherine Garbera

LOVE INSPIRED
Hunted On The Trail Dana Mentink
Tracking The Missing Sami A. Abrams
Larger Print

LOVE INSPIRED
Texas Kidnapping Target Laura Scott
Alaskan Wilderness Peril Beth Carpenter

LOVE INSPIRED
Ambush On The Ranch Tina Wheeler
Cold Case Disappearance Shirley Jump

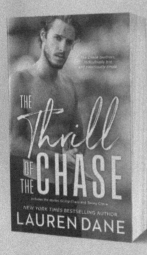 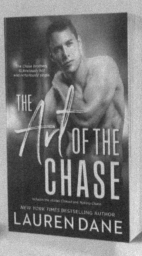

Subscribe and fall in love with a Mills & Boon series today!

You'll be among the first to read stories delivered to your door monthly and enjoy great savings.

WE SIMPLY LOVE ROMANCE